A CLASH OF CROWNS

THE FIVE REALMS VOLUME 3

M.L. DARLOW

ALSO BY THIS AUTHOR

THE FIVE REALM CHRONICLES

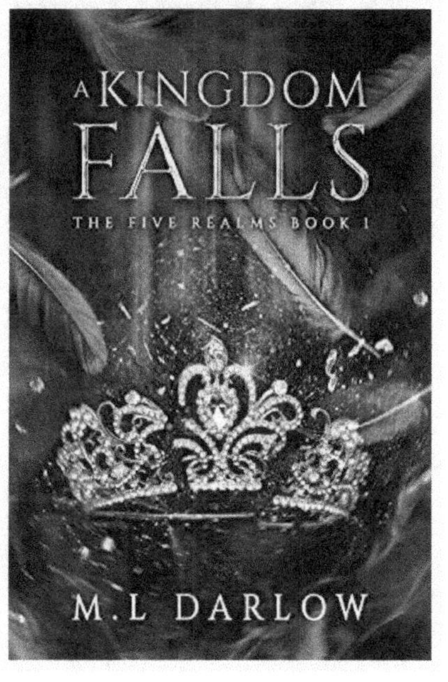

A Kingdom Falls

The Messenger

To my mother, who always finds a way to instill hope in me when I have none. Without you, I would have never considered publishing a single word. You once sat at a computer and typed out my stories for me before I could read a word myself, and now you're the first one to read my five-hundred paged books (and you don't even like fantasy). I love you, mama.

THE SAFE HAVEN
THE FOREST OF FOOLS
SALORIS CITY
THE KINGDOM OF ELVES
THE SKYWARD RANGE
BLACK BAY
LAKELANDS
ARDON LAKE
THE STRI
GOLDEN CITY
COHMDHAIL
MAYFIRE
GRAYSTONE RUINS
DEATH VALLEY
AREN

THE IDONIAN KINGDOM
GALACTIC GATES
THE IDONIAN FOREST
ENDURION LAKE
WITHEROW
REDDING
DRACUS
CRANE
OLAIGON
LORCAN
DAIRTH
THE REGAL MOUNTAINS
THE EDGE OF THE UNDERWORLD
N
W
E
S

Prologue

The Hidden Village of Crane, Year 1031 N.D.
Three months after the Idonian Kingdom's fall

Pat McBride's barn was the only place he found any solace. It was his sacred place, where he buried all his secrets beneath the floorboards and in the hayloft. It was the first structure he'd built on the property he'd chosen for himself. He'd lived in it for two years before he'd completed construction of his house. And, some nights, he still found himself sprawling out on a bed of hay with a good book and a bottle of whiskey.

Today, however, Pat wasn't staring down at a book. He was staring down at a paper that his oldest friend Celine had brought for him. One displaying a picture of Marcus Bonaventure and a group of trackers. The moment he'd skimmed the title for the first time, his stomach had twisted into painful knots. *The Late High Queen's Guardian, Marcus Bonaventure, Begins the Search for the Missing VanCamp.*

"We knew that this would happen," Celine whispered sadly. "All it does is prove what I've said these last three months. We need to take her to the Elves before we put ourselves and all the other villagers at risk. They've been too kind to us, Pat. We can't put them in danger."

"They're already in danger," Pat growled. "Just like everyone else in the Realm. No one is safe."

Celine pursed her lips and turned her gaze to the hay beneath her. "Marcus was a wonderful tracker *before* he became a Draconian. It's only a matter of time before he finds her, and when he does… if any of the Kingdoms catch wind of this place…" she trailed, swallowing hard. "Xavier might come sniffing around. He'll discover that we never escaped Idona before the Galactic Gate's shut, and that Malachai has been lying to him about our location. He'll realize that we've both had children—"

Pat reached for her hand, squeezing it tightly. "No harm will come to them."

"You can't be sure of that!" Celine shouted, her words echoing throughout the barn. "He will stop at nothing to fulfill the Prophecy, and without the blood rushing through our veins and our children's veins, he can't release the fallen."

A wave of nausea rolled over Pat at the mere thought of what would happen if the *Beautiful Mind Prophecy* ever reached fulfillment. "I won't let that happen," he assured her, though he wasn't so sure himself. "Malachai won't either. He's never broken a vow, and he won't start now."

Celine nodded slowly, but her aqua eyes still filled with tears. "What about the baby?"

"She'll be safe here with us," Pat said, reaching for his bottle of whiskey. He took a long swig before handing it off to his friend. "We'll do what the Elves wouldn't. We'll train her. We'll make sure she's ready for what's coming. And one day, when she's old enough, she'll remind Si Realtra just how powerful the VanCamps are."

Six years later, in the midst of another Red Winter, both Pat McBride and Celine Waters died on the same night, in the same room, at the same time. Their fears had come true. Xavier had discovered the truth and no matter how hard Malachai had tried to stop it, he was unable to and was forced to watch his father summon the Dark power he rarely used to end them both. Two people he cared for. Two people he *loved*.

Xavier used his power to manipulate Malachai and his movements as punishment for withholding such crucial information. He'd lost all control of his body and was entirely at his father's mercy. He wanted to close his eyes and wished that he didn't have to witness what he was being forced to do, but that power prevented him from doing anything at all.

Malachai's tears were the only thing he could control while he was forced to slit their throats. They welled in his eyes, blurring his surroundings, offering him a reprieve. Malachai drew in a deep breath as he heard them choking on their own blood; the sound of their heartbeats slowing to a stop and their final labored breaths fading into nothing.

The event was a firm reminder that he was no more than a puppet. That's all he'd ever been, and it didn't matter how smart, skilled, or powerful he came to be. But that night, he made a promise to himself while he stumbled back to Solaris.

One day, he would clip his strings.

CHOICE

THE STRIP

PRESENT TIME

A week after being thrown out of Solaris, forbidden to return without the Idonian Sectra and the High Queen's head along with it, Malachai found himself in the center of the Realm. However, he had yet to decide what he would do while he was there.

Something had snapped in the prince the second he'd met Constance Waters. The harsh words she'd said to him still rang relentlessly in his tortured mind. *When are you going to stop ruining lives? He had cringed. When someone does me a favor and ends mine.*

Memories of those he'd harmed, physically, mentally, and emotionally, weren't the only things plaguing the Dark Prince. He'd suffered from nightmares each time he dared to close his eyes. He'd see Cedric Chamberlain, pinned to a headboard by a lance. He'd hear the Elf's words, clear as day, over and over again, until he was driven to the brink of insanity. *You don't have to do this. You can stop.* But the dream never changed. Malachai fled every time, only to hear Princess Penelope's scream pierce through the atmosphere.

If he wasn't dreaming of that murder, the prince was dreaming of Death Valley. The screams, the smoke, and the flames. He was dreaming of the Idonian Kingdom's fall—of how the ballroom appeared when all was said and done. Drenched in blood, bodies lying in heaps of charred flesh, some still twitching from the shock that ended them all.

Sometimes, Malachai would dream of how Ash's beautiful face had appeared the second he drove that dagger into her side. He could still hear the sounds of Pat McBride and Celine Waters dying by his own forced hand.

There were some nights when Malachai would wake drenched in sweat, his stomach churning enough to send him scrambling into the washroom. There were days where he'd sit at the end of his bed and stare vacantly into nothing for hours until his father summoned him to do yet another terrible deed.

Every horrible thing Malachai had ever done had led him to where he was, waiting in the forest surrounding the East Cliff. He wasn't sure what he'd do when Ash inevitably arrived. It would be easy enough for him to end her while she was weak from her fight with the beast, but could he live with another nightmare?

Shaking his head, Malachai leaned against a tree, pulling in a series of calming breaths. He knew he couldn't go through with it, but where would he go from there? His father's men would hunt him to the very edges of the Galaxy if he ran. There would never come a day where he wasn't looking over his shoulder.

Unless... Ash *succeeded*.

If he were to help Ash fill the Scepter with Moonlight, then he would strengthen the chances of defeating his father, freeing himself in the process. He could swoop in as Xavier's heir. He could order the Dark Army to stand down.

The war would end.

However, there would still be the Idonian Council to deal with, he thought, scratching his head.

Malachai could strike a deal with Ash that would allow him to remain alive and command the Pandora. She could banish them all to the Regal Mountains the same way her ancestors did to the Witches, Trolls, and Giants.

The odds were that Ash wouldn't arrive for another few hours, which gave the prince time to ponder what he would do and say. He sank against the trunk of a tree, exhausted from his journey. His eyelids drooped, growing heavy with each passing second until sleep beckoned him into a dreamless slumber. When he awoke hours later, the sun was setting. Malachai's lips pulled into a frown, and he pushed to his feet, straightening his cloak as he pulled his hood over his head. When his gaze drifted to the forest surrounding him, his heart skidded to a stop.

There she was, beneath a thick forest canopy less than ten feet away.

Ash.

The High Queen.

The scent of her blood lingered heavily in the air. Gashes were visible all over her form, some deep enough to reveal bone. Her uniform jacket was shredded, as was the white shirt she'd worn beneath. Their appearance reminded him of racks of raw meat hanging in a butcher shop's freezer.

Having not expected to find Ash in such a torn state, Malachai grimaced. If it weren't for the fact that she was a Berserker, she'd be dead without question. His fingers twitched with the urge to use an ability he often ignored that he had—the ability to heal.

Snow began to fall in thick flakes from the sky while Malachai slipped into an internal debate. Ash didn't stand a chance filling the Scepter in her condition. He could attempt to heal her while she slept, but it was best to wait. If she woke up to *his* hands on her, chaos would surely ensue.

Minutes later, Ash's eyelids fluttered, slowly opening to reveal her forest-green eyes. She stared vacantly above her for a few moments before she sat up, wincing with each movement, looking all around. The prince stepped further into the shadows, fearing she'd catch sight of him.

Malachai watched as Ash struggled to her feet, slowly turning in place, scanning her surroundings. Curiosity flooded her delicate features, her breath catching audibly in her throat as she kneeled, retrieving the ancient weapon at her feet, a smile beginning to build on her chapped lips.

Malachai's pulse thrummed in his ears at the sight of it. *She did it,* he thought, eyes bulging in awe. *She actually did it.*

When Ash started toward the tree line, stepping out onto the cliff, he knew he had to follow her. He couldn't hide in the shadows forever. Malachai sucked in a breath, filling his lungs to the brim before releasing it all in a single huff. *I can't believe I'm about to do this,* he thought, stifling a groan.

Once Malachai passed through the tree line, he was greeted by warm, fading sunlight shining down upon his face. Ash stood just a few feet away, admiring the view. The second every single one of her muscles went rigid, Malachai knew she'd sensed his presence. His heart hammered, a shiver slithering down his spine. He watched her turn around, eyes widening as realization spread across her face.

The beautiful smile playing at Ash's lips vanished.

"Hello again, Ash." Malachai forced himself to smirk, hoping it was enough to hide his evolving fear.

he allotted hour Ash had given the Allies before sending Aries in to retrieve her had passed too quickly. Quinn paced, lost in his thoughts and memories the entire time. He thought of the shade of Ash's eyes, the way she'd tell stories, of her bronzed skin in the summer months, and the sound of her laugh. He felt as if his heart had been cleaved in two. What if he never heard that musical laugh again?

"I'm taking you back to Olaigon before I go in," Aries said, snapping Quinn's attention back to the present. "Sending you back to Dracus before you have any answers for King Loren and the others won't do anyone any good. I don't want you standing here alone. In case you've forgotten, this place isn't very welcoming. In fact, it's most known to chew trespassers and spit them out. You'll be safer this way."

Quinn opened his mouth to object, but Anastasia cut him a hard look, her charcoal eyes narrowing into sharp slits. He pursed his lips, working to keep his temper in check.

"What will you do if she's…" Cooper trailed, bringing a hand to his open mouth. Alistair squeezed his shoulder reassuringly. The Rider had more or less sat in silence throughout the entire ordeal, as if he were concentrating on something. Then again, he'd almost died in that very place a little over a month ago before Vincent

VanCamp found him bleeding out. It was no wonder why he seemed so detached.

Aries' features softened with understanding. "I'll teleport her to the Safe Haven and summon the Idonian Council."

"King Thaddeus will be all over that Sectra," Ana replied, her mouth pulling into a thin line. "You'll want to put it back in Loren's vault as soon as possible."

"I already have my orders."

Ana's stark-white brows rose. "Oh?"

"This morning," Aries began, his burgundy gaze drifting between the Allies before ultimately landing on Quinn. "She gave me her directions. If the beast were to win, I was to kill it and use her blood to break the spell on the Scepter. I would then give the weapon to Marcus, and the Sectra would go to Vincent. Essentially, she figured out a way to ensure that we could still proceed with the Idonian Kingdom's siege. The only difference would be that she'd have passed the torch to Marcus. He'd be the one to slay the Dark King."

Quinn shivered, goosebumps pebbling along his flesh at the thought.

"Funny," Ana said. "There was a council meeting after we found out that Ash was the Messenger. She was afraid of failing, but Marcus told her to just get the Scepter. He said that if she died, he'd pick it up and drive it through Xavier's heart himself."

Quinn's chest became tight, dread settling in his stomach, twisting it into knots.

"We should go," Cooper mentioned. "Maybe get a drink at that tavern, just to get our minds off of things."

Ana nodded in agreement. "I like the way you think, kid."

THEY FOUND A TABLE IN A DARK CORNER, NEARBY TO A SCREEN displaying a broadcast from the Kingdom of Elves. The Pandora were migrating back to Solaris, likely to start preparing the city for the havoc the Immortal Armies would soon leash upon it. *With or*

without Ash. Quinn grimaced at the thought, bringing a glass of chilled ale to his lips. The other Allies were talking amongst themselves. Anastasia seemed to be the least concerned. Maybe she had faith in the High Queen? Or maybe she'd lived so long that she was used to losing companions to battle.

"You and *Humphrey* are battle companions?" Alistair gawked at her. Ana's lips spread into a knowing smirk as she nodded and rolled her eyes.

"Not so much anymore. Not since the base fell."

"What base?" Cooper inquired.

"Well, you know those bases we took down for the first task were once held by the Idonian Army, right? When the war started heating up, and it was clear that the Pandora were a bigger threat than we'd anticipated, Loren started sending out his best." She paused, reaching for her glass of blood, drinking it deeply. "Humphrey and I were stationed at the Regal Mountain base. The same one the onyx division took out. We'd been there a week when they swarmed us—their numbers were more than triple what we were expecting, and the battle was *brutal.* We fought to hold the base for three days before Loren ordered us out. We fled, forced to leave our dying comrades behind. My leg was broken, twisted in ways you wouldn't believe. Humphrey, who was fine aside from a few scratches here and there, threw me over his shoulder. Dairth was under attack. We had to sneak past, and only found safety when we made it to Lorcan. By then, I had a fever and a blood infection. I was hours away from death."

Shadows danced in the Fire Clan's eyes. She was staring down at the blood in her glass, swirling it.

"Oh," Alistair whispered, his cheeks reddening. "I see."

"See what?" Cooper asked, his face twisting with confusion.

"Things got awkward," Ana continued, her lips spreading into a smile that never reached her eyes. "And Humphrey returned to his position as Draconian Representative in Solaris."

Alistair winced. "That bad?"

"Not anymore," she assured him.

"I'm still confused," Cooper admitted, sinking further into his chair, crossing his arms.

Quinn returned his attention to the screen, half expecting for the broadcast to be interrupted with news of Ash's death. After a few minutes, it *was* interrupted, but the news shared wasn't what he'd expected.

The journalist's complexion paled as she recited the news. "It appears that while Pandora throughout the Realm are running *toward* Solaris, no doubt to defend it in the event that the Messenger is successful in retrieving the Sovereign's Scepter, some people are *leaving* the city. A source has told us a Draconian specialist was able to successfully infiltrate Solaris but we have yet to verify. We are also being told he's since returned to Dracus with a Pandora responsible for the creation of the portal raging above the Idonian Jurisdiction.

"Whether the Pandora was brought to Dracus to answer for her crimes or to aid them in their work to disable the portal is yet to be determined. Meanwhile, the undercover agent heard Xavier address the city to announce the abolishment of his own son. More details to come."

THE BROADCAST FINISHED AND THE SCREEN TEMPORARILY WENT black until it found something else to display—a film meant to be a comedy. But no one in the tavern was laughing. Instead, they were all staring vacantly at one another.

"It's gotta be a lie," someone insisted after a while. "He just wants us to think that he got rid of his biggest asset."

"I don't know," another patron countered. "He's got an Archer now. Maybe the Prince *isn't* Xavier's biggest asset now."

Quinn finished off his ale at the mention of his brother, Lincoln.

"You wanna tell me that recruiter, or whatever we're calling him, is more of an asset than the prince? That bastard has been terrorizing this Realm for decades. I heard he ripped Kurt Walsh's throat out with his bare hands, and that he tore through what was left of the Rebels while his lackeys stood by and watched!"

Anastasia had gone as pale as a ghost, her hand trembling

around her glass. "You think Xavier cast him out because he didn't kill Ash?" she whispered to the others, the patrons continuing to argue in the background. "What if he's hunting her now to finish the job so that he can return to Solaris?"

"What if he was in the cavern?" Cooper's question was spoken so softly that Quinn had hardly heard him. "Waiting."

Alistair shook his head. "No. There's no way."

"How would you know?"

Quinn rubbed at his temples to ward off a coming migraine, his throat becoming too tight for him to breathe between the Allies bickering and the patrons arguing. "I need some air," he ground out. The sound of wood scraping against wood screeched in his ears as he pushed his chair back, rising to his feet without another word. He didn't wait for anyone to reply before pushing the door open with enough force to send it slamming into the tavern's withered siding.

The sun was on the brink of setting, streaks of orange and purples swarming the sky. The Three Moons, all full, were just beginning to show their faces. Quinn stared up at them, trembling with anger he fought desperately to smother. He'd followed Ash to Dracus, despite knowing for two years that wherever she'd wound up going, she was meant to go alone. He'd risked his own head, crossing the Unity Bridge, when he knew the chances of the Draconians killing him on sight were high. Some might say he was a bloody idiot for doing any of it. Some *had* told him that. But the Moons had thought otherwise.

Quinn had gladly accepted the Ally badge. He never complained. Not when he was sent out into the Realm to destroy an entire base with only two other Allies to aid him, or when Craven had nearly died doing so. He remained silent when Lucinda decided to take it upon herself to try and complete the second task alone. He hadn't protested when he'd arrived in the Forest of Fools, only to watch Ash walk into that cavern. For the first time in Quinn's twenty-two years of life, he wanted to complain. He wanted to scream from the top of his lungs, loud enough to shake every mountain in the Realm. He couldn't let her go, even if that was what he was *supposed* to do. What he'd *always* been supposed to do.

The realization hit him so hard that he felt as if he'd been hit with a bag filled with bricks. Quinn fought to control his breathing and failed miserably. He bent over, put his hands on his knees and gulped down haggard breaths. Black dots formed in his vision and Quinn was unsure whether he was going to pass out or wretch into the snow.

The door opened and shut behind him, and footsteps followed shortly after. He didn't bother to look behind him to see who it was. He could sense his kin in a heartbeat.

Cooper didn't say anything right away. Instead, he dropped to a crouch beside him, staring up into the array of colors flooding the sky. When he finally did speak, he said, "Eliza told you to protect her, not fall in love with her."

Quinn stilled.

"It doesn't matter."

"Why?" Cooper asked. "Because of Constance? I thought that ship had sailed."

"I made a promise—"

Cooper cut in. "Fuck your promise. You have every right to break it after what she did. Goodness, if you didn't, Lilly might ring your neck. You deserve so much better. Stop being so gods-damned honorable for once."

Before Quinn had a chance to argue further, Aries appeared abruptly in front of him, Ash's bloody sword in his hand. "This was all that was left," he admitted breathlessly. "The beast, the Scepter, and Ash were all gone. I just spent the last half hour trying to tele-port to her, but I-I can't," he stammered, eyes wide with panic.

Quinn had never thought he'd see the great Blackwing Fae in such a state. "What do you mean, you *can't*? Where is she?" he demanded, every muscle throughout his form, growing stiff. "*Where is she?*"

he coppery taste of blood and revenge lingered on Ash's tongue as she took in Malachai's familiar features. He dropped his hood, and his long, dark hair blew in the breeze. A vicious, animalistic snarl tore from her throat as his vibrant red eyes roamed over her. Her grip tightened around the Scepter, the weapon she'd fought through blood, sweat, and tears to win.

I didn't get through all of that just to die here in the same place my journey started, she thought, lifting her chin and narrowing her eyes.

Ash had been preparing herself for this encounter since she woke up in Dracus after he'd left her for dead. On any other day, she would have already shredded him into ribbons in a fit of Berserker rage, but her entire body screamed with each breath she took. She could feel her blood seeping from every wound, dripping down her arms and legs, pooling in the snow at her feet.

"If you've come here to try and kill me, I'll have you know that I just had a fantastic warm-up."

The prince didn't appear to be amused. That famous smirk he always wore disappeared, and something like genuine concern flashed across his face. It was gone just as quickly as it had come, leaving a placid expression in its wake. "Congratulations on your completion of the three tasks," he said, inclining his head to her.

Ash's blood roared in her ears. "No thanks to you." The longer she could keep him talking, the more time she'd have to come up with a plan. Her Draconian abilities were off-limits. She'd need to drink heaps of blood just to summon a gust of air, but she might still be able to utilize her inner Berserker, or at the very least, connect with the Amulet. A spared glance at her surroundings convinced her otherwise. The last thing she wanted to do was destroy even a blade of glass in the place she loved—the place her mother had loved.

Berserker rage was her best option.

That chained box, buried deep within Ash's gut, slowly unlocked. Little by little, but not enough for the prince in front of her to notice, or so she'd hoped. It took a valiant effort to keep her breathing even. Black spots swarmed her vision. *Heal,* she pleaded. Hartford had said he *thought* she might endure the knitting process. Right now, she needed to.

Malachai continued to watch her. He hadn't moved. Not a step forward, and not a step back. "You shouldn't be able to stand, let alone access that power," he told her point blank.

Ash cursed beneath her breath, watching a flicker of amusement shine in his red eyes. Of all the people to try to deceive… What had she been thinking?

Malachai took a step forward as Ash stepped back. "I'm not here to fight, so don't waste your energy."

"And why should I believe that?" Ash snarled, the words dripping with venom. Her fangs extracted, sharp and aching with the desire to sink into his flesh and drain him within an inch of his life. She'd leave him alive, just long enough for her to fill the Scepter. She needed *someone* to test its ancient power on.

A flicker of indifference flashed across the Dark Prince's face before he shrugged and took another daring step forward. "Because it's the truth. If I wanted to kill you, you'd be dead already."

"Says the man who's already made an attempt on my life and failed," Ash retorted with a withering glare.

Malachai crossed his arms, sighing dramatically. "Again, if I wanted to kill you, you'd be dead. Don't you think that if I *wanted* to kill you, I'd have driven that dagger into your heart?" he asked, lifting a brow.

For a second, Ash considered what he said. Her features softened, her posture relaxing, but then she remembered who Malachai was, and all he had done. "What am I supposed to do, thank you?"

"Well, you *are* the first person I've left alive," he drawled.

Every word that sailed past Malachai's lips infuriated Ash more. The longer she looked at his face, the more vivid each memory of him became. She had despised him the second they'd met in that forest. She'd listened to every terrible thing he had said about Alistair and Cooper, and heard him whistle happily as if he were on a simple stroll on the countryside and not being dragged around by four Allies, each of them with incredibly good reasons to end his miserable life.

All she could see when she looked at Malachai was the way his face appeared when he drove her dagger into her side. The scar he'd left behind began to heat, as if his presence had torn it back open.

Despite each gash decorating her flesh and the pain searing through her body, Ash dropped into a crouch. She set the Scepter down beside her and reached for the enchanted dagger in her boot, throwing it without a second thought.

I should have seen that coming. Malachai rolled, dodging the dagger at the last second. It slammed into the trunk of a tree, not four inches away from his skull. His eyes widened and his breathing staggered as he pushed to his feet, unsure of whether she'd strike again.

A manic laugh escaped Ash's parted lips. Malachai watched her warily, his pulse pounding in his ears. Her chest heaved with each breath she took. "Remember those?" she asked, pointing to the blade. Malachai had never seen someone quite so crazed. Gaping wounds, skin the shade of snow, eyes burning silver. He didn't dare reply. Instead, he curled his hand around the dagger's pommel and yanked it free.

"I should have slit your throat with one when I had the chance,"

Ash seethed, walking toward him. She winced with every wobbly step. Closer and closer she came, until she was standing nose to nose with him. Malachai didn't dare move a muscle.

"I'd let you kill me before I raised a hand to you again," he said, knowing it wouldn't do him any good. "Truthfully, I am not here to fight."

"Looks like you got a fight anyway."

"Would you just look at yourself?" Malachai gestured to her torn uniform jacket, scraps of it fluttering in the harsh winter breeze. Her wild mahogany hair was caked with blood. "Even if I did want you dead, I wouldn't fight you when you can barely stand."

Ash scoffed, now standing so close to him that he could almost smell rage seeping from her every pore. "Am I not good enough for you now?"

In a matter of minutes, Ash would likely pass out from blood loss. Malachai hoped that was the case. She was a lot easier to deal with when she was unconscious. "I can heal you," he offered.

Ash stared at him for a long, painful moment before she began to laugh again. Malachai swallowed the urge to growl at the sound of it, his patience now wearing thin.

"Sure," she said sarcastically, winking at him.

Malachai's eyebrows flattened. "I'm serious."

Shaking her head, Ash scoffed with disbelief.

"I have an ability," he went on. "To heal, I mean."

"And I have *no* abilities," Ash taunted.

"I'm not kidding."

"Pandora don't have abilities," she insisted, her gaze dropping to the dagger in his hand. Her smile wavered, shadows dancing in her eyes. Malachai's heart clenched, and his stomach twisted in coils of dread. He flipped it so that the hilt was out, facing her, the enchanted blade dangerously close to biting his flesh.

Malachai waited for her to take the enchanted blade. "If you want to slit my throat with it, by all means," he said, holding it out to her. "You'd be doing me a favor, anyway. I did tell Constance I'd stop ruining lives when someone did me a favor and ended mine. Help me make good on that promise. I've always been a man of my word." He watched the silver vanish from her eyes, her chapped lips parting.

"Constance?" Ash asked. "Constance *Waters?*" Her voice was so low it was startling.

Fuck, I forgot they might know each other. "Lincoln—"

"He took her, didn't he?" Ash's bottom lip trembled, sending a crack straight through Malachai's heart. "Was it because Xavier wanted him to or because he remembered her?"

Malachai held her gaze, at a loss for words. She had yet to take the dagger or accept the offer that came along with it. She didn't give him a chance to explain before she continued.

"This is all your fault." Tears of anger began spilling from her eyes. She slapped the dagger away, sending it clattering onto the ground before hurling her fist into his jaw hard enough to send him onto his back, his head bouncing off a rock.

Malachai fought to make sense of what was happening, anger bubbling up within him as the scent of his own blood swam into his nostrils. He bared his teeth, making an attempt to stand, only to be shoved back down. Ash drove her boot into his ribs, hard enough to steal the breath from his lungs. He had no time to collect himself before he felt her weight crashing down upon him. She used her lower body to hold him down while he endured the pain of each punch she threw, causing his vision to blur and eyes to water.

For a few moments, Malachai considered letting her continue. She was undoubtedly suffering from a lot of pent-up aggression, and if wailing on him helped her with that…

Ash's punches started to slow until one single fist fell limply onto his chest. He stared up at her, bruised and bloodied, watching her tears fall. He refused to move. Her fist remained where it landed, her fingers twirling in the fabric of his cloak.

Malachai slowly reached for Ash's hands. Gently, he wrapped his fingers around her hand, prying her grip from his cloak. She didn't stop him. Instead, she watched, sniffling, shaking like a leaf.

"Constance and I are cousins," Malachai admitted to her. "That is why she was taken. Our mothers were sisters, and both powerful

Witches. My father believes Constance might evolve to be just as powerful."

The silver faded from Ash's eyes. "Y-you're *related?*"

Malachai nodded and watched her warily. "Yes," he whispered. She remained exactly where she was, staring down at him as if he'd sprouted a second head.

The prince's gaze dropped from her face to the glimpses of bone peeking through the gashes along her ribs. "You should really let me heal you. You might be a Berserker, but you're still susceptible to infection."

"Related," was Ash's only reply. "You and Constance Waters." She shook her head in a daze as her mouth slackened. "No wonder why I was born with a natural hatred for her," she added in a whisper.

Malachai's lips dipped into a deep frown. "You're bleeding all over me and that's what you're thinking about?" Clearly all the blood loss was taking its toll on her. Ash's hands were cold and clammy, and her pulse was becoming weaker by the second. Malachai met her gaze, staring into her glassy, unfocused eyes. *It would be too easy to kill her.*

But he didn't want to kill her. No part of the prince wanted to take another life. Malachai tightened his grip on her hand in an attempt to draw her attention and said one more time, "Ash, let me heal you."

"Okay," she replied.

Surprised, Malachai breathed a sigh of relief. "Good, now I'm going to do this for you, if you'll do something for me," he explained. "Actually, two things. You'll have to get off. I can't concentrate with you on top of me."

It was as if something in Ash had broken. She obeyed him, slowly climbing off his lap. She sat, pressing her back against a tree, her shoulders slumped in defeat.

Malachai shed his cloak, the nip of the winter air chilling him to the bone, but he offered it to Ash anyway. Ash looked at it, her brow furrowing. "Just take it," he ground out. "You have a long night ahead of you, and it is *not* going to be easy. It might even be the hardest thing you've ever done. You don't need to freeze in the middle of it."

Reluctantly, Ash reached for the cloak. She pulled it around herself, eyeing the symbol of three intersecting swords embroidered in red. Her face twisted into a scowl, but she didn't utter a complaint. Warmth was warmth.

"What do you want from me?" she asked.

Malachai pulled off his black leather gloves, cracking his knuckles in preparation for what he was about to do.

"I'm going to use my ability to heal you. Afterward, I'm going to help you fill the Scepter with Moonlight. What I want *you* to do is kill my father with it."

ASH STARED AT MALACHAI, HER MOUTH AGAPE, HER CHEEKS STILL wet with tears. She was no stranger to surprises, especially after arriving in Dracus. It seemed that every fifteen minutes, something shocking occurred. But to hear those words come out of *his* mouth...

Ash gulped. "Is this a trick?" Perhaps the entire ordeal was a lucid dream. She'd lost a lot of blood. There was a trail of it leading from where she'd awoken to where she sat right then.

The prince shook his head, tying his hair back with a thin strip of leather. "I never wanted this war. I never wanted *any* of it. I despise the person it's made me become." He started to tremble, his red eyes fading until they were a familiar shade of vivid green. She fought not to gawk at the transition and failed miserably. He didn't give her an opportunity to ask about it before his complexion started to change as well, from a pale, ghastly shade to golden, as if he lived to stand beneath the sunlight. "*This* is who I really am. Granted, I buried this version of myself the second I awoke as a Pandora. It's always been there, waiting beneath the facade I was forced to live behind."

That face. She'd seen it before in the papers Eliza had collected. The face in front of her was the same one the news clippings portrayed. She could see the title even now, *Would-be Black Knight and*

Galaxy Renowned Scholar becomes a Traitor to the High Throne. A chill crept down her spine.

"Turn around and move the cloak aside," he directed softly. Ash did as he asked without question, too stunned to object. She felt him move what remained of her uniform jacket aside and heard his breath catch in his throat. She fought against the urge to flinch, even when his warm hands landed on her shoulders. The sensation that came along with his touch was indescribable. Warm, yet cold. Calming, yet invigorating. She melted; her thoughts became a scrambled mess. Her stomach erupted with butterflies and her heart skipped into overdrive. Ash bit her lip to keep herself from laughing as her eyes became misty with tears of joy now that her pain had vanished.

When it ended, she opened her mouth to protest. She whirled around to glare at him, but the expression on his face made her forget about... everything. He grinned at her, leaning back on his hands, crossing his feet at the ankles. Nothing about the man in front of her was the same. *Nothing.*

"Now *that's* something you could thank me for," he stated matter-of-factly. His green eyes gleamed in the moonlight. Ash swallowed the lump that formed in her throat and looked down at herself. Her uniform was in tatters but there were no gashes visible beneath the tears.

There wasn't a hint of a scar, even by her ribs where Archibald's claws had dug in the deepest. "H-how?" She fumbled with the word, checking to see if the one he'd given her was still there. It was. A depressive grunt escaped her at the sight of it.

"I can't heal what's already healed," he told her before she could ask. "And, how? I'm not sure. None of the other Pandora received any abilities. It was assumed that I only had one because I was injected with the formula, while everyone else was changed using my venom."

"Interesting," she muttered. "But healing? That seems odd, even for you."

Malachai shrugged. "Not really. I'd just finished training to be a Healer when—" His lips dipped into a frown. "Anyway, I was certified in Idona *and* Erim before the war. Perhaps, this was the Moons' way of allowing me to keep a part of my former self."

The sun had officially set, and all three Moons were full. Ash pushed to her feet with ease and adjusted the cloak, pulling it tightly around herself. Across from her, Malachai stood as well, his gaze drifting to where the Scepter lay nearby in the snow.

"Just so you know, I don't forgive you."

Malachai blinked, his attention shifting back to her. "I didn't ask you to, and I don't expect you to."

Nodding, Ash crossed her arms, reveling in the cloak's warmth and scent. It smelled of pine and campfires. She fought not to smile at how much it reminded her of home. "Thank you," she said so softly, she was surprised he'd heard it at all.

"I think that's the first time anyone has said that to me in thirty years," he admitted, reaching to rub the back of his neck. "Anyway, we have a Scepter to fill and a Dark King to slay. We better get to work and stop wasting precious Moonlight."

Ash snorted and watched him storm out of the tree line. "Not to mention, a war to end and a prophecy to fulfill," she added before following him.

he three tasks had been difficult, but *none* of them compared to filling the Scepter. Malachai was right, though Ash would never admit that out loud. It *was* the hardest thing she'd ever done. It took every ounce of their strength to keep from being driven back into the trees by the force of all three Moons funneling their light into the orb hovering in the center of the Scepter's crescent-shaped blade.

The phenomenon was so bright that Ash needed to keep her eyes shut, or she was sure she'd never see again. She kept her feet planted, and the prince remained behind her, holding on for dear life.

"This beam can probably be seen from everywhere in the Realm!" he shouted excitedly.

Ash hoped it could be. At least that way, the Allies would know she was alive.

THE ALLIES WHO HAD RETURNED TO DRACUS TO START RESEARCHING a cure for Lucinda's eternal sleeping spell had gathered on the roof of the Training Center with most of the Draconian Council. The Realm Prophetess, Valentina Gold, insisted they'd all be able to see

Moons awaken the Sovereign's Scepter from anywhere in the Realm. So, she'd dragged them out there, promising that the roof of the massive, arena-shaped building would have the best view.

Craven consistently checked his chip, awaiting word from the other Allies. He'd sent Quinn at least seventeen messages in the last two hours but received no response. The famed Electric Immortal couldn't escape the knot of despair that pitted in his gut. Something was wrong.

"They're probably just busy," Morghan assured Craven, patting him on the shoulder while Vincent passed him the bottle of rum they'd brought along.

"Drink," the prince demanded. "And fucking relax."

Benjamin Buttler, the Head of Communications, clucked his tongue. "Such strong language from an Idonian heir." A melodic laugh sounded from next to him.

"As if you don't use the same word six times a sentence," King Loren replied.

"Would you all focus?" Valentina hissed, shivering in her white fur cloak. "If my vision proves to be correct, it should be starting in less than ten minutes."

"Speaking of visions…" Marcus mentioned from the Prophetess's side. "See anything about Malachai? Any clue as to what he'll do? I can't be the only one thinking he's gone off to try to finish what he's started in order to get in his father's favor again."

Valentina shook her head, pursing her red-tinted lips. "I'm afraid not."

"What if he's come to his senses?" Richard asked.

Craven snorted at the thought. "Yeah, after thirty years? You think he woke up one day and decided he was good again?"

"Well, no," Richard grumbled, shifting his weight from one leg to the other. "What I meant was that perhaps he's realized that he's just as powerful as his father and is sick of being shoved aside. It's no secret that Xavier played no part in the creation of the Pandora. Malachai is the one who fought all of his battles *for* him. The prince practically *handed* Xavier the High Throne."

An uneasy silence fell over them all. Craven dared to entertain the thought, his breath staggering. Xavier had done well concealing his power after all these years, keeping it close, so that no one would know just what he was capable of. But what if Richard was right? What if Malachai was just as powerful?

"Did anyone else just have the same thought as me?" Craven asked, his heart thrashing against the walls of his chest.

"That depends," Morghan replied, taking the bottle from him, and bringing it to his lips. He took a long swig before going on to say, "Were you thinking that it's as cold as Ryhian ice up here?"

"That's certainly what I was thinking," Princess Penelope admitted through chattering teeth.

Craven shook his head, but before he could go on, a massive beam of light erupted from the Moons, streaming down toward the earth in the center of the Realm. His jaw dropped open as cheers sounded throughout the Kingdom, including those standing around him. People hugged. Smiles lit up every face, tears glistened eyes. As Craven looked about, he noticed that Valentina wept with joy. Marcus soothed her. Loren held a toast to the High Queen. Penelope and Vincent stared at the beam in awe. Morghan howled like the Wolf he truly was. and, all Craven could think was that something was amiss.

Prince Beck Chamberlain stood with his family and Commander, Aveo Calloway, on his father's balcony, staring toward the center of the Realm. Silence hung in the air between them as they sipped their wine, waiting for something miraculous to occur. Everyone in the Kingdom of Elves was watching from their rooftops in silence. The weight of the entire war fell the moment the Messenger filled the Sovereign's Scepter with Moonlight. But there was still no word about whether she'd even survived the third task. The minutes that ticked by felt like hours. Beck wasn't entirely sure what he wanted more, to see the great, white beam of light that was supposed to emit from the Moons, or to know that Ash was alive.

As if his mother could sense his longing, Esmeralda said, "Stop worrying so much. Ash has already exceeded all of our expectations. I'm sure she'll do it again." Beck could practically feel his father's stone-cold glare.

"She's little more than a child," Thaddeus ground out. "They put that Sectra around her neck without having any idea who she *really* was. If that wasn't bad enough, they let her out in the field after what, two weeks in Dracus under Loren's supervision? Then, she's idiotic enough to try and trap the Prince of Darkness, almost getting herself killed, only to be rewarded with the bloody High Crown." If someone didn't stop the Elven King, his rant would continue all night. "The Draconians need to gather some sense and dethrone their king before he drives them all into the ground."

Beck closed his eyes and exhaled slowly. "They made her High Queen so that Xavier could no longer call himself High King. The Sectra Holder was the only person who could legally do it." It took a valiant effort to keep his tone from revealing his simmering rage. "Not to mention, she's had training. A lot of it. You weren't there to witness her take down Aries. *Aries.* And in case you've forgotten, *I* deemed her worthy to be a Sectra Holder."

"And I can't believe you did," Thaddeus barked. "The fact that they chose you as one of the champions she was supposed to fight was our chance at a shred of control. If you'd said no—"

"*What* if I had said no?" Beck fumed, pushing himself off the balcony railing. He whirled around to face his father and didn't dare look at his mother or his sister. Even Aveo was avoiding him, pretending the tile work beneath his feet was far more interesting. "There was no good reason to, no matter how badly you wanted the Sectra to go to Mika." His sister flinched at the sound of her name. "Ash was the one Meera chose, and she earned it. Since then, she's continued to prove herself over and over again. You haven't even met her, yet you dismiss her so easily."

White-hot fury flickered in Thaddeus's harsh, golden gaze. "Mind your tongue, boy, before I rip it out."

Shaking his head, Beck knew he couldn't stand this ill opinion of the Messenger, or the desperate need for the High Throne and *power* another minute longer. "I'd like to see you try."

Aveo choked on his wine, his bulging, bronze eyes darting in Beck's direction. *Seriously?* the Commander mouthed. *He'll throw you off the balcony.* He made a tumbling gesture with one hand before using it to point toward the ground below.

"Don't look at me like that," Beck snarled. "You're the one marrying into their family. It should be you that takes offense, not me."

"Don't you put me in the middle of this," Aveo grunted.

Before anyone had a chance to argue further, the biggest, brightest beam of light poured out from the Moons, sailing toward the earth. The ground trembled beneath Beck's feet, rippling throughout the Realm. The prince's heart leaped into his throat and his eyes burned, but he refused to blink and miss the historical sight before him.

"Would you look at that," Aveo said, finishing off his glass. "Do you think Xavier is shaking in his boots right now?"

"I would be if I were him," Thaddeus admitted.

"Aren't we all?" Beck whispered.

XAVIER HAD ALWAYS KNOWN THIS DAY WOULD COME. WHILE EVERY other Kingdom in the Realm was trembling with applause and cheering, Solaris was silent. No one dared to clap. No one dared to utter a word, for they knew what would soon come. Death. So much death. And with such ancient power awakening, the odds weren't exactly in their favor.

She's done it. Meera laughed the same musical laugh Xavier had heard millions of times throughout the last eighteen years. *I have to admit, I was nervous.*

"You should have been," Xavier replied, his eyes as black as coal narrowing. "And you still should be. This changes nothing."

Meera's snort didn't go unnoticed. *Xavier, it's over.*

"The power racing through my veins is as ancient and powerful as the Scepter she holds," Xavier seethed. "I was made to destroy her, just as she was made to destroy *me*."

A knock on Xavier's study door drew his attention. "Enter," he snarled, turning to face the door in time to watch Lincoln enter, his expression grim. "What do you have for me?" the king asked, gesturing to the letter in the Archer's hands.

Silently, Lincoln approached, getting only close enough for the king to snatch the letter from his hands. Xavier tore into it, skimming the script. His lip curled over his teeth, an animalistic snarl reverberating from his throat that quickly transitioned to a roar powerful enough to rattle the castle, shattering the windows behind him. A harsh winter's breeze sailed in, a soothing chill to his boiling flesh.

"And here I was, believing that Malachai had just been a bit lazy in getting to her on time!" Xavier bellowed, crumbling the letter in his hand. A few seconds later, nothing but ash drifted out. He wanted to do the same to everything around him. To *everyone* around him. *"Summon Savron!"*

Lincoln flinched, taken aback by the voice that gave the command. "Of course, Your Highness," he said with a bow before turning on his heels, fleeing the study as quickly as he could.

What will you have Savron do? Meera asked.

Xavier hadn't quite decided yet, but whatever it was, it wouldn't be pleasant.

JUST AS QUINN WAS PREPARING TO HEAD OUT TO THE CENTER OF THE Realm with a search party made up of Allies and volunteers from the tavern, he caught sight of the beam. His shoulders sagged as relief flooded through him. He fell to his knees, thanking the Moons, the Sovereign, and whoever else's superior hands had played a part in Ash's victory. A hand landed on his shoulder and the Archer looked up to find that it belonged to Aries.

"Looks like we won't need to go searching after all. We know exactly where she is." The Fae laughed.

"I'd say that's a pretty clear marker," Briggs, the barkeep, said from behind. "Won't be needing a map. Just follow the light."

Alistair snorted. "I knew she was alive. You all freaked out for nothing."

"And how would you know that?" Anastasia asked, lifting a brow.

The Rider's cheeks flamed pink at the hidden accusation. Quinn's gaze landed on Cooper, taking in his brother's less-than-thrilled appearance. He quirked a brow to his brother, silently asking what was the matter. He should be just as relieved as the rest of them. And as if on cue, his brother solemnly answered.

"She might be alive now, but every one of our enemies will see that light, and I still can't teleport anywhere near there."

Quinn hadn't considered that possibility. He pushed to his feet, cursing beneath his breath. "If we travel at Immortal speed, we can get there by midday tomorrow."

"I hope that's fast enough," Ana said warily.

Ash awoke with a start. She hadn't meant to fall asleep, there on the East Cliff, just a few feet away from her sworn enemy. A man that had tried and failed to kill her. A man who could very well change his mind and decide to try again. She scrambled to her feet, almost tripping on the loaned cloak, waking the prince in the process. He seemed equally surprised, staring at her for a long moment before he rubbed his tired eyes and turned his attention to the rising sun.

Ash followed his gaze, her breath catching in her throat. The view before her was the same one her mother adored. Eliza had often told stories of how before the war, she and her husband would camp on the East Cliff and watch the sunset. Ash smiled, remembering the way her mother's eyes glistened as she recalled how they would wake with the sunrise. She always thought she'd do the same if Idona ever found peace again. And now, she had her chance to do just that.

Streaks of orange and red painted the morning sky, fading into pinks and blues. There wasn't a cloud in sight, giving a full view of the Three Moons. Snow-capped mountains lingered in the distance, glowing with the rising sun. "The Elves say that their sunrises and sunsets are the best in the Realm," Malachai said. "I beg to differ."

Ash swallowed and silently nodded, shifting her gaze back to the prince. "Where will you go now?"

Malachai shrugged and pushed to his feet, stretching as though he'd slept for days. "I'll stay in the area," he replied. "I like it here."

Ash had to clench her jaw to keep it from dropping.

"Maybe I'll finish building Morghan's cabin since he clearly found another place to live. I'll have to set up Wards against certain creatures like Witches and Warlocks who might wish to hunt me down and punish me for what they undoubtedly know I have done."

"You might want to include Wolves in that too, since Morghan will cleave you in two when he finds out," Ash warned. Malachai lifted a brow as his lips quirked up into a smirk. He turned to face her completely.

"For a second there, it sounded like you were concerned for my safety."

Ash gave him her best scowl. "I don't care *what* you do. You could jump off this cliff and I wouldn't bat an eye. We made a deal, and you kept up your end of the bargain. Now, I have to worry about mine, and that's all. We're still enemies. Just like we were yesterday, and the day before that, and the day before—"

"I get it," he cut in, raising up a hand in submission. Ash met his eyes, glimmering with amusement. She bit her lip to keep herself from smiling.

"Forever enemies," she declared. "Pray that our paths don't cross again."

The corners of Malachai's mouth lifted into a smile. "I'm sure I'll rue the day it does."

Despite herself, Ash snorted. "It's been nice hardly knowing you, Malachai." Turning her back on him and without another word, she started toward the tree line.

"Wait," Malachai called after her. Ash froze mid-step, her stomach flipping on itself. She sucked in a deep breath before slowly turning back around. "Before you go…" he paused, pursing his lips. "My father has someone working for him in Dracus. I'm not sure who it is. We refer to him as the *Rat*. He's been feeding my father information for decades. Whoever it is, they know everything King

Loren does, and they know everything about you and the Allies too. Just… be careful.”

Ash's heart thudded a little harder in her chest as her eyes grew wide. To think that someone in Dracus was feeding Xavier information about her... a shiver crept down her spine.

“W-what?”

“I wish that I could tell you more,” Malachai added, his shoulders slumping. “Really, I do, but my father kept a lot of things from me. He couldn't trust me, and for good reason. If I were you, I'd be *very* careful about what you say once you return to Dracus. You can't trust anyone. Not until you discover who it is and who else might be working for them.”

“And how do you suppose that I do that?” Ash asked through clenched teeth. “How am I supposed to trust you?”

“You don't have to, but I haven't lied to you thus far.” Malachai started to pace before the cliff's edge, his brow wrinkling with thought. “Whether you want to believe me or not, I have a few ideas. The Rat *has* to be handing off his messages to my father's men somehow. The only way to do that would be to cross the Unity Bridge. Start looking for a pattern. Find someone that crosses the bridge at regular intervals and go from there.”

Ash sucked in a sharp breath, holding it for a few moments before exhaling slowly. “Alright,” she growled. “Any more helpful tips before we go our separate ways?”

“I'm willing to help you, Ash. Between the two of us, we could change everything. I made my choice…” he paused, looking away before meeting her gaze. “I chose you.” He pushed his long dark locks away from his face. “The best tip I can give you is to reconsider how you label me. Because, at the end of the day, I might be the *only* person you can trust.”

Without giving Ash a chance to respond, Malachai transitioned into a hawk and flew off toward the mountains. Ash stood there a moment longer, trying to calm her racing heart. *I chose you.* The words echoed in her ears. Guilt began to settle in the pit of Ash's stomach. “I didn't ask you to,” she whispered, turning her back on the cliff. She'd think more about his words after a long, scalding bath and enough blood to sate her carnal needs. Ash sucked in a deep breath, slowly exhaling before she started her journey to the McBride Estate, the pleasant thoughts of home easing her mind.

Quinn smiled as he approached his family home. The McBride Estate loomed just ahead, smoke billowing out of the chimney. *It's good to be home.* He didn't waste any time marching up the stone walkway as the others fought to keep up behind him.

"*This* is where you live?" He didn't need to look over his shoulder to know that Anastasia was gawking at the place. "It's absolutely gorgeous."

"Even nicer than Mayfire Manor," Alistair added.

"I need a nap," Aries complained. "It's been centuries since I've run so fast for so long. One gets used to teleporting everywhere."

Cooper chuckled beneath his breath. "Looks like someone needs to exercise a bit more."

Before Quinn could walk another step, Cooper teleported to the front door. Aries' answering growl echoed throughout the front field. "How long have you been able to do that?" the Fae snapped.

"At least an hour," Cooper replied with a devious smirk.

"Why didn't you say anything? My legs are killing me," Ana whined. "You don't have wine in there, do you?"

"It's hardly noon," Alistair shot at her.

Quinn rolled his eyes and watched his brother open the front door. He followed, holding his breath while his stomach fluttered excitedly. He couldn't keep himself from smiling at the thought of finally returning home. He'd never thought he could miss a place so badly. Then again, he'd never known that he'd have to leave this place to begin with.

The second they all made it into the foyer, Ana collapsed in a heap of flesh and bone on the floor, rolling onto her back, releasing a groan. Aries sank onto a bench, his wings vanishing so that he could relax against it. Alistair looked around, setting his pack aside.

"It's like a cabin in here," he mused. "I like it."

"She must be upstairs," Cooper said.

"You go check," Quinn replied. "I'll look in the kitchen."

The others remained in the foyer, too exhausted to take another step. Quinn imagined they wouldn't be returning to Dracus anytime soon. At least not until Aries had had his nap and Anastasia had her wine. The idea of spending a night at home excited him. Perhaps he'd summon the other Allies.

Reaching into his pocket, Quinn fetched his chip. He grimaced at the amount of missed messages from Craven and the others. He drew in a breath before releasing a sigh and typed out a quick message... *We're in Crane. Ash is somewhere here. Looking for her now. Feel free to join us.*

Cooper's footsteps echoed along the floorboards above Quinn's head. They paced from room to room, telling Quinn that his brother hadn't had much luck finding Ash up there. She wasn't in the kitchen either. Quinn clenched his jaw, his brow furrowing as he began to wonder if she'd headed down to the village. *Perhaps she wanted to see Lilly, Sam, and Constance.*

"I really wish she would have thought to take her pack into the cavern," Quinn grumbled, opening the cupboard. He pulled a few glasses from their spot on the shelves before closing the door. Their liquor cabinet was lacking, but he figured a bottle of rum would be enough to warm everyone's spirits. He'd send Cooper for provisions later.

Quinn ripped the cork out with his teeth, spitting it out onto the counter. The scent of the liquor enveloped him, thrusting him back in time, to an evening he'd shared with his family and friends at Crane's annual Harvest Festival last year. They'd all settled onto a picnic table, where they'd shared a bottle of the same rum. He could still hear Ash laughing at something Cooper had said.

While the Archer poured himself a glass, the back door opened and Ash walked through, lips stained with blood. She didn't notice him right away as she kicked her boots against the doorframe, knocking the snow off. She shivered, her icy breath clouding in front of her. For a second, he allowed himself to enjoy how much she looked like herself, before the crowns, the dresses, and the uniforms.

She was wearing *her* clothes. Her cheeks were flushed, as they often used to be after hours hunting outdoors in the coldest part of the Realm, in the harshest winter conditions.

Bringing the glass to his lips, Quinn leaned against the center island, taking a long sip. Ash shed her coat, her back to him while she hung it on a hook beside the door. She slipped out of her boots, rubbing her hands together to warm them before finally whirling around. Their eyes met, and she practically jumped out of her skin. Her bright green eyes brightened, shining like emeralds.

"Want some rum?" Quinn asked, flashing her a crooked smile.

Ash stood in silence for a few moments, debating whether she was dreaming. She blinked several times before finally rubbing at her eyes and took in Quinn's features. She noted the ice slowly melting in his hair, the emerald division Ally uniform, the shining badge on his chest, and the massive black bow looming over his shoulder. *Real,* she determined, swallowing the lump of emotions welling up in her throat. Tears pricked at her eyes as she fought to steady her ragged breathing. Her heart thundered in her chest and blood roared in her ears until everything became silent. She was *home.*

"Quinn," she breathed, feeling her lips spread into a grin. "You found me." She ran for him, leaping into his arms, hooking her legs around his waist, squeezing with all her might.

"I had a feeling this was where you'd go after the show you put on last night," Quinn said, holding her tighter than he ever had before. "We started running from Olaigon the second we saw that beam. It took us all night and half the day to get here."

Ash pulled away from him so that she could stare down at his face. "Why would you run when you had two teleporters?"

"They couldn't teleport," Quinn replied. "Aries mentioned the possibility of Wards."

Malachai. Ash frowned. "Well, you're here now."

"That I am."

"You can put me down now," Ash added, chuckling.

A blush bloomed on Quinn's cheeks as he released her. He cleared his throat nervously, his eyes falling on the kitchen's threshold. Ash turned around and melted with relief at the sight of Alistair, leaning against the frame, holding a chrome thermos.

"Where were you ten minutes ago, when my fangs were buried in a deer's neck?" Their bond, which was still incredibly new to them and extremely accidental, portrayed the question loud and clear—*is this your blood or a lab-created version?* He winked in response, and Ash wasted no more time opening it, before downing the contents.

"You drank from a *deer?*" Quinn asked, wrinkling his nose.

"Desperate times call for desperate measures," she retorted defensively. "I want no judgment from any of you."

"You won't get any from me!" Ana's voice rang from somewhere nearby. Ash peaked down the hall, getting a glimpse of her lying flat on her back, staring into nothing. "I'd get up to greet you or bow, now that you're High Queen, but I can't move and I'm already on the floor."

Ash cringed and shook her head. "Please, don't ever bow to me. I'll only be High Queen for a month, perhaps a little more. That's all I'll be able to withstand, I can assure you."

"Good," Quinn grumbled. "It's weird thinking of you in that role."

"Get used to it," Aries called from a place where Ash couldn't see. "Even if it's just for a month, it'll be chaotic. Realm addresses, village tours, dress changes, balls, dinners, and whatever else the council decides to throw at you."

Cooper appeared in the kitchen, startling Ash. "Then I suggest we stay here as long as we can. You know, get a small break before that chaos starts."

"I already told Craven where we were, and that they're welcome to join," Quinn admitted, rubbing at his neck. "As long as they can get away."

"It'll be weird," Alistair replied, leaning against the door to the pantry. "Celebrating without Lucinda."

Ash wasn't sure that they should celebrate at all. And, if they knew who had helped her last night, would they still want to? They might shun her. Alistair would likely never speak to her again. Her stomach churned with the thought.

"Looks like you got away from the beast unscathed," Alistair added, which only made matters worse. "At least that makes one of us."

Craven needed a day off.

More than anything, he needed silence. Peace and complete silence. But, as a specialist in the Draconian Army, Interrogator, and an Idonian Ally, it was rarer for him to see the back of his eyelids than it was for a Pandora to sit across from him in their Mortal form, inside Dracus's Communications Center.

And the latter had only happened once.

Craven set his jaw and narrowed his gaze. He sucked in a deep breath and let out a huff. His body tensed, arms crossing as he looked down his nose at the woman before him. His eyes roamed over her body, assessing her. This was no ordinary woman; she was a Pandora. A muscle feathered in his jaw. This was not the usual environment in which he interrogated people, but, considering that the woman was a stolen daughter of a Justice Keeper in the Draconian Jurisdiction, Loren demanded that she get special treatment. Which meant Craven wasn't allowed to shock her. By the look on her face, one would think he already had.

"State your name," he requested, picking up his quill.

"Anderson," she quipped. "Bernardine Anderson."

"What sort of name is Bernardine?" He snorted.

Benjamin hissed from his place down the table. "Seriously?"

Craven smirked, quirked a brow, and gave Benjamin a shrug. "What? I'm curious."

"It means brave as a bear," she said, biting her bottom lip, staring down at the glass table.

You certainly don't look as brave as a bear. Craven's lips pulled down in a grimace. "Is that your favorite Pandora form? A bear?" he asked, his tone hardening. Benjamin shrunk further into his chair, pinching the bridge of his nose between his thumb and forefinger.

"It was a genuine question," Craven insisted defensively. "Excuse me if I've never held a conversation with a Pandora. I don't think anyone has unless you count that stunt Ash pulled with Malachai." Bernardine's gaze lifted from the table. Craven wasn't sure which name had dragged her attention and caused such fear to flash in her burning red eyes.

"She'll kill me no matter what I say. For creating the portal and working for *him*, but I never had a choice in any of it, you know. Xavier learned about my talents, thanks to all of his scouts, watching everyone in all areas of Idona. I was dragged from my bed in the middle of the night a year ago, injected with venom, and two days later I was shoved into a room with a Sorcerer named Storm. He had the knowledge about Magic, and I had the knowledge about tech and astrophysics. We made the perfect pair. After a while, I forgot where I was, or just stopped caring. The idea of creating a portal that size became intriguing. Any scientist or physicist would think the same. But then, Veda had to ruin it with Black Magic. *Everyone* told her not to. *Malachai* told her not to. But she did it anyway. And that's why all these Mortals are getting abilities, and why we can no longer control the portal. Storm was so upset that he tried to attack her. Xavier had him reassigned. I was working alone when Humphrey showed up, holding a knife to my throat."

Silence spread throughout the room. Craven watched her head fall into her hands. Her short, raven-black curls bounced as her shoulders trembled in time with her sobs. Something twisted in his gut. Guilt? Pity? He wasn't sure, but never had he imagined he'd feel anything but hatred for a Pandora.

"Ash won't kill you," Craven told her.

"You're the one chance she has of learning how to destroy that thing," Benjamin added. "Between you, Grant, and I, it'll be taken care of. No one is going to punish you for what you were *forced* to do. Why do you think Humphrey brought you back here?"

Bernardine lifted her head, her cheeks stained with tears. "Then why is he here?" she asked, pointing at Craven.

Clearing his throat, Benjamin said, "We need to make sure you're not a threat."

"It's called *screening*," Craven clarified. "Everyone goes through it when they move into the Kingdom. It's how we keep Dracus safe."

"Though, to be quite honest with you, we haven't asked half of the questions we would need to, and we already know you're not a threat," Benjamin stated. Craven gave him a dazed look of bewilderment, to which he replied, "Do you *seriously* think she's going to inflict harm on anyone?"

"I don't know. She still hasn't answered the question about the bear."

"If you really *must* know, I've never transitioned at all," she revealed, crossing her arms. "I refused."

Craven set his pencil down. "Well then, you should probably learn." She started to shake her head as soon as he said the words. "Come on, that's one *awesome* gift to have. No one wants to say it out loud, but the fact that Pandora can transition into anything with a beating heart is *badass*."

"It's true," Benjamin admitted with a sigh. "Xavier's a genius."

Bernardine scoffed. "You mean Malachai's a genius. Xavier played absolutely *no* part in the creation of the Pandora. Malachai and Pat McBride were the ones who did everything with Veda's help. Well, before Pat deserted the Dark Army."

Craven's stomach hit the floor. "What did you say?"

"Malachai and Pat McBride—"

"You *really* don't need to repeat that," Benjamin told her, sharing a wary look with Craven. "Ever again."

Cowering in her seat, Bernardine's gaze darted between the two of them. "They don't know, do they?" she whispered, eyeing the cameras around the room.

"*We* didn't even know that," Craven admitted in a horrified whisper. "Well, we knew that Malachai likely did most of the work but…" he trailed, wondering how Quinn and Cooper would feel if they found out. Whatever image they had of their father would be destroyed in the blink of an eye.

Bernardine bit her bottom lip again, tapping her fingers on the glass table. "Oh," was all she said.

An awkward silence hung between them, only to be interrupted by Craven's chip buzzing. He retrieved the device, desperately in need of a distraction. His heart skipped a beat at the sight of Quinn's name flashing on the screen. How long had it been since he'd heard from his division leader? A glance at the clock told him well over twenty-four hours. He was quick to read the message, a sigh of relief emptying from his lungs.

"They have her," he said to Benjamin. "Ash, I mean. She's safe."

Benjamin brought his hands together, looked to the ceiling, and said, "Thank the Moons."

"He's asked for us all to join him at their home in Crane," Craven added, looking at the Head of Communications with pleading eyes that said *release me, I beg of you.* He even went as far as to stick his bottom lip out.

"Alright, but if anyone questions you, we examined all the proper inquiries and Bernardine is now the Communication Center's newest officer."

"Got it," Craven replied, springing to his feet.

"Anderson," she corrected before he could leave. "Call me Anderson."

illy McBride and Sam Waters had traveled night and day for over a week. She was frozen to the bone by the time she crossed the famous Unity Bridge. Her legs were stiff and aching, her hair caked with ice. She hadn't slept since Olaigon. Every time she closed her eyes, images of her brothers in danger would snap them back open. Her fear of what would happen once they made it to Dracus consumed her. Now that they'd arrived, her anxiety was at an all-time high, controlling every erratic heartbeat and rickety breath.

The waterfalls surrounding the Kingdom roared in Lilly's ears as she walked past the Black Butterfly fountain. She fought to keep her wits about her when all she wanted to do was reach out and touch it, perhaps even drag her fingers through the water.

Dracus was unlike anything Lilly had ever seen in her mere fourteen years. The city was vast, stretching out farther than her eyes could see, red-roofed houses lining every street. Any shop imaginable was right at her fingertips, containing everything her heart desired.

It was difficult to avoid staring at the beauty of the Kingdom, but Lilly found that it was nearly impossible as Immortals walked by. Lilly had never seen a Draconian up close. They were so beautiful. Their flesh sun-kissed and star-kissed skin glowed as though the

Immortals, themselves, had been blessed by the Moons. Their eyes were bright, their teeth too white. Lilly felt small compared to them. So… *unworthy.*

"We should head straight for the castle," Sam said, his deep voice piercing through Lilly's thoughts. She'd forgotten he was there. "Take my hand. I don't want to get separated."

Lilly nodded and did as he asked, taking comfort in his touch. Compared to her brothers, Sam was the next best thing. She'd never lived a day where she hadn't known him, or his sister Constance. Her heart clenched at the thought of her. How was she fairing? What were they doing to her? Was she cold? In pain? Panic began to set in more and more with every question.

"Still have that book?" Sam asked, motioning toward her cloak.

"Yes," Lilly replied. She'd carried it all the way to Olaigon. Before she left, Lady Evanora had given her a satchel. Now, it hung over her hip, thumping against it with every step she took.

Sam sighed. "That book and what it contains could be what convinces King Loren to accept this alliance," he whispered, looking around nervously, as if he were afraid someone might overhear.

"And keep you out of chains?"

"That too."

"I'm just saying, the closer and closer we get to that castle, the more I remember how close Princess Penelope and King Loren are," Lilly said, matching his hushed tone. "The word *Rebel* won't bode very well with him."

He cut her a harsh look in response. "This is already nerve-racking enough. Try not to make it worse, would you?"

An hour later, they were standing before three people. Two were simple guards, who'd been standing outside the castle's front doors, the red stripes running across their uniform jackets now reminding Lilly of the shade of blood. The third was a familiar face who had been walking by. Lilly wished they had walked through the castle's foyer at a different time.

Vincent VanCamp was too personable and polite to be the stuck-up royal Lilly had imagined him to be. He was tall. *Too* tall. Staring up at him felt like staring up at a massive tree. She was no more than a shrub in comparison. All she wanted to do was shrink into Sam's shadow.

"You would like an audience with the king?" Vincent asked. Lilly stared up into his sage-green eyes, eyes that reminded her of Ash, eyes that shone with kindness. His lips spread into a genuine smile. "Might I ask why, so I can let him know?"

Sam's throat bobbed as he looked down at Lilly, who gave him a confirming nod. "I am—" he stopped himself, pursing his lips. Beads of sweat peppered his brow. His grip around Lilly's hand was tighter than a vice.

"The Rebel General, Sam Waters," Lilly finished for him. It was better to be out with it. "We've come to talk to King Loren about a potential alliance and to answer the High Queen's call."

The guards stiffened in unison. Vincent's smile faltered. His gaze darted between the two of them in their filthy, travel-worn clothes. Lilly wondered if he'd deem them crazy. Sam certainly didn't *look* like a General.

"Before you make your assumptions," Sam started, holding up a hand as if to stop those guards from slaughtering him. "Lady Evanora Ivanenko of the Zerinian Empire sent us. She had faith that King Loren would hear us out and worked directly with Cedric Chamberlain when he started our organization."

Vincent winced at the sound of the name, and Lilly's heart cracked at the sight.

"Ash summoned us," Lilly added. "In her Realm address."

At first, Vincent didn't seem to react to the sound of his sister's name. But after a second, his expression changed. "You called her Ash," he said, turning his attention solely to Lilly. "Do you know her?"

Unsure of what else to do, Lilly squared out her shoulders, held out her hand, and said, "I do. I'm Lilly McBride."

Less than fifteen minutes later, Lilly was sitting on a couch with a warm blanket thrown over her shoulders. Her fingers were wrapped around a hot cup of tea, thawing her frozen hands. She blew on it, watching steam billow from the brim as Vincent paced the confines of his personal suite. He raked his hands through his wavy hair. After convincing the guards downstairs to take a vow of silence about Sam and Lilly's arrival, the prince had brought them up to his personal suite, where he'd asked a maid to hunt down changes of clothes for them.

"Now that I recall, Ash mentioned you both," he admitted, still pacing. "In the library when we first met. She said you were a teacher, and that Sam was a close friend that she'd grown up with. But she did not mention that you were Rebels."

Sam and Lilly shared a wary look before the former said, "Ash and Quinn both left the organization two years ago. I assume that's because Eliza told them about her true nature. I don't blame either one of them for leaving. Walsh and everyone that followed him were dead, but most Mortals in Central Idona are extremely wary of Immortals because they've had little to no interaction with them.

"The rest of us, and by that, I mean, Cooper, Lincoln and I, remained with the Rebels. But we were never allowed to go to the gatherings they'd hold underground. My father was the only one who went. Sometimes he'd bring the baker, Jeremy. You see, we've been pretty quiet after what happened with Walsh. No one else alive agreed with his wicked ideals. We're disgusted by everything he did."

"Is that why Malachai issued a destruction-level attack on Crane, because you're Rebels?" Vincent asked, finally ceasing his pacing to face them completely.

Lilly didn't have an answer for that. "There's no clear reason why Malachai attempted to destroy Crane. We just assumed that he'd had enough of trying to get us to bow down. You know what happened to the other villages who'd outright refused."

"If it was Rebel related, I think Witherow would have been hit by now, too. And Olaigon," Sam told him.

The prince reached to rub one of his temples. "Are those *all* of the participating villages, or are there more?"

"They're just the biggest players," Sam explained. "I'm going to give it to you straight, just because you're Ash's brother and I love her. There are Rebels in every village, town, city, and Kingdom—Mortals and Immortals alike. Our *real* purpose was to keep the peace throughout the Realm and rebel against *Xavier*. No one else. The only reason no one knows about us is because raising an army without the Idonian Council's permission is forbidden."

Vincent's expression remained stony and unreadable. "What happened with Walsh then? Because that's *certainly* not what he was trying to do."

"We're convinced that Walsh was clinically insane." Sam leaned back, crossing his arms. "My father had *just* started bringing Quinn and I into the loop when Malachai attacked the Grimm Estate and sent Cedric running behind those golden walls to lie low. He told everyone else to do the same, putting that psychotic bastard in charge. But Walsh didn't want to lie low. He was sick of waiting. All he did was spew hatred for *all* Immortals, not just the Pandora. Quite frankly, he wanted to rid Idona of Immortals altogether. He thought Mortals deserved their *own* Realm. So, he wanted to speed things up and came up with his own way to find the Messenger. People started volunteering to go into the Forest of Fools. They all died. It was complete and utter madness. *Then,* he and that creep, Hans, came up with this idea that the Messenger was a VanCamp, and well, you know what happened after that. They devised a plan, kidnapped your sister, and then Cedric killed Hans. He started coming to meetings again after that. In secret. But then, Malachai took out Mayfire—another huge statement that said that the prince was on to him. He told us to put down our swords after that. It didn't save him in the end."

Lips pulling into a frown, Lilly watched Vincent stumble toward the nearest chair, sinking down into it. They sat in silence for a while. Lilly sipped her tea, watching the snow fall outside through the panes of the glass wall on the north facing side of the room.

"It all makes sense," Vincent said to no one in particular. His eyes were blank, staring into nothing. "Why he came back to the Kingdom of Elves after so long and everything that happened afterward. Why he lied to us…"

Lilly's heart sank as she watched the prince piece everything together, his handsome features twisting with pain. Her shoulders drooped as she said, "I'm sorry."

"You have no reason to be," Vincent told her immediately, pushing to his feet. His lips spread into a smile, one that Lilly noted didn't reach his eyes. "Neither of you do. But we're going to have to be *really* careful. You can't just walk up to Loren and say you're the Rebel General. You'll have to speak with the entire Idonian Council and your argument will have to be squeaky clean. Maybe we should even give you a new name. *Rebel* will just make them think of Walsh and what he did."

"A new name?" Lilly asked, sitting up a little straighter. She wanted to know more, needed to. "Like what?"

The prince shrugged. "We should summon Lady Evanora and talk to her about it. I don't think anyone has any idea she's still in Idona. But, if she supports you, then the Elves and Draconians will probably lean in that direction too."

"She's a pretty big deal, isn't she?" Sam asked.

"You have *no* idea, do you?" Vincent gaped, shaking his head as if to say *this won't do.* "Lady Evanora was leading *armies* by the time she was seventeen. She's the one who made it, so the surname *Ivanenko* is known in every household, in every Realm. Before, she was essentially nobody. Just a girl from a village who grew up in the middle of a civil war with absolutely nothing. But now, she's had tea with every Royal in every Realm. Rumor states that *she* was offered Zerin's Sectra, but insisted that it go to her brother, Sampson. It's no wonder Cedric chose to seek her out."

Lilly watched Sam's eyes widen, her stomach bottoming out. They'd shared a meal with Evanora and had no idea who she really was.

"The woman is a walking legend," Vincent insisted. "Lucinda said that she once spat in King Maverick's face for so much as insinuating that men were more powerful than women."

"We heard about what happened to Lucinda," Lilly said, her gentle tone taking on a sad note.

"That's why some of the other Allies and I are here while everyone else is out in the field. We're looking for a cure. Morghan has been in contact with the Idonian League of Sorcerers, but no one seems to have been able to come up with anything. Granted, it's only been a few days, but still, even a few days without our Realm Sorceress leaves Idona in a very unstable state."

Lilly reached for her satchel, pulling the book out. Vincent raised his brows as he gazed down upon the cover. "This..." Lilly paused, considering her words carefully, "...was my father's. My brother, Cooper, found it in the barn at the same time he found the bows. He gave it to Ash for her birthday, hoping that it would help her figure out what she was turning into. I brought it along because it's filled with helpful information. I began to flip through it while we were resting the other day." She opened to a specific page that she'd marked with a ribbon. "I found this."

Vincent took the book as Lilly handed it out to him, skimming the page she'd opened it to. After a few moments, he slowly lifted his gaze from it and stared at her. His eyes were wide, almost taking on an alarmed reaction, before his lips spread into a grin, staring at her in awe. "Lilly McBride, you're my hero."

"No, I'm *Lucinda's* hero," she countered. "We need an alchemist. Half of it seems to be in a different language."

"You're right," Vincent admitted. "And in this day and age, alchemists are hard to come by. If anyone knew where one was, it would be Lucinda."

Sam grunted. "Figures." Lilly opened her mouth to say something but stopped short as the front door opened and closed. Her eyes darted to Vincent, whose body became rigid and then slackened a few moments later when the servant Vincent had sent for clothes walked into the living room. He handed the bags off to Sam and Lilly and then with a quick bow, made for his retreat.

"I'll show you to the washrooms," Vincent replied, offering up his arm to Lilly. She flushed before settling her hand in the crook of his arm. Lilly looked up through her dark lashes and smiled. The prince smiled back and said, "Once you're both clean and happy, we'll start figuring out where to track down an alchemist and send a letter to Lady Evanora. I bet she'd know where to find one."

It sounded like a great plan and Lilly was thankful for a warm shower and clean clothes. At first, she'd been wary of the fact that she was standing in a prince's personal washroom, but the second she stepped into the warm, misty shower, all her worries faded away. She scrubbed the filth from her flesh and long, golden locks before standing in the relaxing stream for a few extra minutes, lost in her thoughts.

After she finished, Lilly dressed quickly in the clothes she'd been provided with. A cream-colored, cable-knit sweater, along with a pair of warm black leggings, wool socks, and black boots, all of which were a perfect fit. She braided her damp hair back, fastening it with a red ribbon, tying the perfect bow. For the first time in days, she was able to look into the mirror and feel like herself, not a nomad traveling through a snowy abyss.

When Lilly returned to the living room, Vincent and Sam weren't the only ones waiting for her. Craven Amsterdam had joined them, dressed in the same uniform she'd seen him wear in every paper he'd appeared in. Shadow Strike's silver hilt gleamed, looming over his shoulder. The crimson stripe that ran diagonally from his left shoulder to his right hip stood out in stark contrast against the black surrounding it. The Ally badge shined on his chest beside the Draconian symbol—a Black Butterfly. Other various badges adorned his chest. One, Lilly recognized was a Draconian medal of valor, which he'd been presented with after the Idonian Kingdom's fall.

Lilly swallowed hard. She'd known that once she arrived in Dracus, the odds of encountering Realm-renowned warriors were high. However, there was nothing that could have prepared her to stand in such a legend's presence. Being in the same room as Prince Vincent VanCamp was nerve-racking enough, but in Craven's presence, she forgot how to breathe. She joined her hands behind her back in a sad attempt to hide how clammy they'd become from him and nervously cleared her throat.

No one said anything right away. Instead, Lilly and Craven stared at one another. She didn't take her gaze off of his peculiar, violet eyes.

"Okay..." Craven said, the word dragging on. "Vincent, would you care to explain?"

The prince shrugged. "There really isn't much to explain. I was simply walking through the foyer when they arrived, so I brought them up for tea."

Craven cocked a brow. "How very royal of you."

Vincent cut him a dirty look. "You have yet to explain why you stormed into my suite without any warning."

"Oh, yeah." Craven chuckled, punching him playfully in the shoulder. "They have Ash. We're going to Crane. I came to tell you."

Lilly's heart skipped a beat. "My brothers are in Crane?"

Craven returned his attention to her. "Your brothers?"

"Quinn and Cooper," Vincent clarified in a careful tone.

"Oh!" Craven gasped. "Oh," he repeated, less enthusiastically. Lilly watched him blanch. "Does Loren know she's here?"

"Not yet," Vincent replied. "Why?"

Craven shrugged. "No particular reason. I suppose we'll be bringing them along then?"

Lilly's brows raised. "That way it can appear that you just brought us back," she said slowly to Vincent, turning to face him, earning a knowing smile in return.

"Why would it need to appear that way?" Craven asked.

"No particular reason," Vincent quipped.

Sam chuckled, drawing attention to himself. His smile quickly vanished with both Vincent and Craven staring at him. "So, we're going back to Crane?"

"Yes," Craven confirmed.

"Please tell me we're not walking," Sam pleaded. Vincent's laughter was capable of bringing a smile to anyone's face. Lilly beamed at the sound of it, her heart soaring.

"We have more efficient ways of teleportation," the prince said to Sam. "Don't worry."

8

Marcus slung his pack over his shoulder, prepared to join the others in the Throne Room, where they would use Lucinda's chrome sphere to open a portal to Crane. He couldn't shake the grin that had played on his lips since he'd heard the news. Marcus had been conducting an elemental test at the time, and his cheering was more than a distraction for the new Earth Clan member. But the student was understanding, nonetheless. After all, one doesn't defeat enchanted beasts and fill ancient scepters with Moonlight every day.

As the Mentor passed through the front door of his apartment, turning to lock it behind him, someone tapped him on the shoulder. He whirled around to find none other than Valentina Gold staring up at him, clutching her own pack. She wasn't dressed as she normally was, in a gown that always made Marcus's mouth water. Instead, she was wearing a pair of tight black pants and a blood-red wool cloak that matched the paint on her lips. Her long, golden curls were tied in a loose bun atop her head. He wondered if he'd ever seen her hair up before. If anything, it just made him desire her more. He could see more of the features he adored so much, such as her immaculate golden eyes, plump cheeks, and delectable lips.

"Val," Marcus greeted her, hoping he wasn't as flushed as he felt. "What do you have there?"

"My pack. I'm going with you to Crane," Valentina replied excitedly, taking Marcus aback with surprise. "I'd like to celebrate with Ash and help care for her. This pack is filled with medical supplies Hartford provided. He'll be joining us too."

Marcus's brow furrowed as he scratched his head in confusion. "Quinn didn't say anything about her being injured in his message."

"I had a vision," Valentina replied as her perfect lips pulled into a frown. "I saw how she'd walk out of that battle with the beast. Trust me, she'll need this pack." That smile Marcus had worn for hours quickly disappeared.

"How bad is it? Should I go back inside and fetch her anything?"

Valentina shook her head. "It's bad, but she has everything she needs where she is. It'll be good for her to heal in Crane. After all, that *is* her home."

"As long as she's happy," Marcus said honestly. That's all he wanted for Ash, especially after all she'd done and would do. He felt terrible most days. He'd torn her away from the life she'd known. He wished he could have just knocked on her front door and explained who he was and who she was related to. It should have been her choice, whether she wanted to leave Crane or not.

"You look sad," Valentina said matter-of-factly, interrupting Marcus's thoughts. "Why?"

Marcus shrugged and turned, staring down the Councillor's Corridor. Valentina started down it, a certain pep in her step that he hadn't seen in quite a while. He followed, hoping it wouldn't disappear too soon.

The Prophetess nudged him with her elbow. "Are you going to answer my question?"

"I don't know," Marcus grunted, rounding a corner, headed for the staircase that would lead them down to the castle's first floor. "I feel terrible sometimes. If I had just remembered my training, then I'd have known Ash was transitioning. I could have taken her back home instead of bringing her here. I could have eased her into this new life instead of just—"

"Don't go blaming yourself for her struggles," Valentina cut him off. "Ash was meant to come to Dracus when she did. You and Craven were *meant* to find her at that exact moment. You were *meant* to bite her, or else she wouldn't have turned into what she is now. Being a Berserker is what's going to keep her alive. Everything happened the way it was supposed to." Marcus huffed out a sigh and nodded, knowing that everything the Prophetess said was true. She reached out, taking his hand in hers. His cheeks warmed at the sensation of her touch.

"I despise the fact that that fight with the beast won't even be the worst of it for Ash," he admitted, his voice lowering to a whisper. His stomach twisted and turned. "I just hope that she'll heal quickly. That way, she has time to enjoy herself before she's forced to face all the horrors of the Underworld."

"I'd hardly call Xavier and the Dark Army *all the horrors of the Underworld.*" Valentina chuckled.

"You know what I mean."

Valentina released a weary sigh and said, "I know, but I refuse to think that way. I'd much prefer to think of other things, like letting loose for a change."

"Oh?" Marcus replied, lifting a brow. "And what does letting loose entail?" Valentina's lips curled into a suggestive grin.

"I'm not sure yet," she replied, batting her lashes. "But I suppose we'll find out."

Marcus and Valentina had arrived in the Throne Room, just a few moments before Craven and Vincent walked in with two unfamiliar faces. Before he could ask who they were, Valentina made a strange, gurgling sound at his side, her pack falling to the floor with a thud. His attention snapped back to her, only to find that her eyes had gone completely white, her head tilted back.

The man beside Vincent gaped at the Prophetess, fear dancing across his features.

"It's a vision," Craven stated before the man had a chance to ask. "You get used to it."

The girl didn't appear to be bothered by it in the slightest. She turned her attention to Marcus and offered him a smile as sweet as pie. "You're Marcus Bonaventure."

"I am," he confirmed, his gaze darting between Valentina and the girl. "And who might you be?"

"Lilly McBride."

Marcus could have sworn his heart ceased to beat. Now that she'd mentioned her surname, he could see the resemblance between her and Quinn. If there was a younger, female version of him, Lilly would be it. The only thing different about them was the shade of their eyes. Lilly's were a crushing blue, while Quinn's were a bright cerulean.

"I had no idea they had a sister," Marcus admitted. "You *are* their sister, right?"

Lilly nodded, rolling back on her heels while she turned her attention to the Throne Room around them. Her eyes shined brighter as she took everything in. "So, this is where Ash's coronation and Realm address took place. Sam and I watched it in Olaigon. It's safe to say we were *shocked*."

The man Marcus presumed was Sam chuckled, though he was still watching Valentina with wide, fearful eyes. "Yeah, we certainly weren't expecting that. I mean, we were all under the impression that Princess Penelope would be the next High Queen, not the girl who thought it was funny to throw daggers at unsuspecting people to see if they could move fast enough," Sam admitted.

"Ash did *what?*" Vincent balked.

"Sounds about right," Craven said with a sigh. "I keep encouraging her to train with different weapons, focus on perfecting her swordsmanship. But she can't seem to walk away from daggers, even for an hour. I suppose we all have our weapon of choice."

Sam finally tore his gaze from the Prophetess, looking toward Craven now instead. "You're training her?"

"I'm her Mentor, not that she needs me."

"Man," Sam grunted. "If someone would have told us that Ash would eventually be trained by *you*, we'd have all laughed, including Ash."

"How long do these visions last?" Lilly asked with a curious tilt of her head.

Marcus shrugged. "Should be over soon, but we never know."

"This is the first time I've witnessed one," Vincent admitted. "It's... odd."

"That's *one* word for it," Morghan said, slipping through one of the Throne Room's side entrances. He took one look at Valentina and winced. "I just don't like the way her eyes do that... *thing*."

Valentina blinked, her gaze returning to their normal, golden state. Red soaked the white around her irises, and her breaths came in ragged, shallow puffs. She took in the faces around her, a blush beginning to bloom upon her cheeks. "Sorry about that." She laughed nervously.

"What did you see? Was it about Malachai?" Vincent implored.

Sam's nose wrinkled with disgust. "Why would you want to know about him?"

"It was," Valentina responded. "But, what I saw wasn't *good*."

"Oh?" Marcus quipped.

"Do tell," Morghan drawled. "And please, make sure to include all the gory, sordid details about what's going to happen to him."

Valentina bit her bottom lip, her gaze dropping to her shoes. "Well," she started, kneeling to retrieve her fallen pack, throwing it over her shoulder before rising back to her feet. "I'm not really sure what to make of it. He looked normal. Like he did before he was a Pandora. And it looked like he was being hunted. He was captured." She gulped. "And then... tortured."

An uneasy silence spread throughout the Throne Room faster than a wildfire spread throughout the drybrush in Zerin. Morghan's grin vanished.

"I saw you, too," Valentina added, pointing to Lilly.

"Me?" Lilly squeaked.

"Her?" Vincent added, giving the Prophetess a long, disbelieving look.

"I think. Everything happened so fast that I could barely grasp what I was seeing. It came in vivid flashes. There were more things, too. It was like... like the Moons were dumping all of this information on me at once," Valentina explained warily, reaching to rub the back of her neck. "I haven't had such complicated visions in decades."

"Well, what else do you remember?" Marcus asked.

Valentina wrapped a loose curl around her finger, her brow wrinkling with thought. "The Idonian Council was at odds. Everyone was fighting. But, not all at once, and not all in the same place. A Guardian was being appointed. And then there was a wedding."

"A wedding?" Craven asked quizzically.

"And a funeral," Valentina whispered.

Morghan let out a long whistle. "None of that sounds good."

"Well, a wedding does," Vincent countered. "And a Guardian is always a good thing. But who's getting one? Penelope?"

"No," Valentina said, just as Hartford walked into the Throne Room, wheeling a suitcase behind him, glass bottles rattling within it. "Ash is."

Sam laughed. "Oh, she's going to *hate* that."

While the other Allies slept, exhausted from their Immortal run halfway across the Realm, Ash sat with Alistair on the window seat in her bedroom. She stared out at the falling snow, her breath clouding the chilled windowpane in front of her. Her finger mindlessly drew swirls as her mind raced to catch up with everything that had happened.

"You should rest," Alistair suggested, leaning against a pile of pillows, his long legs stretched out beside her, feet crossed at the ankles.

Ash shook her head, pulling her knees up to her chest, wrapping her arms around them. "I doubt I could, even if I tried." She left out the reasons why for Alistair's own good. She wished that she could tell him everything. It had been less than a day, and she was already drowning in a sea of guilt.

"Don't forget that I can sense you," the Rider reminded her. "Whatever you're feeling guilty about, you can tell me."

If only I could. Ash's shoulders slumped with grief. She met his gaze, wincing at the way he looked at her. As much as he could feel her guilt, she could feel his concern. He wouldn't feel that way if he knew that she'd just spent the night with the man responsible for his family's demise.

"It's about the beast," she said. It was a lie, but not entirely. Ash hated what had happened to him. She hated what she'd been forced to do as a result. "Xavier trapped him there. He was spelled so that he could never leave, and to attack anyone that came close. I spoke with him. He told me everything before the spell to attack me became too much for him to bear. Now, everyone's rejoicing in the fact that I obtained the Scepter. But all I can think of is how I murdered him to get it."

Ash felt Alistair's heart plummet. Bile crept up her throat as she fought against the urge to get sick. She closed her eyes, dropping her head to her knees, allowing her hair to fall around her, shielding her face. It was hard to breathe, and Ash felt tears spring to her eyes as a weight settled on her chest. Her lung burned, begging for air.

"That wasn't your fault, Ash, breathe," Alistair assured her, straightening on the seat, scooting closer to where she sat. "Xavier did that to the beast. If anything, you freed him."

"That's one way to look at it," she murmured, her throat tightening. "But the beast was just one of many."

"One of many, what?"

Ash lifted her face, sucking in a deep breath. "One of many that Xavier never gave a choice too," she spat, pushing off the window seat. "All he does is threaten people to do his will. I'll never forgive myself for any of the things I was forced to do. Did you know that most of the Pandora were *forced* to be Pandora? How many of them have we slayed? How many more will have to be killed? Xavier is the most manipulative bastard to have ever existed in Si Realtra. The word *choice* means nothing to him. Now, we all have to fight for what he started. I had to kill an innocent man, who was forced to harm an innocent man, who was driven out of his own home because innocent men were forced to kill other innocent men!" The rant came forward too quickly for her to stop it. "This war is *bullshit*. And we're all suffering because of Xavier's personal vendetta."

Alistair stared at her, his mouth agape.

"They thought I was turning into a Pandora," Ash added, pointing in the direction of the village. "During that battle that you and Willa saved us from. I started my transition. They thought—" Ash broke off, fighting back a sob. "They thought that one of them had bitten me when I was dragged beneath our line of shields. Because that's how most Pandora are changed. It's no secret. People just like you and I are dragged beneath lines of shields. And just like that, they are doomed." She snapped her fingers for emphasis.

"I guess I never thought of it that way," he replied softly, staring into nothing.

Ash swallowed her urge to scoff. "That's because no one does. We're born and bred to kill them. And, once someone is turned, whether they wanted to be or not, they have nowhere else to run except straight into Xavier's open arms."

Alistair raked a hand through his pale waves and pushed to his feet. He paced before Ash for a few moments and then turned to look at her. "Listen, Ash, I appreciate the wake-up call, but what exactly are you getting at?"

"I want to give them a choice," Ash blurted before she truly had a chance to think it through. Alistair froze, his muscle's growing rigid with surprise. "I don't know how, or really even why, but if we could give them somewhere else to go, someone else to fight for…" she trailed off, her mind whirling with all the possibilities. "Who says that the last Red Winter has to end with bloodshed?"

"Everyone else in the Realm."

Ash groaned, turning her back on him. She rested her head against the chilled windowpane and resumed watching the snow fall. *I made my choice. I chose you.* Malachai's words rang relentlessly within her mind. If the Prince of Darkness himself had chosen her, surely, others would too.

"I'll find a way," she insisted, whirling back around. "My reign might be a short one, but I'll bring peace. I'll make it so that whoever I choose to succeed me is able to lead a peaceful, unified Realm."

"That's a pretty big goal," Alistair said, a subtle warning in his tone. "The Idonian Council will fight you tooth and nail on it. Unity doesn't happen overnight. The Draconians spent centuries trying to be accepted by the other Immortals. The same *might* be possible for the Pandora, but what they've done is much, *much* worse than what the Draconians did during the Scarlet Era."

"I have faith."

Alistair looked at her as if she'd lost her mind. But, after a few silent moments, his features softened.

"The others won't like this," he insisted, crossing his arms. "But you have me. You've had me since the start of all of this, and you'll have me until the end."

A slow smile crept along Ash's lip. Her eyes looked up into Alistair's as her body slumped. "Thank you," she breathed, rushing forward, falling into his open arms. He wrapped them around her, holding her tightly against him before dropping a kiss to the top of her head. Ash stilled. Her stomach fluttered. She bit her lower lip and gazed up at him through dark lashes. Alistair's sky-blue eyes met her stare.

There was no missing the desire that lurked in Alistair's eyes. There was no mistaking his feelings. Ash remained still and cleared her throat as memories of his kiss and touch floated through her mind. They had both agreed to keep it a secret—to forget that it had ever happened. Yet, she knew that they were both thinking of it.

Ash tried to convince herself that it was wrong. That she shouldn't be considering any sort of love life, with so much on her plate already. Other women were often betrothed the second they turned eighteen. Ash's own sister was. But those women weren't *the Messenger*. They weren't about to risk their lives and face the Dark King.

Lost in her thoughts, Ash had almost forgotten that she was still standing there in Alistair's arms. It wasn't until he lifted a hand to brush a strand of hair out of her eyes that she snapped back to reality, her gaze immediately falling to his lips.

They might not survive the siege. Ash's mouth became dry. There may be no future for them, together or separately. But that didn't mean that they couldn't steal whatever time they could. Ash swallowed the lump that had been growing in her throat and licked at her chapped lips.

As if Alistair had known what Ash was thinking, he leaned down to claim her lips with his own, stealing the breath straight from her lungs. His lips were soft but fierce, claiming her entirely. Ash wrapped her arms around his neck, melting against him. There was something intoxicating about the way he moved his lips against hers. Ash had never experienced anything like it. Maybe it was the accidental lover's bond... maybe it was because such interactions were new and exciting... or maybe it was because she cared for him more than she'd admitted to herself.

Alistair's tongue nudged against her closed lips, beckoning to be let in. Ash obliged as Alistair explored her. Their tongues danced in circles as their kiss deepened and they drifted back to the window seat. Alistair collapsed upon it, pulling Ash onto his lap. She nipped at his lip, shuddering from his answering growl. His hands drifted down, landing on her hips. His fingers dug in tight, hooking his thumbs between her flesh and pants.

"We're not alone," he murmured against her lips. But at that moment, Ash didn't care. She straddled him, feeling his hardening length beneath her. Her heart was racing, the feeling of need coursing through her veins. She wanted him. Now.

Alistair grew still beneath her as the front door opened and shut, the sound echoing throughout the house. Ash leaned away and growled frustratedly.

"Great timing," she groaned, pushing off of the Rider.

A glint of mischief flashed in Alistair's eyes. "Oh, don't worry. Where there's a will, there's a way. I'm sure we can find the time to pick up where we left off soon enough."

10

The second Anastasia answered the front door, Craven and the others flooded into the foyer. He paused, taking the place in. It wasn't that long ago that he was sitting in some nearby brush, admiring the estate from an outside view. He'd envisioned having a family in a place like this, picturing his future children running around in the front fields. Now that he was standing inside, he knew this was the *only* sort of place he'd want to raise a family in.

A chandelier forged with deer antlers hung from the ceiling, filling the massive foyer in a soft glow. A grand staircase sat ahead, the railings carved and stained by caring, careful hands. A hall sat beside it, leading into the rest of the estate. To the right sat a parlor with windows that spanned the length of the front facing wall, while the rest were built-in bookcases. A bearskin rug lay centered on the floor. To Craven's left, was a family room filled with mismatched furniture—a large, brown leather sofa, a few comfortable chairs, one of which Aries was sleeping in. A fire roared in the hearth; the wood crackling and popping in Craven's ears. Craven stood there, lost in awe. It wasn't until the Prophetess punched him in the shoulder that he snapped back to reality. Valentina began barking orders, "Take Morghan and go fetch Ash. And be careful."

"What do you mean *be careful?*" Ana asked from where she sat on a bench beside the coat rack. All eyes turned toward the Fire Clan Leader.

"She's injured," Valentina stated matter-of-factly.

"She seemed fine to me earlier," Ana replied, crossing her legs as she leaned back on her hands. "She didn't even have a limp."

"That doesn't make any sense." Valentina's brows wrinkled, her eyes narrowing. She scratched at her head, absent in thought as she spoke aloud. "In my vision, she walked out of that fight with the beast torn to ribbons."

Aries emerged from the family room, rubbing sleep from his tired eyes. "Must you all be so *loud*," he grumbled. "Some of us had to run for over twelve hours."

Craven snorted. "You're talking to people who just spent weeks crossing Idona."

"Yeah, not everyone gets to teleport everywhere they go," Morghan shot at the Fae.

"That *was* the problem," Anastasia retorted. "We couldn't teleport anywhere near here. We had no choice but to run. And, I'll have you know, that finding our way into this place through the mountains wasn't easy. Whoever built the Hidden Village definitely wants it to stay hidden, that's for damn sure."

"And then there's the invisible barrier of course," Aries contributed. "That was a pain in the ass, even for the McBride's."

Valentina shook her head, holding up her hands to stop everyone from talking. "None of this has anything to do with Ash's condition. I know what I saw. I can promise you that she's *not* fine." Valentina closed her eyes, blinking away the shadows that danced across her irises. Whatever it was that the Prophetess saw, Craven imagined that it was unnerving.

"Whatever injuries she has, they're not physical," Aries stated.

Bristling like a cat thrown into water, Valentina replied, "I refuse to believe that."

"Go up and see for yourself."

"While you all argue, I'd like to know if anyone got my message about a change of clothes," Ana said, pushing to her feet, gesturing to her filthy uniform. "And I pray that Marcus thought to bring a meal, because all I want is to shower, dress in clean clothing, and eat until I pass out."

Craven's lips spread into a smirk. "Anastasia," he crooned, waiting for her to look at him. Her gaze settled on him before Craven shrugged off his pack and tossed it to her. Ana caught it with ease, her grin stretching from ear to ear. She took a few steps forward, rising onto the tips of her toes and kissed him on the cheek.

"About food," Marcus said, slipping his own pack from his shoulders. "I need a place to cook it."

"Follow me," Lilly and Sam said in unison, leading him down the hall while Anastasia rushed up the stairs. "You know, I'm a bit of a novice chef, myself."

Craven watched them disappear before his gaze shifted back to Valentina.

"I know what I saw," she said, setting her jaw.

"She's a Berserker," Craven reminded her. "Perhaps she healed herself."

All eyes turned toward Hartford, who shook his head, his arms crossed in front of his chest. "Even *I* don't heal that fast," he explained, pressing his lips into a fine line.

"Well, there's *one* way to find the truth," Morghan insisted, starting toward the stairs. Craven followed him, as did the others. The Wolf's supreme senses would lead them straight to Ash. "I smell blood, but it's pretty faded," he informed the others. "I also smell…" he paused, wrinkling his nose.

"What is it?" Valentina asked once Morghan failed to finish his sentence.

Cooper opened a door, stepping out into the hall, his brows disappearing into his hairline at the sight of everyone crowding it. "Good to see that you all made it here in one piece. I'm going to shower and then fetch some things from the village."

"Wine!" Ana called from a nearby washroom.

"Got it!" Cooper called back before disappearing back into his room, shutting the door behind him.

Morghan continued down the hall, stopping in front of a door on the right side. Craven stood behind him, peeking over his shoulder. "Is this it?" he asked.

"Seems so," the Wolf murmured.

"Well, are you going to knock?" Vincent urged.

To Craven's surprise, Morghan took a step back, bumping straight into him. "What's your deal?" Craven growled, stepping around him, bringing his fist up to the door, knocking three times.

"What if she can't get up to answer it?" Valentina asked, fiddling with her necklace.

"I'm telling you, she's *fine*," Aries argued. "She might be asleep. Moons only know how drained she is after that fight and the two tasks beforehand."

"Well, we should check," Vincent suggested. "Just in case. What if she was hiding her wounds? She really isn't the type to want people fussing all over her."

Unable to disagree, Craven wrapped his hand around the doorknob, twisting gently until he heard it click. He sucked in a deep breath and held it in place, nudging the door open. Inside, Ash and Alistair were sitting on a woven throw rug, daggers spread out between them.

"Oh, hello," Ash said, flashing the pearly whites of her teeth. "I was just about to get up and answer your knock."

Valentina and Hartford pushed past Craven, all but shoving him to the side like a useless rag doll. They stormed into the room; their scrutinizing gazes fixed on the High Queen. Both of their nostrils flared as they arrived in front of her. Ash didn't blink. Instead, she stared up at them, her smile growing wider.

"I wasn't expecting you two, but I'm so glad you're here."

Craven moved further into the room, scanning it curiously. He noted the books piled upon shelves. One lay open on the nightstand beside her bed. *The Adventures of Captain Loch: The Lost Isle.* Jasmine scented candles decorated every surface, along with framed photographs of her childhood with the McBride's.

"You're fine?" Valentina asked, staring down at Ash with sheer disbelief etched into her features. "But how? I saw you—"

"Come out of that fight with the beast shredded?" Ash asked, lifting a single brow, twirling a dagger in her hand. "I definitely did. You're not wrong. But I healed."

Hartford scoffed with disbelief. "No."

"No?"

Vincent and Morghan entered the room, the Wolf scanning his surroundings nervously. Something was amiss with him, but Craven knew it wasn't the right time to ask what. His gaze drifted to where Aries lingered in the hallway, the condescending look upon his face saying none other than *I told you so.*

"I don't believe you," Hartford declared. "I've seen your DNA. I've run it through dozens of tests to discern what your capabilities as a Berserker are. How is it that a stab from one of those daggers," he pointed to a few of the silver ones laid out in front of her, "nearly kills you, but after a fight like that, you heal overnight?"

Ash shrugged. "The beast's claws weren't enchanted?"

"Someone healed you," Hartford accused. "And I want to know who."

11

"No one healed me," Ash insisted, pushing herself to her feet. "I awoke with wounds, but they had already faded when I filled the Scepter. By the time I made it back here, they'd almost vanished entirely. After a shower and some blood, I was back to normal." All the lies felt sour upon Ash's tongue, but she ignored it. If anyone knew the truth, she would lose their respect. Her eyes darted to Alistair and back again. A wave of nausea swept over her as she fought to keep her feelings under control. He'd never forgive her, and, she didn't want to lose him. Not after everything they'd been through and done.

"I don't believe it," Hartford said, staring down his nose at her. Ash lifted her chin, straightened her spine, and fought to appear big, no matter how small she felt next to the mountain of a man.

"Well, you'd better start, because it's the truth."

Vincent cleared his throat, drawing their attention. "Ash wouldn't lie, especially to her Healer." Ash gave her twin an appreciative smile, despite the growing nausea in her gut. Oh, how completely and utterly wrong he was. She was lying, and it was crushing her. She'd promised herself that she wouldn't tell another lie after what had happened to Lincoln. If she had told him the truth, then he never would have stormed off into the mountains. And Lincoln never would have wound up in Xavier's custody. Tears bit behind her eyes as Ash threatened to lose her grip on her emotions. She swallowed the lump that was forming in her throat. She was betraying herself, but for good reason.

"Why would I lie about something like this?"

"I don't know, lass," Hartford retorted.

"Maybe we should drop it?" Aries suggested from where he stood at the threshold. "You're not just accusing one of your patients of lying, Hartford. You're accusing the *High Queen*." Hartford's lips pulled into a tight line as he backed away, turning his back on Ash.

"What matters is that she's fine," Craven chimed as he stepped forward, wrapping Ash in a warm embrace. "Besides, I prefer her more without gaping wounds." Ash chuckled; the sound muffled by his chest.

"You and me, both."

"I don't think there's a soul alive who can heal someone that quickly anyway," Aries added matter-of-factly. "If there was, then I would know."

MALACHAI KNEW THAT THEY WOULD COME FOR HIM EVENTUALLY AND he had prepared. *Wards.* Dozens of them. Each one protecting the property he'd claimed for himself from a different species. No one could teleport to him. No one could use any sort of Magic anywhere near him. Warlocks, Witches, and Wolves couldn't step past the barriers he'd set up.

But that didn't keep Savron from walking straight up to those barriers. Malachai had sensed his presence long before the Warlock had shown his face. So, while he waited for Savron's grand arrival, he cooked himself some venison stew and filled his belly. He watched as the sun dipped beneath the mountains from the cabin's front porch.

Out of the corner of Malachai's eye, he noticed a flicker of darkness in the tree line. Soon after, Savron was standing in the prince's line of vision, armed to the teeth.

"I sure hope you brought some ale," Malachai drawled. "I could really go for a glass."

Savron scoffed. "You think these Wards will keep me out?"

"They are, aren't they? That's why you're standing all the way over there." Malachai rose to his feet and jumped off the porch. He walked over to where the Warlock stood, the barrier he'd created flickering between them. Even so, he was still close enough to taunt him, and he'd always thoroughly enjoyed that. "You look angry. What? Did Veda throw you out of her bed again? Poor thing." The prince stuck out his lower lip. "Tell me, does she ever scream *my* name during your bouts between her silk sheets?" Malachai slipped his hands into his pockets and narrowed his red eyes. "I specifically remember how it sounded, rolling off the tip of her tongue. And *oh,* that tongue of hers..."

A vicious snarl escaped the Warlock's parted lips. He attempted to take a step forward but crashed into the barrier.

"This is just *too* much fun." Malachai snickered. "You might want to thicken that skin of yours. It shouldn't be so easy to get underneath it. Especially when we speak about a four-hundred-year-old woman's sexual exploits and who's been privy of her attention. She's had many lovers and will have many more. The only difference between you and me, is that she'll remember me a century from now."

Savron bared his fangs, resting a hand against the barrier. "Talk about Veda all you like. You're wasting your breath and just putting off the inevitable. You might be able to relish in the fact that Father can't kill you, but that doesn't mean I won't take immense amounts of pleasure in making you suffer."

"Well, then it's a good thing Father's reign is coming to a quick end, and I'm his heir, not you." Malachai's lips curled into a grin. "That might be because you're someone else's bastard that he took a liking to, solely because you're a Warlock." Malachai tilted his head to one side and watched his words hit a nerve. Savron flinched before regaining control of himself. "You were just a replacement for a son he deemed too weak to continue to raise. But at least *that* son shares his blood. Fuck, even *he* has a stronger claim to the throne," the Prince of Darkness hissed.

"I couldn't care less about titles," the Warlock insisted, crossing his arms. "But if family ties mean so much to you, then I suppose I could use what I know to single-handedly destroy any chance of the VanCamps continuing with their claim to the High Throne. Maybe I'll hand my family tree right over to the Elves. I'm sure good, old Thad would get a kick out Auntie Meera's lineage."

A chill crept down Malachai's spine as his blood cooled in his veins.

"Maybe I'll plan a family reunion," Savron continued with a shrug. "I've always wanted to get to know those cousins of mine. Two of them are right down the mountain. Perhaps, I'll go say hello."

All signs of amusement vanished from the prince's face.

"Does that bother you, 'Chai? The fact that the pretty High Queen you're enamored with and I share blood?" Savron taunted. His lips quirked into a devilish smile. "Tell me, was bedding her worth betraying your people?"

"I didn't," Malachai snarled. He wouldn't. That wasn't why he'd chosen to snap the leash his father had on him.

Savron's brows flicked upward. "Oh? Do you think that *weak* brother of yours has? What about Pat McBride's brats? Have *they* had a taste?"

A low growl reverberated in Malachai's throat.

"Either way," Savron continued, glancing down as if to inspect his nail beds. "If I can't get you today, I suppose I'll have to lure you out by killing them instead." Savron took a few steps back in retreat. "But, before I leave the area, I'll make sure to leave the High Queen's head right here, so that you can look at her face a bit longer before it starts decaying."

A portal opened beside the Warlock, and Malachai watched as Storm passed through, worry etched in every one of his features. "We have a problem in Solaris. Your presence was requested." The Sorcerer looked toward the prince, inclining his head to him. "Nice Wards."

Malachai forced a smile.

"What sort of problem?" Savron barked. "What could be more important than—"

"We've been infiltrated," Storm cut in.

"Then why aren't *you* handling it? Or Ryole? Where the fuck is Glen?" the Warlock fumed.

"Trust me," Storm whispered. "You're going to want to handle this."

Malachai's brows lifted out of curiosity. Who could have possibly infiltrated Solaris? Whoever it was, clearly, they were a cause for concern.

"Unless you're not done with your temper tantrum, of course," Storm said to Malachai, who scowled in response. "Very well then. Let's go. You can come back and finish your playdate later."

A snort escaped Malachai as he bit back his laughter. Savron glowered over his shoulder before disappearing through the portal. Malachai watched as it quickly closed, before letting out a sigh. He could breathe a little easier for the time being, and he could only hope that Ash and her Allies had left Crane before Savron returned.

12

Cooper wasn't sure what had made him think of Constance instead of Sam or Lilly. He didn't exactly have time to question it when he found himself standing inside of a bedroom, in the last place in Idona he should be. Solaris.

When he'd appeared, he'd startled Constance so badly that she'd almost fainted. She stumbled backward, nearly knocking a lamp off a nightstand. Once she had recovered, she raced toward him, her sky-blue eyes wider than he'd ever seen them.

"You can't be here," Constance whispered, her bottom lip trembling. "I can't *believe* you'd be so idiotic."

"Where is *here?*" Cooper asked, glancing toward the windows, each of them covered by thick, black curtains. "Why aren't you in Crane?"

Constance's restraint crumbled; tears brimmed beneath her thick eyelashes. "You didn't know," she choked out, turning her back on him. "Lincoln came for me. He brought me here, to Solaris. I've been here for weeks. Trapped. And now, you're trapped too. There are Wards. You can teleport in, but you can't teleport out. The only way to freedom is through the fucking front door."

Cooper's breath hitched. He wasn't prepared for that. His eyes widened and fingers curled into fists at his sides. After all he'd just endured during the three tasks, he'd finally made it home to Crane, only to stumble right into this mess, where the only way to escape was to *fight* his way out.

Out of habit, Cooper reached for his bow, but it wasn't there.

"Shit," he hissed, realizing he'd left it on his bed. After all, he'd thought he was teleporting into the village—not into enemy territory.

"What did Lincoln want with you?" he asked through clenched teeth. "Don't tell me that he's forgotten the rest of us but remembers *you*."

"He doesn't remember me," Constance spat, her eyes blazing. "It's Xavier who wanted me here. His deceased wife was my mother's sister."

Cooper's jaw dropped, a shiver skittering down his spine. "What?"

"My mother was a Witch, Cooper. And a powerful one, at that. So was her sister, and so am I. Granted, I don't know the first thing about Magic," Constance informed him, pacing before the fireplace. "But he's convinced that I'll become just as powerful, if not more. So, I'm stuck here, forced to share meals with him and his demented daughter every day."

Cooper raked a hand through his hair, still damp from his shower, at a loss for words.

"I hope someday I'll get a chance to explain more," Constance continued. "But we need to find a way to get you out of here."

"I'm not leaving you," Cooper said, shaking his head

"You don't have a choice. I'll only slow you down. Besides, I won't be harmed here. One day, I'll find a way out. At least one of us is here for Lincoln, even if he doesn't know it."

They stared into each other's eyes for a long while, enduring a silent argument regarding the matter.

"What about the siege?" Cooper asked. "What happens then when we invade this Kingdom with the Immortal Armies? That's one hundred thousand soldiers who don't know your face. They won't know that you're innocent. I can't leave you here to die. I can't go on and live the rest of my life, knowing that I had a chance to save you."

Constance walked toward him, wrapping her arms around his waist, burying her face into his chest. "I have a friend here," she whispered. "I'll be safe." She pulled away, staring up at him. "It's almost dusk. If you slip out during shift change, you might be able to get through the front door and teleport before being caught."

"Alright." Cooper pulled in a deep breath, before scanning her room for some sort of weapon. His gaze fell on a fire poker leaning against the hearth. It wasn't the most practical weapon, but it would do.

THAT PLAN MIGHT HAVE WORKED, HAD COOPER'S ARRIVAL NOT tripped the Wards. The Dark Army had already known he was there, and they made their presence known the second he opened Constance's door, slipping out into the hall. In a matter of minutes, he was running from a dozen Pandora guards, racing through unfamiliar halls, swinging the fire poker at anyone that came within reach.

Alarms wailed in every direction, blaring in Cooper's ears. He held his breath, every second of his life leading up to that moment, flashing before his eyes. He willed his legs to move faster, faster than they had ever ran.

Cooper rounded a corner, unaware of which direction he was supposed to go in, the hook of his poker colliding with a guard's face, catching him in the eye. The scream that followed would forever haunt the Archer's dreams. As he looked over his shoulder, bile began to creep up his throat at the sight of the gore trailing him.

Cooper impaled guard after guard with his poker, fighting against the nausea as he kept moving. After the fifteenth guard, he stopped counting his kills. It was pointless. More and more guards were waiting around every corner, rushing after him, shouting commands. Some transitioned, picking up speed in the forms of wolves or big cats. Bats swarmed him, slowing him down. He swung, and swung, making contact, listening to the thud of bodies hit the floor. Blood splattered on his face, painting him.

Doubt crept into Cooper's thoughts by the time he found his way to a staircase, flipping over the railing, landing in a crouch on the marble floor below. A long, wide hall lay in front of him. *The way out*. But for every Pandora Cooper killed, six more appeared. He was fighting a losing battle.

Sticky, crimson blood pooled on the floor around him, making it next to impossible to gain any traction as he pushed onward. The Pandora continued to pursue him, determined to keep him from getting any closer to freedom. The ones in the forms of birds clawed at his back, their sharp talons sinking into his flesh. He worked to shove them off while he ran, swatting at any that flew in front of him, with the poker.

To Cooper's surprise, the Pandora seemed to let up. He breathed a sigh of relief, pushing into Immortal speed, every muscle throughout his form burning from the effort it took to keep himself upright. But he soon learned that the reason those Pandora had retreated wasn't because they realized their pursuit was pointless. It was because an even bigger enemy waited in the foyer at the end of that hall.

Cooper slowed to a stop at the sight of the biggest bear he had ever seen standing on its hind legs. Its massive maw opened with a mighty roar that rattled the windows, putting its razor-sharp teeth on full display. Cooper's stomach churned, his heart thundering against his sternum. Rolling his shoulders, he prepared for the throw of his life. He whipped that poker through the air, aimed right for the beast's head.

The soupy, crunching sound the weapon made when it pierced through bone and brain left Cooper's skin crawling. He swallowed the vomit creeping up into his mouth, setting his sights on the front door.

Just as Cooper was about to throw the door open, something pierced his shoulder. A cry ripped from the Archer's lungs as he dropped to his knees, looking down to find that he'd been shot with an arrow. But not just any arrow. An Arebus Arrow.

Slowly, he looked up to find his brother standing at the top of a set of stairs, loading another arrow.

There wasn't enough time to push to his feet. Blinding pain seared through his body, stealing his breath. Before he had a chance to lunge for the door, another arrow sailed through the air, striking him just below the last rib on his right side. Blood poured from his wounds, hot and sticky, but the pain was subsiding. Cooper knew what that meant, hell, he'd seen it in his comrades as they'd fought against the Pandora invasion on Crane and lost. There were more arrows, but by the time the fifth struck him, he'd already started slipping into an unconscious state, his gaze fixed on the door that was close enough for his bloody fingertips to graze.

13

The McBride Estate was buzzing with life. Allies laughed, drank, and enjoyed themselves while they celebrated their success in completing the three tasks. After sending Aries to fetch more supplies in Dracus, Marcus worked hard to create a meal for them. They were short an Ally since Cooper had clearly decided to remain in bed for the evening. Marcus leaned against the counter with a dishtowel slung over his shoulder and let out a breath while dinner was cooking in the oven. Lilly had offered to help and made herself useful by peeling and cutting potatoes. He couldn't help but notice how much promise she showed in the kitchen.

The smell of homemade bread permeated the air, telling Marcus that it was ready to come out. "It's nice to have a fellow chef to work with," Marcus told her, pulling his bread out of the oven. "Usually, it's just me marching around the kitchen while everyone else enjoys themselves elsewhere."

"I rather enjoy cooking. It's always been the highlight of my day." She beamed, emptying her potatoes into a pot of water, and carrying it over to the stovetop. "I think I'll make an apple pie now. It's Ash's favorite."

"I'll assist," he offered. His heart soared. Marcus couldn't remember the last time he'd smiled so much.

The pair worked tediously to prepare the dessert. Occasionally,

Allies would walk into the kitchen, fetching bottles of wine, another thing Aries had been happy to retrieve. Eventually, Valentina made her way in, her golden eyes shining bright with joy.

"You look just like two peas in a pod," the Prophetess commented, walking over to the table where they both worked. Lilly was rolling out the dough for the pie crust while Marcus skinned the apples. "Do you need any help?"

"You could always help me with the apples," he told her.

Two chefs turned into the three. Before long, the ham was retrieved from the oven, the scent of it alone enough to send Marcus's evolving hunger into a mouth-watering frenzy.

"So, you mentioned a wedding," Lilly said to Valentina once she'd finished assembling the pie. "Any idea who's getting married?"

Marcus took the liberty of placing the pie in the oven, all while tuning into their conversation.

"I'm not sure," Valentina admitted. "Back when I first met Ash, I saw her get married, but I never saw who it was. I doubt that it was *her* wedding. It appeared to take place before the siege, and as far as I'm concerned, she isn't seeing anyone. It must be someone else."

Walking back over to the table, Marcus refilled his glass of wine, deep in thought about who Ash might marry one day. Names and faces flashed through his mind, but none of them appeared to be close enough to Ash for such a union.

Lilly wiped her flour-covered hands on her apron and said, "What about you two?"

Marcus almost choked on his sip of wine.

"Us?" Valentina gestured between herself and the Mentor.

"Yes," Lilly confirmed with a subtle nod. "Aren't you two…" she didn't finish the question, her gaze dancing between them. "Oh goodness, I'm wrong, aren't I? I'm so sorry."

Valentina chuckled. "Don't be."

Marcus's brows perked.

"Well, if it's any consolation, you'd make a fantastic couple," Lilly insisted, pouring herself a glass of water without even touching it.

Lilly, you're an absolute angel. Marcus pursed his lips so he wouldn't smile too broadly at the sound of her words. "She's not exactly wrong," he said, surprising himself.

Valentina blinked. "I suppose she's not."

They stared into each other's eyes as the rest of the Realm disappeared around them. If it weren't for Lilly clearing her throat, Marcus would have forgotten that she was still there.

"Valentina, if you intend on staying tonight, you're more than welcome to use my room. I can stay in Lincoln's, seeing as he hasn't been using it as of late." The Prophetess's smile disappeared.

"Oh, you don't have to do that."

"It isn't a bother," Lilly assured her, waving her off. "You'd much prefer my room, anyway, seeing as it isn't an absolute mess."

Valentina snorted.

Not all men are messy. Marcus frowned.

"I'll show you to it now, so you know where to go," Lilly offered, holding out her hand. "Marcus can start making the plates." The two women disappeared, and Marcus was left alone with his fluttering stomach.

Dinner was served shortly after, and everyone ate as though they had been starving for weeks. Conversations were held as the Allies reminisced about their tasks. Craven explained what it was like to nearly boil alive in a well beneath a smoldering Pandora base. Ana told them about Marcus's fall off a mountain. He cringed at the memory. And Morghan gave a detailed explanation of how Ash joined two lakes in the process of defeating the sapphire divisions assigned base.

"So, you two broke out of Dracus to join the others?" Hartford asked, shooting a glare toward Ash and Alistair. "How *exactly* did that go for you? I assume it went well, since that wound of yours seems to have healed."

Neither one of the Allies answered right away. Quinn got up to fetch another bottle of wine for the table, all while the others waited for the story they'd been yearning for ever since Ash and Alistair intercepted them at Veda's cottage.

"Well," the Rider started, shoving another forkful of pie into his mouth. "We started toward the Kingdom of Elves, since that's where we'd been told the rest of the Allies were. That crazy storm was still raging, and we wound up having to stay the night in a cave somewhere on the Strip. After that, the skies were clear. When we arrived in the Kingdom of Elves, Princess Mika told us what had happened with Lucinda and that the rest of you raced after her. And well, you know what happened after that."

"I'm mad at myself," Anastasia said quietly.

"Whatever for?" Craven asked from his place at her right side.

"I should have sensed her leaving," the Fire Clan Leader admitted, swirling the wine in her glass. "We might have been able to get to her sooner if I had. She wouldn't be under that spell."

Vincent perked up at the mention of the spell, which Marcus found to be quite odd. "Don't worry, we found a way to fix that."

"We did?" Marcus balked at him.

"Well, Lilly did," Vincent clarified. All eyes turned to the youngest McBride. She cleared her throat nervously and looked toward Ash.

"That book Cooper gave you for your birthday. I brought it to Dracus."

"Wait." Ash held up a finger, shaking her head. "You were in Dracus? When?"

"That doesn't matter right now. What matters is that in the book, I found a cure for Lucinda's curse. We just need an alchemist to create the formula."

The dining room fell into silence, every soul sitting around the table, staring at Lilly. Quinn walked back in, two more bottles of wine in his hands.

"What did I miss?" he asked, setting them down on the table. There wasn't a specific answer to the Archer's question. The only response he received was the roaring and cheering erupting from everyone in the room as they shot up from their seats. Morghan wrapped Lilly into a bear hug, lifting her off her feet. She squealed as the Wolf twirled her around. Tears swam in Valentina's eyes, and Marcus reached for her hand beneath the table, interlacing his fingers with hers.

"A toast to Lilly McBride!" Hartford shouted, raising his glass.

"Hey, I found it too, ya know," Sam grumbled, raising his own.

"Okay." Craven chuckled. "A toast to Sam Waters as well!" Glasses rang together, joy spreading throughout the room.

"And Pat McBride," Vincent added. "For writing the spell down!" More glasses rang. For the rest of the evening, there wasn't a face that didn't bear a smile.

Ash awoke in the early hours of the next morning to Valentina panting at her bedside. She rolled over, intent on pretending that she wasn't there. How long had it been since she'd had a good night's rest? She'd slept like the dead atop the East Cliff the night before, just a few feet away from a man who could have killed her so easily. She'd hardly call that *good* sleep.

A warm body lay on the other side of Ash's bed, and another at the foot of it. Her division members. Alistair and Morghan. Her heart warmed at the realization. The only person missing was Cooper, but Ash supposed he was getting the sleep he needed in his own room.

"Ash," Valentina growled, shaking her shoulder. "I had a vision. You need to get up. We have a serious problem." Ash groaned and pulled a pillow over her head, cursing into it.

"Can't this wait until the sun rises? Or, better yet, can't you go wake someone else?"

"You're the queen."

"So?" Ash snorted. "Contact my adviser."

The Prophetess tore the covers off of Ash's form. "You don't have one."

"Sure, I do," Ash argued. "You advise me enough."

"So you're suggesting that I talk to *myself?*"

"I suppose," she replied before reaching for another blanket.

A vicious snarl tore from Valentina just before she gripped Ash by the ankles, ripping her from the bed. She landed on the floor with a loud *thunk*, stunned to the core. She had just been assaulted, by her own adviser. "Was *that* necessary?"

"When one of our Allies is in the Dark Army's custody, I'd certainly say so!" Valentina snapped.

Ash's heart skidded to a stop. "What do you mean? We're all here."

"Are you sure about that? When was the last time you saw Cooper?"

"He's been sleeping," Ash argued, working to sit up, back aching from her fall. "He woke up to take a shower earlier and went right back to bed. We're all exhausted in case you haven't realized. You, of all people, should understand after you sent us on a journey with a thousand different ways to die."

Valentina's cheeks began to burn red-hot. Her jaw tightened and fingers curled into fists. She glanced toward where the Sovereign's Scepter sat, leaning against the wall beside Ash's vanity, her face twisting into damning glare. "I had a vision of him inside Solaris with a woman named Constance."

"No," Ash insisted, refusing to believe it. "*No.*"

"See for yourself. He's not here." Pushing to her feet, Ash stormed toward her bedroom door, bursting out into the hall with little consideration for the individuals sleeping around her. She rushed toward Cooper's bedroom, not bothering to knock before she flung the door open, stepping inside to find the bed unmade, and the room empty aside from the Arebus bow and quiver set on top of it. Dread settled in her stomach, her heart leaping into overdrive.

"No," Ash repeated, staring at the ruffled sheets. "*No!*"

The coppery taste of blood lingered on Cooper's tongue. He could feel it filling his lungs, drowning him. Every nerve throughout his body screamed in agony. It wasn't enough to just toss him in a cell, not after what he and the other Allies had done to the Dark Army's forces. He'd pay for each Pandora he'd slain. They'd make sure of it. If Cooper survived this encounter at all, it was for the sole fact that he was of use to the Dark King.

After his initial beating, where Savron had taken great pleasure in ripping every arrow Lincoln had fired from Cooper's flesh, he had blacked out again. The entire ordeal could have lasted ten minutes or ten hours. He no longer knew the difference.

Cooper woke sometime later, bound by chains, his eyes swollen shut. He could still hear the sound of those arrows flying through the air, headed right for him. Memories of the moments leading up to his graphic capture would plague him for the rest of his life.

Sweat dripped from his brow to his jaw, coating his flesh beneath his shirt and pants. White-hot pain flared in his lungs every time he dared to draw in a breath. All twenty-four of his ribs felt like they'd been ground into dust. For the amount of discomfort he was in, Cooper thought that they could have crushed every bone in his body.

But they had not shattered his will to fight. No matter how broken and battered he was, Cooper would find a way out of there.

After drifting in and out of consciousness for an unknown amount of time, the swelling in Cooper's eyes had gone down enough for him to see. His surroundings were exactly what he'd thought they'd be. A large cell, surrounded by iron bars. A table sat on the far side, covered in the sort of weapons that appeared in nightmares. He swallowed, feeling a chill skitter down his spine.

This is bad. He pursed his bloody, torn lips, and fixed his gaze on a whip. *Really fucking bad.*

Footsteps sounded down the corridor, drawing the Archer's attention. Savron Phantom was storming toward him. Cooper held his breath.

Payback.

That's what this was.

However, he wasn't alone. A woman with long dark hair and piercing green eyes walked at his side. She was dressed in a long, black velvet gown and trailing on her heels was Lincoln. And behind him was a man Cooper had recognized from the papers. It was an effort not to stare at his brother. The very sight of what he'd become made Cooper sick to his stomach. He'd caught a glimpse of him in Olaigon, but up close like this... those red eyes...

"It's good to see you awake, old friend," Savron drawled as a set of guards pulled open the doors to the cell. "I have to admit, we weren't expecting your visit."

"Neither was I," Cooper ground out, his voice hoarse.

A vicious snarl escaped the woman beside Savron. "You don't think we know who sent you?"

"No one sent me."

Savron slowly shook his head, clicking his tongue. "Cooper, Cooper, Cooper. Surely, you should know better than to lie to us. Tell us what we already know and I'll give you only fifteen lashings instead of thirty," he offered, nodding toward the whip on the table.

Cooper swallowed. Twice. "I'm not lying. I swear it. I thought Constance was still in Crane. I only teleported to retrieve her and my sister. I didn't expect to wind up here."

"I retrieved Constance weeks ago," Lincoln replied. He narrowed his red eyes into dagger-like slits. "And you expect us to believe that he didn't tell you she was here? That *he* didn't send you?"

"I don't know who you're talking about."

"Either he doesn't know or he's playing dumb," Lincoln growled, turning his attention back to the Warlock. "Thirty lashes, it is."

Cooper's pulse pounded in his ears, and his heart thrashed against the walls of his chest. While the Warlock walked over to the table, he found himself looking toward the only person who hadn't said a word. The man from the papers. "I don't know what they're talking about," he said, the words coming out weaker than he'd intended.

The man lifted a brow.

"Ignore him, Storm," Savron ordered. "You're only here to tighten his chains." Cooper's shoulders slumped with defeat as the man walked forward, a wand falling from his sleeve, landing perfectly in his grip.

"Don't let them do this," Cooper pleaded.

Storm did as he was asked, tightening Cooper's enchanted chains. A shout escaped the Archer as they bit into the raw flesh around his wrists and ankles. He moved onto the chains binding him to the stone wall, unfastening them so that he could be brought forward. Cooper was shoved onto his knees.

"Was this worth it?" he snarled as Savron stepped forward with the whip in hand. Storm stared back at him with no emotion visible upon his familiar face. "What did they do? Pay you off? Did they promise you riches and glory? Was all of it *so* appealing that you'd turn on everyone who loved and cared for you?!"

Finally, Storm's stony facade cracked. If only for a mere second, Cooper saw pain flash in his blue eyes.

"If you let them do this to me, you'll be twisting the knife you drove into Penelope's back," Cooper fumed, baring his teeth. "And when they come for me, and they *will* come for me, the first thing I'm going to say when I get back to Dracus is that—"

Crack!

Savron's whip came down hard on Cooper's back, slicing right into his spine, stealing the air from his lungs. He opened his mouth to scream, but not a single sound came out. Tears were already flowing down his cheeks by the time the whip came down again.

And again.

And again.

And again, until the Warlock eventually said, "When you get back to that queen of yours, you can show her your new scars, and tell her that she might as well have been holding this whip herself." Another strike tore through Cooper's flesh, grazing bone. A scream roared from Cooper's throat, his body sagging against the bindings. "Because the second she decided to trust my brother, she betrayed you all."

None of the words coming out of the Warlock's mouth made any sense. Cooper ignored them entirely, staring only at the Sorcerer in front him.

"Fuck. You!" he thundered between lashings. "I hope she's the one that snaps your fucking neck one day."

CHANGE

here would be no Allies headed into Solaris to retrieve Cooper. While this infuriated Ash to no end, she understood why. There were only eight of them left, and they would all be needed for the Idonian Kingdom's siege. However, Ash would still risk the lives of plenty of people she cared about that day. Her throat became thick as she watched Sam arm himself to the teeth.

"Are you sure about this?" she asked, wrapping her arms around herself. They were standing in the foyer of the Waters' family home. Pictures of Sam, Constance, and their parents were hung along the walls. To think that Constance was trapped in Solaris, and that Sam might very well be at the end of the day…

She sucked in a breath, wincing as her sinuses burned. Tears sprang to her eyes, and a sneeze threatened her near future. "We can send someone else. Humphrey was more than willing to go back to Solaris."

Sam shook his head and finished strapping his sword along his back.

"If Quinn can't go in there for Cooper, I will," he declared. "And if you're going to insinuate that because I'm a *Mortal*, that my survival chances are slim, then you should probably know that I'm *not* a Mortal."

"Wait, what?" Ash gaped.

"Constance is a Witch," Sam said. "What do you think that makes me?"

"B-but Warlocks are rare," Ash whispered. "Most men born into Witch families turn out to be Mortal."

"*Unless* someone awakens their gene," Sam countered, pointing to her Sectra. "Something like that could do the trick."

Looking down at the Amulet, Ash's brow furrowed. "I don't get it."

"It's all explained in that book," he told her. "When I get back from this mission, we'll look into it. For now, you're just going to have to have faith in our training. If you were deemed a good enough fighter to be made the Sectra Holder *and* the Messenger, then I think I'll be okay. Besides, my swordsmanship skills have always been better than yours."

Ash scoffed. "No, you just always *said* they were better."

"Want to have a duel and prove it?"

"I'm afraid we don't have time," she retorted, heading for the front door. Outside, the village was buzzing with preparations for the mission. The schoolhouse was in the process of being turned into an infirmary. Benjamin had sent Grant and their new Pandora partner over to assist in person, and they'd set up a war tent in the village square. The tent flaps were left wide open, and Ash could easily see the pair pouring over a table with Marcus.

As the Draconian General's second, Craven was placed in charge of the mission. He would spend the entirety of it in that war tent, communicating with the specialists using the various forms of technology Grant had brought along with him.

Jeremy, the baker, did his best to make everyone feel at home, as did the other villagers. Even though for most of them, the only Immortals they'd seen were Pandora, they treated all the Allies and their comrades with kindness.

As she walked over to the war tent, Ash noticed that while she'd been inside with Sam, the last of the reinforcements had arrived. She slowed her pace, eyeing the massive Elf. He was at least five times her size, with long, honey hair braided at his temples in traditional Elven fashion. The uniform he wore was a steel gray, and while he wasn't wearing a cape at the moment, Ash could tell by the various badges adorning his chest that he normally would be.

"No shit," Sam breathed, paling at the sight of the Elf. "They sent *him?*"

Perhaps Ash wasn't as familiar with the high-standing Immortals in Idona as Sam. "Who is he?"

"Who is he? Who is *he?*" Sam spluttered.

"That's Aveo Calloway," Alistair said from behind, startling Ash. She whirled around. "Sorry to sneak up on you."

"That's the man Penelope doesn't want to marry?" Ash whispered.

"Can't say I blame her," Alistair replied, matching her soft tone. "He's not exactly filled with rainbows and butterflies. That's mostly because he takes his position as a Commander *very* seriously. But I will say that he's probably the best person to send on this mission."

A sigh of relief emptied from Ash's lungs. They resumed their walk toward the tent, Sam practically vibrating with excitement to be in the presence of such a legend.

"Man, it was exciting just meeting Craven, Marcus, and Alistair," he admitted. "But Aveo 'fucking' Calloway? The Moons have blessed me."

There was no missing the pride shining in the Rider's eyes.

"At least you can find something to be joyful about today," Ash replied, entering the tent. Both men followed in on her heels. Grant and Anderson straightened at the sight of her, while Marcus continued to pour over the map on the table. Aveo didn't look Ash's way. He was too busy glaring at the Pandora.

"Your Highness," Anderson squeaked, bowing at the waist.

"Ash," Marcus mumbled without looking up from the map.

Ash's gaze slid over to the Commander, who now stood with one hand resting on the hilt of his sword. She didn't blame him. It proved that following through with her plan to give the Pandora a choice would be difficult. *Extremely* difficult.

"There will be no slaying Pandora inside Crane's borders," Ash said coolly, gesturing to that hand of his. Finally, the Commander's bronze gaze met her own. "At least for today."

Craven snorted, sipping the coffee Jeremy had provided him. "Anderson is harmless," he insisted, inclining his head to the trembling Pandora, who had now realized how badly the Elf in the tent wanted her dead. "She's an astrophysicist who's never transitioned. I wouldn't be worried about her. Besides, she's now a Draconian Communications Officer. Benjamin won't be pleased if she doesn't return to Dracus." There was a warning in Craven's tone that hadn't gone unnoticed.

"And she's here because she's familiar with Solaris and its current state," Marcus added. "Humphrey only saw bits and pieces. Anderson has seen far more."

"Will she be attending the mission then?" Sam asked.

"Unless we can find a better replacement, then yes," Craven said. His forehead wrinkled as he steepled his fingers to his lips in deep thought. "We need someone on this team that knows their way around any traps Xavier might set up. Anderson is our best bet."

Ash knew if they sent Anderson back into Solaris, the odds of her coming back out were slim. "Can you fight?" she asked, but there was no answer. Her blood quickly came to a boil, the heat radiating off her was enough to melt the snow covering the ground beside her feet. "Did anyone bother to ask her?"

"We don't have another option, Ash," Craven told her, raking a hand through his black, shoulder-length hair. "There's no one else."

"Pandora or not, I'd rather risk going in blind than allowing someone with no clue as to how to protect themselves lead us in and out," Aveo growled, taking them all by surprise.

"We could break the 'no Ally' rule?" Marcus offered. "I mean, Solaris has, no doubt, changed these last eighteen years, but I grew up there. I know those streets like the back of my hand."

"No," Craven replied tersely. "No council members either. So, even if the no Ally rule was broken, you'd still be benched."

"Aries is an *Idonian* Council member, and he's going," Marcus argued.

"*Aries* can teleport," Craven snapped.

Marcus cursed beneath his breath, kicking at the snow.

"Who else is attending the mission?" Aveo grunted.

Sam waved at him. "I am."

"He was trained by the same people I was," Ash told the Commander before he had a chance to object to Sam's mortality and weakness. "He can hold his own."

"Hartford is going too, as extra muscle *and* as a medic," Craven added. "Aries will be teleporting you in."

Aveo's shoulders relaxed. "That's not the worst team I've heard."

"But we still need eyes," Marcus insisted. "You may not be an Ally, or a Council member Aveo, but you still command an entire legion of the Elven army. You're not exactly expendable."

"And there's that whole possibility of becoming the next High King thing. You know, in the event that Princess Penelope takes Ash's place on the High Throne," Grant quipped. "It probably wouldn't be a good idea to go and get yourself killed."

"I'd say Princess Penelope has had her fill of perishing betrotheds," Ash mentioned.

At the mention of *possibly* becoming the next High King, Aveo's bronze gaze shone a little brighter. "Fine," he said. "There has to be *someone* alive who knows their way in and out of that castle."

Grant pursed his lips and scratched at the back of his neck. "As crazy as it sounds, Malachai would be the best person for the job."

Craven choked on his coffee. "Okay, first of all, no one knows where he is or *what* he's planning. For all that we know, he could just be biding his time until he can strike Ash again."

"He could have," Anderson blurted. "He knew everything about the Prophecy. He once said that he even knew where the Scepter was going to take her after she broke the spell. He would have known where to wait. So, if he was going to make another attempt on her life, he would have done it then."

Ash pulled in a deep breath, her heart skipping a beat.

"You seem to know a great deal about him," Marcus said to Anderson.

The Pandora nodded; her red eyes flitting between all their faces. "I worked with him directly on a few occasions. Well, him and Storm. All he really did when he was in Solaris was work in his lab, which was right next to ours. So, conversations took place."

"If you know him well, what do you believe he did once Xavier threw him out of Solaris? Where do you think he went?" Aveo asked.

"Honestly," Anderson started, biting her bottom lip. "I think Malachai would have taken that abolishment as an opportunity to clip his strings. He mentioned that once—that all he wanted to do was clip *'his strings and be free.'* I bet that's what he's doing right now. Being free."

Alistair scoffed. "Okay, he's still committed countless war crimes, so being *free* isn't exactly an option for him.".

"Technically, he hasn't," Anderson replied. "Xavier *did* occupy the High Throne. No matter how he won it, he still *won* it. Which means that anything Malachai was ordered to do from the moment the Idonian Kingdom fell to the moment Ash's coronation took place was an order from the High Throne."

Craven stared at the Pandora, his mouth agape. "Why does it seem like every word that comes out of your mouth is the equivalent of throwing grease on a fire?"

"She's not wrong," Marcus said, slowly shaking his head. "He's—"

"Don't finish that fucking sentence," Alistair snarled, baring is fangs. "That man is *not* innocent."

"Maybe not in the moral sense," Anderson told him softly. "But he can't be charged with any crimes committed during the last eighteen years." Alistair's rigid body slowly began to shake. He set his jaw and curled his fingers down at his sides.

Ash had never seen Alistair quite so angry. And now that she could feel his emotions, she was furious too. She swallowed hard before saying, "Excuse us," and shoved the Rider out of the tent, afraid he'd blow the entire structure to bits with the fire now engulfing his hands and wrists.

"Calm. Down," Ash demanded. She fought to control her own emotions, separating them from Alistair's. The villagers were staring at them now, probably remembering precisely why they didn't trust

Immortals. But all Alistair's anger did was intensify until it was a fiery storm fueled by his rage.

Ash felt her fangs extract without permission. This was too much. She reached for Alistair's wrist, biting back a cry as she burned her hand. Tears sprang to her eyes, silently spilling down her cheeks as she began dragging him away. It took every ounce of her strength to get him as far as she did.

They stood on a forest trail with the village still in view through the tree line, but they were far enough away to where no one would be harmed by Alistair's outbursts, or witness what Ash was about to do to him.

Using her ability to manipulate air, Ash blew him into the trunk of a tree, holding him there. The fire around his hands and wrists dissipated, smoke lingering in the air.

"Calm. Down," she hissed through clenched teeth. Twigs snapped beneath booted feet, announcing the arrival of Aveo and Marcus. Ash knew they would have followed her, wanting to defuse the situation.

"Ward," Aveo greeted him, eyeing the way Ash was holding him against that tree without any hands. "I'm no more a fan of this than you are. But what matters more to you? Your need for vengeance or the life of a fellow Ally?"

Ash's brows flicked upward, her fangs retracting.

"Obviously, Cooper's life," Alistair barked. "You can let me go now, Ash."

She stared at him for another moment before deeming him safe for release and let go of her invisible hold.

Marcus took her burned hand in his own, examining it. His eyes narrowed and lips pursed as he scowled. "We should get you to Hartford."

Alistair followed Marcus's gaze. "I-I'm—"

"Save it," Ash snapped, eyes blazing. "It doesn't matter. What matters is that you get a hold of yourself. Your outbursts don't only affect you." That was her way of saying something she knew the Rider would understand. She was forced to deal with *everything* he felt. "We all have reasons to despise Malachai. But you'd be surprised what I'm willing to do for the people that I love. Even if that means making deals with Dark Princes."

There was no arguing with that. Alistair silently nodded; his cheeks burning with shame.

"You seem to forget that we need to find that prince in order to make a deal with him," Aveo said.

Ash would much rather deal with the aftermath of the Allies finding out that she'd lied to them than waste another minute. "I know where he is," she revealed, biting her inner cheek as she waited for impact. No one said anything. "He's not far. We could get to him within an hour."

The Commander stared down at her, his expression unreadable.

"Marcus, take Alistair back to the McBride Estate. Inform the other specialists that's where they'll be gathering. Make sure one of the Communications officers is there to set them all up with the tech to communicate during the mission." Ash pulled in a breath before finishing her orders. "Warn the other Allies who'll be arriving, and tell them if they so much as scowl, they'll be sent back to Dracus."

The Mentor gave her a nod, reaching out for Alistair's arm. "What about your hand?"

"I'll be fine," she told him, looking toward Aveo. "You're with me. Let's go."

16

Sleep had escaped Malachai during his first night at the cabin. He hadn't been able to bring himself to stop wondering who had infiltrated Solaris. His stomach churned at the thought of how they fared now, especially since Savron had been summoned back to handle their punishment.

"It *has* to be an Ally," the prince mumbled to himself, sipping his morning coffee. "And if it's not, it was likely a teleporter. Aries. Goodness, what Savron would do to his wings?"

Malachai's stomach churned at the very thought. He set his coffee down, unable to stomach it anymore, and moved into the washroom. Thankfully, all the plumbing had been finished, and he was able to bathe in hot water before standing in front of the mirror, gazing at the same reflection he had thirty years ago.

The only difference between now and then was the length of the prince's hair. Malachai made the decision to cut most of it off.

After sharpening a dagger with a slab of whetstone, Malachai returned to the mirror and started hacking away at his dark-choco-late locks. Strands of hair fell, drifting down onto the tiled floor. By the time he'd finished, the sun was already high in the sky, and the prince's hair only fell to his collarbones instead of his waist.

"That's better," he insisted, tying it back with a strip of leather. There was no doubt that he would still be recognized, but at least people would now have to do a double take in order to discover who he was. It gave him a higher chance of being able to slip back into the shadows before they came to the realization.

Knowing that he'd need to travel somewhere for provisions, Malachai dressed in simple, warm clothes. He looked as if he'd been born and raised in Central Idona once he'd finished, clad in denim pants, a pair of boots, and a green-plaid flannel shirt. When it came to arming himself, he opted for a sword belt instead of strapping the weapon to his spine, giving off the appearance that he wasn't a warrior, just a simple man who wanted to protect himself. He kept the daggers he wore to a minimum, most of them strapped beneath his wool cloak, out of sight but not out of mind.

After filling a pack with necessities, Malachai threw it over his shoulder and prepared to take his leave. He waited until the fire in the hearth died down, unwilling to burn the only roof over his head to the ground, before walking out onto the front porch, and locking the front door behind him. When he turned around, he soon learned that he would not be headed to Witherow for provisions. Ash VanCamp and Aveo Calloway were waiting for him in the front yard.

Frozen in place, Malachai's mind whirled. Why was she there? Why was she with an *Elven* Commander?

Dropping the cloak's hood, Malachai made sure to give her his best scowl, green eyes quickly transitioning to red. "I'm armed and I will not go easily," he assured her, fingers curling into fists at his sides. She'd betrayed him. He'd asked her to reconsider, and she'd turned against him.

"I need to make another deal with you," Ash said, stepping forward while the Commander remained behind, hand resting on the hilt of his sword.

"If that's the case, why did you bring *him?*"

Ash looked over her shoulder, meeting the Commander's gaze. "It turns out everyone else was too emotionally involved, and there was no way they were going to let me go to you alone."

"Excuse me if I have a hard time believing that you're not here to detain me," Malachai spat, wrapping a hand around the pommel of a dagger sheathed at his hip. No part of him wanted to kill either one of them. He was done with death.

But he would if he had to.

"Do you have a place where we can talk?" Ash asked.

"Right here is fine by me," Malachai growled at her, his gaze dropping to her burned, right hand. "Who did that to you?"

The Commander and Ash's eyes both followed Malachai's line of vision. Ash's lips dipped into a frown as she held it out in front of her, turning it over, the scent of her burned flesh, seeping into the air. If she was in pain, she didn't show it. Instead, she said, "This doesn't matter. What matters is the fact that Cooper McBride is trapped in Solaris, and we need your help to get him back."

ASH WAS IN AGONY. IT WAS A MIRACLE THAT SHE HADN'T RUN RIGHT toward the prince, begging him to heal her. But in order to prove her point, she kept still, bearing no expression upon her face while all Malachai did was stare at her in complete and utter shock.

"*Cooper* was the one who infiltrated Solaris?" He shook his head slowly, snorting in disbelief. "Why the fuck would he do that?"

The Commander at Ash's side stepped forward, his bronze eyes narrowing accusingly. "If you cut ties with your father, how do you know Solaris was infiltrated at all?"

Malachai climbed down the porch steps, pausing once his boots landed upon the snow beyond them. His gaze was still fixed on Ash's hand as he said, "My father knows I betrayed him. He sent Savron Phantom to bring me back. But the Wards I set up kept him from getting anywhere near me. No Witches, Warlocks, or Wolves allowed," he explained. "I still spoke with him, though. Taunting him has always been a guilty pleasure of mine. While he was here, a Sorcerer called Storm opened a portal to fetch Savron. That's how I found out Solaris was infiltrated."

"It was an accident," Ash started, the searing pain in her hand causing her words to catch in her throat despite her best efforts to hide her pain. "We believe he thought of *Constance*," she paused to glare at the Pandora, "while he was teleporting."

"Oh," Malachai said, the color draining from his cheeks.

"We're sending a team in to get him," Aveo announced. "We need eyes. Someone who knows Solaris's current state. As much as I'd rather cut you down right now, I know you're the best person for the job."

Ash nodded in agreement. "We can strike another deal," she offered, grinding her teeth. "I just want him back. I'd do anything."

The Commander at her side shot her a disapproving look.

"I don't want anything," Malachai admitted, still staring at her hand.

Aveo scoffed. "Yeah, right."

"I'm serious," the prince growled. "All I want is to put this war behind me. So, unless you can do that…"

"I'm doing my fucking best," Ash imploded, throwing her hands up into the air, grimacing in the process. "But I can't do that without Cooper. So, if you're willing to help, then help!"

Malachai walked toward her. The sound of Aveo unsheathing his sword seared through the air, causing birds to leap from the tree limbs they perched upon. "Fine," he told her. "But I suggest that we head to Solaris immediately. The more time we waste, the more damage will be inflicted upon your Ally."

"I'm aware," she seethed. "Do you have any armor? A uniform of some kind? You can't walk into this mission wearing a flannel and jeans."

"Would you believe me if I said that I'd burned it?"

Pursing her lips, Ash started to think of an alternative. She looked the Pandora up and down, examining his height and size. "I have an idea."

"Am I going to like it?" Aveo grumbled.

"Not one bit," Ash informed him. "Follow me. Both of you."

No matter how hard he tried, Quinn couldn't sit still, calm his racing heart, or control his breathing. He'd entered a state of complete and utter panic the second he'd learned about what had happened to his brother, all while he'd thought he was asleep upstairs. Guilt gripped him like a vice, seeping into his every thought, overpowering any other feeling. And while he tried to appear unfazed for his sister Lilly's sake, he knew that she could see right through him.

"It's no one's fault," Anastasia assured Quinn as he stomped into the kitchen, pouring himself a glass of water with shaking hands. "Stop pacing around, blaming yourself. If it makes you feel any better, blame Morghan. He was one of the last people to see him."

The Wolf flinched in his seat at the kitchen table.

"I'm not blaming anyone," Quinn replied. "How were any of us supposed to have known that Lincoln had taken Constance until Sam and Lilly told us? Cooper was likely already gone before they even explained what happened. Why he thought of Constance instead of Sam or Lilly, we'll never know."

Ana nodded, her expression grave. "Constance is your betrothed, right?"

Quinn shrugged. "She was. We never really ended things before I left, but I think we both know it's not going to work."

"Because you're an Ally now?"

"No," Morghan said softly. "Because she slept with his brother."

"Oh," Ana said, the word dragging on. "*That's* why he thought of her."

"Not Cooper," the Wolf explained. "Lincoln."

"It doesn't matter," Quinn told them both. "I never wanted to marry her anyway. But that does not mean I am not bothered immensely every time I think of the fact that she's in Solaris, with no one familiar but a brainwashed Lincoln."

The front door opening and slamming shut caused everyone to jump. The sound of stomping feet and curses being uttered rang in Quinn's ears before Alistair and Marcus entered the kitchen, both of them equally bothered about something. The Dragon Rider appeared to be absolutely devastated, while the Mentor behind him looked about ready to tear his head off his shoulders.

"He's your responsibility now," Marcus grumbled to Ana.

"What happened?" Quinn ground out. The last thing he needed was for something else to go wrong. He was barely holding it together as it was.

All Alistair did was fall into an empty chair at the table, lay his head down on his arms, and shielded his face from everyone.

"We needed to add someone who knows Solaris's current state to the team we're sending after Cooper," Marcus explained, grinding his teeth. "Originally, we were going to send in Anderson, but Ash wouldn't allow it. She's untrained in combat. Then Malachai came up, and Alistair lost his shit. Ash tried to defuse the situation and wound up burning herself because this fuck can't control his emotions *or* his fire."

Quinn's heart stilled to a stop, his blood immediately beginning to boil as he turned his harsh gaze toward Alistair. "You burned her?" he asked, his tone dangerously low, anger rippling off him like a waterfall.

"I didn't realize I'd even summoned my fire." Alistair's voice was little more than a whisper. "She grabbed my wrist. That's how it happened."

"Where is she now?" the Archer snarled.

"Retrieving Malachai," Marcus said, a muscle feathering in his jaw. "Apparently, he's nearby."

Astounded, Quinn gaped at the Mentor. "And you let her go?" Unable to help himself, he stepped forward, fingers curling into trembling fists. "First, *he* injures her," he snarled, pointing in Alistair's direction with nothing but disdain for the Rider. "And then *you* let her go after the same man who's already attempted to kill her once?"

Marcus took a step back, eyeing Quinn's readying fists. "She's not alone."

"Who's she with?" Ana asked curiously. "Craven?"

Shaking his head, the Mentor said, "Aveo."

"Oh," Morghan said, sighing subtly with relief.

"Aveo *Calloway?*" Quinn fumed.

Marcus nodded. "I wouldn't be worried about her safety."

There was no doubt in Quinn's mind that Ash was safe, but that didn't deter him from boiling over with rage. The only interaction he'd had with Sir Aveo Calloway, back in the Kingdom of Elves, had left a sour taste in Quinn's mouth that would take centuries to fade. The Commander had not only disrespected Quinn by refusing to allow him to enter the Golden City, but also by speaking ill of his late father. Without Lucinda at his side, Quinn would have torn the Elf in two.

Now, that same Commander was alone with Ash, somewhere upon the Strip, seeking out the Prince of Darkness.

Quinn's stomach flipped, his heart thrashing against the walls of his chest. "I'm going after them," he declared, storming out of the kitchen to retrieve his bow and quiver and attach a simple, nameless sword to his belt before he exited the estate through the back door.

A gut feeling told Quinn to head south. He walked around to the front of the house, only to find three people walking up the snowy stone path leading up to the front porch. Pausing, Quinn's hand flew to the hilt of his sword. His cerulean gaze darted between their faces. Aveo, Ash, and ultimately the prestigious Prince of Darkness, who appeared to be far too *normal* to have ended so many lives.

"Quinn," Ash said, slowing her pace, taking in the look on the Archer's face. Her gaze dropped to the hand he held his sword with. "Going somewhere?"

Frowning, Quinn advanced a few steps. "After you."

Malachai and Aveo shared a quizzical look, as if they were trying to figure out which one of them the Archer despised more. The truth was that he didn't know, but he *remembered* Malachai. He could still see the Pandora standing in the estate's foyer, getting quite the tongue lashing from Pat. Up until that moment, Quinn had never put the puzzle together. He'd never realized that the Prince of Darkness was the same *Chai* who had once known his father.

"Go inside," Quinn directed.

All three individuals took a step forward, but Quinn held up his hand, causing them all to stop. "Ash and the prince," he clarified, summoning his worst glare for the Elven Commander. "I'm afraid I can't allow you to enter."

Ash blinked. "What?"

"Go inside," Quinn repeated, nodding toward the front door. "Don't let him near Alistair."

While Ash had every right to disobey Quinn's order as High Queen, she didn't utter a single word. Instead, she gave Aveo a sympathetic look and nudged Malachai toward the porch. The second the Archer heard the front door shut he asked, "How does it feel?"

The Commander lifted a single brow. "I outrank you," he said simply.

"Not here." Quinn chuckled. "Crane is the only place in Idona that doesn't belong to a jurisdiction. You're on my property now, and considering how disrespectful you were to me last time we met, I'd say I have every right to make you stay where you are."

Aveo's lips twitched toward a smirk. "I'm fine where I am. Nice house, by the way. It looks incredibly peaceful. Pat did well for himself."

"Fuck off."

The Elf snorted. "It was a compliment. And I thought *my* temper was bad."

Quinn snarled, baring his teeth. "I don't want to hear my father's name coming out of your mouth again," he warned, fighting the extreme desire to wrap one of his hands around an Arebus Arrow and drive it straight into the cocky bastard's—

Aries teleported, arriving right in front of the estate, startling Quinn so badly that he stumbled backward. The Fae had brought along Sam, Hartford, and a Pandora, Quinn knew to be Anderson —a petite young woman with short black curls and pretty eyes, despite their red coloring.

"I assume we're all here?" Aries asked, his gaze dancing between the Archer and the Elf.

"If by that you mean if Malachai is inside, then yes," Aveo answered.

"We brought a light meal to eat before we go," Hartford began to explain. "And of course, Anderson will need to prepare to set us all up with our bugs."

"Bugs?" Quinn lifted a brow.

"Communication devices that fit perfectly inside the ear canal," Anderson explained. "They allow users to hear directions and communicate verbally, yet also inconspicuously."

"I hope we're inconspicuous altogether," Sam said, visibly shivering. "Either way, let's eat quickly, arm ourselves, and get Cooper back."

Everyone nodded in agreement, and though he didn't want to, Quinn allowed Aveo to enter with the others. If the Elf was willing to attend such a dangerous mission to get his own brother back, the least he could do was let him eat first.

ASH HAD LED MALACHAI TO A BEDROOM UPSTAIRS, WHERE THERE was already an onyx division Ally uniform laid out on the bed. He dressed quickly, pleased with the fit. Whomever she'd instructed to lend him one had a strikingly similar build.

While arming himself, Malachai heard a knock on the door. He finished strapping his sword along his spine as he said, "Come in."

Malachai had expected that it would be Ash, coming to retrieve him. But it wasn't her at all. It was Morghan Henning, and a young woman with a long, golden braid and sparkling blue eyes. *Pat's eyes,* the prince thought, his mouth growing dry. A tray with a sandwich and a cup of tea sat in her trembling hands.

"This is for you," she said, her voice surprisingly strong despite how timid she appeared.

"As much as I'd love to see you starve, it isn't in good practice to send a man into battle on an empty stomach," Morghan added.

"Thank you," Malachai told the girl, refusing to give the Wolf the time of day. He watched her walk further into the room, setting the tray down on a desk. Unwilling to be a rude guest, he waited for her to rejoin Morghan in the threshold before walking over to pick up the sandwich. Salami. Not his favorite, but anything other than venison stew was pleasing to his taste buds.

"Once you finish, we'll take you down to the dining room where the others have gathered," the girl explained. "In the meantime, do you mind if I ask you a question?"

Morghan shot her a look of warning, but she ignored him.

"Ask away," Malachai replied, if only to get under the Wolf's skin.

"You've been all over the Realm, so you must know where I can find an alchemist."

Brows rising, the prince finished swallowing his most recent bite, nodding in confirmation before he said, "I'm an alchemist."

"Of course, you are." Morghan rolled his eyes. "Lilly, might I remind you that your brother told us to only deliver the food, not to start a conversation?"

"What do you need one for?" Malachai inquired, sipping the tea.

Lilly sighed heavily, wrapping her arms around herself. "We found a way to break the Realm Sorceress's sleeping spell, but we don't know anyone who can understand the required formula. Even Hartford can't make sense of it."

Though he tried not to show it, Malachai knew exactly what Lilly was referring to. He also knew where she'd found that formula. But telling her the truth would only ruin whatever image she had of her father. So he did his best to feign ignorance.

"I can have a look at it," he offered.

"Wonderful!" Lilly chirped. "I'll retrieve the book it's written in right now." With that, she scurried away, leaving Malachai alone with one of his oldest enemies.

Morghan leaned against the door frame, glaring at the prince. "You're not fooling me." His nose wrinkled with disgust. "I don't know what game you're trying to play by getting close to Ash and doing all of these good deeds, but don't think for a second that I won't rip your throat out the second you step out of line. These people have worked too hard and lost too much, to be betrayed. Your very presence here has driven a rift in my Allies. The mere mention of your name resulted in an injury for Ash."

The Wolf's last sentence caused Malachai's appetite to vanish.

"Also, might I add that a Werewolf's senses are superior to those of any other Immortal? But I'm sure that you're aware of that," Morghan sneered, a smug smirk playing on his lips. "They're so strong in fact, that I could smell if a woman is with child, and who the father of that child is. Which means I can also smell when a pair of individuals share blood."

Malachai's heart skidded to a stop, every one of his muscles becoming tense.

Morghan's gaze dropped to the uniform the prince was wearing, chuckling softly. "I might be able to smell better than others, but that doesn't mean they won't see. Especially now that you've changed your appearance. I hope you realize what you're risking. Your reputation might not matter to you, but for some people, it does. And if people start to put the pieces of that puzzle together, you will *ruin* his."

"That's the last thing I want to do," Malachai hissed before he had a chance to stop himself. "I've done *everything* I could to save him from the life I was forced to lead."

"Just be careful," Morghan warned. "No matter how badly you want to escape your father and change your ways, you have to consider whether your freedom would be worth his downfall. I would suggest that after this, you stay the fuck away from these Allies. Stay the fuck away from Ash, and *especially* stay the fuck away from Marcus."

They stood in silence, staring each other down, until Lilly returned with an all too familiar book in hand. She went on to show Malachai the formula needed to break Lucinda's spell, and he told her that he'd help. However, he hadn't told her *how* he'd help. And, adding yet another task to the mission Malachai was about to endure would be dangerous. But Morghan had made it entirely clear that the prince was better off disappearing altogether. So, if making that formula into a serum capable of waking the Realm Sorceress was the last thing Malachai ever did, at least he could say that he died doing something that would better the Realm of Idona. For once.

18

Xavier should have been thrilled that yet another Arebus Archer had arrived in his custody, but the second he set his sights on Cooper McBride, his stomach lurched with disgust.

"What have you done?" he snarled viciously, whirling around to face Savron.

The Warlock shrugged. "Every wild horse must be broken."

"And you think that after you've *mangled* him, this man will gladly serve us?" Xavier could hardly breathe. Thoughts of how badly he wanted to strangle the man in front of him flooded his mind. "In the end of all of this, when all of our fallen are released to join us, *that* man will be the one to lead the Archers. And you just whipped him into oblivion! Give me one good bloody reason why I shouldn't have your fucking head!"

Savron blinked, every single one of his muscles growing visibly stiff. "Father, he almost killed me."

"And you've almost killed him!" Xavier thundered. "Wars are not won by getting an eye for an eye."

Well said, X.

Xavier flinched, having forgotten for once that Meera remained within his mind, chiming in whenever she felt necessary. *Thank you,* he added and meant it.

What will you do with him?

Cooper or Savron?

Both, I suppose.

"This was a perfect opportunity to speak with him," Xavier informed the Warlock. "We could have detained him just long enough to tell him the truth, and then send him on his way to ponder it. His Amorian blood would have roared in his veins. He would have realized what had been done to his people, and that we all deserve this redemption. He would have joined us in the end. Now, he never will."

Savron scoffed, shaking his head in denial. "His own father betrayed us. What makes you think he wouldn't realize that too? Start to think about why it was that Pat left the Black Legion, hmm?"

"If Pat sided with anyone, it was the Erminians. He was never one of us. Not when his father practically sold him to Queen Raina," Xavier explained. "He lived over a hundred years with that bitch whispering in his ear. He was lost to us. But that young man in there is just barely eighteen. He's fresh. Moldable. And he's a teleporter. A bloody rare treasure, and you've turned him into a bloody mess!"

"He'll live," was Savron's response. He turned his back on the cell and the limp heap of flesh slumbering within.

Before Xavier could beat the Warlock to a pulp for his dismissive attitude, Ryole stormed down the hall, a letter in hand. Xavier sighed with relief, snatching it from the Commander before he'd even had a chance to announce who it was from.

X,

They're sending people after him. I'm not sure on the specifics, but I know one of them is Aries. They won't send in any Allies, so it could be anyone. I'm told Loren requested Elven assistance.

The Allies are still in Crane.

Valentina has had some interesting visions. She predicts that the Idonian Council will be at odds, and that Ash will receive a Guardian. She also mentioned a wedding, and a funeral. Since she returned to Dracus, she's had three more visions, but she hasn't spoken about them to anyone. The only company she keeps is Penelope, who's all nerves. We had dinner last evening, while everyone else was gone. Sweet girl, really. You should resend that offer to marry her, though now you'll have Aveo Calloway and Loren Mason to contend with.

There's no word on Malachai. If Valentina decides to share about her visions, I'll be sure to let you know what they entail.

Your Humble Servant

"Well, this is hardly helpful," Xavier grumbled, tossing the letter back at Ryole. "Either way, at least we know to prepare ourselves. They're sending people after Cooper. One of them is Aries."

Savron cursed beneath his breath. "If he decides to use his Magic, we're all fucked."

"He'd never disobey his queen," Ryole drawled.

Ryole is right. Aries would never disobey Cleo. But if he did... after centuries of bottling that Dark Magic up...

Xavier cringed. *There's no need to finish that sentence.*

"I'm removing you from your post," the king informed Savron. "Storm and Soroya will oversee the Archer from now on. You may return to the Regal Mountains and ready our forces there. I'll see you at the siege."

Savron's face crumbled. "But I was supposed to go to the island *before* the siege."

"You've proved that you're unworthy of the Dark One's blessing," Xavier told him matter-of-factly. "Soroya will receive it instead."

"*Soroya?*" Savron balked.

"She's my heir."

"But I'm older," the Warlock argued. "And I'm more experienced. The Pandora *listen* to me."

Ryole snorted. "I don't listen to you."

"Sod off, Ryole."

"Fetch Storm," Xavier ordered. "And when you return to the Regal Mountains, inform your sisters that they're to be on standby. After what the Allies did to our numbers during that first task of theirs, we'll likely need reinforcements."

The Commander at the king's side bristled. "Pardon me, Your Majesty, but the Witches are meant to fight in Erim, not Idona. There they'll only have to worry about the Elves. The Draconians here in Idona will tear right through them."

"We need the numbers," Xavier spat at him. "Update the Rat."

Ryole bowed at the waist before retreating without another word. Savron lingered a moment longer, as if expecting Xavier to change his mind. "Irina won't allow it," the Warlock warned. "You seem to forget that she's our High Priestess, not Veda. She will not send her Witches into battle against the Draconian Elemental Clans. She'd condemn them to their deaths by doing so."

"Did I ask for your opinion?" Xavier inquired, lifting a brow. "I don't recall doing so. Another word from you, and I'll lower your rank even further. So, unless you intend on being a grunt on the front lines, I suggest you walk away. And before you embark on your journey home, inform Glen that we're to have company."

Scowling, Savron did just that. He stormed back down the hall, quickly fading from Xavier's view.

That poor man, Meera started again once they were alone. Xavier could sense her looking through his eyes, staring at what had become of Cooper. *He's hardly breathing.*

"I'm aware."

Why not just let him go? Or at the very least, allow Storm to use a healing spell on him.

A heavy sigh escaped Xavier before he said, "You know I can't do that. While I am extremely displeased with Savron's behavior, we need the Archer. Not to mention, with him in our custody, we have one less Ally to deal with. What Veda did to Lucinda was a real treat, but this... it must be my birthday."

While Lilly remained upstairs to keep Alistair company, Morghan led Malachai down into the dining room, where the others were waiting to review the plan. Upon entering, the prince was met with tension so thick that even an enchanted sword would have trouble slicing through it. He'd expected as much, but that didn't make it any easier to stomach. Not when every soul seated around the table had their weapons well within reach. The only people that *didn't* appear to want to kill him were Ash and Anderson, who was the last person he'd expected to encounter at the McBride Estate.

"Malachai," she greeted, offering him a wry smile.

"Anderson," he replied slowly, his brows pulling together.

"I take it you haven't seen the news," Morghan said from behind, pushing him toward an empty seat beside Aries. The prince dropped into it, biting back a growl at the sight of the Wolf's smug smirk. "Every journalist in the Realm is either talking about how your father threw you out of Solaris, or how Anderson betrayed him and ran out of the city to swear fealty to the Draconians."

"And soon enough, they'll be talking about how Xavier is holding an Ally captive," Craven's voice rang from a device in front of Ash on the table. "Now that we're all here, can we focus? Time isn't exactly on our side."

Ash nodded, shifting uncomfortably in her seat. Malachai's lips curved into a frown at the sight. She could try to hide the fact that she was in pain all she wanted, but he saw right through her. He opened his mouth to offer her help, but the scowl she gave him led him to shut it.

"Alright, here's the plan so far. Aries will teleport everyone in. Thanks to Anderson, we know that there are Wards preventing anyone from teleporting out. We're certain that's how Cooper wound up in this predicament. If we can disable the Wards, all you'll need to do is get to Cooper and then teleport out," Craven explained.

"We are, of course, aware that it won't be that simple," Anderson added. "Those Wards are airtight. Disabling them isn't something that we can do remotely. Whoever takes on this task will need to get into the powercell, and the code to do that changes every fifteen minutes. Grant will be able to hack into it and provide you with the proper code, but that's just step one. Once you're inside, you'll have to know what you're looking for. These Wards aren't physical. They're technological. And, as I'm sure you can imagine, there are thousands of different Wards placed around the castle. Finding a specific one would be worse than trying to find a needle in a haystack if you're not able to read code."

Someone cursed beneath their breath. Malachai's gaze shifted over to Aries, who was currently massaging his temples. "What ever happened to *normal* Wards? Why is everyone so deterred by runes these days?"

"I'll admit that I know nothing about any of this," Aveo said, leaning back in his chair. "What about you?" he asked Hartford.

The Berserker shook his head. "I'm with Aries. The only Wards I understand are created with Magic, not technology."

"I don't understand *any* Wards," Sam said with a frustrated grunt. "In case you haven't noticed, Crane's a little behind the times."

"I do," Vincent frowned, "but I can't participate."

People started to murmur, growling about the Ally ban on the mission. Malachai observed them while waiting for all the chatter to stop. As far as he was concerned, most of these people were strangers a month ago, yet they acted as if they'd known each other for years.

"There's a kill switch," Malachai revealed after a while, causing all the chatter to stop abruptly. "For the Wards," he clarified.

Anderson perked, curiosity flashing in her eyes. "I was never made aware of that, and I was the one in charge of the powercell."

"That's because no one knows about it," he told her. "When my father asked me to place the Wards after he won the Kingdom, I made sure to create a fail-safe. I never told anyone I did it. Until you, no one worked in the powercell. I handled everything, hence why my lab was built around it. Anyway, I can disable all the Wards at once, but it'll incite complete and utter chaos if I do."

Ash tilted her head curiously. "If you're familiar with coding, why can't you just disable the Ward we need?"

Malachai cocked his head, a small smile blooming on his lips. "Well, Your Majesty, if I disable *all* of them, my father will lose every layer of protection he has in an instant. Anyone would be able to walk straight into Solaris *and* the castle. There wouldn't be any Wards for him to activate to stop them." He tapped his fingers along the table, watching the realization expand across her face.

"I see," Ash drawled, a glint of mischief shining in her eyes.

"Without me or you, Xavier won't have anyone to replace the Wards," Anderson concluded, shaking her head in amazement. "But, if you disable them all, you won't have anything to hold back any reinforcements with. We can assume that Cooper's being held in the same area Lincoln was—the old dungeons. Of course, we won't know for sure until Grant succeeds in hacking into Solaris's mainframe, gaining access to their security footage. But, if he is where we think he is, there could be any number of people guarding him. Even if you defeat them easily, more will come. *Unless* you activate a Ward that prevents them from entering that floor."

Malachai nodded, biting his inner cheek. "That's possible, but I fear that I can't be two places at once. The others will need my assistance. The second we teleport inside, we'll trigger the Wards. They'll know that we're there. I have an advantage over the Pandora, but my father has more in his arsenal. My sisters are all powerful Witches, and I'm not sure how many are in Solaris. All three of them could be now, not to mention Savron. I'm sure that Ash has already told you about his involvement. There are also Sorcerers, the most notable being Storm and Cade."

"Magic wielders," Aveo murmured with a deadly scowl.

"How long would it take for you to use the kill switch and enable a protection Ward over the castle's bottom floor?" a new voice asked. Malachai could only assume that it was Grant.

"Ten minutes at most," Malachai told him.

"Have you had any luck hacking into Solaris's mainframe?" Anderson inquired.

"I'm getting there. You didn't exactly make it easy to do this."

Anderson's prideful smirk didn't go unnoticed.

"Disabling the Wards is just one task," Malachai said. "There's something else that I need to be able to do while I'm there."

"This mission isn't an excuse for you to tie up loose ends," Aveo snapped.

"It isn't a loose end," Malachai started. "Lilly showed me the formula for Lucinda's cure. I have the ingredients in my lab, and the knowledge to make it."

Ash's eyes grew wide across the table, her lips parting slightly. Beside her, Quinn's expressions changed rapidly from anger to confusion, then to outright shock.

"But you just said you'd be needed elsewhere," Ana countered angrily. "So now you're supposed to be *three* places at once?"

"I don't have to be," Malachai replied, reaching to rub the back of his neck. "Technically, anyone could make the formula."

Anderson's brows wrinkled with thought. "I could set up a separate channel and have someone here read the ingredients and measurements to whoever's making it. I could also install a camera in their uniform too and connect the feed to one of the screens back in the village so we could see what they're doing."

"Any volunteers?" Ash chirped.

"I can do it," Hartford replied. "I'm confident enough in medicine. I know a great deal about Magical cures, but I'm attending this mission as a medic."

"And for brute strength," Aveo added.

The Berserker gave him a nod. "That too."

"Aren't you a Healer?" Anderson inquired, her curious gaze falling on Malachai. "Don't you have an ability or something?"

Ash went rigid in her seat, the color draining from her cheeks.

"Before I became what I am, I was a Healer," Malachai confirmed, forgoing any mention of his ability after watching Ash's reaction to Anderson's question.

"Great. Malachai can take Hartford's place as the medic and Hartford can take Malachai's place as the alchemist, Craven chimed. But that still doesn't solve the Ward problem."

"We need more people," Sam insisted.

"I could always handle the Wards," Anderson offered. Aveo and Ash immediately shook their heads in protest, but the Pandora continued anyway. "I'll stay in the powercell and won't see any action. And, if Hartford is going to be working in Malachai's lab, then we'll be right next to each other. It'll take some of the weight off everyone else. If I'm doing that, the others can head straight for Cooper. By the time they make it to his cell, the Ward problem will be solved, and I can move on to helping Hartford with the cure."

There was no arguing with that. Malachai sank back in his chair, watching Ash and Aveo share some sort of silent conversation. Why *he* was the one she was looking to made no sense to the prince.

"Fine," Ash reluctantly agreed. "But you'll need a uniform, and I'm arming you to the absolute teeth."

"Why? She's a Pandora, can't she just transition?" Anastasia asked with a snort.

"That's a long story," Craven said.

"Back to the healing though," Anderson started again. "You have an ability. I remember, because everyone talks about how weird it is that you got one and no one else did."

Malachai swallowed his groan. Of *course*, she'd circle back to that. Out of the corner of his eye, he watched Ash shrink further into her seat, grimacing, likely because of her hand. "I'm a certified

Healer in Idona and Erim. Whether I have an ability for it or not doesn't really matter. I'm still qualified."

"I've never heard of an ability like that," Aries commented. "So, if it's true that you have one, I'd like to see how it works."

"It could make the world of difference for Cooper," Quinn added, now staring toward the prince with pleading eyes. "He tried to kill Savron. I know your father won't want Cooper dead, but that doesn't mean that sick fuck isn't enacting his vengeance some other way. By the look on your face right now, I know that I'm right in assuming so."

Pursing his lips, Malachai averted his gaze from the Archer's face. "I do, but it might not be enough if what you're assuming is true. Savron is known for torturing his enemies, healing them, and then starting all over again. He likes to bring people to the brink of death. Knowing him, he'd rather Cooper die than escape. My father would feel the same. Historically, teleporting Archers are the Arebus leaders. They're so rare that only two others have come before Cooper. Your father Pat, and his father Sylvian. The truth is that Cooper is your biggest asset, and one of my father's biggest threats."

"Why would Cooper be a threat to your father?" Aveo asked, his bronze eyes narrowing. "I thought Queen Ash was his only true threat."

Grinding his teeth, Malachai thought of how to respond. He'd need to choose his words carefully unless he wanted to cause an uproar. "It would take me far too long to explain why, and we need to focus on Cooper's safety. Like I said, my father would rather him be killed than handed back to the Allies. My ability might not be enough to help him. If you want him to live, you'll have to think of a backup plan. My suggestion would be Marcus's venom."

Gasps sounded around the table. Marcus, who'd been silent throughout the entire meeting, slowly shook his head. "You can't be serious."

"You yourself were in a similar position, were you not? The only reason you're alive right now is because Lucinda got you to Dracus in time." Malachai sucked in a sharp breath, exhaling slowly before he continued. "I'm just saying, it would be another fail-safe. A precaution."

Marcus growled, baring his teeth. "Either King Loren or I would have to be present to administer the venom," he replied. "It's Draconian law."

Nodding, Malachai said, "I'm aware of that. But, if we're being honest, that law creates a huge risk. Far more lives could be saved if people didn't have to rush to Dracus in order to escape an early death. You got lucky. If we have to teleport Cooper to Dracus when he's already in a fragile state, he might not be."

"If Draconians were able to choose who they change at will, the result would be pandemonium. That law is in place for a reason," Craven argued.

"You don't think I know that?" Malachai grit out. "I'm not asking you to petition Loren to repeal the law. What I'm asking is for an exception. Unless you would rather me use *my* venom. In which case, problem solved."

Morghan's nostrils flared. "Absolutely not."

"Great, we're in agreement for once," Malachai shot back before he turned his attention to Ash and said, "You wouldn't have come to me, putting your entire reputation at risk, if you weren't willing to do anything to save Cooper. This might very well be your only way to do that."

Ash clenched her jaw. "Are you *certain* that your ability won't be enough?"

"It's hard to say without knowing what his condition is," the prince explained. "But I've known Savron his entire life. If I'm telling you that I think it might be necessary, then it's necessary. Not everyone's a Berserker. We don't all heal as easily as you do."

Hartford shot to his feet just as Ash's eyes began to bulge, her jaw dropping. Malachai recoiled, the realization of what he'd just done hitting him like a bag of bricks. He opened his mouth to apologize, but closed it quickly, knowing that nothing he said would make a difference. Everyone seated around the table was now staring at her the same way she'd once stared up at him, the moment he drove that dagger into her side. He wasn't sure what she'd said to them, but it was evident that they felt betrayed. Even Quinn was looking at her as if *she* was the Prince of Darkness.

"You knew where he was," Hartford said so softly that it was startling. "He has the ability to heal. You *lied* to us. Straight to my face, lass."

Vincent's face crumbled. "How?" he asked, his gaze darting between his twin and the prince. "What, have you two been working together or something? First, you let him live when you had the opportunity *everyone else in the Realm* has been waiting for. Now this?"

"No," Ash snapped defensively. "I was injured. He helped me. That's the beginning and end of it. I knew where he was, yes, but I chose not to detain him as a thank you. Don't read too much into it."

"But you *lied*," Morghan growled. "And after what he *did* to you, I can't believe you'd let him anywhere near you."

A crack seared through Malachai's heart. He fought to ignore it. He deserved every harsh word they had to say.

"I'll have you know that he's the *only* reason I was able to fill the Scepter," Ash seethed, pushing to her feet. "I did what I had to do to finish the fucking tasks. If you want to crucify me for it, go right ahead."

"We don't have time for this!" Quinn thundered. "Right now, you should be preparing to leave. Marcus, can they take your venom with them or not? I'd prefer to get my brother back *alive* more than I would prefer lighting into Ash."

Marcus nodded, his expression grave. "Aries will have to teleport to Dracus to retrieve a syringe of it. He can say that the High Queen demands it."

"I'm on it," Aries declared before he vanished.

"As for you," Hartford fumed, his gaze burning with hatred meant for the prince, "heal her hand. I want to see just how much you helped my kin. Depending on what I see, I might not rip you apart and scatter your limbs around the Realm for the wolves to gnaw on. I happen to know one that would be *thrilled* to tear into you."

Morghan's responding smirk stretched from ear to ear. Malachai dared to roll his eyes, pushing to his feet and walking around the table. He arrived at Ash's side, taking her injured hand in his. She refused to meet his gaze, her features contorting with fury; however, she relaxed once he summoned his ability. The others watched in awe as her blooming blisters and charred flesh faded back to normal.

Releasing her hand, Malachai stepped away. She dropped back into her chair as if she'd been struggling to stand, her gaze fixed on the table in front of her. Shame flushed her cheeks, and guilt twisted Malachai's stomach into knots.

"If you're going to tear me apart," the prince said to the Berserker, "at least let me do what I came here to do first."

20

When the meeting ended, Anastasia took Anderson upstairs to get her in uniform while Quinn headed to the weapon's closet to find things to arm her with. Lilly came downstairs with Pat McBride's book so that Malachai could get started on translating the formula into something easy enough for others to understand. Vincent started equipping the mission attendees with tech per Grant's instructions, and Ash found herself desperately in need of fresh air.

The party would leave in half an hour, which gave her time to collect her thoughts somewhere out in the fields before she would return to see them off. She'd much rather stay outside and freeze instead of remaining where everyone else could look at her as if she'd chosen to fly the Dark King's flag.

Once everyone else was busy, Ash slipped out of the back door. Over forty acres of snow-covered fields sprawled out before her, sparkling in the late afternoon sun. Ash headed out into them, picturing how the property appeared during Spring Solstice, when the snow turns to rain, leaving sprouts on the once bare trees. The snow melts, revealing miles of luscious green grass beneath. Everything about the Realm is vibrant and full of life—a new beginning after another gruesome winter.

Next year, however, when the snow began to fall, there would be no bloodshed. No one would be afraid the second delicate flakes fell from the clouds above. Winter Solstice would become just as beautiful and peaceful. By then, no one would care if Ash had aligned herself with the Prince of Darkness to heal her wounds and save one of her oldest friends. They'll be too busy building snowmen and starting snowball fights. But would her Allies forget? Would they forgive her lies so easily?

Groaning, Ash wrapped her arms around herself. She shouldn't have lied. She knew that. At the end of the day, she wasn't entirely in the wrong. She'd needed help. It wasn't her fault that the only person there was the one person no one trusted—the person everyone had one reason or another to despise. And, for good reason. Would they have preferred for her to be too weak to fill the Scepter?

Lost in her thoughts, Ash hadn't noticed anyone approaching. When Alistair stepped in front of her, Ash staggered backward, her boot catching on a patch of ice. She recovered, just in time to keep herself from tumbling down into the snow.

"I heard everything," he fumed, nothing but hatred burning in his eyes. His emotions slammed into Ash hard enough to rip the breath straight from her lungs. Her knees wobbled beneath the weight of them all, threatening to give way. "Of all the people for you to lie about…"

Ash set her jaw, her fingers curling into fists at her sides. "If I wanted to be berated, I'd have stayed inside." She pushed past him, unable to withstand staring into those hateful eyes for another minute longer. How he could kiss her one day and look at her in such a way the next was beyond the limits of her imagination.

One of Alistair's hands wrapped around her wrist, stopping her from taking another step. Ash whirled back around, baring her teeth. "I'm sorry that I lied, but I won't apologize for anything else," she snapped. "Quite frankly, I'm appalled by the fact that you would all prefer to rage about *how* I was healed instead of being thankful for the fact that I *was*. Would you rather me stand before you now, bleeding and broken? Would you rather me have missed my shot at filling the Scepter eternally?"

Releasing her hand, Alistair took a step back, his lips disappearing into a hard line before he said, "You don't know what it was like to find you the way we did. Bleeding out, buried beneath all that snow. I was terrified that you would die on the journey back to Dracus. That I wouldn't make it there in time. Morghan is right, and he wasn't even the one who had to bear the weight of saving your life. How you could let Malachai anywhere near you after all of that, we'll never understand."

"I didn't have much of a choice," Ash told him miserably. "You know what it's like to be attacked by the beast. Can you imagine how it would feel to go through what you went through and still be expected to do what I had to afterward?" She waited for a response, crossing her arms defensively. Alistair didn't give her one. Instead, he averted his gaze from her face, a muscle feathering in his jaw. "This prophecy has done nothing but put me in danger. It has pushed me relentlessly to do the impossible. Every corner I turn, there's another merciless task waiting for me. Even if I'm shredded by a beast, I'm still expected to move forward. There is no time for me to sit and lick my wounds. I did what I had to so that I could succeed."

The Rider turned away from her, raking a hand through his pale hair. "I get it, okay?" he spat. "I just don't understand why you would let him live. After what he did to you and everyone else, you just let him walk away because he healed you. Why? Do you think that he's changed all of a sudden?" He whirled back around, anger heating his cheeks. "Does nothing that happened to anyone else matter because he did *one* good thing? Can you really be that inconsiderate?"

Ash's stomach and jaw dropped in unison.

"My sister was six years old," Alistair fumed as despair flooded his features. "And he stood there and let his fucking brutes *slit her throat.*"

Dropping her gaze to the toes of her boots, Ash's cheeks began to heat with shame.

"He destroyed Morghan's entire species," Alistair continued. "He murdered your sister's betrothed and *my friend* in cold blood. He captured Lincoln and injected him with something to erase his memories and turn him into an unfeeling, relentless *monster*. He created a species that's killed hundreds of thousands of people over the last three decades. Hundreds of villages across the Realm have been leveled because of him. He single-handedly turned our Realm upside down, but because he healed you, I suppose all is well then."

Hot, angry tears began to puddle in Ash's eyes. She tried to blink them away, but a few slipped past, rolling in steaming streams down her chilled cheeks. "You know that's not true," she said, swallowing a sob. "You know I don't feel that way. You can feel it. Why say such harsh things when you already know the truth?" She took a few steps back, her heart shattering. She knew he could feel that too, but nothing about his expression changed.

"I don't know what the truth is anymore," Alistair shot back, his nose wrinkling with disgust. "I thought you were different. I pinned you as the *last* person to betray anyone. To think that I actually *fell* for you—" he stopped himself, scoffing.

Ash's breathing slipped out of her control, panic setting in. Alistair could clearly tell how he was making her feel, but that didn't stop him from continuing, anyway.

"If you like Malachai so much, go be with him," he threw at her. "You must, right? What was it, love at first sight? Is that why you didn't kill him when you had the chance the first time, back in that forest when you met? You know, when you carted him along, allowing him to belittle us day after day. I mean, he did stab you, but for all I know, you *could* be into knife play—"

Unable to stop herself, Ash slapped him. The palm of her hand collided with his cheek, the sound of the impact echoing through the fields. He staggered backward, his hand flying to his cheek, eyes bulging. "How dare you?" she seethed, her vision blurring as tears continued to pour from her eyes. She sniffled, wiping them away with the back of her hand. She stepped back, trembling with rage, her blood roaring in her ears. "It's always been the two of us. Together. We arrived in Dracus within hours of each other. We took our elemental test together. We were put on the same Ally division. You saved my life. You were the only person there when I became

High Queen. I *gave* the most *precious* thing a woman can give *to you.*" She tried to breathe, but her throat was too tight. Her chest felt heavy, her stomach twisting and turning in knots.

Ash knew she couldn't withstand sticking around to hear whatever he had to say next, so she turned around and headed back toward the barn. He followed her, clearly unwilling to relent.

"I didn't know," he insisted, reaching for her wrist. Ash snatched it back. "Please, stop. I shouldn't have said any of that, I know. I'm sorry."

"It's a little late for apologies," Ash snapped. "I'd like to collect myself. Alone. Go inside and tell Marcus and Quinn that you're being placed on another division. They can fight over you and your dragon. While you're at it, tell everyone else that there's no reason to ream me out. You did that enough for them all."

A low growl reverberated from Alistair's throat. "You can't be serious."

"Oh, I'm serious," Ash replied, fighting against the urge to summon air, turn back around and blow him onto his back. "No one has *ever* spoken to me that way. Sure, I made a temporary alliance with the most terrible person to walk upon Idona's soil. But I did it to fulfill a prophecy, and now I'm doing it to save someone that I've known my entire life. Someone that I shared a *cradle* with. If you want to condemn me for it, go right ahead. No one ever said that I needed to make friends or fall in love to be the Messenger. I was expected to do whatever it takes. I'm doing it."

"I get that," Alistair insisted.

Shaking her head, Ash bit back a laugh. "If you did, you wouldn't have questioned my loyalty or my motives. Now, leave. Please. You've said enough."

Though it was clear he didn't want to, Alistair walked away. He left Ash in the barn with only her misery to keep her company. In silence, she worked on unraveling the knots twisted in her stomach.

Dropping down onto a bale of hay, Ash scanned the barn around her, hoping to change her train of thought. She could recall a day where the horses used to live in the empty stalls across from her, before the stables were built a year back. A memory came to mind at the sight of them, one from two summers ago, before she'd learned the truth about her origin and the blood rushing through her veins.

Ash and Lincoln had just entered the barn after a long day watering and tending to the plots. Cooper and Quinn were still out in the fields, harvesting garlic and onions. Lilly's lessons hadn't ended for the year, and Eliza was too ill to see to the animals, so it was up to the two of them. They started with the horses, refreshing their hay and water.

After finishing up with her favorite *noble steed*, as Lincoln liked to call them, Ash left the stall, turning to lock it behind her. When she turned back around, Lincoln kissed her.

It happened so fast that at first, Ash hadn't registered that it had happened at all. "Did you just kiss me?" she'd asked to be sure.

"That depends," he'd replied with the same dashing crooked smile that had always made her heart jump into a skittery dance. "Are you mad?"

Ash had shrugged and said, "I don't know. Maybe you should do it again."

Back then, everything made sense. Sure, the Pandora were still a threat every Red Winter, and during the other Solstices, their days were filled with the same mundane tasks, but they were happy. There were no secrets between them, or distance. There were no prophecies or injections. No Ally badges or crowns. No Dragon Riders, Dark Recruiters, or Dark Princes.

What Ash would give to turn back time, at least for a day. She'd even settle for an hour if that meant she could relive that moment. That simple, trivial moment where she shared her first kiss with the man she'd thought she would be with forever. Perhaps they could have been if they'd just told one another the truth. If they had, would she be suffering from such heartache now?

Ash shook her head, willing those painful thoughts away. This was her mess. No one was at fault for it but her. She wiped what remained of her tears away and shot to her feet, sucking in a breath so deep that it filled her lungs to the very brim before she let it loose in one, sharp huff. From that moment on, she would no longer entertain the idea of a future. Not until she was able to put this prophecy, and this war behind her. She wasn't entirely certain that she *had* a future. Spending what could be her last few weeks or months suffering from a broken heart once again was foolish. There was work to be done, and Ash knew better than anyone that time flew by far too fast.

Once she was sure that she wouldn't burst into tears the second she met anyone's gaze, Ash prepared to leave the safety and silence of the barn. She'd nearly made to the doors when she started to hear the shouts. A ripple of fear stroked Ash's spine as she pushed the doors open and rushed back to the house, skipping into Immortal speed.

The shouts continued, and ideas of what might be happening swarmed Ash's mind. Had they decided Malachai had already helped them enough? Was Hartford making good on his promise and tearing the prince limb from limb? Ash's stomach turned sour at the mere thought.

As Ash drew closer, the sounds of sobs greeted her ears. Her heart sank into the depths of her roiling gut as they flooded her ears. *Lilly,* she concluded, slowing her pace. If Lilly was sobbing…

Ash's sinuses started to burn with her own coming tears. Part of her wanted to turn back around and retreat to the barn's safety. Perhaps she'd crawl into one of those empty stalls, put her hands over her ears, and shut her eyes tight, pretending this was all some nightmare.

There was no hiding from this. Ash knew that, so she forced herself to continue and rounded the side of the house just in time to watch Aries appear, a syringe of Marcus's venom in hand.

"What happened?" the Fae asked, his gaze dancing between Ash and the house.

"I don't know," she told him. "I was out back when I heard the screams."

Before Aries could reply, Willa pierced through the clouds, aiming to land out in the fields. Ash's heart shuttered right along with the ground once she succeeded. Next, Quinn barreled out of the house, his cheeks stained with tears, his cerulean eyes brighter than Ash had ever seen them. He took one look at her and his features crumbled. He hurried down the front steps, crashing into her. He wrapped her in an embrace so tight, it was almost as if Ash were an anchor, the only thing keeping him from blowing away in this storm.

"Grant got into Solaris's mainframe," Ana said, now standing on the front porch. "He gained access to the security footage." She didn't need to say another word. Instead, she pressed her lips into a grim line, slowly shaking her head, confirming all of Ash's suspicions.

"Oh." The word came out cracked. Broken.

Steeling herself, Ash swallowed the sob creeping up her throat and turned her attention back to Quinn. He was shaking so terribly one might think an earthquake was triggered within him. She wrapped her arms around his waist, steadying him.

Willa crept around the side of the house, her massive form quickly swallowing the front lawn. Ash met the beast's solemn, sapphire gaze just before her attention was diverted by Malachai storming out of the house, Aveo on his heels.

"What, you're just going to leave now?" Anastasia snapped, gesturing angrily to the pack slung over the prince's pack.

"Yeah," Malachai replied, matching her tone. "For Solaris."

"Why?" Sam asked, the question wavering. "You saw the footage—"

"I refuse to believe he's dead," the prince cut in. "And even if he is, the least I can do is return his body to his family. If you don't want to join me, then don't."

"We still need Lucinda's cure," Lilly mentioned, her voice dry and worn. Ash eyed her, noting how hard she was trying not to shed another tear. Her small fists were clenched, her chin lifted with determination.

Aveo nodded. "We'll get it."

Malachai's brows shot upward. "We?"

"I would move mountains if Cooper was one of my men," Aveo informed him, his bronze eyes narrowing. "If he was my brother, I'd tear through hordes of Pandora with only a rock to defend myself with to get to him, whether he be dead or alive. No man deserves what I just watched on that footage."

"I agree," Anderson said, now in uniform and armed to the teeth just as Ash had demanded of her. "We don't know for certain if he's dead. And, even if he were, he deserves far better than to be tossed into some unmarked mass grave."

Ash's blood chilled at the mere thought.

"I'll still participate," Hartford declared.

"So will I," Sam added.

"I say that we act as if this mission hasn't changed," Aries suggested. "We go with our current plan."

"Agreed," they all said in unison.

Ash watched in awe as they all joined hands before disappearing right before their eyes. Just like that, they were gone, and she had no clue whether she would see any of them again. As guilty as it made her feel, she realized how horribly she'd feel if Malachai lost his life in Solaris, or wound up in chains, forced to serve his father for the rest of his days.

Lost in her thoughts, Ash hadn't noticed Willa creeping closer. Like a cat, she nudged both Ash and Quinn with her massive muzzle. She wondered how the Dragon had known to come and offer comfort. Had Alistair summoned her? Or, had the Willa known that Ash was in distress because of her bond with the Rider?

Quinn pulled away, reaching to run a hand along the scales above Willa's nose. He'd never met the Dragon before, but that didn't seem to stop him. There was no fear etched on his face. Only devastation. "Thank you," he said.

Have hope.

Ash could have sworn that Willa's voice rang in her mind.

21

ries teleported Malachai and the others straight into his former lab. Upon their arrival, Aveo and Sam were quick to shoot out all the camera's positioned around the room with arrows, but that wouldn't do them any good. Their arrival had already tripped the Wards, and if Anderson didn't trigger the kill switch, all hope was lost. They'd be sitting ducks, and Malachai refused to let everything end that way. Not just for his sake, but for the others as well. His failure couldn't be the reason these people perished.

"Grant, the code," Anderson pleaded, pounding on the power-cell door.

"I've got it, Grant replied. I was able to change it to a permanent code. 13IA-AMCA-QCLM-3MAV."

Anderson typed it in quickly, the sound of the large steel door unlocking, echoing throughout the tiled lab. Malachai rushed inside after his fellow Pandora, sliding into the operator's seat, typing in his code for the kill switch as quickly as his trembling fingers would allow.

"There," Malachai said, shooting to his feet. "You know what to do next."

Alarms started to ring in every direction, rattling in Malachai's ears as he made his way over to his desk where Hartford was already trying to sift through the ingredients lining the shelves beside it.

"Here," Malachai said, his nerves rattling his tone. He plucked each ingredient from their places and set them down on the desk. After, he pulled open the drawers and retrieved a few measuring instruments and a corked vial. "Make sure to pocket extra just in case you fuck it up."

Hartford gave him a withering glare in response, but the prince was under too much pressure to sneer like he normally would. Throughout his fifty-five years of life and thirty years as an Immortal, he'd completed hundreds of risky missions. But never before had he done something as daring as infiltrating his father's Kingdom *after* he'd betrayed him so terribly.

"The new Ward is up," Anderson called, bursting out of her office. "How's the cure coming?" she asked the Berserker.

"I'm moving as fast as I can, lass. 'Tis a tad difficult with two sets of people bickering in my ear."

Anderson snorted, using a device on her wrist to switch her bug's feed. Her eyes bulged, brow flicking upward. "Whoa," she said.

"See my conundrum?"

"Just get it done," Aveo barked. "Are we ready?" he asked the others.

Sam shook his head.

"Forget I asked, then," the Commander quipped, heading for the door, bringing a finger to his ear to activate his own bug. "Grant, do you still have a visual on McBride's cell?"

"Yes," Grant replied. "There's only one man guarding it. I'm going to connect the feed to the chip Ash gave Aries."

The Fae retrieved the device from his pocket, holding it out to Malachai, who stared down at the footage, squinting as he worked to get an ID. "My father really needs to update his cameras," he uttered beneath his breath. "But I'm almost certain that's one of the Sorcerer's I mentioned, Storm."

"Fun," Sam drawled sarcastically. "I take it we're going to go introduce ourselves now?"

The sound of two swords unsheathing drew Malachai's attention. He looked toward Aveo in time to watch the Commander twirl them both, rolling his shoulders. "If you call what we're about to do to him an *introduction,* then I suppose so."

Malachai drew his own sword, sucking in a breath and holding it while the Commander kicked open the lab door. Aries moved to the front, and the prince took his place beside him. They were less susceptible to Magic attacks than the Elf and the Mortal—Aries, because he possessed his own Dark Magic, granted he wasn't allowed to use it, and Malachai because Black Magic played a large part in the Pandora's creation. They weren't immune, but they were as close as they could get to it.

The four men made their way across the castle's bottom floor to the dungeons. There were no other prisoners inside the iron cells, just rusty shackles and a mixture of dried blood and dust. They rounded one corner, passing the cell where Lincoln had once been held, chained to the far stone wall. The scent of bodily fluids and vomit lurked in the air, unforgiving and undying.

"We're almost there," Malachai warned. "Be ready. My father doesn't commission just *any* Sorcerers. This one specializes in weather. He can do anything from freezing you where you stand to plaguing the entire Realm with tornadoes and electrical storms with one bloody spell."

"His name seems fitting, then," Aries murmured. "That's some top-notch creativity."

Sam snorted, despite the circumstances. Malachai didn't dare to smile.

"I knew a Sorcerer like that once," Aveo admitted, hate tainting his tone. "For all I know, his bones are turning to dust in some slum village ditch."

"You're talking about Abernathy," Aries presumed. "Not a fan?"

"I wasn't a fan *before* he was banished. For good reason, might I add," Aveo said.

Malachai's stomach turned sour, anxiety beginning to grip him like a vice, ruling his every breath. Regret coiled in his gut. He should have warned them. There was no time left to change his mind, as they were approaching the final corner. Perhaps he could play prince and lie. Say that he had paid no mind to the people working for his father. He cared about himself, and himself only. But that had never been true. He simply wasn't built that way.

They rounded the final corner, finding Storm standing outside Cooper's cell, his hood pulled tight over his head, concealing his face. He didn't look at them. Instead, he continued to gaze inside the cell, his hands wrapped around the iron bars.

"Come on," the Sorcerer urged through clenched teeth. "Look at me. Breathe."

Malachai's heart stuttered, his shoulders drooping. This was a trap. Not for the Allies or their associates, but for the prince and the Sorcerer as well. His father wanted to pit them against each other, and he'd get his wish.

"Storm," Aries called, retrieving two twin daggers from his belt.

The Sorcerer ignored him. "Please."

"Step away from the cell," Aveo ordered, the sound of his voice causing Storm's attention to snap in his direction. There was only one window, at the end of the hall, barred and just big enough for a small child to fit through. Moonlight spilled through the panes, casting light upon the Sorcerer's face as he turned around to face them. The quick movement caused his hood to fall around his shoulders, revealing his head of long light brown hair dusted with gold.

Malachai didn't need to look behind his shoulder to know that Aveo had recognized him, and that he was furious.

"Abernathy," the Elf seethed.

Without any warning, the prince and Aries were shoved aside, stumbling into the stone walls. Malachai steadied himself, just in time to watch the wand slip from Abernathy's sleeve, landing in his grip. Before he had a chance to use it, Aveo slapped it away with one of his swords, slicing a deep cut across the Sorcerer's hand. The wand fell to the ground with a clatter, sliding into Cooper's cell. That wasn't Abernathy's only form of defense, however. He drew a short sword from his belt just in time to block a second strike from the Elf. The sound of the two blades colliding rattled and echoed throughout the corridor.

COOPER AWOKE FROM WHAT FELT LIKE AN ENDLESS SLEEP TO THE sound of a brawl outside of his cell. His eyes drifted open, the scent of his own blood flooding his nostrils. Black spots danced in his visions. He could hardly move, even if he wanted to. His breathing was slow, and labored. Each time he tried to inhale was more difficult than the last. He was dying. Slowly but surely.

How many hours had it been since his last lashings? How many times had Savron come to heal him, only to whip him over and over again? Every event muddled together into one, long, gruesome memory. Had he only been in Solaris a day? Or had more time passed? The fact that Cooper was still alive was some cruel, sick joke.

Silently, Cooper prayed for death. He was admitting defeat. All he wanted was for this horror to come to an end. Even if he were to survive, he knew he would never be the same. Every time he closed his eyes, he would see Savron's face. He would hear his pleas to the Sorcerer. His threats. He would feel Lincoln's arrows and the whip slicing through his flesh, grazing his bones. He would taste the coppery tang of blood on his tongue.

The ground shook. A crack seared through the stone, stretching from the hall to the end of Cooper's cell. A wand slid into Cooper's line of sight. His heart skipped a beat, but he didn't try to reach for it. He couldn't, even if he wanted to. Moving was impossible, darkness already creeping along the edges of his vision.

Would Cooper see his mother and father again when this was all over? Would Eliza be waiting for him, wherever the afterlife lay, her arms outstretched and ready to hold him?

Hot tears began to slip past Cooper's eyes at the thought of what he might find when the darkness swallowed him whole. He was ready, no matter how truly terrified he was to feel his last breath empty from his lungs, but fear wouldn't stop his heartbeat from becoming any more sluggish.

The brawl continued outside his cell, and while Cooper would rather focus on his final prayers, he couldn't stop himself from turning his head to get a view of it. If he weren't so weak, he might have yelped from shock at the sight of the massive Elf holding the Sorcerer by the throat. Around them, the corridor was a mess. Bits of stone were thrown about, more cracks splintering the walls. Clouds of dust billowed in the air.

Cooper watched the Sorcerer struggle, his face turning beet red, his blue eyes bulging. The Elf strangling him was vaguely familiar. Cooper was sure he'd seen him in the paper as well.

"Just let me explain—"

Before the Sorcerer could finish, the Elf kicked him hard in the ribs. Another crack of bone seared through the air.

"As if I'd accept any sort of explanation from you!" the Elf roared. "Do you have any idea how much pain this will cause Penelope? How long she's looked for you? To think you've been here the entire time…" He paused to kick him a second time. The cry that escaped the Sorcerer sent a shiver down Cooper's exposed spine. "Is this what you were doing while she was writing you letters, hoping even the most skilled and expensive of hawks would be able to track your worthless life down?"

The Sorcerer pushed himself to his feet before the Elf had another chance to kick him, snatching a broadsword from the ground in the process. The Elf laughed at him for it, reaching for yet another of the same sword.

"It isn't what you think," the Sorcerer insisted.

"What I *think* doesn't matter," the Elf barked. "It's what I know. And what I *know* is a worthless traitor when I see one." He struck at the Sorcerer so quickly that if Cooper had blinked, he might have missed it. One second, the sword was hanging at the Elf's side, and the next, it was less than an inch away from the Sorcerer's throat.

Cooper watched in awe as the Sorcerer blocked the weapon with his own, shoving it away with ease before striking the Elf, tearing the fabric of his uniform just below his shoulder. Scarlett blood dripped from the wound, but that didn't seem to faze the Elf.

A sword fight ensued, one where the Sorcerer could barely hold his own. The Elf was too strong, too fast, and too skilled. He was unmatched, and it would be the death of him. The hatred burning in the Elf's bronze eyes told Cooper that odds of the Sorcerer perishing before his own heart gave way were great.

"She despises you, you know? She always has," the Sorcerer said through clenched teeth, narrowly dodging a strike to his neck, one that would have surely sent his head rolling onto the ground. "She'll *never* marry you."

"What she does or doesn't do is none of your concern!" the Elf spat, hurt momentarily flashing across his features as he tossed his broadswords to the floor, taking the Sorcerer by surprise, which left him stunned enough for the Elf to advance, wrapping his bare hand around the Sorcerer's blade, ripping it from his grip. Cooper's stomach churned at the sight of all the blood dripping from the Elf's hand as he threw the Sorcerer's sword into the air. It landed perfectly in his grip, and within a matter of seconds, the Elf rose a single foot, kicking the Sorcerer hard enough for him to fly out of Cooper's view. The sound of him crashing into a nearby wall rattled in the Archer's ears.

"You knew about this!" the Elf whirled toward someone else, baring his bloody teeth.

Whoever he was speaking to only said, "Open. The. Cell. Door."

Cooper flinched at the sound of the tone.

"You do not give me orders," the Elf snarled.

"I do," Aries barked. "Open the fucking door, Aveo."

Aveo, Cooper thought, his heart seizing. Stunned, the Archer brought a hand to his chest, his mouth opening in a silent scream as blood surged up his throat.

"It's spelled," the Sorcerer wheezed. "So are his chains."

"Unspell them, Storm," the unknown, yet familiar voice said. "Now."

The Sorcerer scoffed with defiance.

Cooper fought to breathe, but it was useless. He was choking on his own blood, darkness threatening to swallow him whole. *This is it,* he thought, just as someone moved in front of the cell, shoving the Elf aside. Cooper could barely make out his face, but he knew who it was. "M-Malachai? S-Sam?" the Archer managed to ground out, terror causing his voice to tremble. He stared at them both, silently pleading for help, but it was no use. He felt himself grow limp, no longer able to feel his arms or legs. His lungs constricted, refusing to allow any more air to invade them.

The prince was rattling the bars to Cooper's cell, snarling like the beast he truly was within. "Storm, open the fucking doors. *Now!*"

No, no, no, Malachai internally screamed, whirling around to face the other four men crowding the hall. "He's dying, and if I don't get to him *now,* we'll have to return to the Allies and explain to them that Cooper *was* alive but since Aveo couldn't control his temper, we had to bring them back a body instead!"

The Commander gave him a long, deadly look.

"If you think that glare of yours is going to scare me in the slightest, you might want to remember who it is you're looking at," Malachai sneered, his tone dripping with malice. "Now, open the doors."

Storm wobbled forward, holding a hand to a gaping wound at his temple. "My wand is inside the cell," he said breathlessly.

Transition, Morghan practically pleaded, his voice projecting through the bug in Malachai's ear. *Into something small enough to get through those bars.*

Malachai growled. He'd never appreciated being in the form of a mouse, but he'd do whatever it took to get to the Archer inside. Once he'd completed the transition, he scurried through the bars, returning to his Mortal form once inside. He wasted no time diving toward the wand, tossing it to Aries instead of Storm before he kneeled beside the Archer, bringing his fingers to his neck.

The Fae had a vast enough knowledge of Magic to open the doors within a matter of seconds. Once they were open, Sam rushed inside, sliding over to where Malachai sat on his knees while Aveo remained in the hall, scowling at the Sorcerer.

"I don't feel a pulse," the prince announced, summoning his

abilities, praying to whoever might listen that he might be able to save him. Before he laid hands upon Cooper, he reached into his pocket, retrieving the syringe filled with Marcus's venom, handing it over to Sam.

Sam stared down at the syringe; his face paler than a sheet of paper.

"I want it ready," Malachai told him. "The whips they used were essentially flexible swords," he explained, his expression grave as he lowered his hands onto Cooper's shoulders. "I'll heal what I can, but due to his loss of blood—"

Do it. It was Quinn's voice that rang in the prince's ears.

Surprise flooded Sam's face, the syringe now trembling in his grip.

"Marcus," Malachai said, pursing his lips.

Do it, the Mentor agreed, his voice cracking around the words.

Please, Ash added, causing the prince's heart to crumble.

Malachai looked toward Sam, offering him a nod. "Take off the cap," he directed, continuing to use his abilities to heal what he could. But it wasn't enough. Cooper's pulse had yet to return.

Sam tore off the cap, his brow wrinkling with determination, eyes growing misty with tears. "What now?"

"Find a vein in his neck," Malachai said.

Aveo had abandoned Storm in the hall and was now standing behind the Mortal as he brought the syringe's needle to the most prominent vein he could find. "There," the Commander said softly, his lips dipping into a deep frown.

"Insert it," Malachai ordered.

Sam moved to do as the prince asked with terribly shaking hands. His face crumbled, before he said, "I can't."

Aveo knelt beside him, placing a kind hand on Sam's shoulder as he gently removed his grip from the syringe, replacing it with his own. Malachai watched with wide eyes as the Commander pushed down upon it, releasing Marcus's venom into Cooper's veins.

The second it was confirmed that Cooper's pulse had returned, Ash watched Quinn slump with relief before rushing out of the tent. She followed him, tears of her own relief pricking her eyes, leaving the other Allies to raise their glasses to the mission's success.

"Where are you going?" Ash called, hurrying to catch up with him.

He didn't answer her. Instead, he changed directions, headed toward the north facing watchtower. Ash's brow furrowed with confusion at the sight of him starting up the ladder. While she wasn't sure whether she should follow, she did anyway.

Once they arrived at the top, they stood in silence, staring in Solaris's direction. Willa flew in front of the Moons with Alistair and Lilly on her back. The Rider had offered to take her for a ride in hopes to get her mind off things. While Ash was furious with him, she was thankful all the same, and hoped that the Dragon might have been able to make Lilly smile.

"You know," Quinn said after a while. "If you hadn't involved Malachai, Cooper would have died. Anderson wouldn't have known how to help him, or about the kill switch. No one would have thought about bringing Marcus's venom. I just hope you realize what you've done to your reputation by involving him."

"I don't regret it," Ash blurted, her grip tightening around the railing in front of her. "I never will. I already lost Lincoln. I refuse to lose you, Cooper, or Lilly too. I'd do anything to keep you all safe and breathing. Cooper's alive, and that's what matters. If I have to drown in judgment because of that, well... I don't really care."

To Ash's surprise, Quinn snorted. "At some point, you're going to have to realize that you're not just Ashlyn Snow, a nobody from a village no one knew about. You're Ash VanCamp—Messenger, Idonian Ally, Sectra Holder, and High Queen. As much as I appreciate how much you care about us, and what lengths you're willing to go to for us, I can't just let you ruin your life on our behalf."

Ash lifted a single brow, angling her body to face him. "My life isn't ruined, Quinn. How could it be with you in it?" She could have sworn she caught a hint of a blush on the Archer's cheeks. Normally, she'd tease him about it, but she decided to refrain.

Silence fell upon them again. The only sound to be heard were the nearby villagers chatting in the streets, purchasing bread from the bakery, or milk from their farm, which their old friend Billy sold from a stand as a way to help.

Willa flew in front of the Moons a second time, the sound of Lilly's giggles echoing throughout the night.

"I take it that you and Alistair got in a bit of a spat earlier," Quinn mentioned. "When he came inside, he seemed pretty rattled and upset. Want to talk about it?"

Ash's lips dipped into a frown.

"Lover's quarrel?"

"No," she retorted

Quinn chuckled. "Oh please, Ash. You two are close. I mean, everyone is with their division members, but you two seem *really* close. You *did* spend all that time alone together between the first and second tasks. Besides, he seems like a great guy—handsome and of noble blood. He isn't exactly the *worst* person to be courted by."

Ash scowled. *I beg to differ.* "It's nothing."

"Are you sure? It certainly seems like something."

"I told him earlier to talk to you and Marcus about changing his division," Ash admitted, crossing her arms in front of her chest. "I can assure you, it's nothing. At least not anymore."

Quinn went rigid at her side. "Really?"

"I knew he wouldn't react well to Malachai's presence. Let's just say that he went beyond my expectations," Ash groused, eyeing the Dragon dipping in and out of the clouds. "I won't go into details. The less you know, the better for Alistair."

If Quinn knew all that Alistair had said to Ash, he'd pummel him the second Willa landed, and would likely be eaten by the Dragon as a result. "That bad?"

"I was an idiot to think that I could entertain the idea of a love life, all while knowing what I'd eventually have to do, and that I might not survive it," Ash said, changing the subject. "Besides, even if I do survive, I'll be matched with someone the Idonian Council approves of. Idona is being rebuilt, not only physically, but politically too. We need to appear strong when the Galactic Gates open. The odds are, I'll be married to someone with a powerful family, like Prince Beck. Or someone known throughout the Realms, like Craven. A love match isn't in my cards."

"Thinking like a real queen, I see," Quinn mused, nudging her with his elbow. "Beck and Craven aren't horrible, but I still think it should be your choice. Any man would be glad to have you. I'm sure Sam would leap with joy. I bet you that even Malachai wouldn't deny you."

Ash rolled her eyes. "You were just telling me that *involving* Malachai would ruin my reputation. Now you're suggesting that I marry him? Have you lost your mind?"

"I was just using him as a reference. *Anyone* would fall for you. You're everything—beautiful, strong, selfless, talented, powerful. The list goes on. Whoever gets your hand is going to be the luckiest man in Si Realtra, I'm sure of it," Quinn proclaimed with a prideful grin.

It was Ash's turn to blush now. "You're lying."

"You could always test my theory," Quinn suggested. "Go walk up to anyone inside that war tent and ask them if they'd marry you. I bet you even Ana would say yes."

Ash laughed. It was the first time she had all day, and she reveled in the feeling. "Or I could save myself the trouble and just test the theory on you," she joked.

Quinn froze, his lips parting for words that never came out.

"Sorry," Ash murmured, her stomach flipping. "Bad joke." She averted her gaze from his face, turning it back toward the sky. *Really bad joke,* she added silently. Quinn was betrothed. He always had been, and while he and Constance had their fair share of problems, he wasn't one to break a promise. "Maybe I'll ask Grant," she said, hoping to lighten the sudden depressive mood.

Quinn didn't laugh as Ash expected him to. She glanced in his direction, only to find that he was clearly deep in thought. "Lincoln and I got into a fight one day over this," he admitted in a whisper. "He was so convinced that we were—" he cut himself off, cheeks heating with shame. "I suppose Constance felt the same way, and that's why they did what they did. Perhaps it was vengeance. Maybe it was out of a need to be loved in that way. But, if we're being honest, I don't feel guilty. I sound horrible, but after what has happened to Lincoln and Cooper, if there's one thing I've learned, it's that life is too short to waste doing things you don't want to do. Even for Immortals."

Ash's breath caught in her throat as he reached for her hand, wrapping it in his own, pulling her so that she had no choice but to look at him. She wanted to make herself let go, especially after all that had happened earlier with Alistair, but she couldn't bear to. Instead, she found herself staring up into his eyes, still shining bright despite their dark surroundings. Moonlight danced across his features, the same way it would when they'd wind up on watch together atop that very tower. Just a few hours ago, he'd held her as if she were the only solid thing in the Realms. And now, she was looking up at him, remembering when he was the only person she trusted. That not all that long ago, *he* had been the only solid thing for her.

Someone lit off a firework out in the valley surrounding the village. People were starting to gather out there, carrying lanterns and bottles of wine to celebrate Cooper's rescue. The Allies were joining them, whooping, and hollering.

"To Sam Waters!" Ash heard someone cheer.

"To Sir Aveo Calloway!"

"To Lord Aries Blackwing!"

"To Hartford of Dairth!"

No one mentioned Malachai or Anderson. At least not until Ash heard Anastasia scream, "To Prince Malachai Trevayne and Bernardine Anderson!"

At first, no one clapped or drank to those names, but they softened after a few moments. Ash heard more shouts of joy and praise to the Moons and the Great Sovereign of Light.

Willa landed nearby, and Lilly and Alistair rushed to join in on the fun. Ash watched them, her lips twitching toward a smile at the sight of Vincent twirling Lilly around in a big bear hug. Willa sauntered up, startling quite a few villagers, but a few daring people decided to approach her, and she had no complaints about them rubbing her scales.

Fireworks erupted; their colors so incredibly vibrant against the black velvet night. Ash had had no idea that anyone in Crane had even possessed such things, but, with Grant in the area, anything was possible.

"Ash," Quinn said softly, reminding Ash that she wasn't alone, and that her hand was still wrapped within his. "I want to thank you."

"For what?" she asked, snorting disbelievingly. "Today, I've done nothing but piss people off."

"I'm sure that they're not as pissed now that they know your idea to involve the prince is what saved my brother's life," Quinn argued, offering her a kind smile. "But I wanted to thank you for letting me help you for those two years. I know we weren't particularly close before Eliza summoned us to tell you the truth. I was always older and felt that I needed to be wiser—the man of the house. But Eliza saw what I couldn't back then. That together, we were meant for so much more. She trusted me with your well-being, and because of that, I am here today. The Realm has opened up around me to show me that there is more to life than just Crane, farming, marriage, and children. Following you to Dracus is what made me... more. So, thank you."

Ash's heart had melted the second he'd said, *That together, we were meant for so much more.* To think that now, they were leading two separate divisions made up of living legends, working alongside people who've already made so many differences in Idona.

"I'd also like to apologize," Quinn admitted, sadness slipping into his tone. "I never meant to drive a wedge between you and Lincoln. I should have never stopped you from telling him the truth each time you tried. I can only blame myself for where he is now."

Another firework, another boom. The sky lit up. Cheers of joy flooded Ash's ears, all while a crack seared through her heart. "It's alright," she assured him. "If Malachai was willing to help us save Cooper, he should be willing to help save Lincoln too. We'll get him back, and then we can make everything right."

Quinn shook his head, pursing his lips. "After all he's done... I don't know how he'll ever be the man we knew again."

"Don't lose hope," Ash demanded. "Not now, not ever."

"Ash!" Morghan called in a panic.

Stunned, Ash released Quinn's grip, moving back toward the railing to peer down at the Wolf. The others were making their way back toward the war tent. Ash's heart skipped into an unhealthy rate.

"What is it?" Ash asked urgently.

"Malachai."

MALACHAI HELD HIS BREATH, WELL AWARE OF HOW BAD OF AN IDEA teleporting into Dracus would be. He arrived in the Infirmary, kneeling beside Cooper's lifeless body, his hands covered in the Archer's blood. Healers screamed with surprise and horror at the sight of what had arrived in front of them, but the prince paid them no mind. Instead, he looked up at the Elven Commander standing in front him and instantaneously admitted his defeat.

"Thank you," Malachai ground out. "For what you did back there."

Aveo stared down at him, holding out the enchanted chains he'd stolen from the cell. "Stand up."

"What are you doing?" Sam barked, his voice muffled by all the Healers and guards scrambling around them.

"What I must," Aveo replied, bearing no expression upon his face.

Hartford bared his teeth, rage flickering in his golden gaze. "Without this man, we'd have failed our mission three times over!"

The Healers now surrounding Cooper's body flinched.

"You seem to have forgotten that at the end of the day, he's still our enemy," Aveo said calmly. "He can't be trusted inside the walls of any Kingdom. He must be detained."

Malachai nodded solemnly, pushing to his feet. He would not fight Aveo. Not there, or anywhere. He knew the second he left Solaris that he would find himself in chains at one point or another. He had just hoped that now wouldn't be that time.

"You and I both know that without the two of us, an Ally wouldn't be alive," the prince said to the Commander. "If it's any consolation, before you throw me in a cell, I believe we made a good team."

The Commander simply stared at him.

"You can't be charged with any crime," Sam told Malachai.

"This man is *beyond* crime," Aveo barked

"Detaining him goes against the High Queen's wishes," Aries reminded him warily.

Aveo looked toward the Fae, clenching his jaw. "I have no quarrels with High Queen Ash VanCamp," he stated, loud and clear for all to hear. "My only goal here is to protect her and those she cares about, including my own betrothed. As a Commander of the Elven Army, I have every right to detain whomever I like, whenever I wish, unless someone of a higher authority within the *military*," he added, clipping the words as if to get a point across to Aries, "says I am not to."

"Like a General?" Sam snapped.

"I don't see either Axel Graves or Prince Beck Chamberlain stepping in to stop me from putting this man in chains," Aveo retorted.

Sam stiffened, his cheeks flaming red. "Well, then I have news for you, Commander," the Mortal started, squaring his shoulders. "I am the General of the Idonian Alliance army, appointed by Lady Evanora Ivanenko of the Zerinian Empire, and I hereby command you to lower those chains and obey the High Queen's orders at once."

Malachai deadpanned. *Did he just say Lady Evanora Ivanenko?*

"There is no Idonian Alliance army," Aveo argued.

"Oh, there is," Sam spat, crossing his arms. "Fifteen thousand men and women willing to fight on behalf of the Messenger."

Aveo blinked, shock flooding his face.

"Formerly known as Rebels," Sam continued daringly, stepping forward. "Created seventeen years ago by Lord Cedric Chamberlain with the help of Lady Evanora Ivanenko. Until recently, this army had no one to lead them. Now, here I am."

The prince pulled in a deep breath, filling his lungs with desperately needed air.

"*Rebel?*" Aveo spat, cutting a harsh look to the prince. "I thought you took care of that problem."

Malachai held his hands up in defense. "So did I."

"The king is coming," one of the Healers informed them. "So, whatever you three are planning on doing, do it quickly. Just get out of my hall."

"You may detain, if it makes you feel safe," Malachai offered.

Aveo wasted no time at all, wrapping the enchanted chains around Malachai's wrists, despite the protests coming from the others. Shortly after they were set in place, King Loren arrived with General Axel Graves, who was more than happy to cart Malachai away, while everyone in the Infirmary stood in silence, watching with wide eyes.

The prince was led to the castle, paraded throughout the Kingdom for all Draconians to see. Some cheered, some gasped, and others remained as silent as the night around them.

Once they arrived in the castle, Malachai was brought down to the bottom floor and escorted inside a plain apartment, complete with a living area, a bedroom, a small kitchen, and a washroom. Once he was left alone, he sank down onto the sofa, placing his head in his hands, and started to rethink every decision he'd made that day.

Loren watched as Hartford approached Lucinda's bedside, a vial filled with glowing white liquid in his hands. The Berserker plucked the cork out, lowering it to the Sorceress's lips, emptying the contents of that vial into her mouth.

While they waited for the formula to take effect, the Berserker explained all that occurred that day in great detail. He told the king how Ash had enlisted Malachai's help, and how the prince's presence had not only saved Cooper's life, but the Realm Sorceress's as well.

"Aveo was the one who injected Marcus's venom into Cooper's veins," Hartford revealed, staring vacantly at where Lucinda lay on a hospital bed. "For a second, we were all unified, despite that Sorcerer's betrayal. We managed to do the unthinkable—infiltrate Solaris and bring an Ally back from the dead. Yet now we are no longer unified."

"That was to be expected," Loren replied, crossing his arms. "But the help that Malachai gave will be taken into consideration when we move forward with... whatever we plan to do with him."

The Berserker turned to give the king a long, serious look. "Something isn't right with him, King Loren." He shifted his weight uncomfortably from one leg to the other. "He was nothing like what the papers made him seem."

"Have you forgotten so quickly what he did to Death Valley? To Gideon? To Ash? That man isn't innocent," Loren insisted, his stomach knotting. "And even if he was, I couldn't just release him. Thaddeus would have my head."

"Stop worrying so much about Thaddeus," Hartford growled.

"You are just as much a king as he is, and it's time not only he realizes it, but you as well."

Lucinda coughed, startling both of the men standing at her bedside. Loren's attention darted back to her just in time to watch her eyes flutter open. "Am I dead?" she croaked, running her tongue over her dry lips.

"Not yet," Loren told her kindly, reaching to take her hand in his. "But Ash might kill you."

The Sorceress chuckled nervously. "Rightfully so. What I did was reckless, selfish, and downright foolish."

"We can talk about your many mistakes later," Hartford assured her. "For now, let's work on getting you back on your feet. You have an entire league of Sorcerers to prepare for a siege. Besides, Loren has more pressing matters to deal with. Like the fact that we have the Prince of Darkness in custody and an apparent Rebel General walking the streets of Dracus."

"Rebel General?" Lucinda gawked at the Berserker. "I thought Malachai took care of that problem."

Hartford snorted. "So did he."

23

While she waited for her siblings to return to Dracus in one piece, Penelope did her best to keep herself occupied. She'd hardly seen Loren or Valentina during the last few days, but the Prophetess had provided her with a task. She'd asked the Princess to start planning a celebration for the Allies, to congratulate them on completing the three tasks.

Simple enough. Or so Penelope had thought.

After spending the last two days, darting to different areas of the castle and city, meeting with members of Loren's staff, bakers, chefs, designers, and more, Penelope finally arrived back to her own suite. By the time she passed through the door, her legs felt like gelatin.

Penelope's Lady's Maid, Yvonne, was waiting for her in the foyer. She helped the Princess out of her cloak, hanging it on a hook in the closet while Penelope tugged off her gloves and stepped out of her slippers.

"Would you like me to run you a bath, Your Highness?" Yvonne asked, following Penelope out into the vast living area.

Shaking her head, Penelope said, "That won't be necessary, Yvonne. Head on home. It's late."

Surprise flashed across the maid's features. "Are you sure, Your Highness? Have you eaten? I could fetch you something."

"I'll request for someone to bring some chocolate cake up from the kitchen," Penelope told her. "Now, go enjoy what's left of the evening. When I was out and about, I heard something about a Giving Day wrapping contest over in the shopping district. You should attend. I'm sure you'd win. I've seen your cross-stitching. You must be pretty crafty."

Yvonne waved the compliment off, a blush dusting her cheeks. "Oh, I'm not *that* good, Your Highness."

"I beg to differ," Penelope replied, offering her a kind smile. "Now go and have fun. I'll see you in the morning."

Yvonne bid her goodbye, dropping into a perfectly executed curtsey before she fled out of the front door. Once she was alone, Penelope opted for a shower instead of a bath. She stood beneath the stream of water for a while, lost in her thoughts.

Since the Allies had left for the three tasks, Penelope had seen little of Loren. Of course, it was normal for kings to be busy from dawn until well after dusk. She knew that, after being raised by Thaddeus. But the Elven King had always made time for his queen. He never missed a meal with her. They always retired at the same time. There were days where he'd clear his schedule just to spend quality time with his queen.

Penelope had her quarrels with the Elves. She couldn't trust them, and she knew that. However, when she thought of a good marriage, she thought of theirs—undying, unconditional love. With Loren, Penelope wasn't entirely sure that she could have that. She'd fallen in love with him, but as the days dragged on without setting her eyes upon him, thoughts of the mistake she might be making crept into her mind.

The day before, when Penelope had visited the royal designer, Henry, to review the designs for Ash's celebratory dress, she'd asked him about Loren's mother, the late Queen Sofia Mason.

"Is this what Sofia did? Plan parties?"

"No, dearie," Henry had replied. "Queen Sofia was the face of this Kingdom. It's because of her that the Draconians were able to gain the trust of the Mortals and extend the borders of our jurisdiction. There wasn't a soul in Idona and beyond who didn't think highly of her. Well, aside from the crazed Elf who murdered her, of course."

"An Elf murdered her?" Penelope had gaped. "I thought she died during the Giant's Rebellion."

"That was the time period, yes," Henry confirmed. "But it wasn't a Giant that killed her. It was an Elf by the name of Delmuth Tralar. Sofia had been in the Regal Mountains with the rest of the Idonian Council to negotiate a peace treaty with the Giants. Delmuth used the conflict as a cover. He pushed Sofia off a cliff and made it appear as if the Giants were at fault. This caused quite the uproar. But Realm Prophetess Amelia used her connection with the Moons to view the past and discovered the truth."

"Why would Delmuth want to kill Sofia, if everyone loved her?"

Henry had given her a long look, one that made her feel daft. "Delmuth refused to say. In fact, he cut out his own tongue to keep himself from saying a word about it. The Elven King and Queen, Esmeralda's mother and father, said that Delmuth had been banished to the Regal Mountains thirty years prior. But no one believes that, especially since they abdicated the throne to their daughter less than three months later before making the ascension."

"You think they hired Delmuth?" Penelope had asked, her stomach churning with disgust.

"Esmeralda's parents ruled the Kingdom of Elves during the Scarlet Era. They had their opinions about the Draconians, as I'm sure you know. If it's one thing they didn't want, it was for the Draconians to become unified with the rest of the Realm. Dracus exists because of our first queen, Lexa Hathaway, one of the original Draconians, and the first Prophetess. She's the one who petitioned the Idonian Council for land. Sofia was finishing what Lexa started, and the Elves likely hated it. I wouldn't be surprised in the slightest if they'd had her murdered."

If the Elves were willing to murder Loren's mother, what would they do if they found out about Penelope's plans to marry him? Her stomach lurched at the thought as she stepped out of the shower, reaching for a plush white robe to wrap around herself.

Ash and Vincent were out there, doing incredible things every day, making progress in the war that hadn't been made in decades. Yet there Penelope was, planning parties, and willing to ruin all their hard work, all to avoid an arranged marriage.

"I'm selfish," Penelope admitted, running a comb through her damp hair. "So unbelievably selfish."

Vincent was right. If Penelope were to marry Loren, she could very well start another war. Could she do that? Could she put Idona through a civil war?

Groaning, Penelope walked out into her bedroom and retrieved a set of comfortable clothes—a cream cashmere sweater, a pair of black leggings, and comfortable socks. She dressed quickly, eager to slip into her study and distract herself by reading someone else's story until the wee hours of the morning. Most of the preparations for the celebration were in order, therefore she had most of the day to herself tomorrow and planned to sleep through most of it.

Penelope had just retrieved a bottle of wine and a glass from her wine cellar when she heard a knock on her door. Brow furrowing, she glanced at the time on her chip. It was half-past nine at night. Who would visit at such an hour? Ash, Vincent, and the other Allies weren't supposed to return until the next morning. At least, that's what Valentina had said to Penelope in passing earlier in the day.

"Maybe they decided to come back early," Penelope thought out loud, her heart soaring as she rushed to answer the door. Her socks were so soft that she nearly slipped on the foyer's hardwood floors, risking the bottle of fine red wine clutched in her grip. She recovered, sighing with relief.

The visitor knocked again, far more urgently than they had before.

"I'm right here," Penelope groused, yanking the door open, only to find none other than Aveo standing on the other side. Her heart took a flying leap off a cliff at the sight of him. His honey-blond hair was caked with blood, the Elven braids adorning his temples an unraveling mess. Multiple lacerations decorated his form, staining the steel-gray fabric of his uniform. Bruises were beginning to develop along his sharp jawline and beneath his right eye, where a slit in his eyebrow dripped with dark crimson blood.

If Penelope hadn't had a good grip on her wine, she might have dropped it right along with her jaw. "W-what happened to you?" she stammered. "W-what are you doing here?"

"I need to speak with you," he said, his voice wavering. For the first time, Penelope noticed that he was shaking. She'd never seen him do such a thing in all the years that she'd known him. "I know that it's late, but may I please come in?"

Penelope looked him up and down, assessing his injuries. "How about we go to the Infirmary instead?"

"I just came from there," he revealed, the lump in his throat bobbing. "I'd have stayed to have these wounds addressed, but I needed to see you immediately."

Nodding, Penelope gestured for him to come in before popping her head out of her front door, spotting one of the guards roaming the corridor. "Hey," she called, grabbing his attention. "I need you to find me a change of clothes for Sir Calloway."

"Right away, Your Highness," the guard replied.

Penelope watched him scurry away before she shut the door, turning back toward the Commander. "Start talking," she directed before heading toward the washroom beside the kitchen. He followed her, standing at the threshold while she retrieved a med-kit from beneath the sink.

"I'm not exactly sure where to start," he replied as she pushed past him, heading out into the kitchen where she set the kit on the island along with her bottle of wine.

"Sit," the Princess demanded, tapping the island's surface.

Aveo gave her a long disbelieving look. "*You're* going to patch me up?"

"No," she drawled sarcastically. "I'd prefer for you to bleed all over my kitchen floors."

"Funny," he replied, eyebrows flattening as he hopped up onto the island, pulling off his uniform jacket before discarding the shirt he'd worn beneath. Penelope tossed the shirt in the trash before plucking all of his badges off the jacket and carrying them over to the sink, where she rinsed them off and set them in a rack to dry.

"Thank you," Aveo said softly.

Penelope shrugged on her way back over to him, where she dumped the kit's contents on the counter and took inventory of the supplies. "Don't thank me yet. I'm sure some of this will hurt."

"I bet you'll enjoy that."

"Perhaps," Penelope said with a wicked grin.

While the Princess started to clean and dress his wounds, Aveo explained what had happened throughout the day. "Early this morning, I reported to the barracks to oversee the training of a new legion of recruits. An hour hadn't passed before Beck arrived in a panic. King Loren had requested Elven assistance for a rescue mission. Something like that *never* happens. I immediately offered to help, without knowing the mission's details. Beck told me to head to the portal rooms, where I found Craven waiting for me with a tele-portation sphere. Right then and there, I knew that it was an Ally. I didn't know who.

"He took me to the Hidden Village, Crane, where I arrived to complete and utter chaos. Turns out that yesterday evening, Cooper had decided to retrieve a few people from the village. He thought of the wrong one, and wound up in Solaris, where there were Wwards set up to keep him from teleporting back out."

Penelope's heart stumbled, the color draining from her face. She found it difficult to concentrate and decided to take a small break, pouring herself a glass of wine and then a second one for Aveo. He drank it greedily, his hand trembling around the glass.

"I had no idea any of this was happening," Penelope admitted in a whisper, anger beginning to blossom deep in her gut. Why had no one said anything? She'd spoken to Valentina that morning, and the Prophetess hadn't mentioned it. Loren hadn't so much as sent her a message that day, let alone told her about what had happened to Cooper. "Why did they send you when there are eight other Allies?"

"There was an Ally ban on this mission," Aveo informed her as she refilled his glass. "There were five of us at first—Hartford, Aries, a man named Sam Waters, me, and the Pandora Humphrey brought back to Dracus from Solaris. She wasn't battle trained, and both your sister and I were uncomfortable with sending her. Without her, however, we wouldn't have anyone who knew Solaris's current state. We needed a new set of eyes, and Ash knew where to find a pair."

Penelope set her wine aside, her heart thrashing against her sternum as she examined a gash along Aveo's arm. "Where? Who?" she asked, unsure of whether or not she wanted to know the answer.

"Malachai," Aveo admitted, grimacing as she applied a liquid bandage to fuse his flesh back together. The sound of the name led Penelope's stomach to churn, her chest growing tight. "She knew where he was, and we went to retrieve him together. He looked... normal. His eyes weren't red, he wasn't pale, and he was dressed like a farmer. He agreed to help, and we brought him back to the McBride Estate, where together we all devised a plan."

Penelope halted, her eyes bulging. "You *worked* with him?"

"Without him, we wouldn't have known... well... anything. He was the one who told us about Savron Phantom's involvement. Because of that, we knew that Cooper would be in even graver danger than we thought. He gave us the information we needed to disable all of the wards and set up new ones that would prevent anyone from interfering with the rescue. Without him, we wouldn't have thought to bring Marcus's venom along with us, and Cooper would be dead."

Bile lurched up Penelope's throat, but she forced herself to continue with his wounds.

"We wound up bringing Anderson—the Pandora Humphrey rescued—so that she could handle the wards and help Hartford create Lucinda's cure. Yes, he helped us with that too," Aveo added. "But when we all approached Cooper's cell..."

Penelope climbed up onto the island, pushing Aveo back so that he'd lie down. She focused on the gnarly gash across his chest, sitting on her knees at his side. "What about the cell? What had happened to him?"

"Abernathy was guarding it.".

Penelope froze, horror twisting her features. "*What?*"

"The second I saw him, I forgot about the mission. Cooper was lying there, dying in his cell, and all I could think about was how Abernathy had betrayed us all." Aveo shook his head, swallowing hard. To Penelope's surprise, she saw tears beginning to dampen his eyes. "I fought him. He's at fault for all these wounds. I didn't kill him, but I'm sorry to say that I wished I had. Malachai snapped me out of it. He got inside Cooper's cell and next thing I knew, the doors were unlocked and Sam had joined him. Malachai has healing abilities, but they weren't enough to bring Cooper back. Sam was supposed to inject Marcus's venom, but he couldn't. I—" he caught himself, lips quivering. "I did it."

Penelope stared down at him, at a loss for words. She absent-mindedly left her hand resting on his chest, her thoughts a panicked clamor. Abernathy had inflicted each wound she'd just cleaned, glued back together, and bandaged. She hadn't realized she'd begun to cry until she noticed her tears falling and landing on Aveo's shoulder. A sob started to crowd her throat, the realization of where Abernathy had been all these years while she tried to find him, hitting her like a bag of bricks, stealing the breath straight from her lungs.

Suddenly, Penelope was standing in Thaddeus's study, noticing the mysterious man lingering in the corner. She could feel his hand around her own as they were introduced. *I'm Matt Abernathy,* he'd said with an awkward smile. The next second, she was standing beside him at the golden gates, where she met Cedric for the first time. In a flash, they were all in the library again, searching for a clue as to where the Rebel's stronghold was per Aveo's demands. In the blink of an eye, Penelope was *in* the Rebel's stronghold, listening to Walsh and his delirious rants, all while knowing that Abernathy would find a way to get to her. That he'd save her, eventually. She had escaped, and the next thing Penelope knew, she was walking out of the Forest of Fools to find that her Guardian, Cedric, and a team of extraordinary people were waiting for her.

Penelope's vision grew blurry as she recalled the few moments before her eighteenth-year ceremony, when she'd noticed that Abernathy was wearing *her* family sigil instead of his own. *"You're my favorite person, and this is the symbol of your family. Not your family's reign, but your* family," he'd clarified. *"And you're my family."*

Shaking her head, Penelope worked to rid the memories from her mind. She wanted to bury them in a place she would never dare to look again, but they wouldn't relent. She was still there, like a ghost fluttering through the past, watching as Thaddeus banished Abernathy from the Kingdom of Elves. She watched him walk away all over again, never to see him again.

Panic clawed at Penelope's insides, preventing her from drawing in a decent breath. Her chest was too heavy, crushing her heart, constricting her lungs.

"Penelope," Aveo called, taking the hand she'd left on his chest and wrapping it in his own. "Words can't describe how sorry I am. I wish that we could have both remained oblivious. Truly, I do. But you deserved to know the truth."

Nodding, Penelope tried to blink away her tears, but they were forming too quickly for her to control. She pulled in a shaky breath, barely gathering enough to fill her lungs. She opened her mouth to thank him but found that she was unable to form any words. Anything she tried to say would just come out as a sob instead.

Aveo pushed into a sitting position, releasing her hand. "What can I do?" he asked in a whisper.

Penelope couldn't think of anything other than the Sorcerer who she'd loved and trusted. She sat frozen on the island, trembling from head to toe. The only thing she wanted was to travel back in time, to play a game of cards with him and listen while he told Vincent elaborate stories about his training in Ryiah. But she'd settle for a hug, to feel something other than pain, regret, and the bitter sting of betrayal.

Though he was the last person Penelope would run to for comfort, she surged forward and hooked her arms around Aveo's neck anyway, burying her face in his bare, bandaged, and bloodied chest. He returned the embrace, wrapping his arms around her, pulling her closer, resting his chin in the crook of her neck.

"Thank you," Penelope murmured against him. "For telling me

the truth." She felt his fingers beginning to run through the ends of her hair and immediately relaxed, finally finding herself able to forget everything that occurred before that moment, where they were nothing more than two people without a past. Two people with cracks in their hearts and scars on their flesh.

24

Xavier stared down at his latest message from the Rat, slowly shaking his head. He wasn't sure whether to laugh or roar with rage. The desire to scream at the top of his lungs burned through him, but there was no more time to waste. The rest of the Dark Army was arriving in Solaris, and they'd expect a greeting from their king. Unfortunately, their cherished prince would be absent—permanently.

"It's a good thing I have you, dearest," Xavier said, holding his hand out to Constance. She took it without question, interlacing her gloved fingers with his. In the weeks since she'd first arrived, she'd adapted to her surroundings, and every time the king saw his beloved niece, she seemed to fit in with those surroundings more and more.

The pair walked out of the castle, slipping into the carriage awaiting them. Constance was as silent as ever, her beautiful face failing to portray a single emotion. Her guard, Alrich, followed on horseback behind, watching the carriage like a hawk. Lincoln rode alongside him, dressed in his Arebus uniform, his massive black bow strapped to his back beside its matching quiver. Soroya would meet them there, having left earlier that morning to meet with the Commanders regarding the fortification of the city.

"How will you punish that Sorcerer?" Constance asked, tugging at the cuffs of her black velvet gloves. "Will he be banished to the Regal Mountains like Savron?"

Xavier shook his head. "I knew what would happen if I put Storm in charge of guarding Cooper, which is why I did it."

"It was a trap, wasn't it?" She gave him a long, disapproving look. "You wanted him in front of that cell, because you knew that whoever they sent after Cooper would recognize him."

"Now, we are his one and only home," Xavier declared with a sinister smirk.

"Did you not believe him when he took his oath?" Constance pressed.

"Oh, the oath *he* took was different compared to others," Xavier explained to her. "And I didn't necessarily do it just to ruin any chance he had to change his mind. I did it because now that it's known that he's here, most of the Idonian Council will blame King Thaddeus for casting him out to begin with. Thaddeus will likely take offense and refuse to lend his army to the siege, which will cause friction in his own household because Prince Beck certainly won't stand for that. And that's just *one* reason everyone will find themselves at odds. There's also the fact that Ash publicly enlisted Malachai and supposedly a Rebel General's help to get Cooper back. That won't sit well with the Council either. Ash won't know what to do with them all at each other's throats, and hers. Oh goodness, this should be fun."

You're a psychotic piece of shit, you know that? Meera snapped.

Xavier swallowed his urge to laugh.

Constance pulled her arms around herself, her face twisting into a scowl. "The Royals leading this Realm shouldn't fall for a trick like that so easily."

She is right, they shouldn't, Meera growled.

"But they will," Xavier countered, reclining in his seat. "The Realm seems to forget that I once had a seat on that very Council. I worked alongside those kings and queens, and I know what makes them tick. Perhaps, once the Idonian people start to see what I always had—a fragile council made up of self-serving Immortals— they will finally realize that this Galaxy is due for a serious change.

There is no good reason to have all of these royals and their crowns constantly clashing against one another. There should be one king, and one king only to rule over all of Si Realtra."

"And that king should be you?" Constance ground out.

"No," he said, the smirk vanishing from his lips. "Our one true king is trapped, and it is my responsibility to free him. Before I can do that, I must prepare each Realm for his arrival."

You'll never make it that far, Meera reminded him harshly.

I might not, Xavier agreed with her. *But you seem to forget that I am one of many. It will be done, whether I am alive to see it or not.*

"W-who is it? How are they trapped?" Constance stuttered. Xavier might have told her if they weren't arriving in Solaris's city square, where thousands of Pandora and Mortals dedicated to Xavier's cause had gathered to hear their king speak.

"You will know all in time, darling," Xavier replied before he exited the carriage.

THERE WAS SOMETHING SO... EXHILARATING ABOUT STANDING UPON A dais, with every soul in Solaris kneeling around it. Xavier would never get used to it. The excitement surging through him each time he stood before his people would never dwindle. Sometimes, it was easy to forget all he'd done, and how hard he'd worked to stand where he was.

Constance and Soroya stood on either side of the king, their backs as straight as boards, their eyes colder than the ice in Ryiah. Xavier's heart swelled to have them both there. The daughters of the notorious Trevayne sisters, in the flesh, taking their rightful places in society, reminding those that looked upon them of their lineages' success.

Lincoln McBride stood on the dais' first step; his hands clasped behind his back.

All three Bloodlines, Xavier thought, his lips spreading into a wicked smile. *Here, for all the descendants to see.*

Meera snorted within. *If only two of them weren't here by force.*

Choosing to ignore her, Xavier began his speech. "When I was a boy, some seventy-odd years ago, my father said to me; *It'll be you, Xavier. You will be the one to bring us out of the shadows after centuries of hiding. The fate of our people falls upon your shoulders.* And when I was a young man, just barely eighteen, Soroya Trevayne and I were tasked. We were told to marry and move to Idona, where we'd do the unthinkable. We'd gain the trust of the High King.

"It was easier said than done. Simply getting a job in the castle was more difficult than one might ever fathom. Gregor VanCamp was a frightening force to be reckoned with, but when he perished at the end of the Five Realm War and his fifteen-year-old son was set to take the High Throne, I saw an opportunity and I took it. Within a year, he'd named me his leading adviser and second-in-command. Truthfully, I didn't hate him. I rather enjoyed Gideon's company and looked upon him fondly."

Xavier listened to the gasps sounding throughout the crowd and took in all the confused expressions contorting the faces of his following. He laughed in response. "I am not cruel. I was not born with a hatred for Idonians, Erminians, Zerinians, and Ryiahns embedded in my heart. Gideon was not a horrible man. His soul was pure, but the burden of all our ancestor's mistakes weigh upon our shoulders. Gideon was, unfortunately, the man who had to pay the price for what all his predecessors had done to our people. This is war, after all. Sacrifices must be made."

Silence enveloped the square as Xavier pulled in a deep breath, pondering his next words.

"For the last eighteen years, we have waited to proceed into the other Realms," Xavier went on to say. "In order to do that, we must face a final battle between ourselves and the Idonians, and most importantly, I must face the Messenger. This battle will either make or break us. We will find out, once and for all, if all of this tiring work has paid off, but it won't be easy. In fact, it'll be the hardest thing any descendant has ever done. We will face the Draconian Elemental Clans. We will face the Elves and their brute force. We will face Si Realtra's strongest league of Sorcerers. We could very well face the Fae and their Magic as well. But we will *not* fail. Not now. Not after all we've done.

"So, I thank you for the faith you have in our shared cause. I thank you for your willingness to sacrifice your own lives to see it through. Most importantly, I thank you for your undying loyalty. As we proceed into the other Realms, we will be joined by more descendants. Our army will grow, but please know that I won't forget the men and women who helped me start it all."

Applause and chants followed the king's speech. He closed his eyes, listening to them shout his name, reveling in the way their cheers rattled the city.

When the applause died down, people began to ask questions, most of which Xavier was happy to answer, such as *When do you think the battle will take place? Or, when we win, can we choose where we live? Could I build a home wherever I like?* But it wasn't until a man stepped forward, clearly of low rank, that Xavier grew uneasy.

"Has the prince truly abandoned us?" the man asked.

Xavier set his jaw, unsure of what to say.

"Is it true that the castle was breached twice?" a woman inquired.

"If the prince has abandoned us, who will take his place as your heir?" another man pressed. "Who will command the army and the Pandora?"

Xavier drew in a breath, his blood beginning to boil, the monster buried deep within him inching toward the surface at the thought of his traitorous son. "Don't worry about the prince, or my heir. Does this army truly need his direction after decades worth of experience? Are you all truly so misguided that you need someone to tell you left from right?" he thundered.

There was no response.

"Your Commanders will provide you with your assignments for the battle and your stations. Listen to them," Xavier barked, turning toward Soroya. "I want you to meet with Veda to start strengthening the city walls. Leave immediately," he demanded.

The princess nodded, bowing at the waist before snapping her fingers, disappearing.

What an inspiring speech, Meera snickered as Xavier led Constance off the dais and back to where their carriage waited with Lincoln and Alrich following close behind. *It's a shame how Malachai's absence will affect your army. Sooner or later, they're going to remember who won this city to begin with, and it wasn't you.*

Xavier swallowed a vicious snarl. *I killed you, therefore I'm the one who won the throne.*

And you couldn't even do that correctly, might I add.

The King slid into the carriage, pounding his fist against its roof to inform the driver he was ready to leave. He didn't respond to her. Instead, he sat as silent as a still winter's night as the carriage lurched forward.

He appeared to me before you did, Meera informed him. *He told me to aim for your heart.*

Xavier's breath caught in his throat, his eyes bulging. *You're lying.*

One of Meera's memories began to flash before his eyes—one of her standing in the Throne Room the night the Idonian Kingdom fell into Xavier's grasp. He watched Malachai approach the queen, only to receive a harsh slap across the face. His heart ceased to beat in his chest as he heard their conversation unfold. He listened as Meera chastised his son, telling him that he was *brilliant* and that he could have been so much more had he not followed in his father's footsteps. But, as Xavier heard the words *aim for his heart* sail past Malachai's lips, he felt as if his own son had taken a dagger and driven it straight into his back. He'd never felt so betrayed.

You see, Meera started again as the memory faded away. *He was* never *the man you thought he was. He was better. He always has been. And now, the Messenger isn't your biggest threat. He is.*

25

The second Ash had heard about Malachai's arrest, fury began to grip her like a deadly vice. Detaining the prince was never part of the plan, but after all she'd heard about the Elves, she should have known that they couldn't be trusted. Penelope's decision to marry Loren instead was beginning to make a lot more sense.

"The second I find that Elf, I'm going to ring his bloody neck," Ash fumed as she paced angrily in front of the other Allies while she waited for Aries to arrive and retrieve them.

Craven gave her a dazed look of bewilderment. "Why? Because he did what every other Immortal and Mortal in the Realm wishes they could do? Ash, Malachai was going to get arrested at one point or another. I don't see why you're so angry."

Ash stopped dead in her tracks, anger sweeping over her. "I understand that, but this is *not* how we repay people who help us. Without him, we'd have been as good as blind when it came to rescuing Cooper and getting that cure for Lucinda. We'd still be down two Allies. But sure, let's thank him by leading him to his execution. Sounds honorable to me," she spewed sarcastically.

"Ash is right," Ana added. "As much as I hate to say it, we should have allowed Malachai to walk away, just this once, with a warning that if we ever saw him again, we'd flay him."

Ash waved her hands dramatically in the air. "See? That's a *much* better idea."

"There's also the fact that Aveo deliberately disobeyed the High Queen's orders," Grant mentioned, fiddling nervously with his fingers. "Not that we really specified what was to be done with the prince once the mission was through."

Frowning at the realization, Ash cursed beneath her breath. Grant was right. They never discussed what was to happen with Malachai once all was said and done. Perhaps that was why Aveo took the liberty of detaining him.

"What do you think will happen to him?" Lilly asked, her chin trembling.

"Technically, as Anderson said earlier, all the wrongdoings he committed throughout the last eighteen years were done because he was following the High Throne's orders," Marcus explained, pointedly avoiding eye contact with Alistair, who scoffed and rolled his eyes in response. "I'm not saying that makes him innocent on a moral standard, but as far as the legal standard goes, he's untouchable. You can't execute someone who hasn't committed a crime."

Ash swallowed her urge to sigh with relief.

Before their conversation could continue, Aries appeared, and the next thing Ash knew, she was standing in a private waiting room in the Draconian Infirmary.

"How is he?" Quinn urgently asked the Fae.

"Alive," Aries told him, falling into a chair. "If Aveo had injected him with Marcus's venom a second later, that wouldn't be the case. Thankfully, Cooper's vitals are climbing now. He's stable. Ebony will stay with him through the night. She can't confirm anything, but she's confident that he'll make a full recovery."

Ash gave into that urge to sigh with relief. "So, he'll be a Draconian, then."

"As far as we know," Aries replied, raking a hand through his dark, silky locks. "Much like you, Cooper will be the first of his kind. Ebony has no idea what Draconian venom will do to an Arebus Archer. She's already reached out to a few Elven Healers to get their opinion."

"Speaking of Elves," Ana drawled. "Ash is looking for Aveo. Where is he?"

"I suspect that he's gone to see Penelope," Aries said, a hint of sadness creeping into his tone, shadows dancing in his burgundy eyes. "He was in such a rush... didn't stay to get any medical attention. He was only here long enough to put Malachai in chains and then he was gone."

Alistair moved forward, arriving at Ash's side. She spared him a sidelong glance, noting his solemn expression. "He went to tell her about Abernathy," he presumed with a deepening frown.

"Her heart will shatter," Marcus said, slowly shaking his head in disbelief. "I don't understand. Granted, I didn't know him well, but I thought I knew him well enough. How could he join the Dark Army? Why? What could he possibly gain from working with Xavier?"

Aries grimaced. "Aveo didn't exactly give him a chance to explain. Can't say I blame him, though."

"I'd have done the same," Alistair admitted, a muscle feathering in his jaw. "But I wouldn't have left him alive."

"There was no time for Aveo to defeat him," Aries explained. "Cooper was dying, or quite possibly already dead. They ceased their fighting to focus on him. However, I will say that when we arrived to find Abernathy in front of Cooper's cell, he was trying to get his attention... to wake him up... telling him to breathe. I think Xavier put him there on purpose. It was almost as if he knew that Aveo was coming. I don't know how that would be possible, but it felt like a trap."

Ash's heart dropped into her stomach. "I think I know," she said, biting her inner cheek. "There's a Rat in Dracus."

"*What?*" everyone in the room asked in unison.

"Malachai told me before we went our separate ways after we filled the Scepter," Ash began to explain, staring down at her feet, afraid to meet any of them in the eye. "He said that he didn't know who the Rat was. His father never told him. He found out last month when it was discovered that I was the Messenger. I planned to tell you all and Loren, the second I made it back to Dracus, but I never got the chance. I'm sure that you can understand why I might not have thought about it."

Silence fell over the room like a wet blanket, causing Ash's anxiety to fester. After the day she'd had, she expected someone to berate her in some way, shape, or form. No one did. Instead, Marcus said, "You need to tell us *everything* he said. If this intel turns out to be correct, then I'll buy that man an ale."

ONCE ASH TOLD THE OTHER ALLIES EVERYTHING THAT HAD transpired between her and Malachai from start to finish, they sat in silence for a time. There were no questions or accusations. There were no harsh or berating words. There was only deafening silence and vacant stares.

Ash sat on a cushioned chair; her knees pulled to her chest. She allowed her thoughts to drift back to the moment she woke up after the final task to find him waiting for her. She was weak, afraid, and in excruciating pain, but she would have fought him anyway. She'd have tried if she needed to, but he wasn't there to inflict more pain. He was there to erase it. If he hadn't, would Ash have succeeded in filling the Scepter? Or would she have bled out, falling into a hibernated state until the Berserker knitting process was complete? When would she have woken if that had been the case? Days? Weeks?

"Years ago, back when Xavier was still Gideon's adviser, he brought Malachai to an Idonian Council meeting," Aries revealed, leaning forward in his chair, bracing his elbows on his knees. "At the time, he was nineteen and attending university to become a Healer. He was at the meeting because Queen Ren Richmond of Erim had heard of him and his skill and was requesting that he attend university there." Aries chuckled, shaking his head slowly. "Malachai was so brilliant that two Realms were willing to fight for him. Something like that has *never* happened before."

One of the nurses brought in a tray containing blood and coffee. Everyone grabbed something to drink, eager to stay awake to hear more.

Aries took a sip of his coffee and said, "Malachai wasn't just brilliant, though. He was kind," he revealed, his lips twitching toward a smile. "Meera had presented him with an offer to train as a Black Knight shortly after. I'd heard that he'd accepted and planned to begin training once he finished certifying as a Healer in Erim. He never came back. Then, all of a sudden, Xavier resigns as Gideon's adviser due to a family emergency in Erim. Naturally, we all assumed that something had happened to Malachai, but we never heard anything. Next thing we know, three years have passed and Malachai resurfaces as... well... what he is today. No one understood. Meera was heartbroken. Absolutely none of it made any sense. As much as I hate to say it, I'm not at all surprised that Malachai's chosen to return to the light. I don't think that he ever intended to leave it."

"If that's the case, why did he do the things that he has?" Alistair asked, though his tone wasn't nearly as angry as Ash had anticipated it would be.

Morghan cleared his throat, drawing everyone's attention. "I've been a nomad a long time. I've lived everywhere in Idona and have met a lot of people. There's one thing that I've learned and carried with me all these years, and it's that everyone has one simple thing in common—we all have a story. We have no say in how it begins, but how it ends... that's up to us."

"Malachai is trying to change his ending," Anastasia concluded.

"The question is whether or not we help him," Vincent said, scratching at his temple.

"Should we, after all he's done?" Marcus asked.

Most people in the waiting room shrugged in response, but Ash and Aries both nodded. "If we help Malachai, he'll help us. We completed the three tasks, but now we have the siege to worry about. The intel that he can provide could improve our chances at succeeding tenfold. Not to mention, he did help us save Cooper. He didn't have to risk going back to Solaris on *our* behalf. But he did. We owe him a life-debt, whether we like it or not."

"Agreed," Quinn said.

"As do I," Aries contributed.

"Me too," Ana said.

"Same," Vincent chirped.

"I don't like it, but I'll do what I can," Marcus informed them.

"What Marcus said," Alistair grumbled.

Craven sighed heavily. "Ditto."

"I should have never set foot in Dracus," Morghan complained.

"So, it's settled then," Ash said, finishing off her blood. "Malachai will not die in Dracus."

Everyone nodded, leading Ash's heart to soar. As High Queen and Sectra Holder, she knew that she could prevent Malachai's death on her own. Would it make her look terrible? Yes. Would everyone's opinion of her across the Realm dwindle? Absolutely. Did she care? Not a chance.

26

While the Allies all agreed that Malachai was owed a life-debt, the next morning, Ash learned the hard way that they had no say in the matter. At sunrise, she was awoken by a trio of lady's maids who informed her that she'd been summoned by the king for a council meeting. They helped her get ready, dressing her in a pair of black leather leggings with a high-collared satin crimson overcoat designed to be shorter in the front and longer in the back. Golden buttons lined the front and matching thread was embroidered along the hem, long bell-shaped sleeves, and fitted bodice. The ensemble was one of the most stunning things that Ash had ever seen, let alone worn, but even its beauty couldn't keep her mind off what was to come in the next few hours.

After she was deemed presentable, with half her hair braided into a crown atop her head and a golden circlet resting on her brow, Ash was whisked away to the Round Table Room.

Upon entering the room, all Ash could think was about the Rat sitting somewhere around the table. She scanned everyone's faces, sucking on her teeth. Her heart felt heavy once her gaze fell on Loren. She could only imagine how his own heart would shatter once he found out about the Rat's betrayal.

Lowering into her seat, Ash looked toward the people she knew weren't working for the enemy. Marcus met her gaze, offering her a small smile. Anastasia did the same, though it never reached her eyes. Ash returned the expression, fiddling with her fingers beneath the table. They had already made up their mind about Malachai, but now it would come to a vote. There were only three of them against seven other council members who would love nothing more than to watch the prince burn.

"Now that we're all here," Loren started, reaching for a pitcher of water to fill his glass. "We should start this meeting by saying that as of this morning, Cooper McBride's condition has remained stable. So far, he shows no signs of waking, but that's normal for this stage of transition. As for Sam Waters, the supposed Rebel General, he is currently residing on the bottom floor and will remain there until Lady Evanora answers her summons."

"I received a response from her this morning," Richard revealed, his lips spreading into a genuine smile. "She needs to tie up a few loose ends, but she should be here by lunchtime tomorrow via a teleportation sphere."

"Great!" Valentina chirped. "If she's truly involved with the Rebels, which by now we can all assume that she is, she'll be able to answer a lot of unanswered questions and provide some closure to people who adored Cedric Chamberlain."

Ash thought of Penelope and wondered how she was doing after Aveo told her about Abernathy. She didn't know a great deal about her sister, as they'd hardly had a chance to get to know each other, but everyone in the Realm knew how close she had been with her Guardian and her first betrothed. There were countless pictures of the three of them displayed in papers during their time together.

"If Lady Evanora can clear Cedric's name, that would be wonderful," Ariel insisted.

"Let's not forget that his murderer is currently a few floors below us," Axel growled. "What are we going to do about him?"

"That's what we're here to figure out," Loren assured the General. "What we decide today will affect whether or not an Idonian Council meeting will take place on Comhdhail at week's end. Personally, I would prefer we handle it ourselves and keep the Elves out of it."

Richard snorted. "I hate to break it to you, but now that Queen Esmeralda has requested that Aveo remain here as an Elven Representative, I'd say that they're already *in* it."

Loren's nostrils flared, a vein throbbing at his temples. Ash watched him warily, wondering what thoughts were swimming around beneath his matte-black, ruby-encrusted crown. Aveo's presence would only complicate his relationship with Penelope, or worse… he might find out about their relationship to begin with.

"Since when are Commander's representatives?" Anastasia asked, scoffing. "Doesn't he have a fraction of the Elven army to prepare for... I don't know... the *siege?*"

"Supposedly, he'll only be staying with us for a short time," Loren said, crossing his fingers, which made quite a few council members laugh. "Anyway, once we execute Malachai, he'll have no reason to remain here."

Ash's stomach bottomed out, her eyes growing wide. Before she had a chance to hide her surprise, Richard took notice of it. He gave her a long, questioning look before he said, "You seem a bit shocked. I don't know why you would be. What else did you think we would do with him? Throw him a welcome party and grant him citizenship?"

Frowning, Ash shook her head. "I simply thought we'd use him for intel, is all. He *is* Xavier's son, and no one knows Solaris better than he does. Whatever knowledge he possesses could improve our chances at success tremendously. I can't be the only one who feels that way," she said, glancing about the table, searching for signs that someone agreed.

"Ash is right," Marcus said, drawing attention to himself. "Why would we kill an asset like that when we could use him first?"

"I'm sure he'd be incredibly helpful if he weren't *who* he is," Axel grunted, leaning back in his chair, crossing his arms in front of his muscled chest. "What makes you think that Malachai would help us so easily? You act as if he would sell his loyalty to the highest bidder. He didn't leave Solaris willingly. Humphrey said so himself. He was there. Why do you *think* Xavier would toss out his strongest asset? Did you think it was because they had a little spat?

No, it was because he failed to kill *you* and he's here to finish the job."

Ash nearly opened her mouth to object but bit her tongue instead. She *wanted* to inform Axel that she already knew that was why Malachai was abolished. She wanted to tell the Council all about their encounter on the East Cliff, and how he had every right and motive to try to end her but chose to help her. She wanted to scream about how they'd slept just a few feet apart, and how he could have taken that opportunity to slit her throat and steal the Scepter. She awoke the next morning in one piece, only for him to tell her that there was a *Rat* sitting at *that* very table.

Instead, Ash sighed exasperatedly, feigning boredom. "Now that I have the Scepter, a small fish like Malachai is no match for me," she insisted, offering the General a sweet, teasing smile.

"Don't get cocky," Blade warned. "The moment you think you're undefeatable is the moment you're most vulnerable."

No part of Ash believed that she was undefeatable. In fact, she was almost certain that she wouldn't survive the coming siege. These could be her very last days, weeks, or months—however long it took to plan the ordeal. She wouldn't spend such precious time holding her tongue or worrying about what other people thought of her.

"If Malachai wanted to kill me, he would have," Ash declared, reaching for her glass of blood, bringing it to her lips. "Anyone with a brain knows that he doesn't leave people alive unless he wants to. He could have driven that dagger straight into my heart or head, killing me instantly, but he didn't."

"Ash…" Loren trailed. "Tell me you're not defending his actions against you—"

"I'm not!" Ash blurted defensively. "Trust me, I'd *love* to do to him what he did to me, but I don't act on vengeance. I act on my gut, and my *gut* is telling me that he'd help us if we gave him a chance to."

Loren sucked in an audible breath before going on to say, "Even if you're right about that, we can't have the rest of Idona thinking—"

"Why don't we worry about what the rest of the Realm thinks

after we end the war," Ana interjected, earning quite the glare from the king. She didn't so much as flinch and instead lifted a brow in his direction. "Don't look at me like that. You know just as well as I do that if Malachai was arrested in the Kingdom of Elves, they'd be draining information from him as we speak just to get a leg up on us."

"They really do turn everything into a competition," Shay said with a depressive huff. "Honestly, I think that executing Malachai would be just as beneficial as using him. We won't have to worry about him turning on us, which he undoubtedly will. And, we wouldn't have to worry about him outsmarting us during the siege, which he undoubtedly would also do. He's too much of a risk and more powerful than he makes himself seem. For all we know, he could be waiting for Ash to defeat his father just so he can take his throne."

Everyone around the table grimaced in unison. For the first time, after hearing Shay's words, Ash began to doubt Malachai. What if she was right, and the second Ash rid the Realm of Xavier for good, Malachai swooped in, and the war continued anyway? Her stomach became sour as she considered all the possibilities.

"I agree," Shadow said, tapping his fingers along the table's polished surface. "We can't take any chances. Not with him."

"Let's not forget that through Sam Waters and Lady Evanora, we could gain fifteen thousand more soldiers," Blade added. "Ash, if you're looking for something that could improve our chances, think about what that would do for us."

Blade wasn't wrong. Fifteen thousand more soldiers to add to the hundred thousand the Immortal Armies already had would make a huge difference. She didn't technically need Malachai's information now that they'd outnumber the Dark Army.

"Valentina," Loren called, tearing Ash from her thoughts. "Have you seen anything recently that might be of help to us right now?"

The Prophetess shook her head, her shoulders slumping. "Unfortunately, nothing about Malachai. The last vision I had about him was one where he was being chased and tortured. Then again, that can be prevented if we choose to... you know."

"You all seem to think that we have a choice," Richard spat in a tone so aggressive that it sent everyone shrinking further into their seats. Ash stared at him, her fingers curling into fists around her overcoat beneath the table. "Every moment that Malachai remains in Dracus puts us all at risk. He needs to be executed immediately, whether Valentina receives another vision about him or not."

Ash swallowed against the growl creeping up her throat. "I'm the High Queen *and* Sectra Holder. You won't do anything unless I say to."

"Very well," Richard said with a snort, waving her off. "Doom us all."

"Ash," Loren said, drawing her attention. Her heart sank once she saw the way he was looking at her, with sunken, sympathetic eyes. "I don't know what's transpired between the two of you, but you have to realize how upset the people would be if you didn't take this chance to protect them from him forever. They could revolt."

"Nothing transpired," Ash lied. Plenty had. Enough for her to want him alive. She found herself looking toward Marcus for help, but he seemed to be at a loss for words. All he did was shake his head, a grim expression upon his face. "Without him, Cooper would be dead. Lucinda would still be under that curse. We can't overlook that."

"So kill him quickly," Richard suggested nonchalantly. "Make it merciful."

Ash's eyes bulged, her jaw dropping. "You want *me* to execute him?"

"You're the High Queen," Richard retorted, clearly bothered by how she'd waved her titles in their faces a few moments prior. "Not to mention, if you're the one who does it, it'll squash any rumors flying about. You do realize that the entire Realm is talking about all the reasons why Malachai would be wearing an onyx division Ally uniform, right? Some are saying that you two have known each other a lot longer than you're letting on, and that this is all part of some grand scheme that Loren is involved in. Others are saying that you're betrothed, and that your marriage will form an alliance with Xavier and end the war. No one will think such things once you decapitate him."

Bile crept up Ash's throat, a cold sweat developing beneath her attire. Her overcoat's fitted bodice was beginning to feel more like a vice crushing her ribs and the fragile organs beneath them.

"All for executing the prince," Loren said, his voice sounding far away, like an echo bouncing off rolling hills.

A murmur of yesses rattled in Ash's ears, but her hand remained down, limp at her side. She could stop this and remind them that she had the final say, but every time she formed the words, they vanished on the tip of her tongue.

"We'll schedule it for two days' time in the city square," Richard announced, pushing to his feet.

"I'll inform the Elves," Valentina said solemnly.

Before Ash knew it, everyone was leaving the room. By the time she broke out of her trance, the only people remaining were Ana, Loren, and Marcus. She looked at each of them, spots swarming in her vision, either from rage, lack of oxygen, or shock.

"You look ill," Loren mentioned, concern flashing in his slate-gray eyes. "Marcus, maybe you should get her back to the apartment."

Ash didn't fight when Marcus pulled her from her seat and guided her out of the Round Table Room. The second she heard the door shut behind her, she reached for the golden circlet resting on her brow and ripped it off her head.

"Ash," Marcus said warily. "Maybe this is for the best. Fighting to keep him alive would do more harm than it could ever do good. He's caused too much pain. Whether his father was High King at the time, and he was following orders doesn't matter. Idona will *never* accept him, and if you choose to ignore that and work with him anyway, they won't accept you either."

Ash spared him a glance before she picked up her pace, tears of anger pricking her eyes. "You can't honestly look me in the eye and tell me that nothing about this feels wrong," she accused. "You were there yesterday. You saw how helpful he could be.

You've met the man behind the nefarious facade he wore for decades."

"Whether he was wearing a facade or not, he's still the enemy," Loren reminded Ash from behind.

Scoffing, Ash glanced at the king over her shoulder. "Yeah, well, sometimes the enemy isn't all that bad, and the hero isn't all that good. You never know someone's true colors until they slap you in the face. Oh, and that reminds me, there's a Rat on your council." She added the last bit far more bitterly than she'd intended and cringed. "Sorry," she admitted, pausing mid-step to turn around and face him, just in time to watch the color vanish from his face. "I was going to tell you sooner, but you called the meeting for such an early hour—"

"What do you mean there's a *Rat* on my council?" Loren asked, rage flickering in his hardening gaze.

Gulping, Ash glanced at Marcus and Ana, hoping one of them would step in and explain. Neither of them did. Sighing, she said, "Malachai told me that his father has been communicating with someone inside Dracus for an unknown amount of time. He had only just found out about it himself last month, so he wasn't able to tell me who it was. Given the information this Rat provided Xavier, involving me and the Allies, it would have to be someone on your council."

Loren stepped toward a nearby decorative table to brace himself, his complexion taking on a green hue. "Are you certain that he was telling the truth?" he asked, his voice a far higher pitch than Ash was used to.

"Malachai is many things, but I wouldn't take him for a liar," Marcus contributed.

"He has no reason to lie," Ash added.

"Are you sure about that?" the king spat. "I feel as if he would have plenty of reasons to lie. His life is on the line."

"Why don't you ask him yourself?" Ash inquired, crossing her arms. "I'm certain that he'll tell you everything that he told me, and maybe more if you ask nicely. Afterward, you might understand why I'd prefer not to decapitate him."

Loren scowled at her, pursing his lips. "Unless you want to paint yourself as an enemy to the Idonian people as well, you don't have much of a choice," he informed her, pushing off the table. "At least you have two days to suck all the intel you need from him. I suggest that you start now. I want to know who this Rat is by sundown tomorrow."

The King stormed down the hall, raking a shaking hand through his raven-black locks. He had turned a corner before Ash opened her mouth to reply, leaving her growling frustratedly.

"What's gotten into him?" Marcus asked Anastasia, who simply shrugged in response.

"If I had to guess, I'd say that it has something to do with Malachai being detained in his kingdom, Aveo staying until further notice, and the apparent Rat on his council," she replied, staring down the hall. "However, I suggest that we stop worrying about Loren and start worrying about that Rat and what Malachai can tell us before his untimely departure."

27

Ash decided that it was best that she return to the apartment to decompress and eat some lunch before she paid Malachai an unpleasant visit. Marcus escorted her in silence while Ana went off to hunt down the other Allies to inform them about what had occurred. While they had all agreed to try and keep Malachai alive, Ash doubted any of them would be too upset about his execution. If anything, some would be envious of Ash and wish they'd been given the opportunity to perform it themselves.

It was easy for Ash to become lost in her thoughts as she walked, her shoulders slumping, and her head hung low. The challenges that she was facing now were the same challenges that every ruler before her had faced at one time or another. However, Ash hadn't expected to be High Queen long enough to have to deal with something like this. Then again, had she chosen not to follow Richard and Loren's advice, there was a strong chance that she would have had to swing the executioner's blade anyway.

The Messenger had always been a symbol of hope for the Idonian people. For decades, they had waited for her to surface and lead them all out of the darkness. Even Ash herself had spent her life praying each night to awake the next morning and learn that the time for the prophecy's fulfillment had come. Now that *she* was that symbol of hope, she needed the people's faith in her just as badly as she needed to keep faith in herself. How could they trust her with their livelihood in her hands when she would rather keep the man responsible for their pain alive than give them the peace his death would bring?

"Are you alright?" Marcus asked in a hushed tone as they ascended the staircase that would lead them to the castle's fourth and final floor.

Shrugging, Ash thought of what to say. She wasn't alright. How could she be? "I'm as alright as I could possibly be under these circumstances. Malachai's execution aside, how are we supposed to figure out who this Rat is in less than forty-eight hours? Moons only know how long they've been trading Loren's secrets. For all we know, this has been going on throughout Xavier's entire reign, maybe longer. Not to mention, Cooper isn't exactly out of the woods yet. Even *if* he pulls out of this transition in one piece, he's going to have to endure a lot of change. It isn't easy becoming dependent on blood." She paused her rant, exhaling slowly. "And here I thought that completing the three tasks was a challenging feat. These last two days have been just as troublesome, if not more."

Marcus nodded, pressing his lips together. "I wish I could say that things will get easier."

"Don't bother," Ash replied with a snort. "You'll just jinx any chances of that happening."

They rounded the final corner, arriving in the councilor's corridor where they found an unexpected visitor waiting outside their apartment door. Ash stopped dead in her tracks at the sight of Aveo, leaning with his back against a wall. The second their eyes met, her blood came to a boil, just as his cheeks heated with what appeared to be shame.

"Don't rip his head off," Marcus warned as Ash pressed onward, her fingers balling into trembling fists at her sides.

"I'm not making any promises," Ash shot over her shoulder.

Aveo scanned Ash up and down and went rigid. "Ash," he said uneasily. "I came to explain—"

"Explain what? How you deliberately went behind my back and made a call that you knew no one would agree with, especially me?"

Marcus arrived at Ash's side, his features contorting with worry. "Why don't we take this inside, where there are fewer chances of acquiring any witnesses?"

"I arrested Malachai *for you,*" Aveo argued, ignoring Marcus's suggestion.

"For *me?*" Ash snarled. "All you've done is back me into a corner, and now I'll have to thank Malachai for his help saving Cooper and Lucinda's lives by severing his bloody head, meanwhile, forgoing any chances I have at saving Lincoln!"

Aveo grimaced, dropping his gaze from her face. "I thought for certain that they would keep him alive, perhaps use him as a pawn to ensnare Xavier in some sort of trap," he admitted, slowly shaking his head in wonder. "You have to understand that the only reason I chose to detain him was because of how it would have looked for everyone if Aries teleported him out of Dracus with all of those witnesses. You think the headlines are bad today? Imagine what they would have said if we'd set Malachai free."

The Commander had a valid point, but it didn't improve Ash's mood, or her aggressive demeanor. "How am I supposed to believe a word you say when we've only known each other twenty-four hours and you Elves are known for your conniving bullshit?" she asked point blank.

Aveo's brows shot upward. "Conniving bullshit?"

"Ash," Marcus said again, a warning, audible in his tone. "Inside. Now," he demanded, opening the apartment door and urging them to follow him inside. They did but failed to take their scowls off one another in the process.

Ash waited for the apartment door to shut before she said, "You don't think that everyone in the Realm knows why King Thaddeus and Queen Esmeralda chose to betroth Cedric, and then you to my sister? To finally put an Elf on the High Throne, that's why. If it can't be a Chamberlain, it might as well be a Calloway, right?" Ash scoffed, shaking her head. "They didn't call off the search for me because they were worried Cedric and Marcus were putting my siblings in danger. They called it off because they didn't *want* me to be found, so that the Sectra could go to *their* daughter after the deadline passed. I have no reason to trust you, and you've done the opposite of giving me one."

Marcus choked on what could have only been his own breath, his vivid green eyes bulging.

Aveo stared down at Ash, baring his too-white teeth. "I have nothing to do with whatever my King and Queen have done. Like any loyal subject, I follow orders. You failed to give me one, and I made a call that would protect you *and* everyone else involved."

"Everyone *but* the one solely responsible for that mission's success," Ash retorted. "I know Malachai's one of the two most hated men in Idona, and that his execution is warranted. He's far from innocent, and I have my own scar to prove it. If anyone should want him six feet under, it's me. However, something in my gut, which I trust entirely, tells me that he is of more use to us all alive than dead, and that there's more to his story than just creation, obliteration, and damnation. Thanks to you, I get to go tell the man that he'll die in two days. Before that happens, he needs to tell me literally everything he knows until I've sucked dry each and every one of his brain cells, so that I can figure out who the Rat on Loren's fucking council is!"

Aveo blinked, his lips parting for words that didn't come out.

Marcus pinched the bridge of his nose, squeezing his eyes shut. "First, you accuse the Elves of conspiring and then you tell one an incredibly sensitive piece of information. Nice work."

"There's a Rat in Dracus?" Aveo whispered.

"Yes," Ash whispered back in a teasing manner. "Malachai told me so, which is why I'm going to talk to him shortly. I'd planned to do so anyway, but now I get to look him in the eye, knowing that I'll have to separate his neck from his shoulders in forty-eight hours. This might surprise you but being the Messenger doesn't mean that I'm a malicious murderer. I'd prefer not to kill at all. If the Moons wanted a remorseless killer, they should have picked someone more like you."

Scowling, Aveo said, "I may be a Commander, but I don't kill for sport. I do it because someone has to. No one has a choice in the matter. If you want to survive in this day and age, you pick up a fucking sword. You're no different than I am, and neither is the average Mortal. The fact that taking a life *bothers you* means that you still have honor. The moment you can slit someone's throat without batting an eye is the moment you've become too far gone."

Ash's features softened, her anger fading away. "Are you too far gone?"

It was a serious question. This man in front of her was a stranger, but at the same time, he knew her own family members better than she did. Penelope might dislike him, but she respected him, and Vincent spoke highly of him. Was this man too far gone? Is that why when people spoke of him, they described a cruel, angry man on a mission to save the Galaxy in the bloodiest of ways?

"Not yet," Aveo replied, a hint of sadness seeping into his tone. "To prove that to you, I'll help you figure out who this Rat is. If Malachai can show Loren and his council how helpful he can be, it might save his life."

"Why would you help her?" Marcus asked, taking Ash by surprise. She looked toward him, noting the sincerity etched in his handsome features. "You said it yourself. You're one of King Thaddeus and Queen Esmeralda's loyal subjects, yet you're saying that you'd help Ash attempt to save the Prince of Darkness. Why?"

"All titles aside, in time, Ash and I will call one another family, and family comes first," Aveo explained, meeting Ash's gaze once more. "I lost all six of my brothers and my parents in the Ballroom Battle. I've lived each year since then attempting to convince myself that I'm fine on my own. I'm not. I want a family again. I would do anything to protect that possibility. Why do you think I requested to stay here in Dracus? I've spent far too much time honing my skills as a warrior, but not a brother, husband, or father. I want to make up for lost time. You can trust me. I'll help you, no matter what it is you need help with. If you want to save Malachai, then that's what we'll do."

Ash blinked, her jaw dropping. Something in her heart cracked as she examined his face and the shadows now lurking in his eyes.

This man, the big, bad Commander, was more than the blades he was known to wield. He was lonely. "I just want to save this Realm," she admitted. "Can you help me do that?"

Aveo perked, his lips stretching into a smile. "It would be my pleasure."

"Good," Ash said, offering him an approving nod. "Let's start with catching this Rat and keeping Malachai's head on his shoulders. Something tells me that without him, we'll be flying blind when the time comes to end this war."

Marcus snorted, drawing Ash's attention. "Well, he did *start* it, so one would think he'd know how to finish it."

28

Malachai had spent the last twelve hours under constant surveillance. While he couldn't see anyone, he knew that they were watching him, waiting for him to do something rash like transition into a tiny bug and escape. He could do that if he felt the desire, but the truth was that he wanted nothing more than to stop running. He'd rather face his fate here and now than spend the rest of his days as an outlaw.

Though he wasn't sure what was going to happen in the coming hours or days, Malachai was determined to make the best of what little time he had left. He showered, put on a pair of sweatpants, tied his hair back, and got to work.

With piles of paper resting on his kitchenette table and three vials of ink, Malachai started writing. He knew in his heart that if it was up to Ash, he'd remain alive, but knew that the Idonian Council would back her into a corner. The least Malachai could do for her was create a cure for Lincoln. In fact, that wasn't the only mistake that he wanted to undo before he met his maker.

If Malachai could create a species once, he could do it again. He couldn't bring Morghan's relatives and all the other Werewolves back from the dead, but he could create a way for him to make more, or at least something *close* to a Werewolf.

To create the Pandora, Malachai had used DNA from a Werewolf, a Draconian, and Black Magic. "There has to be a way to do the same thing without Draconian DNA," he murmured to himself, his quill scraping against the parchment at top speed. "Perhaps if I remove Black Magic from the equation and replace it with Fae Magic or Light Magic…" he trailed off, his brow wrinkling with thought.

When the Prince became stumped on his Werewolf predicament, he focused on Lincoln's cure. It would be a lot easier for him to create one if he had his notes from when he first created the injections, but he'd have to make do with his memory. "Everything has an opposite," he reminded himself, scribbling away with his quill so ferociously that the tip snapped. After retrieving another, he kept going. "If I could just remember every ingredient used, then I could create a list of more ingredients that would counteract those…"

While Lincoln's cure was serious enough in its own right, there were more things that Malachai needed to apologize for. While he had nothing to do with the death of Alistair Ward's family, he was still present when the event took place. There was no way the Rider would ever forgive Malachai. In fact, he was certain that the only marks on his grave would be the boot prints Alistair would leave once he danced on it, but that wouldn't stop the prince from doing something nice for him.

"Armor and a saddle," Malachai said, his lips spreading into a wide smile. "If he expects to ride that Dragon into battle, then I might as well find a way to protect them both."

It was difficult to make a proper design for such things without Willa's measurements, so Malachai resolved to create a will and hoped that the Draconians would acknowledge it once he passed. Over the decades, the prince had acquired so much coin that he might as well be named the richest man in Si Realtra, for he never spent a dime of it. However, he was smart enough to put all his coin in an account that only *he* could access, therefore he left directions for Anderson.

Once he finished the will, Malachai sat back and read it. He'd donated an unspecified amount to Willa's armour, and what was left over to the VanCamp family so that they could use it to rebuild Solaris and other cities and villages destroyed by the war. Coin wasn't the only thing that Malachai wished to give away, though. If recovered, he left all of his research to Vincent, his arsenal to Marcus, and the contents of his personal Library to Penelope. As for his biological sisters, Trixa was the only one who would receive anything—his Regal Mountain home and everything inside of it.

"Savron can go fuck himself," Malachai murmured, just before he heard the alarming sound of a key twisting inside of a lock. He shot to his feet, his heart skipping into overdrive as the door creaked open. His mind raced with thoughts about what might happen next. Was this it? Had the Prince of Darkness finally run out of time?

Nothing compared to the relief that washed over Malachai once he set his eyes on Ash. His shoulders slumped, his heart calming like the sea after a storm. However, once Aveo followed her inside the apartment, the prince became as still as a marble statue. Marcus sauntered into the room last, shutting the door behind him. All three of their expressions remained neutral, which worried Malachai even more, seeing as he had no way of knowing where this meeting would take him.

"You look nice today," he told Ash, gesturing to her attire. "Red suits you."

Ash lifted a brow. "I'd say the same to you, but you're lacking a shirt."

"Doesn't mean I don't look good," Malachai replied, smirking devilishly. "What are you doing here?" he asked, his attention shifting over to Aveo. "I thought you would have run back to the Kingdom of Elves by now, eager to be showered in gold and praise for your recent accomplishments. I must have made you one massive pile of coin. Last I knew, my bounty was worth more than Solaris itself."

Aveo shrugged. "I'll make sure to spend it all wisely."

Ash cleared her throat, shooting the Commander the dirtiest of looks.

"By spending it wisely, I mean donating it to Justice Keepers across the Realm, working to rebuild what your beasts destroyed," Aveo said, lowering to sit on the couch, making himself at home. "Not that it's any of your business what I do with any of my finances. Instead, you should be more concerned with keeping your head attached to the rest of your body."

Growling, Ash's eyes momentarily flashed silver. "You're not being very helpful."

"Let's not beat around the bush," Aveo suggested, leaning forward in his seat, placing both his elbows on his knees. "We need you to tell us everything you know about the Rat here in Dracus. If you play your cards right, we might be able to help you avoid an execution in two days' time."

Malachai's heart skipped a beat, the color draining from his face. "Oh," he uttered beneath his breath, returning to his chair. It wasn't that he was surprised. He'd known that he was living on borrowed time, hence why he'd chosen to write a will. That didn't make it any easier to hear, though. One could never mentally prepare themselves enough to lose their own life. "Why would you want to help me *avoid* the execution when you arrested me in the first place?" he asked the Commander, narrowing his eyes accusingly. "You're incredibly confusing, you know that?"

"I prefer the term *unpredictable*," Aveo told him with a shrug of his shoulders.

"I can't disagree," the prince admitted. "Not when you're helping the Draconians just as much as you're helping me. That's a plot twist if I've ever seen one."

Marcus nodded agreeably. "You're right. However, I don't know about you, but I grew up knowing not to question the help others give."

It took a valiant effort not to recoil as the words left Marcus's lips, considering how painfully they stung. He tried his best to keep his expression placid and said, "Forgive me for being a tad hesitant when it comes to Calloway the Cruel."

"Is that what they're calling me these days?" Aveo inquired, seemingly unbothered.

"Well, that amongst other things…" the prince trailed, fighting against a teasing smile. "I'd be happy to review all of your recently acquired titles, but I'm afraid Ash would rather spend her time focusing on more important matters."

"You mean like how to figure out who this Rat is by tomorrow evening?" Ash inquired, sauntering into the kitchenette where she poured herself a glass of water and sipped it gingerly. "Now, I know from past experience that you provide intel but only if it benefits you. I can't assure you that helping us with this will improve your circumstances at all, but I have faith. That's all I have left right now. I won't force you to do anything, but if you could help lead us in the right direction—"

"Say no more," Malachai interjected, holding up a hand. "I'm sad to say that I hardly know a thing. As I told you before, I only just learned the Rat existed a few short weeks ago. My father hasn't always been upfront and honest with me. Rightfully so, honestly. However, I have a hunch that this Rat has been feeding him intel for far longer than I originally thought."

Ash frowned, her grip tightening around her glass. "You truly witnessed just one message?" she asked, frustration tainting her tone.

"A few," Malachai replied. "Ryole, my father's most trusted Commander, delivered the first message I knew of during a family dinner. Soroya and I were both present. Our father was so stunned by its contents that he showed us the letter. It spoke all about how you were found, and that you were the Messenger. There were mentions of Alistair as well, which he was equally infuriated about."

Ash and Marcus shared a puzzled look before the latter asked, "Why would he be just as furious about Alistair surfacing as the Messenger?"

"Well, that's a long story," Malachai admitted, immediately regretting his choice of words. He hoped they'd drop the subject, but the way all three of his visitors were staring at him proved otherwise. After a long, dramatic sigh, the prince gave in and continued, "My father was under the impression that Alistair had died with the rest of the Ward family. When it came out that he was alive, he learned that I had lied to him."

"So a Rebel slipped through the cracks," Aveo said with a shrug. "If I were your father, Alistair would be the least of my concerns."

Shaking his head, Malachai said, "It isn't that simple. Sure, Lord Angus Ward had a few Rebel connections, but his affiliation with the organization wasn't what put him at the top of my father's to-kill list. His blood did."

"Dragon's blood," Marcus concluded.

"No," Malachai corrected. "Cavanaugh blood. Alistair's great-grandmother was one of the First High King's younger sisters, and a member of the first Idonian Council—Mackenzie Cavanaugh, first in line for the High Throne. When Aiden died, she abdicated the throne to his daughter Evangeline, who married a Grimm, and moved back to Mayfire to live out the rest of her days. Mackenzie's daughter, Louise, married Anachi Ward. Together, they had Angus. After High Queen Evangeline passed, the Idonian Council approached Louise, as her family still held first rights to the Throne, considering Evangeline had never produced any children. Louise followed in her mother's footsteps and abdicated as well, solidifying the Grimm's claim to the throne. They maintained that claim for hundreds of years, until Blair Grimm married Graham VanCamp, whom she met during a tour of Mayfire. She passed unexpectedly four years later before producing any heirs. Three years after that, Graham remarried, and you know what happened next."

"Thanks for the history lesson," Aveo mused, crossing his feet at the ankles. "I don't think you've told us one thing we don't already know. What does any of this have to do with Alistair? You said so yourself, when Louise abdicated, the Grimm family's claim was solidified."

Malachai nodded, sucking on his teeth while fighting to keep hold of what was left of his patience. *Why did Ash need to choose Aveo, of all people, to work with?* He grunted frustratedly. "When my father stole the throne, and all the remaining VanCamps were three sheets to the wind, the only other people in the Realm that lay claim to it were the Wards. Angus Ward, in particular. People would give *anything* to have another Cavanaugh on the throne, and Angus knew that. My Father got wind that he was planning a rebellion of his own, and that he was working with the Rebels to make it happen. During my mission to rid the Realm of the organization, my father sent word that I was to temporarily cease my hunt, head to Mayfire, and wipe the Ward family off the face of the Realm, ridding Si Realtra of the Cavanaughs for good. You can imagine how furious he was when it came out that Alistair was still alive—and a Dragon Rider, just like his ancestors. His claim to the throne is even stronger than Ash's."

"That makes no sense," Aveo argued. "Even if what you say is true, the VanCamps have held the High Throne for over a century. I understand how pivotal the Cavanaugh's were to Si Realtra's evolution, but just because there's one left doesn't mean they should be able to just walk into Solaris and ask for the crown."

"You're right," Malachai confirmed, nodding slowly. "However, who do you think the people would choose? It was the Cavanaughs who rid the Galaxy of Darkness a millennium ago, bringing on the New Dawn and an era of peace unlike any the Realms have experienced. Surely, a Cavanaugh could inspire enough people to do the same thing now."

Out of the corner of his eye, Malachai watched Ash become as frigid as ice, the color draining from her face. "He has no idea," the prince explained, meeting her shadowy gaze. "As far as Alistair knows, his father was just the Justice Keeper to the second biggest city in the Realm, and that title put a target on his back. He never has to know if that's what you want... if you're worried about him overthrowing you."

"Alistair would never," Marcus argued abruptly. "The Moons made him an Ally—"

"Alistair is emotionally unstable," Aveo said, a bit of sadness slipping into his tone. "He isn't the same man we met in Mayfire three years ago."

To Malachai's surprise, Ash nodded in agreement. "Yesterday, he treated me in a way I never thought him capable. That was *after* the incident in the war tent. Don't get me wrong, I still believe he was meant to be an Ally. That's precisely why I didn't take his badge, and instead suggested that he transfer to a different division. He's unhinged."

"That's putting it mildly," Aveo muttered.

Marcus shook his head, clenching his jaw. "Alistair wouldn't betray the VanCamps, especially Penelope. He may be dealing with some personal matters, but he's loyal."

"No one is saying that he isn't," Ash assured him, now pacing in front of the couch where Aveo was still relaxing. "While all this Cavanaugh business is a bit shocking, we came here to focus on a different matter. We need to figure out who this Rat is. For all we know, now that Malachai's here, they could have assumed that their cover is blown and that it's time to abandon ship."

"Or worse," Malachai added. "They could be planning some sort of strike against Loren. If they've been working for my father for as long as I think they have, they have to have worked their way up the Draconian social ladder. It *has* to be someone close to him, and close to you as well, given the information he was providing my father with. This Rat knew about the Messenger and Alistair surfacing before the population did, which means they have to be a council member."

Marcus choked on his breath, his eyes bulging. He didn't say anything, but Malachai could tell what he was thinking—that this Rat was potentially a person he'd put all of his trust in. Someone he never would have thought would drive a knife into his back or betray their king.

"Not just any council member," Ash contributed, clearly having already come to this conclusion herself. "One that was in the room, at the Communications Center, the moment Valentina revealed that I was the Messenger."

When Malachai was beginning to think that Marcus's complexion couldn't get any paler, he watched what was left of his color drain from his face. "Benjamin... he has access to every form of communication possible. He designed all of our tech. He would know how to get a message out without anyone having a clue."

"They were handwritten, not electronic," Malachai informed him, reaching to rub the back of his neck. "Which makes sense. All the messages sent electronically, no matter the device, can be traced, downloaded, archived, and what have you. Paper can be burned."

"The Draconian Communications department is one of the biggest departments across the kingdoms," Aveo added, straightening in his seat. "There are what, hundreds of people working under Benjamin? Is it possible he's using one of those little worker bees to get written messages across the bridge?"

"Unless he's created some sort of mechanical messenger bird that we don't know about," Malachai joked, hoping to invoke a smile. No one's lips so much as twitched in response. "I'm kidding. I know for a fact that Ryole was the one who received the messages and delivered them personally to my father. He has his own worker bees. Quite a few of them, actually. The odds are that he'd send a pair here to wait in the forest near Redding for one of Benjamin's."

Marcus groaned, squinting his eyes shut. "I hate how much sense this makes."

"So do I," Ash said with a grim expression. "But the only other council members in the room were you, Valentina, Richard, and Loren himself. Richard hardly leaves Loren's side. Valentina would never turn her back on her kingdom. Clearly, we know it's not you. Benjamin is all that's left unless we start considering Alistair and Craven."

Shaking his head, Marcus said, "No, it has to be Benjamin. Alistair might be a tad bit unpredictable, but he would never work for the man responsible for his family's demise. As far as Craven goes, he's been a decorated soldier for decades. He's a household name. I trust that man with my life."

"We trusted Benjamin too," Ash retorted with a depressive huff.

"Well, there's one way to find out. Check the Unity Bridge's security footage for the day you found out you were the Messenger and keep an eye out for any of those worker bees," Malachai suggested. "I'd help, but I think the last thing King Loren wants me near is his security systems. Or any sort of technological device, for that matter."

"You got that right," Marcus confirmed with a snort. "In the meantime, we'll keep you updated."

Malachai's eyebrows flattened, his smirk vanishing. "On what exactly, the Rat or my pending execution?"

"Both," Ash quipped.

29

Obtaining security footage from over a month ago wasn't as easy as Ash thought it would be, especially without Benjamin's help. As it turned out, neither she, Aveo, nor Marcus were fluid in the language of technology, therefore they needed assistance from someone who was. They couldn't trust anyone in the Communications department either, seeing as they had no idea who Benjamin had gotten to do his dirty work.

Thankfully, there was one person who hadn't worked for Benjamin at the time Malachai witnessed that message being delivered to his father. Anderson. She was in Solaris at the time. There was no way she was involved with the Rat at all.

"I don't know," Aveo said as they re-entered Marcus's foyer. "Involving her in this seems like a risk. She was working for Xavier, and Benjamin added her to his team far too easily in my opinion. For all we know, they could have already been working together before she arrived here."

"He has a point," Marcus declared, leading them through the apartment and into the kitchen. "The next best option is Vincent, but he's classified as a resident of the Kingdom of Elves and doesn't have the sort of clearance we need to access that footage. Not to mention, he's close with Benjamin and Grant. There's no way that he'll believe Benjamin's capable of something like this. It's best we keep this newfound knowledge to ourselves until we know for sure."

Nodding, Ash couldn't disagree with that. "Well, either we summon Anderson, or we sneak Malachai out of his cell and allow him to hack into the security systems via the bottom floor's control room."

Aveo shook his head, sliding onto a barstool. "There's a million different ways that could go wrong. If we *have* to pick the lesser of two evils, then I say we go with Anderson."

Marcus drove his hand into his pocket, retrieving his chip. "I'll send her a message."

"Good," Ash said, forcing a smile. "In the meantime, I'm going to go change, inform Loren that we have a lead, and pray that when I wake up tomorrow, this was all some sort of twisted dream."

In the months that followed Cedric's death, Penelope had found it difficult to get out of bed, let alone shower and get dressed. For the first time in years, she found herself enduring the same thing. The moment her eyes had opened that morning, her heart had crumbled all over again, leaving it impossible to take a deep breath. Her tears started as simple drops but soon turned into rivers. She let them fall free, vowing to never shed another tear for Abernathy once they stifled.

Around noon, Penelope forced herself to leave the safety of her bed and allowed her lady's maid to help her get ready for the day.

"Sir Calloway left early this morning," Yvonne informed her in the midst of braiding her hair. "I have to say, I was surprised to find him making coffee in the kitchen. Care to explain?"

"Not really," Penelope said matter-of-factly.

Yvonne nodded, accepting the denial. She went on to help Penelope into a silky pale blue, empire-waist gown with a pair of matching slippers. Once Penelope was finished, the maid let loose a slow sigh, drawing the princess's attention.

Frowning, Penelope considered ignoring her, but once the maid failed to leave the room and instead lingered by the door, she couldn't bring herself to. "What is it, Yvonne?" she asked, hoping her annoyance wasn't too audible in her tone. The last thing she wanted to do was take out her horrid mood on anyone, especially someone as sweet as Yvonne.

"It's just…" she trailed off, gnawing at her bottom lip. "I worry for you. We all know how much Lord Chamberlain meant to you, and with his murderer residing just a few floors down, across the hall from the Rebel General—"

"Rebel General?" Penelope blurted, every muscle throughout her body becoming stiff. "What are you talking about?"

Yvonne's eyes grew wide, her jaw dropping. "I figured that you knew. One of the men that participated in yesterday's mission came forward as the Rebel General in an attempt to undermine Sir Calloway's authority in the Infirmary last night. All the Healing assistants have been talking about it… news spread to those of us working here in the castle. Turns out, this General was appointed by Lady Evanora Ivanenko, and he was trying to stop Sir Calloway from arresting Prince Malachai—"

"Stop," Penelope requested, holding up a hand to silence her. "You mean to tell me that this man was appointed as General to the army that Cedric created by Lady Evanora *Ivanenko* and chose to *use* that title in an attempt to stop my—" she caught herself, cringing around the word. "Betrothed from arresting the man responsible for Cedric's death, who was also supposed to have wiped this army off the face of the Realm?"

"Yes, Your Highness," Yvonne whispered. "Supposedly, there are still fifteen thousand Rebels left."

Momentarily closing her eyes, Penelope started to consider the idea that she hadn't woken up that day at all. "Where is King Loren?" she inquired, sucking in a breath to calm her raging emotions.

"Last I knew, he was in his study," she replied. "Should I request a meeting?"

"That won't be necessary," Penelope assured her, heading through the threshold and out into the hall. It was infuriating enough when he failed to inform her about what had happened to Cooper, but to not tell her that the organization that led to Cedric's death had resurfaced and that the man in charge of it was *inside Dracus?*

Penelope was aware that compared to Ash and Vincent, she was simply a princess, meant to live out her days inside luxury castles, marry, and produce heirs. There was no real reason for why she should involve herself in such complicated politics. However, the Rebels were responsible for a lot of her trauma and pain. She had every right to know if and when they ever resurfaced.

In short, the Rebels had ruined her life in more ways than one.

It took Penelope little more than five minutes to make her way from the Royal Corridor where she resided to Loren's personal study on the third floor. When she arrived, she didn't bother to knock. Instead, she twisted the knob and threw the door open in a fit of frustration and evolving fury, her features set in a scowl so sharp that by the look on Loren's face, one might have thought she'd cut him.

"Penelope," Loren said, shooting out of his seat.

Richard, who sat in a comfortable chair across from the king, didn't bother to stand. Instead, he turned his attention back to his info-tab and started to type something with his fingers.

"Can I have a moment?" Penelope asked through clenched teeth.

The lump in Loren's throat bobbed as he turned his gaze over to his adviser. "You wouldn't mind, would you?"

"Well, we *are* planning Malachai's execution. One would think something like that would take precedence over... whatever is happening here," Richard said, gesturing between Penelope and the king.

"It can wait," Penelope snapped before she had a chance to stop herself.

Richard's brows lifted with surprise. "I'm sorry, but did you just say that Malachai's *execution* could wait?"

"I don't believe that I stuttered, Richard."

"Well, then," Richard said, rising to his feet. "We can finish this discussion at dinner this evening."

"Fine," Loren replied.

The adviser made his way out of the room, offering Penelope a smile that failed to reach his eyes before he shut the door behind him. She returned her attention to Loren, crossing her arms in front of her chest. "I take it our dinner plans are canceled, then," she presumed, watching as he winced at the sound of her words. "It doesn't matter. What *does* matter is that the Rebel General is supposedly residing on the bottom floor, and that he participated in a mission to rescue an Ally that I had no idea was missing at all." She felt her cheeks heat with both rage and embarrassment, but that didn't stop her. "You didn't think that I would like to know about such things? It's bad enough that I had to hear about everything from Aveo, but for over a half a day to pass by without even a *message* from you, or any other council member for that matter? Loren, you can't keep me in the dark. If all you want me to do is play the part of the perfect, oblivious princess, then you might as well send me back to the Kingdom of Elves."

Loren recoiled, surprise flooding his features. "I'm sorry. I know that my mind has been preoccupied since the second task began…" he trailed, as if trying to decide what to say next. "In the last twenty-four hours, my kingdom has turned entirely upside down. I would have told you all about it this morning had it not been necessary to hold a council meeting regarding everything that happened yesterday."

"And the days beforehand? It seems like ever since Ash left for the second task, you've avoided me. While everyone else is working themselves to the bone for the Allies and preparing for the siege, you have me planning a party." Penelope sucked in a deep breath, fighting to regain what remained of her composure. Unfortunately, days, weeks, and years' worth of her pent-up frustration were surfacing all at once. "I want to do more. I can help. I've spent my life studying politics, laws, policies in every kingdom in every bloody Realm. I know the structure of both Immortal Armies like the back of my hand. Utilize my knowledge, for Moon's sake. And, if you're avoiding me because what Vincent said at dinner is finally getting to you, then we should talk about it."

Frowning, Loren dropped back into his seat. "He's not exactly wrong. The Elves have been looking to start a war with the Draconians ever since we were granted territory by the Idonian Council. This would give them a reason to."

Penelope's stomach flipped as she listened to each word sail past his lips.

"That being said, I think that you should be able to marry who you want to," he continued, shifting uncomfortably in his seat. "I'd go to war for you any day of the week. You know that."

"That would make me the most selfish woman in Si Realtra," Penelope insisted, swallowing hard against the lump crowding her throat. "I can't willingly send the Draconian Army to war after they've spent decades trying to defeat the Pandora. I wouldn't be able to forgive myself if I started another war after Ash and the others have worked so hard to finish one."

Loren's expression turned grave, but he nodded, nonetheless. "If you want to change your mind, I respect that. Just know that I'll love you anyway."

Penelope felt tears beginning to swarm her eyes again and blinked them away before they escaped. "This is one thing that I can do to help. It'll strengthen the peace that ending the Dark War will bring. It'll squash any conflict between the Elves and the Draconians and strengthen the bond between Solaris and the Golden city. We Idonians are the strongest among every other, Loren. When those Galactic Gates open, I want the other Realms to know that."

"I agree," he admitted to her, though his expression was still solemn.

"I'm sorry, Loren," she whispered, biting her inner cheek.

"Never apologize to me," he blurted, sincerity etched in his features. "I was wrong to put you in this position to begin with. All I want is for you to be happy for a change."

"I know," Penelope assured him with a sweet smile. "I will be, one day soon enough."

"Good," Loren said happily. "Hopefully the same will go for me the moment these Malachai, Rebel, and Rat problems are through with."

Penelope blinked, her brows pulling together. "I knew about Malachai and the Rebels, but a Rat?"

"Unfortunately," he replied with a depressive sigh. "Malachai told Ash that someone here in Dracus is reporting confidential information back to Xavier. I found out about an hour and a half ago. I've tasked Ash with finding out who it is by tomorrow evening. She and Marcus paid Malachai a visit. Supposedly, Aveo joined them. I'm not entirely sure about how I feel knowing an Elf knows that there's a Rat somewhere on my council, but I need all the help I can get, and I can't exactly ask the other council members—"

"Hold on," Penelope interjected. "Aveo is still in Dracus?"

Loren rolled his eyes. "He's going to remain here as an Elven Representative throughout the duration of Malachai's trial... well... execution."

"Oh," Penelope said, nerves beginning to swarm like butterflies in her stomach. From the moment they were betrothed, she'd done her best to distance herself from Aveo. The only time they spent together was to train, and since she'd returned to Dracus, those lessons had been canceled. Now that Aveo was in Dracus as well, he would undoubtedly want to start them again, or at the very least try to spend time with her. After last night, she didn't despise him as much as she thought, but that didn't mean she was ready to entertain him on a daily basis. "Wonderful," she said, hoping she didn't sound too sarcastic.

Loren snorted, shaking his head. "If you say so."

CHAOS

30

Nine hours had passed since Anderson had arrived at Marcus's apartment. Upon her arrival, she had set up his family room screen so that they could view the security footage from the first day of Winter Solstice—Ash's birthday—and the day she had found out she was the Messenger. They'd set the tapes to start around noon that day, shortly before Ash's elemental test had begun. Since then, they'd replayed them four times, searching for anything out of the ordinary.

"Maybe we should extend them to the next day," Anderson suggested between yawns.

"That would take another nine hours, if not more," Marcus groused, rubbing his tired eyes. "I'm starting to think that we should have let Malachai do this."

"Was that an option?" Anderson squeaked, a glint of hope momentarily shining in her red orbs.

Ash frowned and shook her head. "No. He has to stay where he is, far away from any tech."

"Oh please," Anderson scoffed. "If he wanted to escape or break into the Communications department, control rooms, or what have you, he'd have done it by now. That man can't be contained. I don't see the point in chaining him up at all. Clearly, he doesn't want to run."

Ash ground her teeth. "Yeah, well, we're the only ones who see it that way."

Aveo stood up, groaning pleasurably as he stretched. "Maybe we should call it a night and resume this fiasco in the morning."

"Wait," Marcus called, pointing toward the screen where the footage continued to play. Anderson paused it in a flash, zooming in on the figure he was focused on—a cloaked man, with just a shred of his face showing beneath his hood.

Ash squinted, examining the hint of a sharp, scruffy jawline and a thin nose. "I don't remember seeing him during the last six times we watched this footage," she admitted, her brows pulling together.

"Neither do I, but his cloak is just as dark as the night," Anderson explained, pursing her lips. "I think Marcus just barely caught a hint of his jaw. That's luck if I've ever seen it."

"Who do you think it is?" Ash asked the Mentor.

Shrugging, Marcus stared at the frozen image of the strange, cloaked man for a while before he said, "I have no idea. It could be anyone."

"No matter what, it looks suspicious enough to me," Anderson insisted in a high-pitched, nervous tone.

Everyone fell silent, deep in thought. Ash's gaze danced between them all as she wondered what they might be thinking of her. Did they believe she was going mad? Why else would she be going to so much trouble to save a man who'd once come so close to becoming her murderer? *Why* am *I doing this?* she asked herself, clenching her jaw. After a while of contemplating, she couldn't seem to find an answer to that question. Sure, Malachai had been helpful over the last few days, but what about the decades before that? Maybe it *was* time for Malachai to die, after all.

"I have an idea," Aveo said, snapping Ash out of her racing thoughts. "Today was a big day here in Dracus. This Rat is bound to send another message to Xavier. I say that we head to the forest in Redding and see if we can catch them in the act."

Though she was exhausted, and it was getting closer and closer to midnight, Ash found herself standing up, her lips curling into a devious smirk. "Suit up," she directed. "Let's go set up a Rat trap."

ARMED TO THE TEETH, ASH AND THE OTHERS ARRIVED IN THE forest surrounding Redding via Aries' teleportation. The night was silent, and the air was frigid. Winter was reaching its apex, and ice coated each tree limb in thick, shiny sheets. Their black uniforms stood out vividly against the snow blanketing the ground. Their only option was to stick to the shadows, hiding behind trees in pairs.

"And here I was beginning to think that I'd actually get a chance to relax for an evening," Aries murmured beneath his breath from where he crouched beside Ash. "I take it you've had a busy day?"

Rolling her eyes, Ash said, "You don't even want to know."

"Ana came to the Infirmary earlier and told us everything that happened in the council meeting," he whispered, a hint of sympathy slipping into his tone. "I can't believe they're going to make you execute him. If this were the Safe Haven, Cleo would do no such thing. She believes everyone deserves a second chance. Even people like Malachai."

"Even Xavier?" Ash inquired.

"Well, maybe not him."

Ash chuckled lightly, pulling her knit cap tighter over her chilly, pointed ears. "I thought as much," she replied, momentarily allowing herself to picture the small Fae Queen boiling with rage directed at the Dark King. "I'm sad I couldn't make it to the Infirmary today. How is he?"

"Quinn or Cooper?" Aries asked, exhaling slowly. "I swear, I've never seen a man so out of his own mind. I'm not sure that he sat down even once. He paced the whole day, flagging down Healers whenever one dared to walk by. As far as Cooper goes, he's still in a deep sleep. We had a scare earlier when his oxygen dipped. Ebony is beginning to worry that the transition is too much on his respiratory system, but with the Elven Healers aide, they were able to stabilize him. They're talking about transporting him to the Kingdom of Elves tomorrow to soak him in the Healing springs."

Ash's heart fell, her smile vanishing. "Really?"

"Really," Aries confirmed, his wings drooping in a depressive fashion. "That's the only thing they can think of. The only other option would be the Elders in Ryiah. Unfortunately, they're out of touch."

"What could they do to help him?"

"The Elders have lived longer than any other beings in this Galaxy. Their leader, Gailand, has developed very rare, and specific skills. She can heal any ailment, and even bring people back from the dead," Aries explained in a low, hushed tone.

A chill swept down Ash's spine, her eyes widening. "You're messing with me."

"Not one bit," he assured her.

"Guys," Marcus growled. "Keep it down, someone's coming."

Ash stiffened, sucking in a deep breath, and holding it while she scanned her surroundings. The sound of subtle footsteps crunching on snow filled her sensitive ears, sending her heart into a frenzy. At first, she wasn't sure which way the steps were coming from—the west or the east—but after a few moments, she realized they were coming from *both* directions.

"Fuck," Aries uttered beneath his breath. "We'll take the east with Craven. Marcus, Anderson, and Aveo will take the west," he directed into the earpieces they were all wearing.

Ash began to move toward the east using slow, and careful steps. She remained crouched, using shrubs, shadows, and trees for cover until she caught sight of a man wearing the same cloak as the one Marcus had noticed in the footage.

"That's the one. Brace yourselves," she warned.

"Ash, wait—" Craven started to say, but Ash was already gone, flying through the trees, aiming right for the mystery man. In a matter of seconds, she crashed into him. They fell to the ground with a thud, squirming and hollering, rolling around in the snow.

The man she tackled wound up beneath her, but that didn't last for long. He threw Ash off him, sending her into the trunk of a tree. She felt one of her ribs crack and cried out in pain while Aries and Craven pushed forward, throwing the man onto his stomach, holding his hands behind his back. Toward the west, more shouts arose, but were silenced so quickly that it was unnerving. The scent of blood wafted through the air, filling Ash's nostrils. Her mouth watered, providing a slight distraction from the white-hot pain searing in her right side.

Despite the agony, Ash pushed herself up, standing straight as she approached the culprit. She kneeled, ripping his hood off, only to reveal none other than Axel Graves.

Craven gasped, releasing his superior at once, staggering backward in the process.

Aries kept his grip on the General's wrists, his burgundy eyes narrowing into slits as sharp as daggers. "Check his pockets," he barked, and Ash did as he asked immediately. In one of his back pants pockets, she found a letter sealed with a wax symbol portraying three intersecting swords. Xavier's symbol.

Bile crept up Ash's throat as she tore the letter open, skimming the contents. Sure enough, he'd written about everything that had occurred in the council meeting— details about Malachai's coming execution were involved, as well as Ash's conflicted behavior. She bared her teeth, crumpling it in her hand.

"It's not what you think," Axel revealed, huffing and puffing as if she'd knocked the wind straight out of his lungs during her takedown. "I'd never willingly—"

"You look guilty enough," Craven interjected, flashing his fangs.

More footsteps approached, revealing the forms of Marcus, Aveo, and Anderson. They arrived at Ash's side, staring down in shock at the man lying on the frozen earth at their feet.

"At least give me a chance to explain," Axel begged. Aries tightened his grip around his hands, causing him to whelp in response. "I was tricked into a Blood Oath, and forced to obey... I can't say his name, it was part of the contract I unknowingly signed. You have to believe me."

"A Blood Oath," Aries said, his brow furrowing with confusion. "Blood Magic is forbidden across the Realms."

"That doesn't mean people don't practice it," Anderson said. "Plenty of Xavier's Witches do."

"What exactly *is* a Blood Oath?" Ash asked, her cheeks heating with embarrassment.

"In the past, Sorcerers and other Magic Wielders would use Blood Magic to create contracts that are bound to the soul of another. Most were done willingly. Apprentices would sign Blood Oaths to Realm Sorcerers, promising never to stray. It was a way to show sincerity and commitment. Some marriages in certain cultures involved them as well, promising one's heart to the other for all eternity," Aries explained while simultaneously detaining the General, who struggled beneath him. "It wasn't uncommon, however, for foul play to be involved. Hence, why Blood Magic is now forbidden. If what he says is true, then he has to obey every word written in the contract, or he'll die."

Ash winced, goosebumps pebbling along her arms.

"If what he says is true, the Rat is an incredibly scared Sorcerer," Aries added. "We may be in deeper shit than we thought."

"What do we do with him then, if we can't interrogate him?" Craven asked.

"Lock him up," Aveo suggested. "Ensure that the Rat can no longer use him while we figure out who it is."

"He'll find a way," Axel insisted. "Nothing you do will stop him."

"Wanna bet?" Ash asked.

"You don't get it," the General snapped. "He isn't *what* you think he is. He's too powerful."

Chills raced across Ash's skin. "What kind of powerful?"

"You don't want to know," he rasped. "Powerful enough to go on as long as he has ratting out Loren at every turn. Powerful enough to trick me into a trap like this, forcing me to do things that I would never do. This mess is larger than you could ever dream."

QUINN WAS ATTEMPTING TO REST IN THE INFIRMARY WHEN HE HEARD the alarms again. The moment they started to ring, his heart leaped into overdrive. He shot out of his seat, nearly tripping over his own feet as he burst out of the waiting room, only to be met by a sea of Healers all rushing toward his brother's room, Draconian and Elven alike. His heart jumped into his throat as he attempted to follow, but one of the Healers took notice of him and gestured for him to stay put before hurrying back into the fray.

"What's happening?" Quinn demanded as another group of Healers rushed by. "Someone, tell me what's happening!"

"He's coding," one of them said before they vanished into the crowd.

Coding, Quinn thought before repeating the word over and over again in his mind. "Did they just say *coding?*" he asked Morghan, who'd arrived at his side. "*Coding?*"

The Wolf nodded, dropping his gaze from Quinn's face.

In that moment, Quinn refused to follow the Healer's directions. He would *not* stay put. He would run to his brother's side and do whatever it took to keep him alive. He'd already lost Lincoln. He refused to lose Cooper too. He barreled out into the hall, following the Healers to Cooper's intensive care room, where he found Ebony and a reputable Elven Healer bringing electrical paddles to his chest in an attempt to restart his heart. Every blinking line on every screen had gone still, his flesh as pale as the snow falling outside.

The Healers attempted to revive him once and then twice before the Elven Healer holding the paddles took a step back, her expression grave.

"No," Quinn snarled, pushing further into the room. "Don't you dare fucking stop."

The Healer's eyes widened, her jaw dropping.

"Quinn, you shouldn't be in here," Ebony said frantically. "I don't want you to see—"

"We're running out of options, Ebony," another Healer warned, wiping the sweat off his brow with the back of his hand. "We need to get him to the Kingdom of Elves. Now."

One of the Elves shook her head. "I'm afraid the Springs won't do what we need them to."

Bile crept up Quinn's throat as he listened to them all go back and forth while others worked to continue chest compressions. His mind swam for another option, though he knew little about anything medicinal. Cooper was within inches of his life once again, and they were all stumped.

"Malachai," Morghan said, the name sending the entire room into an eerie silence. "Yesterday, Aries was telling us how he was such a profound Healer that he wound up certifying in two different Realms—"

"Absolutely *not*," Ebony ordered. "Loren would lose his mind—"

"My brother is *dying*!" Quinn interrupted. "Do any of you have any other ideas? Right now, I'd be glad to hear them." The only response was more decrepit silence, proving his point. "Morghan, go get him. Tell anyone that tries to stop you that there's an Arebus Arrow with their name on it."

The Wolf gave him a curt nod before running out of the room and down the hall. "I sure hope you're right about this!".

"We're going to intubate him," Ebony informed Quinn. "The machine will breathe for him while we wait for... er... his Highness. You might want to turn around."

"I've seen worse," Quinn retorted. "I grew up in Central Idona, for Moon's sake."

"You'll stay in here until we get to the bottom of things," Ash informed Axel as she guided him into one of the rooms on the bottom floor, right next door to Malachai's. He didn't respond to her and instead shed his cloak, tossing it onto a table before sinking into one of the chairs, allowing his head to fall into his hands. For a moment, Ash felt terrible for him, caught up in this Rat's web of lies and deceit, forced to do things he would never dream to do otherwise. "Also, I apologize again for tackling you."

Axel snorted at that. "For someone so small, you pack a lot of force."

"It's a job requirement," she replied jokingly.

"I need you to write down everything you *can* tell us," Craven directed from behind her. "If you're telling the truth, and you were really tricked into a Blood Oath, then you'd be willing to help us any way that you can. We need you to do that. We have until the end of the day tomorrow to figure out who this Rat is."

Axel nodded, lifting his face from his hands to meet his Second's violet gaze. "What do you know so far?"

"It's a council member," Ash whispered, hoping none of the guards roaming the halls overheard. To her surprise, Axel nodded. "We think that it might be *Benjamin*." She made sure to mouth the name.

"No," Axel said, though it was clear he was struggling.

"No?" Marcus chirped.

"*No*," the General confirmed, forcing the words through his clenched teeth.

"Maybe the Blood Oath can be broken," Anderson suggested from where she lingered out in the hall. "Perhaps you should speak with Lucinda about it."

"There's no point," Aries informed her. "I'm well versed in Magic as well, and I've read a plethora of different books about Blood Magic specifically. The only way to break a Blood Oath is for the creator to willingly release the contracted being from the contract. Or, for the contract to be found and destroyed, tossed into the Edge of the Underworld."

Ash shivered at the thought of going anywhere near that dreadful place. "We can't just burn it with *normal* fire?"

"It won't work," Aries insisted.

"What if another Magic Wielder destroyed it?" Aveo asked.

"You're all assuming that the contract could even be found," Axel growled. "It would be easier to locate the Forbidden Isle in Minora."

Ash flinched at the sound of the location. After spending years of her life reading novels written about the notorious Captain Loche and his loyal crew, she knew exactly what the Forbidden Isle consisted of, and why it was forbidden.

Before their conversation could continue, shouts started to come from down the hall. Ash's brow furrowed as she stepped back out into it, staring in the direction they were coming from. As they grew closer, she began to recognize Morghan's deep, raspy voice. "What in the Four Solstices is happening *now*?" she asked Marcus, who moved to stand at her side.

"King Loren said that under *no* circumstances was Malachai to set foot outside of his cell!" a guard growled. "If I let you do this, I could lose my job and maybe my head!"

Morghan rounded the corner with a sea of angry guards following him, but by the serious look on his face and his strong, determined steps, Ash knew that there was nothing they could do to stop him.

The Wolf met her eyes and a shred of relief washed over his features.

"What happened?" Ash asked in a rush, her heart slipping into overdrive.

"Cooper's coding and we need Malachai," he said quickly, pushing past everyone to arrive in front of the Pandora's door. "Open it," he ordered no one in particular.

Craven, who'd obtained Axel's keys, hurried to do as he asked. The door swung open and Morghan rushed in. "Good, you're already dressed," he said. "It's time to go."

"Go where?" Ash heard Malachai ask.

"The Infirmary."

The Pandora didn't ask any more questions and instead walked out into the hall, his brows rising with surprise as he took in everyone standing there.

"I'll stay here and deal with Axel," Craven offered. "Aveo and Anderson, you're with me. The rest of you head to the Infirmary with Aries and keep me updated."

Ash nodded, reaching for the Fae's hand, tightening her grip around it. She shut her eyes for a second and when she opened them, she was met with complete and utter chaos. Healers and nurses were swarming the halls, alarms blaring on full blast, rattling her ear drums. She followed Morghan and Malachai forward, her heart crowding in her throat, her pulse thrashing in her veins. They arrived in front of Cooper's room, where she caught a glimpse of her oldest friend lying still on a table, his complexion pale, purple veins visible beneath what looked like translucent flesh.

Malachai got to work, ignoring the looks every other Healer was giving him. He read the chart before tossing it aside and jumping into action. Ash watched in awe as he took over intubating Cooper for another Healer, who stepped back in relief. They all watched in shocked silence as the prince worked. He started giving orders, and while at first the others seemed surprised, they started following them.

"Quinn, you need to get out of here, unless in the last day you've managed to attend six years of university and certify as a Healer," Malachai advised.

Ash hadn't noticed that Quinn was in the room at all, but once she heard his name, she searched for him, her heart dropping at the sight of him pressed into a corner, as frozen as Ryhian ice.

"Someone, get him out of here," Ebony demanded.

Alistair had arrived and moved to follow the Healers orders, gently guiding Quinn back out into the hall. Ash watched them walk toward a waiting room, shocked that the Archer hadn't tried to protest. She'd go to him later once Cooper was in the clear and Malachai was returned to his cell. In the meantime, she would fight to control her festering anxiety and try to remember how to breathe while she watched Cooper fight for his life.

Quinn stormed into the waiting room and immediately started to pace while pulling at his sandy locks. He fought to remember how to breathe, though such a feat was impossible to accomplish during that moment. He'd just watched his brother seize on a table while every machine indicating whether he was still alive screamed with alarm.

"Have some faith, Quinn," Alistair directed in a near whisper, lingering by the door as if to stop the Archer from bursting through it to run back to his brother's side. "I know that's a hard thing to ask of you, but if you lose what's left of your faith, how can the rest of us keep ours?"

"All I've had is faith," he blurted angrily, meeting Alistair's gaze, his cerulean orbs bright with tears. "For years, I've relied on it. First, I had faith that Ash and I would figure out what she was turning into and get her somewhere safe or find a way for her to stay. Then, each Red Winter, I had faith that it would be our last. Of course, I had faith that Lincoln would return to us in one piece, and that we'd make it through the tasks unscathed. All this faith I've had has yet to pay off."

Alistair stared at him, shifting his weight uncomfortably from one leg to the other.

"The funny thing is, for the most part, we made it out of the tasks unscathed," he continued, chuckling with disbelief. "Of course, it was after they were all said and done that Cooper managed to get himself captured. All because he thought of Constance. *Constance.*"

At a loss for words, Alistair kept his mouth shut, glancing about the room as if to avoid eye contact.

"What is it with my brothers and her anyway?" he asked.

"Well, I'm sure that he wasn't thinking of her *that* way—"

"You know, I've been thinking about that a lot lately," he interjected, sniffling. "I should be furious. I should have ripped Lincoln to shreds for what he did, but I didn't. You want to know why? Because I had *faith* that some miracle would happen where I'd wake up in charge of my own life."

When the Rider didn't reply, Quinn turned his attention back to him, noting his thoughtful expression. "Let me guess. You feel the same?" He let loose a long breath, dropping his gaze to his hands. "We've found ourselves in *quite* the predicament, haven't we? Not to mention, your very obvious fight with Ash. That can't be helping anything."

Alistair lifted a brow. "I'm not sure what you're talking about."

Quinn scowl was answer enough, but still, he said, "Now isn't the time to lie to my face."

Gulping, Alistair wiped his hands on his jeans, clearing his throat. "Those aren't just my secrets to tell, and Ash is right down the hall. I could go get her—"

Shaking his head, Quinn ceased his pacing and chose to sink into a chair. "Don't bother. I'd feel like a jerk for tearing her away from what she's doing to answer that sort of question." He fiddled with his fingers, fighting to calm his racing heart. "Distract me. That's all I want. She's requesting that you join another division, and I'd like to know why."

"I said some things that I'm not proud of. My emotions were getting the best of me that day, and I hurt her," Alistair admitted, his voice breaking. He continued to avoid Quinn's eyes and stared at his feet instead. "I feel like a proper idiot. Every time I try to talk to her, she all but shuns me. I don't know how to apologize at this point. Even if I did, she wouldn't let me. I crossed a line."

Quinn's face twisted into a deadly scowl. "How? What line?"

"I'm not entirely sure," Alistair admitted, as he began to pace. "To be honest, I don't see how it matters right now." He gestured to the hall, which was still being swarmed with medical personnel.

"I need the distraction."

Alistair paused in front of the sliver of a window in the waiting room's door, putting his back to Quinn. "If you *must* know, we managed to acquire a lover's bond. Now, I feel everything that she does, and vice versa. When she chose to ask for Malachai's help, I could feel the hope that the thought of him brought her, and it drove me mad. I reacted the same way anyone in my position would have. I was infuriated, and unfortunately, she was the reason why. The thought of Malachai alone always sends my blood to a boil, but to *feel* her want for him... I lost every ounce of my composure. She chased after me and grabbed my flaming hand in an effort to slow me down. Watching him heal that burn..." the Rider shivered with disgust. "She went out for fresh air after our meeting in your dining room. I followed her, but I don't remember leaving the house. The next thing I knew, I was accusing her of things I never would have normally. I'm sick to my stomach even thinking about it, and every time I'm in her presence, I feel how much she despises me. I can't stand it."

Quinn was still stuck on *lover's bond*, unable to rid the term from his mind. "What's a lover's bond, and how do you get one?"

Alistair flinched, glancing at Quinn over his shoulder. "I figured that you knew all that, already." His voice wavered around the words. "We drank one another's blood after a fight with Pandora during that crazy, Magical storm. For Draconians, drinking the blood of another... well... it's an intimate act. One thing led to another. We awoke the next morning in the same predicament we're in now. Connected to one another, forced to feel each other's emotions."

Quinn's chest tightened, his stomach churning. "A lover's bond, so you—" he stopped himself, a wave of nausea sweeping over him at the idea of all they must have done. "At least tell me you were respectful enough to protect yourself."

"I wasn't exactly anticipating anything to happen between us," Alistair informed him. "One doesn't think when they walk out into the field that they're going to wind up in a cave and—"

"Please don't finish that sentence," Quinn groaned.

Nodding, Alistair shut his mouth, swallowing hard.

Sighing, Quinn sank further into his chair and crossed his feet at the ankles. "My family is already in shambles, Alistair. I've spent the last two years of my life doing everything that I could to ensure that in the end, Ash was happy. Without realizing it, I neglected everyone else in the process, so much so, that I drove my own betrothed so far away that she slept with my brother. Now, Lincoln and Constance are both gone, and Cooper's hanging on for dear life. The last thing that I need is for you to stand in the way of Ash's happiness on top of it all, so you'd better hope that lover's bond is the only thing you created, because if it's not, I might very well kill you."

The color drained from Alistair's face, and the sight of it led Quinn to feel guiltier than ever.

"Alright, I won't kill you," he assured him. "You didn't have to tell me any of this, but you did. I respect that."

"Well, you did ask for a distraction," the Rider pointed out.

"You certainly gave me one."

32

Ash fell asleep that night with hope filling her heart and butterflies fluttering around in her stomach. She dreamed of the future, one where the war had ended and everyone, including Malachai, were leading peaceful, profitable lives. No matter what happened next, after dreams like that, nothing could bring her mood down. At least, so she thought until she was awoken at the break of dawn by Loren and Richard, urging her to get ready as quickly as she could.

For the second day in a row, Ash's ladies' maids hurried to get her dressed, this time in an elegant, deep blue gown studded with diamonds designed to look like constellations. While she was being fussed over, she begged for Loren or Richard to tell her what was going on, but neither of them said a word. It wasn't until the maids had placed a sapphire encrusted crown atop her perfectly curled hair that they finally revealed that day's festivities.

"Where are we going?" Ash asked in her most demanding tone as they led her out of the apartment with Marcus on their heels.

"To the city square," Richard informed her. "Late last night, King Loren and I had a meeting with the Chamberlains and their adviser, and we all agree that Malachai's execution is to be moved up to this morning."

Ash's heart stopped dead in its tracks, the color draining from her face. "What?" she snapped, hurrying to keep up the pace. "You can't be serious!"

"We are," Loren replied in a cool, calm tone. "Benjamin will deliver your Scepter to the square, and that's what you'll use to... do the job. He hasn't blessed it with the Moonshade you retrieved during your second task yet, so it should be quick and relatively painless for him."

"I don't understand," Ash admitted, shaking her head in confusion. "How can you have me kill him after what he did for Cooper last night?"

Richard glanced over his shoulder and said, "His temporary release last night is what made the Elves push for an earlier execution. The longer he remains alive inside the kingdom, the more people he'll be able to convince that he's a victim. Clearly, that's what he's done with you and the Allies. Who, might I add, are supposed to be the strongest among us."

"That's not true," Ash snarled. "No one sees him as a victim."

"I find that difficult to believe," the adviser drawled. "Especially when you're willing to stand between him and giving the people what they want. This needs to happen, Ash. If it doesn't, you're going to paint yourself as the enemy, and that's the kind of paint you can't wash off."

Biting her tongue, Ash fought against the urge to roar and throw him into the nearest wall. "You're making a mistake. If we struck an alliance with him, he'd be able to lure the Pandora away from Xavier. Ninety percent of them aren't Pandora by choice. We could offer them a choice, give them a chance to change, and avoid so much more chaos. Xavier could potentially lose more than half of the Dark Army. We could *crush* him. Not to mention, save Lincoln in the process."

"We'll crush him no matter what," Loren told her. "We don't need his firstborn son to assure it."

"So, you'll willingly let go of the chance to add tens of thousands of people to our ranks and keep one of the three Arebus Archer's left in Si Realtra in his grip?" Ash asked, balling her fists around her silky skirts just to keep herself from letting them swing.

"What about the Draconians, and where they started? I may not be well versed in Idonian history, but I know for a fact that they didn't evolve inside some gorgeous meadow. We were just as savage as the Pandora, if not more—"

"That's enough," Loren interrupted, venom dripping from his words. "This is happening right now, whether you like it or not. Either Malachai dies today, tomorrow, or the next day. No matter what, he'll meet his end. If you don't do it, someone else will, and I can assure you that they won't show him mercy like you would."

"At least let me talk to the Elves and see what they think about my idea," Ash pleaded. "You don't know. Thaddeus could agree with me. He's battle-driven. He wants to win this war more than anyone!"

"Thaddeus already gave us an option number two and I doubt you'll like it," Richard revealed as they embarked down their first flight of steps.

Ash's heart shuttered, a shred of hope enveloping her. "What was option number two?"

"Marry him, legally binding him to the VanCamp family throne," Loren said, visibly shivering. "No one is going to subject you to that. This is your best option."

Slowing her pace, Ash looked toward Marcus, who was already shaking his head in warning. "Fine, I'll do it," she declared, nearly choking on the words. "Whatever it takes not to kill one of the few chances at success that we have. Xavier tossing him out of Solaris was a miracle. I won't willingly squash it before it has a chance to manifest."

"It's too late," Richard said. "The execution has already been announced to the public. The people are waiting."

Ash scoffed, her blood heating to a quick boil, singing through her veins. "So, you made my decision for me? That isn't fair. You're the one who made me High Queen. I have the right to decide for myself!"

"I'm sorry you won't get the chance to marry Si Realtra's most vicious war criminal," Richard spat, sarcastically. "Beck is still incredibly available. If you want to devote yourself to a prince, pick that one."

A low growl reverberated in Ash's throat, silver flooding her green gaze. "I didn't name you my adviser," she reminded him, making sure she sounded as cold as she felt within. "You had no right to make this choice without consulting me, and I can promise you that you'll be punished for it, one way or another. The Moons chose *me* to choose what was best for this Realm and the Galaxy beyond. They chose *me* to protect and defend it, not Loren, not the Draconian Council, not the other Allies, and especially not *you*."

Loren slowed his pace, looking over his shoulder to meet Ash's gaze. Practical flames flickered in his eyes; his lips pressed together into a fine line. "You may not realize it yet, but we're doing what's best for you. Malachai would have died on sight in any other kingdom. We've shown him mercy when he didn't deserve a shred of it. Now, it's time for us to do what needs to be done, as the people Idonian citizens trust us with their lives and well-being."

"Can't you see? I *am* worried about their well-being!" Ash thundered as they arrived in the foyer, where a thick flock of guards were waiting to escort them down to the city square. "Malachai might no longer be a member of the Dark Army, but the Pandora still follow him. He's their originator, creator, and their Alpha. If we kill him—"

"Another Alpha will be appointed," Richard cut in. "Not that it matters much. They'll all be dead by Spring Solstice, anyway."

"And if you make us slaughter Malachai, so will we," Marcus finally contributed. "I say we rethink this, throw him Nahmaim instead, where we can still use him for intel."

Loren shook his head. "It's too late for that. The Idonian Council has come to an agreement."

"You only mentioned Thaddeus and Esmeralda," Ash reminded him. "You never said anything about what Lucinda, Cleo, Aries, and Valentina think about this."

"Valentina and Lucinda know what's happening, and I sincerely doubt that Cleo and Aries will try to stand in our way," Richard said. "Have you forgotten who we're dealing with here? One good deed, and you act as if it makes up for every one of his wrongdo-ings. It doesn't. No matter how many good deeds he does, he will never outrun his monstrous past. In time, you'll understand that you're doing him a favor."

Ash clamped her jaw shut to keep herself from saying another word. She would never see this as doing Malachai a favor, and she would never forgive herself for what they were about to make her do. She was backed in a corner; one that she couldn't escape. No matter how many points she made, Loren and Richard made four more. Arguing any further was a waste of time. Ash could only hope that in whatever afterlife Malachai arrived in, that he would forgive her, for she had tried her best.

Malachai hadn't expected to die that day. He'd gone to sleep with a shred of hope to comfort him. He'd helped Ash search for the Rat, and he'd proven how beneficial he could be to the Draco-nians in the Infirmary. Even *Elves* applauded his work. He was more than just the *Prince of Darkness*. He had been someone else before this Dark Age descended upon his life, and he intended to be that man again. Or, so he had, until Craven unlocked the door to his cell and stepped inside with the most solemn expression that he'd ever seen a man wear.

There was no denying what was to happen by the look on Craven's face, therefore Malachai didn't utter a word. He didn't try to talk his way out of it or plead his case. His time had come, so he stood up, squared his shoulders, and walked out of that cell just as he was about to walk out on his very life.

"I'm sorry," Craven mentioned as he chained Malachai's wrists and feet. "Ash couldn't stop it. She tried."

Malachai forced a smile for him. "Truth be told, I never expected for her to succeed. Let's hope that she has better luck fulfilling the Prophecy, eh? I took the time to write down everything I believe would help her defeat my father. I don't know how powerful he really is, but I hope what I wrote will be of some assistance. I also wrote down the formula for Lincoln's cure, my financial information, and instructions for my legacy."

"Well, you're certainly prepared then," Craven noted, guiding the prince down the hall.

"What can I say? I like my ducks in a row," Malachai replied nonchalantly. "Can I ask you a favor?"

Craven gave him a long look in response.

"It's nothing too extreme," Malachai promised. "My family is incredibly complicated, and I doubt most of my siblings will mourn me. Trixa will, though. My death will shatter her, and her grandmother Irina as well. If there's any way that you could... maybe deliver the letter that I wrote for them…"

"I'll tell Ash about it. I'm sure that she'll track Trixa down for you," Craven told him. "Anything else?"

"Yeah, make sure I'm cremated so Veda or Savron Phantom can't locate my corpse and bring me back as an undead servant," Malachai requested.

Craven shivered from head to toe. "Would they really do that?"

"You haven't met them, have you?"

"No, and I'm alright with that."

Ash stood on a dais in front of the Black Butterfly fountain, trying her best to ignore the Giving Day decorations lighting up the city. They were beautiful, but their presence felt wrong. The snowflake-shaped lights strung from building to building and wrapped around lamp posts twinkled against the bright, warm sunrise. Ornaments adorned the trees, all shapes, colors, and sizes. Even the dais itself was decorated with holly and garland. None of it fit. One would not think when they crossed the Unity Bridge during that moment that they were about to witness a historical execution.

The Allies had arrived, taking their place near the front of the evolving crowd with the Draconian Council. Ash met Quinn's gaze and tried to smile for him but couldn't manage to. He gave her an understanding nod, or perhaps it was meant to be reassuring. Either way, Ash didn't feel sure about anything. Everything about that moment felt wrong, like some sort of nightmare that she couldn't wake up from.

Cameras flashed, lights blinking from red to green, signaling that her face was being portrayed on every screen in the Realm. Loren had decided that it was best for Ash to remain silent, and she didn't blame him.

"This morning, on the thirty-fifth day of Winter Solstice, year one-thousand and thirty-one N.D., we will all bear witness to the end of a deadly era. For nearly three decades, Malachai Trevayne has wreaked havoc upon our blessed Realm, changing the way of life for everyone residing in Idona, and in some cases beyond. He is responsible for the deaths of thousands of Idonian soldiers and civilians as the result of a species that he created right beneath the Idonian Council's nose. He is solely responsible for every casualty that has occurred as a result, and the war that was brought on by these relentless creatures. Since the start of the Dark War, he has driven species to the brink of extinction, torn countless families apart, and wiped dozens of towns, villages, and cities off the map. He is at fault for the deaths of High King Gideon VanCamp and Lord Cedric Chamberlain. Not two weeks ago, he made an attempt on our current High Queen Ash VanCamp's life as well. Had he succeeded, this war could have continued onward for centuries, bringing on even more pain and grief."

Loren became angrier and angrier with each sentence, his fury reflecting in his eyes and aggressive demeanor. The hairs rose on the back of Ash's neck and arms at the sight of it, and she found herself wishing she could take a few steps back.

"Two days ago, the capture of Idonian Ally, Cooper McBride, led us to Malachai. He played a vital part in Cooper's rescue, undoubtedly as an act to defy his father, who recently had Malachai excommunicated. Once the mission was through, and Cooper was safe, thanks to Sir Aveo Calloway, Malachai was detained before he had a chance to escape. Without his quick thinking, we wouldn't be where we are today, and I, along with every other Draconian and

Idonian beyond my borders, will be eternally grateful for the opportunity he provided us all."

The cameras momentarily flickered to Aveo, who was standing beside Penelope and Vincent in the front row. He acted as if he wasn't on screen at all, and instead inclined his head to the king and wrapped his hand around Penelope's. Ash fought not to gape at the sight of the interaction.

"Malachai's death will bring the peace we've been craving for decades," Loren went on to say. "Finally, after all these years, we are taking monumental steps in the right direction. Now that the Messenger has surfaced," he gestured to Ash, who shifted uncomfortably as a result, "and with the Prince of Darkness out of the way, we can advance on Solaris as one, and end this war once and for all."

The crowd applauded. Ash was sure everyone else in the Realm was, and she clapped her hands softly, a wave of nausea sweeping over her.

"Benjamin," Loren called. "Bring forth the Sovereign's Scepter."

Gasps sounded throughout the square as the Head of Communications stepped forward with the ancient weapon and handed it to Ash. She took it, wrapping her clammy hands around the silver staff, fighting to keep them steady, despite how badly they wanted to tremble.

"Lord Amsterdam, bring the prisoner forward."

Ash shut her eyes and sucked in a series of breaths, her stomach roiling. She didn't want to watch Malachai approach her in chains, climbing the dais steps to his death.

"I highly advise all of you to deter any children and or squeamish individuals from watching the screens," Loren added, the comment sending bile spewing up Ash's throat. It hadn't occurred to her before that moment that the Realm address wouldn't be the only thing they were broadcasting. Her eyes flew open, and just as she was about to confront the king on such vial behavior, she saw him.

Malachai stood off to the side of the dais, dressed in the same sort of clothes he'd always worn in the past—black fitted pants, black shirt, boots, and a cloak with Xavier's sigil. Ash found herself staring at the cloak, her mind drifting back to when he'd offered one to her a few days before. She'd started off that interaction with the intent of cutting him down, yet now the very idea of doing that detested her. So much had changed in such a short span of time, she could hardly wrap her head around it all.

"Step forward," Loren directed the prince. He did as he was asked, his face revealing no emotion. "Drop to your knees."

Malachai hesitated, shifting his gaze to meet Ash's. She wasn't sure what she saw lurking in his emerald gaze. At first, she thought it might be something like sympathy, or maybe regret, but after a moment, she realized what he was trying to say. *Thank you.*

Don't thank me yet, she thought, watching him sink onto his knees before she stepped forward, Scepter in hand. Her thoughts raced rapidly, searching for a way out of this. The crowd kept silent, watching her expectedly. Ash gulped, ignoring the sensation of walls closing in around her, and of a phantom hand reaching for her own, lifting it up, up, and up, until the Scepter was hanging above his head. The weapon's sharp, pointed edges gleamed in the light of the rising sun, sparkling so brightly that it was nearly blinding.

The moments that passed went by in a blur. It was almost as if Ash had slipped out of her body, and was standing beside herself, watching everything unfold, screaming for her to stop.

I have to do this, Ash reminded herself. After everything Loren had just said to the Realm, she had no choice. If she didn't execute Malachai, she would brand herself as an enemy *just* like him.

"Do it," Ash heard Malachai say.

Grinding her teeth, Ash's muscles strained with the weight that came along with holding the Scepter up.

"Ash, please," he begged. "Just do it and save yourself the trouble."

The crowd disappeared, and for a moment it was just the two of them. Ash trembled with restraint. She fought to bring upon the memory of him driving that dagger into her side. She *wanted* to become angry enough to kill him, just as she had been many times before, but no matter how hard she tried, it didn't work. She wasn't angry with him. In the days that had passed, she'd become thankful for him. She'd grown to *need* him.

"No," she declared, blinking against a swarm of tears beginning to flood her eyes. "I can't."

"You need to," he retorted.

"No," Ash repeated, baring her teeth.

"Yes," Malachai argued.

"*No!*" she bellowed, lowering the Scepter just enough to where it grazed his neck, drawing a thin line of crimson blood before it fell limply to her side.

Gasps echoed throughout the square, thrusting Ash back into reality. Afraid to look anywhere else, she looked toward Quinn, who was staring at her in shock. Lilly, who stood beside him, was grinning from ear to ear. Alistair, who stood at her other side, was rubbing his temples as if to ward off a headache. Ash could feel through their bond that he was uncertain and riddled with worry. To his left stood Anastasia, who sported a sinister smirk that matched the same one Morghan was wearing beside her. Craven, who remained by the dais side, looked to be holding his breath, as well as Valentina, who had gone as pale as the snow beginning to fall upon them.

Ash caught Aveo sharing a look with Vincent and Marcus, who both shrugged, likely clarifying for him that they had no idea what Ash was going to do. Penelope appeared to be close to fainting, and she reached for her brother to steady herself.

The rest of the Draconian Council seemed to have taken on a bit of a green hue. The crowd behind them was as silent as the morning before the birds awoke. The only sound to be heard was someone coughing, and another's chip vibrating in their pocket. The entire Realm had gone still.

"Ash," Loren said, an unmistakable warning in his tone. Richard only scowled, clearly appalled by her behavior just as Ash expected he would be.

In an instant, Ash was brought back to the dinner they shared after she returned injured from the first task. It was their idea to make her interim High Queen, and she would do with that title as she pleased. She would use what little time she had on the High Throne wisely. She would use whatever tools the Moons provided her with. In that moment, Malachai was the tool she needed to create peace between *every* species in Idona, not just the Draconians, Elves, Fae, Witches, Giants, and Dwarves, but the Pandora too.

"You will pledge yourself to me and the VanCamp family lineage for as long as you live," Ash declared, turning her gaze back to where Malachai stared up at her in shock. "You will spend the rest of your life doing exactly as I say. You will not take one step, think one thought, or blink unless I direct you. Most importantly, as a way to make up for some of what you've done, seeing as some things can never be made up for…" she paused, daring to glance at Penelope, who was looking at her as if she'd just driven a knife straight through her eternally broken heart. "You will do whatever it takes to aid us in defeating your father and his Dark Army. And afterward, because we *will* succeed, you will personally travel to every village, town, and city to aid in any reconstruction. You will spend your days curing the sick, housing the homeless, and on top of all that, you will vow to never take another life outside of necessary battle. Do you understand?"

Malachai sat still for a moment, processing all she'd just said, before he nodded. "I understand."

"One wrong move and I won't hesitate to finish what we started here today," Ash informed him, tightening her grip around the Scepter.

"You can't be certain that he'll stay faithful to this agreement," Penelope blurted. "What happens if he betrays you? He will, I'm sure of it!"

Ash nodded, relaxing her shoulders to release some of the tension that had begun to build up within them. "I thought ahead," she revealed. "Aries, did you receive my message?"

"Cut the cameras," Loren ordered.

"Don't," Ash countered, shooting him a dirty look. "Aries," she repeated. "Did you receive my message or not?"

"I did," Aries replied, stepping forward with a scroll in hand. "Are you sure about this?" he added in a whisper.

"Positive," Ash replied, gesturing for him to step onto the dais.

"What are you doing?" Richard demanded.

"Performing a Blood Oath, Richard." Ash angled her head to view him, noting how red with anger his complexion had become.

"You've lost your mind!" the adviser accused, just as Aries arrived at Ash's side and unrolled the scroll. "Blood Magic is forbidden! You'll show the entire Idonian population how little you think of our well-founded laws!"

Shaking her head, Ash said, "No, what I'm showing the Idonian people is that they no longer have to fear him. They will see, in time, why I'm choosing to do this."

Before Richard could say another word, Aries reached for Malachai's hand, grasping one of his fingers between two of his own and running it across the crimson line on his neck where Ash had previously struck him. Afterward, Malachai placed his bloodied fingertip toward the bottom of the scroll. As soon as his finger made contact with the parchment, he froze, his eyes growing wide with fear.

Next, Aries handed Ash a small dagger, which she used to slide across her palm in one swift movement, grinding her teeth against the pain. She dipped her finger in the stream now flowing from the wound and put her fingerprint right beside Malachai's on the paper. A strange, tingling sensation swept over her, causing her breath to catch in her throat and her heart to stumble in her chest.

After that came the quill. Aries dipped the tip of it in Malachai's blood first before handing it to him. He stared down at it for a second, clearly contemplating whether he wanted to follow through with this.

"It's a big decision," Aries reminded him. "This binding is stronger than any other bond known to man. Until Ash releases you from this contract, or it's destroyed via the Underworld, you must obey her. Right now, you're giving your life to hers, unless you would rather die."

Malachai nodded, scribbling his signature across the parchment.

Someone squealed, and another fainted. The cameras were shut off, leaving the rest of the Realm to wonder about what might happen next.

Ash took the quill, dipping it in her blood before signing the parchment. The second she finished, the quill disappeared in her hand, turning to dust that was swept up and carried away by a chilly winter's breeze.

Rolling up the contract, Aries whispered a few final words before it vanished, off to the hiding place Ash had chosen—Pat McBride's barn, beneath the hay loft's floorboards.

"You have no idea what you've done," Richard snarled, pushing forward until he was standing right in front of Ash. "Blood Oaths are far more complex than you could ever dream. You might as well have had someone bind your wrists together with enchanted chains and then kill them so that they could never be removed!"

Ash's brows raised with surprise. "You sure must know a lot about Blood Oaths, then," she presumed, her eyes narrowing.

"What does that matter?" Richard snapped. "My knowledge has nothing to do with what you've just done!"

"Sure, it does," Ash countered, willing the Scepter away. It disappeared right before everyone's eyes, invoking more gasps from the crowd. "Mostly because we know for a fact that whatever Rat has been handing over classified information to Xavier about the Messenger Prophecy and all those involved managed to trick General Axel Graves into a Blood Oath. So, excuse me if I find it a tad bit suspicious that you know so much about them."

Out of the corner of her eye, Ash watched Loren pale, hints of pain and betrayal flashing across his features.

"You know, now that you bring that up," Aries said to Ash, "it makes even more sense why he'd push so hard to get Malachai out of the way, now that he's become such a risk to his father's empire. Tell me, Loren, was it your idea to execute Malachai without providing a trial first, or Richard's?"

Loren clenched his jaw, the lump in his throat bobbing.

"Why wouldn't one of Xavier's Rats want their beloved prince to receive a trial before his untimely death?" Ash asked Aries.

"Would it be because they were concerned the prince might disclose confidential information through it? Was he worried that Malachai would walk free after the Idonian people learned the truth about what he was forced to do all these years?"

Aries nodded, clucking his tongue. "I think so, Ash. Now that I think of it, Xavier was one of our fellow advisers, and if I remember correctly, he and Richard were rather close. They'd have private lunches, excluding Griffon and me on a bi-weekly basis."

Richard scoffed. "Solaris and Dracus have always had a very specific alliance throughout the VanCamp reign. It's only natural that we met more frequently than we did with the other advisers."

"That's funny, because I recall you at our family home, having frequent meals with my parents and Pat McBride," Malachai snapped. "I don't recall anything that you were saying being related to politics."

The mention of Pat McBride sent an eerie chill spreading throughout the crowd. Ash looked toward Quinn and Lilly, who's jaws were hanging open in unison. She gave them both a sympathetic look before turning her attention back to the adviser, who looked furious enough to burst.

Had Richard possessed any fire abilities, Ash was certain that he would have been engulfed in flames. Instead, however, a wand dropped out of his sleeve, aimed directly for where Malachai still kneeled in chains. The Allies lurched forward, moving toward the dais steps, but they weren't fast enough. A strange, orange light began to emit from the tip of Richard's wand, radiating waves of immense heat that led Ash to believe that it was intended to fry the prince alive.

"Loren, get back," Shadow ordered, moving to get in between the adviser and the king, who was frozen with fear and shock.

"No, Loren, use your abilities!" Valentina shrieked.

The king held his right hand, but Richard was too fast for him. He aimed his radiating wand at Loren, and in an instant, the king's hand was severed, twitching on the ground beside Ash's feet, all while slicing across Aries' thigh in one shot. A scream began to build in Ash's throat, but she swallowed against it once she watched Loren fall to his knees, clutching his exposed wrist, blood pouring out of it in thick streams, pooling on the dais' floor.

The crowd was dispersing in a fit of fear, panicked people running in every direction while Richard went straight for Ash's throat. Before he had a chance to use his wand again, Aries reached out, using his ability to teleport it away from them to an unknown location. The Allies fought to restrain him, but it was no use. He was too strong, and he made it to Ash before they had a chance to stop him, his fingers curling around her throat before he used his strength to throw her onto the ground, hovering over her while he attempted to crush her windpipe.

"Get. Out. Of. Here," Ash fought to get out, well aware of what she'd have to do next. The Amulet's power was already building within her to a point where it was boiling over, but she knew if she used it, she'd hurt everyone within a mile radius.

"Get him off her!" Ash heard Marcus shout, fighting to get past the council members and Allies working to keep Loren from bleeding out.

Someone threw themselves into Richard, but he tossed them aside like they were no more than a rag doll. Behind Ash, Malachai struggled against his chains, yearning to break free to either run or assist. Craven must have noticed. he rushed forward to try and unlock them with his keys. He succeeded, freeing Malachai's wrists. The prince lurched forward, trying to pry Richard's fingers off of Ash's throat.

"Traitor," Richard snarled, spitting in the Pandora's face.

Malachai retaliated by sending his fist flying into Richard's jaw, causing his head to recoil, his eyes momentarily rolling into the back of his head. Craven came up from behind, kicking the adviser in the ribs. Between the two of them working to free her, Ash was able to steal a few breaths before Richard tightened his grip once again, leading her to see stars.

"She's going to blow!" Ash heard Morghan shout. "Get everyone out of here!"

The Wolf was right. Containing the power begging to be released for a moment longer would do more harm within her than it would in the city square. She could barely hang on, but forced herself, so she could give the others time to escape.

Ash caught sight of Loren being carted away by Shadow and Blade, a strangled sob escaping her before she accidentally released the power. The next thing she knew, she was surrounded by bright, glowing blue light. She wasn't sure who'd made it far enough away, or if anyone had, but it was too late. The city square erupted. The Butterfly Fountain shattered, sending shrapnel spewing into the bodies of anyone standing close enough. The scent of blood filtered through the air, the screams of the injured rattling in Ash's ears. She allowed her eyes to shut just as she felt someone's strong arms wrap around her, and suddenly she was floating above all the pain and destruction she'd caused, flying through a crisp winter's sky into the unknown.

33

Ash awoke to the sound of thunder crackling in the sky. Her eyelids felt leaden, but when she finally forced them open, she found that she was surrounded by a set of soft, feathered wings. She shuddered, pain radiating down her right side. Every breath she took felt like shards of glass embedding in her lungs. Faded memories of all she'd done back in Dracus flickered before her eyes, reminding her of the monster she was.

Snow covered the ground beneath where she lay. She shivered, but she was alive. She might have been relieved had she not noticed how cold the body beside her was.

After a valiant, painful effort, Ash twisted around to face the Fae. His skin was pale, his veins black. She brought a shaking hand to his chest, holding her breath as she waited to feel his heart's rhythmic beat.

It wasn't there.

Ash's heart skidded to a stop, panic beginning to churn her stomach. "Aries," she whispered and took his face in her hands, scanning his unmoving features. "Aries," she repeated, tapping his cheeks gently. "Wake up," she ordered, tears beginning to prick her eyes. She fought to sit up, ignoring the pain throughout her tattered form, placing her hands on both of his shoulders. "Wake up," she pleaded, shaking the Fae.

"No, no, no," Ash ground out. Her breathing slipped out of her control, her pulse pounding in her ears. "*No!*" she bellowed, her fingers curling into fists that she drove into Aries' chest as tears flooded her eyes. He didn't budge. "I did this," she insisted, her words barely more than a brush of air.

A horrified scream began to build in Ash's throat as she scrambled away from the Fae's body. "This is all my fault." She wiped her tears from her cheeks with a trembling hand. "I-I lost control a-and n-now—" she couldn't bring herself to finish the sentence and clamped her mouth shut.

Ash sucked in a breath, filling her lungs with icy air. She looked around, examining her surroundings. They were in the middle of nowhere. There wasn't a village, city, or landmark in sight. The stars above led her to believe that she was somewhere in Western Idona, but there was no way of being sure. She'd only gone beyond the Lakelands once, a few days ago with Alistair, but they'd traveled in the morning.

"I need to find help," Ash said, her voice wavering as her gaze fell on the Fae once again. She shivered at the sight, her heart crumbling into ashes. *This is my fault.* Her bottom lips started to quiver, her sinuses burning with more tears. Shaking her head, Ash willed them away. She would lose herself in her sorrow the second she got Aries body out of the cold. "We can't stay here."

To find help, Ash would have to leave Aries body, and she couldn't bear to do that. Not when the clouds forming above were likely filled with snow. His body would undoubtedly be buried by the time she returned.

Ash shivered and looked down at the dress she wore. The fabric was torn in various places, and one of her slippers was missing. Blood was dripping from a gash along her right thigh, nearly identical to the one Aries had received from Richard. She could tell by how painful every breath was to inhale that she'd obtained more than one broken rib. She was so sore all over that it felt as if she'd just walked out of her fight with the beast all over again. She could hear Malachai's voice in her head saying, *You may be a Berserker, but you're still susceptible to infection.*

Traveling in Ash's condition would be more than trying, especially with Aries body. Using the Amulet's power to such an extent had left her weak. She felt frail, like one of her bones could snap at any given moment.

No matter what, Ash refused to leave Aries behind. She couldn't. Not when she blamed herself. As she started preparing for a journey she had no idea how long it would take, she started thinking about what she could have done differently. She tore off a piece of fabric from her dress and tied it around the wound along her thigh, reliving every moment of what happened in the square and beforehand in her mind.

Had Ash figured out that Richard was the Rat, he'd have never set foot on the dais. Loren would still have his hand, and Aries would be living and breathing. Had she been strong enough to keep the Amulet's power at bay, Aries would have never had to fly her away from the destruction. Had she sent him home to the Safe Haven, where he should have been all along, he wouldn't have been in Dracus to begin with.

Ash sucked in a painful breath, holding it before exhaling slowly. There was no sense in thinking about what she could have changed. At the end of the day, she was still stranded, and Aries was still dead. So Ash did what any warrior would do. She grabbed one of the Fae's ankles, and she started walking.

Thunder clapped overhead once again, causing Ash to go still. Her brow furrowed as she scanned the skies in search of a dark storm cloud, but she found none. After another few moments, lightning struck a few miles to the west.

That's odd, Ash thought, grunting as she pushed onward. Unable to help herself, she started in the direction where it had struck. There was only one explanation for such a phenomenon. Magic. She could only hope that the source of it was friendly, and not another monster she'd be forced to slay.

The Realm around Malachai had gone hazy, and his ears were ringing so loudly he couldn't manage to form a single thought. Smoke and ruin surrounded him; the scent of blood so thick that he felt as if he could choke on it. He pushed himself up to a sitting position, grimacing at his throbbing head. Concerned, he lifted a shaking hand to inspect it, his stomach growing sour at the sight of hot, sticky blood coating it once he pulled it away.

Healers were already swarming the square, carrying stretchers and bags filled with first-aid supplies. A fire had broken out at a nearby floral shop, the roof already engulfed in flames. The dais Malachai once stood on was now just a pile of shredded wood and glass. The historical Black Butterfly fountain had vanished, what remained of it now mixed in with the rest of the debris.

The Allies were scattered, working to guide civilians out of the square. Most of them appeared to be uninjured, aside from a few cuts, scrapes, and evolving bruises. Alistair's Dragon was hovering in the sky above, observing the chaos. Malachai could tell by her demeanor that she was worried, her gaze fixed on where Alistair was helping Ana to her feet.

No one paid Malachai any mind as he fought to stand up on his wobbly legs. The Healers, Council members, and everyone else were far too busy focusing on the injured to notice him walking further out in the square, toward the burning floral shop.

It would be far too easy for Malachai to transition into a hawk and fly away. No one would know that he was gone until it was too late. Ash would eventually use the Blood Oath to demand that he return, but until then, he could find a sense of freedom. However, the Healer deep inside of him screamed to help. He'd ignored that part of himself for far too long, and after helping to save Cooper, it had begun to surface whether he wanted it to or not. He *was* a Healer. He had known from as young as five years old that that was what he wanted to become, and he'd done it. He'd spent countless, sleepless nights studying, and unending hours training.

All that hard work had turned out to be for nothing the moment Malachai became the monster he was today. He'd fought to bury that side of himself in the past where it belonged, but perhaps it didn't belong there anymore. Ash had seen something in him, and she'd chosen to keep him alive because of it. Malachai wouldn't make her regret it.

"What can I do?" Malachai asked a passing Water Clan member, who was working with the fire brigade to smother all the fires breaking out across the square.

He stopped, eyeing the prince warily. "Anything. Jump in wherever you fit, just don't do anything stupid. We can't handle another catastrophe right now." With that, he walked away, off to use his abilities to save what remained of the square.

Malachai looked around, searching for his first patient. The council members and those standing closest to the blast were already being taken care of by other Healers. However, Penelope and Aveo were both refusing treatment despite Vincent's pleas. Frowning, Malachai made his way over there, well aware of how the Princess would react to his presence. Once he was close enough, he caught sight of a piece of shrapnel protruding from her right shoulder and could tell that Aveo's left shoulder was dislocated.

Penelope took notice of him approaching and froze, her hazel eyes narrowed into slits. Vincent, on the other hand, appeared relieved. "Good, maybe *you* can find a way to convince her to get her impalement taken care of," he said, shooting his sister a damning glare.

"As if I'd listen to a word he says or let him anywhere near me," Penelope snapped. "Have you lost your mind? Who are you and what have you done with my brother? The one that I was raised with would *never*—"

"Penelope," Aveo growled. "Did you not just watch Ash bind him to a Blood Oath? There's nothing he can do to harm you without life-threatening repercussions. It may be difficult to believe now, but he's harmless."

Malachai frowned. "I wouldn't say I'm *harmless*."

"As far as we're concerned, you are," Vincent clarified.

"Blood Oath or not, I don't trust him, and I'm appalled that the rest of you have changed your minds about him so easily," Penelope seethed. "Had you not, none of this would have happened!"

"There would have still been a Rat on Loren's council, and Moons only know when he would have struck," Aveo reminded her, matching her harsh tone. "Clearly, Richard has been practicing Sorcery in secret. We have no idea what he's really capable of. For all we know, he could have performed some spell that would have killed you all in your sleep!"

Vincent shivered. "And now we have no idea where he went, or whether he's going to make an attempt to retaliate."

"Stop focusing on Richard," Malachai ordered, gesturing to Penelope's wound. "You need medical attention, and whether you like it or not, I was once a Galaxy renowned Healer who can help you, seeing as that shard could have severed your brachial artery. It could be the only thing keeping you from bleeding out, and if we don't remove it carefully, you could die in less than ninety seconds."

Penelope's jaw dropped, her balance wavering for a moment. "What?" Her gaze dropped to the shard in her shoulder, her complexion taking on a green hue a moment later.

"Luckily enough for you, I have a healing ability and you won't die," Malachai added, which only made her scowl more.

"I'd prefer to wait for another Healer," Penelope replied, crossing her arms in defiance. "I find it difficult to believe that you're capable of saving any lives after the amount that you've taken."

It took an effort not to flinch at the sound of her words. Malachai fought not to show her how much they bothered him and kept his expression as indifferent as possible. "You're more than welcome to suit yourself. I'm sure there's someone else in this square that cherishes their life and family enough to accept my help." He started to turn away, but Aveo reached out, stopping him.

"Do you hear that?" the Commander asked, his bronze gaze darting across the square before ultimately focusing on the burning flower shop. The roof was already engulfed in strange, blue flames. Thick plumes of black smoke seeped out of every available crack before ascending to the sky, overwhelming the snowy clouds above.

"Hear what?" Malachai asked, staring into the blue flames.

"Someone's crying... no, screaming," Aveo informed him,

starting toward the shop, his limp arm dangling at his side. "A child... maybe a baby."

Malachai's heart skipped an uneasy beat.

"Did you say you heard a baby?" a civilian woman asked, rushing toward them. "A man owns that shop. He has a two-year-old daughter."

Aveo didn't wait to hear another word before he took off. Malachai raced after him. Penelope and Vincent followed them out of concern, but by the time they caught up, Aveo had already made it to the burning shop's steps.

The cries had become loud enough for Malachai to hear, and the sound of them immediately chilled him to the bone. "Don't," the prince said, gesturing to Aveo's shoulder. "I'll go in. You find help." He didn't wait for an argument to begin before he kicked the door down, causing all the smoke to rush out in thick waves.

Malachai pulled his cloak over his mouth, ignoring how badly the smoke stung his eyes. He could hardly see, but he followed the sounds of the cries toward the back and crept behind the sales counter where he found the shop's owner lying dead on the floor, a large piece of glass protruding from his neck. Bile crept up Malachai's throat at the sight of him, but despite how badly he wanted to drag the man's body out before it caught fire, he had to focus on the cries.

Carefully stepping over the body, Malachai made his way to what appeared to be a stockroom. The threshold was surrounded by intense, blue flames, but the rest of the room appeared to be intact, although filled with smoke.

"Hello?" Malachai called as he passed through the threshold, peering through the smoke as he shuffled through crates filled with white roses. The cries continued, now so loud that he was certain the source of them was in that room. He continued to search, moving boxes aside until he found her curled up in a corner. He grabbed her and pulled her beneath his cloak, pressing her face against his chest to help prevent smoke inhalation while he searched for a way out.

The ceiling started to crackle and pop as the shop's structure began to give way. Malachai fought not to panic, flames beginning to spill into the stockroom. There was a window on the far side of the room, but he'd have to travel across a sea of crates and boxes to get to it. The wave of power Ash's Amulet had set off must have knocked everything off the shelves and shattered the windows, killing the girl's father as a result.

Malachai pushed onward, yearning to get to that window. He kicked boxes aside, nearly tripping over one before steadying himself. His breathing quickened, his heart thrashing against the walls of his chest. His pulse drummed so loudly in his ears that he could hardly manage to form a thought. The only thing he *could* think of was how the building was about to crumble down on top of him and the girl if he couldn't manage to get out in time.

Someone appeared on the other side of it, though Malachai couldn't see who it was due to all the smoke and fire. The sound of it crashing followed a moment later, just as Malachai was getting close enough to feel cold winter air flow into the room.

"Come on!" he heard a familiar voice growl.

Malachai picked up the pace despite how heavy his body was beginning to feel. He made it to the window and held the girl out, sighing with relief once she was freed from what was once her pending death. He climbed out next, falling onto the ground below before someone grabbed a hold of his cloak and pulled him away just before the building began to crumble right before his eyes.

"That was close," Quinn breathed as he released the prince's cloak. "Too close for comfort."

"Nothing about that situation was comfortable," Malachai grit out, pushing to his feet while examining his new surroundings. Vincent was holding the girl, who was sobbing in between coughing fits. Alistair was kneeling beside him, working to catch his breath while Willa hovered above them like an overbearing parent. Clearly, it had been the Rider who'd broken the window and retrieved the girl, given his current condition. If Malachai had to guess, he'd say that Alistair had run as fast as his Immortal body would allow to get there on time.

Penelope and Aveo hurried over to where they were all standing while the fire brigade swarmed the sight, accompanied by Water and Earth Clan members. "You did it," the Commander said, observing the girl.

"What about her father?" Penelope asked warily.

"I found him behind the counter," Malachai admitted in a hushed tone, slowly shaking his head.

Penelope's plump lips dipped into a deep frown. "That's heart-breaking."

"Here," Vincent said, handing the girl over to Malachai. "Do that thing you do."

Nodding, Malachai held the girl close to him and summoned his abilities. Her sobs started to slow to a stop, as well as her coughing fits, leaving her sleepy enough to shut her eyes and lay her head against his shoulder.

"She should be okay, but I'd like to examine her properly," the prince explained, whispering out of fear that he'd wake her. "We should get both her and Penelope to the Infirmary."

"I don't need to go to the Infirmary and take a bed away from someone who needs it more," Penelope argued defensively. "Aveo's the one who should go and have someone put his arm back in its socket."

Aveo scoffed. "I'm not the one who was impaled."

Willa swooped down, now flying so low that it was startling. Malachai took an uneasy step back, tightening his grip around the girl. As magnificent as Willa was, she was still a member of the most dangerous species in Si Realtra, and her eyes were flashing with rage.

"Go," Alistair said, causing everyone else's brows to wrinkle with confusion. "Don't worry about me. Go. Now!"

"What's going on?" Quinn asked in a demanding tone as Willa ascended back into the skies and disappeared.

Alistair swallowed hard before he said, "Willa picked up on Ash's scent. She's going to follow it, but she has a bad feeling."

"Didn't Aries teleport her to the Safe Haven?" Penelope inquired.

"No," Malachai replied. "I watched him grab her and fly off. He's likely far too injured to teleport."

"That's a long way to fly for someone that's injured," Aveo mentioned.

"Desperate times call for desperate measures," Malachai replied, adjusting his grip on the toddler. "In the meantime, let's get everyone else taken care of."

Everyone nodded but Penelope. She followed the group all the way to the Infirmary, nonetheless. The toddler was immediately admitted into the children's ward, and Quinn had opted to stay with her while Malachai was asked to head down to the Intensive Care Unit to assist with the overflow of patients. Penelope was his first, and while she fought him tooth and nail, eventually she allowed him to medicate her and remove the shard from her shoulder. Thankfully, he hadn't severed the artery the prince was most worried about, and all it took was a series of stitches and some pain medication to get her comfortable.

Afterward, Malachai assisted Aveo with his dislocated shoulder before showering and dressing in the set of deep blue scrubs that the nurses provided for him. He jumped straight in the fray the same way that he would have thirty years ago when he was first certified as a Healer. After a while, he lost track of how many patients he treated and just kept moving from one room to the next, stitching and dressing wounds, as well as using his abilities when they were needed.

Within a few hours, most of those who could be discharged were sent home, and most patients in need of intensive care were comfortable. By the end of it all, the sun had set, and all Healers, nurses, and medical personnel sulked with exhaustion. Malachai himself felt as if he could drop dead at any moment, but as he passed by a row of floor-to-ceiling windows and gazed out at the smoky Kingdom beyond, he realized that they were all in the midst of the calm after the storm and couldn't escape the feeling that it wouldn't last for long.

34

Ash walked for what felt like hours but was certain that only minutes had passed. She kept pushing through mounds of snow with only one shoe. After a while, she'd lost feeling in her left foot, and the wound along her thigh felt as if it was on fire. Her legs barked, and her arms felt like jelly. Every time she spared Aries a glance, another sob escaped her. The only warmth she had was from the tears continuously rolling down her cheeks.

Not long ago, Ash's biggest concern was keeping the crops alive during the heat of summer and defending the village against the Pandora during the winter. Aries was a stranger to her until she'd been forced to fight him to prove herself worthy of the Amulet. That was weeks ago, but it felt like yesterday. They'd fought dirty but had managed to form a bond in the process. They'd understood one another. Had they had the opportunity to strengthen that bond, she was sure that he'd have become one of her most loyal friends. She'd grown to cherish him, even though they'd only known one another a little over a month. She wasn't ready to lose him, yet he was gone, and she was dragging his body through a snowy abyss in search of shelter and help.

Lightning stuck every few minutes, guiding Ash to an unknown place. There were still no signs of life. Empty fields stretched beyond where her Elven eyes could see, blanketed in snow and ice. She fought not to think about how long she'd have to travel, and instead focused on every memory she'd shared with Aries instead.

Ash thought of how grumpy he always appeared, but how every time she caught him with a smile, she'd find herself smiling as well. She remembered how they'd shared a dance at the Fire and Ice Ball, specifically because her dress had matched his black, feathered wings so well. Every time she'd summon him, he'd come and do whatever she needed without question. While other Idonian Council members were wary about her temporary ascent to the High Throne, he'd been nothing but supportive. How would she finish her reign without his guidance?

They were supposed to be getting an eleventh Ally. Ash had thought it would be Aries. Who would that badge go to now? Would they be anywhere near as deserving as he was?

Lightning struck once more, pulling Ash from her thoughts. She was getting closer, but it wasn't close enough. Every step she took became harder than the last until her legs gave out and she found herself losing her grip on Aries' foot and stumbling face-first into the snow. She remained there for a while, her tears of sadness turning into tears of frustration. A growl began to reverberate in her throat before it transitioned into a scream, the sound echoing throughout the snowy fields.

As if in answer, lightning struck again. Ash scowled at it, baring her teeth. "I'm moving as fast as I can!" she shouted, pushing herself back onto her frozen feet. The sun was beginning to set, and soon the temperature would drop. How much colder could it get when it was already below freezing?

Sucking in a deep, calming breath, Ash retrieved Aries' ankle and started walking again, her legs barking in protest. To distract herself, she began to sing songs from her childhood. She could hardly speak due to the cold, and her words came out jumbled, but she sang anyway.

"Deep in the mountains where no one goes, sits a village that no one knows," she started, her heart warming as she recalled her mother singing those words while she cleaned. *"Down a path of twists and turns, in a*

location the naked eye can't discern. Be careful not to be led astray, for one wrong turn and you won't live to see another day."

Ash scanned her surroundings, her lips dipping into a frown. "*Deep in the fields with nowhere to go, stranded and no one knows,*" she sang and grunted frustratedly. "*On and on I walk with nowhere to turn, in a location that I can't discern.*"

The songs continued, offering Ash some mental and emotional reprieve. She kept walking, following strike after strike of lightning, until a small structure appeared in the distance. She gasped, blinking to ensure that it was real. Flakes of ice fell off her eyelashes, falling and disappearing into the snow below. She started running, no matter how painful it was. Her feet, one so frozen that it had taken on a blue hue, pounded against the ice. She slipped a few times but caught herself before she hit the ground. Aries' body became heavier and heavier to drag, but she wouldn't let go. Not when they were so close to a haven—to warmth.

As Ash drew closer to the structure, she realized that it was a small barn. Where there was a barn, there was usually hay, and a farm surrounding it. She began to hear the moos of cows and neighs of horses. Her heart skipped a beat, and she found herself smiling.

It wasn't until Ash made it to the barn that she realized the lightning had stopped. Whoever, or whatever had been guiding her must have realized she'd made it and had slipped off into whatever shadows they'd crawled out of.

"Hopefully, one day, I'll get a chance to thank you," Ash said, pushing the barn doors open and dragging Aries' body inside before shutting them quietly. There were a few horses in the stalls and a pig nursing piglets in a pen. The animals looked at her, eyeing her curiously before going on about their day. None of them paid her any mind when she moved into an empty stall, setting Aries body in a soft patch of hay before she went off in search of a blanket.

While she searched for anything to keep her warm, Ash noticed that the pig's trough was empty and poured some feed into it. "Nursing mamas need extra nutrients," she said to the pig before tucking a wool blanket under her arm and returning to the stall, where she positioned herself between two bales of hay to rest.

When her eyes drifted shut for a moment, she was unaware that they would remain that way, and that she'd enter a deep unconscious state, where she found herself standing in a field of lavender in the height of Spring Solstice. A dream. A *peaceful*, perfect dream.

ASH RAN HER FINGERS OVER THE LAVENDER, BREATHING IN THEIR scent, allowing it to wash over her. She was calm. Calmer than she'd been in years. Her lips spread into a wide smile, a dreamy sigh escaping her. Everything about the place she'd found herself in was perfect. The grass beneath her feet was soft. The sky was the perfect shade of cornflower blue. Every color was vibrant and full of life.

Butterflies flew through the sky, a few landing on Ash's outstretched hand, greeting her. Birds of all kinds chirped, perched on the limbs of nearby trees. Forest animals frolicked throughout the field with their mates and their young.

Ash began her adventure, losing herself in her stunning surroundings. She laughed at the sight of baby ducks following their mom, one of them falling out of line momentarily before scurrying back into place. She followed too, out of pure curiosity, and found herself at the edge of a sparkling pond.

The ducks swam into the center, quacking along the way. A few deer were drinking the water on the other side, one so small that it could have been born earlier that day.

"It's beautiful," Ash breathed, kneeling to dip her hand in the water. She moved it back and forth, admiring the way it sparkled, and caught sight of her reflection and froze.

While her hair was normally wild, now it was longer, with smooth, perfect curls. Her eyes were brighter, her complexion glowing as if her soul was a star. A silver circlet with a single, shining moonstone at its center sat above her brow. She wore a white, shimmering gown so stunning that her jaw dropped in awe.

Ash had never been a fan of dresses, but she couldn't stop

staring at her reflection. It was the most beautiful thing she'd ever worn. She looked like a bride, or the queen of the Moons. She ran her hands down the fabric, watching it shimmer in the bright sunlight.

"Enjoying yourself?" a male voice asked, causing Ash to startle. She whirled around, only to find herself facing a man wearing a jet-black Arebus uniform with startlingly familiar blue eyes. His dark hair was tied back, aside from a few waves that had fallen free, framing his handsome face. She stared at him, her breathing staggering.

"Lincoln?" she asked, her voice wavering with uncertainty.

The man snorted. "Close, but not close enough."

"Pat?"

"You're getting warmer," he acknowledged, crossing his arms in front of his chest.

Ash scowled, setting her jaw. "I'm not in the mood for games," she growled, walking past him in the direction from which she'd come, toward the vibrant lavender field.

The man followed, his shadow stretching out before her. "My name is Jay," he revealed, arriving at her side. "I've been hoping that you'd show up, eventually."

"This is my dream, of course I'm going to show up in it," Ash retorted. "And, if you'll excuse me, I'd like to enjoy it before I wake up and have to find help so that I can get my friend back to the Safe Haven where he belongs and bury him."

Ash felt Jay wince and spared him a glance. "I hate to break this to you, but this isn't a dream. You've entered your mindspace. See?" He pointed to where the Sovereign's Scepter was leaning against a tree. "It's where you store that, amongst other things like memories."

"If it's my mindspace, why are you in it?" she asked, lifting a brow.

"It's the only place where I can talk to you, and I've been waiting for quite a while. Over fifty years, as a matter of fact."

Ash slowed her pace, surprise flooding her features. "Fifty years? I'm eighteen."

"Oh, I know," Jay replied, slipping his hands into his pockets. "But fifty years ago, I left a few daggers for you in some strange village in the mountains. I take it that you've found them."

Ash's head jerked back, her eyes growing wide. "You're *that* Jay?" she squealed, looking him up and down. "How? You're an Arebus Archer. Almost all of them perished during the Five Realm War. You should be dead."

"Sometimes I wish that I was," Jay admitted, his gaze dancing around the meadow. "It's funny, really. I was once convinced that this gift would be the end of me. Now, it's my only way to escape the horrors of the Underworld."

Dozens of questions arrived on the tip of Ash's tongue, but she found herself unable to pick which one to ask first. Ash, along with every other soul in Si Realtra, knew what happened to the Arebus Archers during the Five Realm War. Lucinda had caught them fraternizing with the Erminians and opened up the Underworld beneath their feet. Ash was having a difficult time believing that Jay was alive. How could anyone survive the flames and whatever else lurked beneath them?

They stared at one another for a while with intent, as if trying to read one another's minds. Jay rolled back on his heels, whistling a happy tune. "Oh, look, a cardinal," he observed, pointing toward a pine tree.

"How are you alive?" Ash blurted. "What sort of gift do you have that allows you to enter my mind?"

"Lucinda didn't have enough time to kill us before she drove a knife into our backs," was his response, a hint of resentment distorting his tone. "My soul didn't enter the Underworld. My physical form did. Therefore, I'm living and breathing, yet trapped for eternity. It's quite irritating."

Ash opened her mouth to speak, but no words came out.

"As for how I'm here, that's an even longer story. One that I'll have plenty of time to tell you. I mean, you're an Immortal. *I'm* an Immortal. I'm sure that we'll have a plethora of different opportunities for you to learn about every one of my misfortunes. Right now, I'd much prefer to discuss the daggers. I can see that you haven't killed Xavier yet, and I won't lie when I say I'm both relieved and disappointed that it's taking you so long. We'd all love to see the war end... well, the Archers, anyway. Then again, no one wants Xavier down here."

Scoffing, Ash said, "You don't have much of a choice. He'll be down there soon enough, but I don't see what the daggers have to do with how he gets there."

Jay clucked his tongue, dropping to sit on a soft patch of grass. "Let me guess, when Amelia Stone wrote down that prophecy, she left out one tiny, crucial detail," he started, patting the ground beside him. Ash remained standing and stared down at him expectantly. "Suit yourself," he said with a dramatic sigh, waving her off. "You weren't the first Messenger."

Ash's stomach dropped. "What?"

"It's true."

The need to sit came over Ash, and she found herself sinking down onto the grass beside him. "How... what... who?" she asked in a rush, her mind whirling.

"There's a lot you don't know about Xavier and why he's doing this. I can promise you that it isn't because he was a disgruntled adviser who craved more power. It's much, *much* more than that. He's the grandson of the last Amorian King, Xanthius Bonaventure. Xavier and his father before him have both tried to follow in Xanthius's footsteps by tainting themselves with the Dark One's power. It's become something of a family tradition, and that's what makes them so hard to kill. The only real difference between Xavier and his father, Xander, is that he's managed to live long enough for that power to peak." Jay paused, clearing his throat uneasily. "I was tasked by the Moons to defeat Xander. They used my gift for Dreamwalking to guide me to the daggers. I found them hidden in Aiden Cavanaugh's original Round Table Room, took them to Erim, and slayed Xander in his sleep. Had I known that Xavier would become such a problem, I'd have killed him too."

Ash hadn't realized how fast her heart had begun to beat until the sound of it was the only thing she could hear. She turned her gaze toward the lavender and felt Jay's eyes on her, as if he were waiting for her to say something. When she didn't, he chose to continue.

"Aiden was the first Messenger, tasked by the Moons to slay Xanthius when he was little more than a carpenter in Mayfire, long before he became the first High King and restored order to Si Realtra. Almost a thousand years later, I was tasked. Now, it's your turn," Jay explained. "The daggers were designed by the Sovereign of Light to obliterate the purest form of Darkness. Her Scepter can nullify Xavier's power, but he won't be defeated until you drive one of the daggers into his heart."

"You said Bonaventure," Ash managed to get out, her breathing staggering. "Xavier's surname is Trevayne."

Jay laughed at that. "What, did he think if he took his wife's name that no one would discover his secret? I find that hilarious. What's the point in hiding? Why plan a war for almost a millennium, only to hide it's true purpose?"

Ash shook her head, unsure of what to say. "There was a rumor that Xavier had more than one son—"

"As enthralling as that is, it's not what matters right now. What *does* matter is that you know what you're up against," Jay insisted, tossing the blade of grass he'd been fumbling with aside and pushing to his feet. "Luckily enough for you, I can be of assistance. Well, right now. I'm not sure when we'll get the chance to speak again before you do the heroic deed."

While Ash wasn't sure how much she could trust this stranger, she knew that she needed all the help she could get. "Tell me everything you know about this power he possesses, and what he's capable of," she requested, leaning, adjusting herself so that she sat in a more comfortable position.

Jay offered her a striking crooked smile before he started again. He went on to tell her everything that he knew about the Dark One, and where to find more information on it in Idona, the Kingdom of Elves, and the Safe Haven. Ash tried not to think about how helpful Aries would have been regarding this matter but found it impossible to rid his face from her mind.

"I don't understand why Malachai didn't tell us any of this,"

Ash admitted after a while. "He seemed so willing to cough up anything that might be of help. I guess I was wrong about him, after all."

"He doesn't know a damn thing," Jay told her abruptly. "Xavier kept him in the dark on purpose. He wanted him to be oblivious, when really, it's *Malachai* that the Amorians have been waiting for. There's a second prophecy, one that intertwines with yours. It was predicted by the original Draconian Prophetess, Lexa Undergrove. She named it the *Beautiful Mind Prophecy,* and Malachai's at the center of it."

The last thing that Cooper remembered was Malachai fighting to get inside his cell while he sucked in his final, labored breaths. During those decrepit moments, Cooper was certain that the next time he opened his eyes, it would be to the afterlife. Instead, to his surprise, he found himself in a stark-white Infirmary room. He remained still for a while and stared up at the ceiling, attempting to sort through the tangle of thoughts racing through his mind. How did he get there? Why wasn't he dead? He *should* be dead.

While he tried his best not to, Cooper found himself lost in his memories of Solaris. He could still hear the snap of Savron's whip and feel the way it bit into his flesh and bone. The scent of his blood and the damp, musty underground cell they kept him in still lingered in his nose. He flinched every time he pictured Lincoln, bow drawn and ready to shoot. He'd felt more than agony when each arrow barreled in his flesh. He'd felt betrayal, and heartbreak.

Tears began to well in Cooper's eyes. He flipped onto his side, pulling his knees upward, and allowed a few of them to fall. A few nurses passed his room, but they took no notice of him. *Good.*

An alarm blared down the hall, and more personnel rushed to attend to whatever patient was in need. They each smelled so strongly of blood that Cooper coughed, his stomach burning with hunger. He ignored the symptoms, even as his mouth started to water.

"This is a bloody mess," he heard a familiar voice say, their words barely audible over the sound of Cooper's pulse drumming in his ears. "We have ninety percent of the council in Infirmary beds, and those that aren't here have gone missing, right along with Ash and Aries."

"I take it Willa hasn't found them yet," another replied.

Lucinda. Cooper's eyes widened. *She's awake.*

"Last I heard, Willa confirmed that they were in Western Idona. Beck and a large group of your Sorcerers started a search party."

"I have a bad feeling, Humphrey," Lucinda whispered. "She's with Aries. Why haven't they teleported back? They should have found a way to one of the kingdoms by now, or at least a city. I can't escape the idea that something terrible has happened to them. My Sorcerers reported that there's been an increase in Witch sightings all the way from the Regal Mountains to Solaris. They suspect that Veda and the Crimson Coven have sworn themselves to Xavier. If that's the case…"

"The Draconians will tear through the Witches like a hot knife through butter," Humphrey insisted. "There's a reason they've never tried to go to war with us. Their Magic is no use to them once they've been buried alive by the Earth Clan."

Lucinda snorted. "I'd love to see that. Anyway, since I was removed from *my* Infirmary room, I've been tasked to watch over Cooper since everyone else is busy doing damage control out in the square and hunting down missing council members."

Cooper closed his eyes and waited for the inevitable. He heard Lucinda's light footsteps approaching and caught a whiff of her jasmine perfume. He could feel the heat radiating off her body and hear the stream of blood rushing through her veins. His mouth went dry as a dessert, beads of sweat beginning to form along his brow.

Shivering from head to toe, Cooper opened his eyes and watched her beautiful face flood with shock. The sight of her made him want to cry either tears of joy or relief. He wasn't sure. Every one of his emotions was so strong that it was unbearable, and impossible to tell which one was the strongest.

Lucinda took notice of how he was crumbling and reached for his hand. Cooper flinched at the sense of her touch but allowed her to take it anyway. He despised how much his skin crawled, when all he wanted was to be held.

"I'll summon Quinn," she said, giving him a reassuring squeeze before she let him go.

"No," Cooper said, snatching her hand back, pushing down any feelings of disgust. He'd force himself to get used to touch again, no matter how painful of a process it would be to endure. "Wait. Just... wait." He moved over, hoping that she'd sit on the bed beside him for a while.

Lucinda took the hint and settled in next to him, wrapping an arm around his shoulders, running her fingers over his mess of sandy locks. He shivered again, but after a while, her touch became soothing. His breathing became easier, and his anxiety faded little by little. He tried his best to ignore how loud her pulse was, and how badly he wanted to sink his teeth into the crook of her neck.

"I'm a Draconian, aren't I?" Cooper rasped after a while.

"Yes," she replied softly. "Well, Hybrid would be a better word to describe what you've become."

Cooper swallowed hard, nodding slowly. "Okay."

"Just okay?"

"Just okay," he confirmed. "Tell me everything, please. Something tells me I've missed quite a bit."

"You and me both, my friend," Lucinda chuckled. "We'll start with what I remember." She went on to tell him how sorry she was for trying to complete the second task on her own before she explained everything that had occurred during the last few days regarding Malachai, Ash, and Richard the Rat. "In short, Dracus has turned upside down. I feel like we've entered some sort of alternate Galaxy, where Malachai's saving babies from burning buildings and Penelope and Aveo are actually getting along for a change. To be honest, I'm not sure which is more shocking."

Cooper wished he could laugh, but he couldn't bring himself to.

Instead, he forced a smile for her and said, "Maybe it's all for the best. Things can only get better from here. They have to. I don't think they could possibly get any worse."

Beck had watched the Realm address just like every other Idonian from start to finish, and he was still riddled with shock as a result. He'd suspected that Ash was going to do *something* unexpected, but the last thing Beck thought she'd do was bind her and Malachai to a Blood Oath.

To Beck's surprise, Thaddeus wasn't nearly as furious as he thought he'd be. Instead, he was the epitome of calm. The sort of calm before a storm, at least. Before Beck had a chance to ask what he was thinking about the matter, Alistair had reached out to let him know that Ash and Aries were somewhere in Western Idona. He'd jumped into action, forming one of the biggest search parties that the Realm had ever seen.

They were leaving the golden gates when Thaddeus approached on horseback, clad in armor he hadn't worn since the end of the Five Realm War.

"What are you doing?" Beck asked, pulling the reins back to slow his own steed.

"What does it look like? I'm joining you."

Beck stared at him for a long moment. "You haven't left the Golden City in decades."

"Well, with Aveo in Dracus playing hero, I figured you could use the assistance," his father explained, breaking into a trot. "Wipe that stupid look off your face and get moving. We have a lot of ground to cover."

Beck clenched his jaw and drove his heels into his horse, taking off after his father. The search party split up into various sections, all heading in different directions. Beck chose to head northeast toward Blackbay, and instead of leading his own faction of the party somewhere else, Thaddeus followed. He took the lead, leaving Beck further behind with Red, the Gatekeeper, and a sea of Elven soldiers and Sorcerers.

"What do you think he's trying to do?" Red whispered. "Bond?"

"Who knows," Beck groused. "Someone, send a message to Aveo and tell him that he needs to get his ass back here before my father decides to relive his old war days."

Red chuckled. "Sorry, Aveo's too busy trying to woo Penelope with his heroic acts."

"Yeah, two years later." Beck rolled his eyes, shifting on his saddle until he found a comfortable position. "I wonder how he feels about this Ash and Malachai business. This was the *wrong* time to become an Elven Representative."

Nodding, Red reached for his canteen and took a long sip before he said, "I don't know what he thinks, nor do I care. All I know for sure is that today, I fell in love."

Beck whirled to look at him. "With whom?"

"Ash, of course," Red replied, using a tone that made Beck feel daft. "I'd like to know who *didn't* fall in love with her today. She made the bloody Prince of Darkness her bitch in front of the entire Realm!"

All the Sorcerers and Elves accompanying them nodded and murmured their agreement. Beck caught Thaddeus glancing over his shoulder disapprovingly. The look didn't go unnoticed by the party, and they kept quiet, keeping their eyes peeled. Occasionally, they'd catch sight of Willa dipping beneath the clouds before she landed a few miles ahead.

"I think she's found her," Thaddeus called, snapping his reins, picking up speed. Beck hurried to catch up. His horse's hooves pounded against the earth, frigid wind whipping through its mane and against the prince's face, causing his eyes to water. His heart started to race once he could see the Dragon, pacing outside of a small farm while the family of three that owned it watched from the back steps of their small cottage. Surprise expanded across their faces once they saw the small army approaching their property on horseback, the Elven King at the lead.

"Search the barn," Thaddeus ordered Beck, throwing himself off his horse. "I'll go speak with the family."

A few guards accompanied the king while the others dismounted and scattered, searching throughout the property. Beck and Red started toward the barn, his heart crowding his throat once he threw the doors open. At first, all he could see were animals and supplies, but once he decided to check all the stalls, he found them.

"Fuck," Red breathed behind the prince. "Aries…"

There were no signs of life from the Fae, but Beck approached his body anyway. He brought his fingers to his neck, checking for a pulse. He found none. "He's gone." His voice broke around the words.

"What do you think happened?" Red whispered.

Beck slowly shook his head before going across the stall to check on Ash. "No idea," he replied. "Once we get his body back to the Kingdom of Elves, I'm sure the Healers will tell us everything we want to know. In the meantime, go and fetch one of those carts and inform the others that she's been found. We'll need to travel quickly," he explained, lifting her into his arms while Red hurried off to do what was asked of him.

Ash squirmed, her eyes opening slightly. She gazed up at Beck for a moment, as if trying to figure out who he was. His chest started to feel heavy as he stared down into her forest-green eyes, something twisting deep in his gut. "You're safe now," he told her. She uttered something inaudible in response, her eyes drifting shut again, her head falling against his chest.

"Beck," Thaddeus said from the barn's threshold. "Let's get her into the cart and get her warm."

Nodding, Beck turned to walk toward his father, whose gaze had drifted to where Aries was lying lifelessly in the stall.

"What a shame," he said softly. "Your mother's heart will break."

"Many hearts will break," Beck replied as he passed through the threshold, where he found the search party waiting, their eyes all on Ash. They brought their fists to their hearts as he passed them by, on his way to the cart where Red was setting up furs and blankets for her to lay in.

Shortly after, a group of soldiers retrieved Aries' body and put it in a separate cart before covering it. The family who owned the property came forward once everyone was getting ready to leave, paying their respects to the Fae. Once they were finished, Thaddeus approached them, his coin purse in hand. Beck watched him from where he stood beside Ash's cart, his lips twitching toward a smile at the sight of his father setting it in the father's hand.

"I apologize for all the chaos. Take this, for your troubles," he directed in a kind tone. "Tomorrow, I'll send someone with a flock of sheep and a new workhorse for you." He turned his attention to Willa, who was lingering in the outer fields, sulking with guilt now that everyone was staring at her.

"Thank you, Your Highness." The man's voice cracked as he stared down at the coin purse in such a way that Beck doubted, he'd ever seen so much coin in one place. "We're eternally grateful. Please, let us know if there's anything that we can do for you. My wife makes amazing macramé."

The wife nodded excitedly. "I'd be honored to make something for the Council, Your Highness. Perhaps something that will serve as a reminder for…" she trailed, shifting her weight uneasily from one leg to the other.

"That would be very kind of you," Thaddeus told her. "Please, feel free to visit us at any time. We'd love to provide you with a feast. I'm sure that the High Queen would love to meet you and show you her thanks."

"We should be thanking her, as well," the man admitted.

Thaddeus's brow furrowed. "Whatever for?"

"Well, Your Highness, she fed our pigs."

Beck swallowed his urge to laugh at the look on his father's face. "She fed your pigs?"

"Yes, Your Highness," the couple said in unison.

Beck turned his attention back to Ash, who had yet to move. "You're something else," he uttered beneath his breath.

After Thaddeus finished bidding the family goodbye, Beck

hopped in the cart with a medic to help address Ash's wounds while the party got moving. She didn't wake up, even as the medic injected her with an anesthetic to numb her thigh so he could perform a series of stitches. Every once in a while, she'd mutter something and everyone in the cart would freeze until she settled again.

By the time they had finished stitching Ash up and cleaning her wounds, snow had begun to fall, and the clouds were indicating that a storm was approaching. A Sorceress came forward with a change of clothes, but they didn't dare undress her. Instead, they put a pair of fur-lined pants on her along with some warm, wool socks. Beck held her for the rest of the way, buried beneath furs and blankets, yet still shivering to the core.

They arrived back in the Kingdom of Elves before morning. Ash started to wake as they passed through the golden gates. She tried to sit up, but Beck kept her still. At first, she had no idea who was holding her back, but once she realized it was him, she relaxed.

"Where are we?" she asked, her voice so weak that it broke Beck's heart.

"The Golden City. We're going to take you to the Healing Springs," Beck explained.

Ash nodded, pursing her lips. Beck could tell by the way that she was blinking that she was trying her best not to cry. He frowned, pulling her tighter. "You were so brave, Ash," he declared. "Don't be afraid to cry now. You survived, and now you're safe. With me."

36

Penelope awoke the next morning to what she *thought* was good news. Beck and Thaddeus had found Ash and Aries on a farm close to Blackbay. She couldn't be more excited and chose to get ready without waiting for her ladies' maids so that he could get down to the Throne Room and meet with the Allies as soon as possible. She dressed as quickly as she was able, careful to avoid her injured shoulder, and flew out of her suite's front door.

More guards trailed her than normal, which was to be expected given the current circumstances. Ariel Manchester, the Air Clan Leader, had vanished shortly after the Realm address, and no one had seen her since. It was now being assumed that she was one of many working along with Richard, and that she'd escaped Dracus right along with him. Her younger sister, Emma, was indefinitely taking her position at the head of their Clan while everyone waited to find out the truth.

Blade, the Light Clan Leader, had openly admitted to being blackmailed by Richard and forced to do things that he never would otherwise, like spying on Valentina, and sabotaging missions out in the field.

"So far, it's just the two of them," one of the guards explained as they walked. "We don't believe that any other Council members were compromised, other than Axel. Right now, he's being screened. Once his charges against the Draconian Throne are dropped, he'll be able to return to his position as Draconian General as long as King Loren still sees him fit. In the meantime, Craven will be acting as General in Axel's place, and Sir Calloway will be assisting him with some of his former duties as a specialist, and an Ally."

Penelope's brow furrowed. "Why Aveo? He's here as an Elven Representative, not a Commander."

"You're right, but he has double the experience than most of *our* Commanders. Craven is the only one that compares to him, and he's clearly in over his head. Lady Evanora is the one who made the decision to change Aveo's position here. She arrived earlier this morning and immediately got to work. Her goal is to maintain a sense of normalcy throughout this odd transition. She said, and I quote, '*this isn't my first mutiny.*'"

Penelope slowed her pace, shock flooding her features. During all the chaos yesterday, she'd forgotten that Lady Evanora was coming at all. "She's here?" she squeaked, glancing down at her appearance. Why, of all days, had she chosen to wear a simple pair of black leggings and a red hooded sweatshirt? Groaning, she pulled the hood over her head, pulling the drawstrings right.

"Yes, Your Highness. She'll be meeting with the Allies in the Throne Room as well, along with Sir Aveo and, well… Malachai."

"Why in the eight layers of the Underworld was *he* invited?"

"I suppose it's regarding something that involves him," the guard replied with a shrug.

"Nothing that involves *me* involves *him*," she growled.

Nodding, the guard said, "Of course, Your Highness."

They made it to the Throne Room a few minutes later, where Aveo was already waiting with Marcus, Alistair, and Craven. There was no sign of Lady Evanora, or Malachai for that matter. Instead, the rest of the room was empty, and the only sounds to be heard were the low whispers shared between the four men.

"Morning," Penelope called, walking up to them. "How did you all sleep?"

"You're assuming that we slept," Craven replied, rubbing his tired eyes while Marcus and Alistair yawned in unison. If Aveo was tired, he didn't show any signs. Instead, he appeared like the serious, loyal Commander that she knew him to be.

"Did you sleep well?" Aveo asked, eyeing her shoulder.

Penelope followed his gaze, her lips dipping into a frown. "Better than I expected to. I suppose that I was too exhausted to keep my eyes open for another second, pain or no pain."

"At least one of us got some rest," Craven groused. "I knew the second that we found Loren's safe open that I wouldn't be sleeping for *at least* a few days."

"You found Loren's safe open?" Penelope and Aveo asked at the same time, surprising one another. "But it's DNA protected. His thumbprint would be needed to get in," she added with a furrowing brow.

Craven and Marcus shared an uneasy look before the latter said, "We never found Loren's hand in the square, and now that Ariel is missing, we're beginning to think that she took it, used it to get into the safe, and then took off."

Dread began to settle in Penelope's stomach. "That's disgusting."

"Do you have any idea what she took?" Aveo asked.

"We plan on asking Malachai if he knows of anything his father might want of Loren's after this meeting." Marcus said. "Right now, Grant's scanning the safe for fingerprints. It won't help us figure out what's missing, seeing as Loren's the only one who really knows what's supposed to be inside it, but it'll help us confirm whether or not Ariel is really at fault."

Penelope swallowed her urge to growl and pressed her lips together. She kept silent and listened to the men exchange ideas about what they thought might have been taken. She couldn't come up with any ideas herself, and instead thought about how infuriating it was that everyone was becoming so willing to accept Malachai's help. Blood Oath or not, she couldn't stand him, and would never trust him. Whatever path to redemption he was trying to pave for himself made her sick.

The others started to arrive in groups. The McBrides were first, and Penelope couldn't help but be surprised to see Cooper. She had figured that after his ordeal, he'd remain in the Infirmary for at least a few days, yet there he was, appearing to be as good as new. However, there was no missing the shadows dancing in his eyes. They were different than Penelope remembered them. Before, they had been the same shade as Quinn's—cerulean that looked almost jade in the direct sunlight. Now, they were a bright, icy blue that reminded Penelope of pictures she'd seen of Ryiah. As if that wasn't strange enough, he seemed taller. Someone who hadn't seen him recently would think he'd endured a growth spurt, not an unwelcome transition into a Hybrid.

"I don't think I've ever been so happy to see someone," Alistair said as the brothers arrived before them all.

Cooper smiled, but it never reached his eyes. Penelope could only wonder how he was feeling. She'd been in his position before, a few years ago, after being kidnapped by Hans of the Mist and the Rebels. They hadn't hurt her, at least not physically, but the months that followed her rescue weren't easy. Even now, she'd wake from nightmares where she'd find herself at the bottom of a gap in the earth, staring up at an unreachable sky.

If Cooper was anything like Penelope, he'd put on a front, and lead everyone to believe that he was alright, when really, every time he closed his eyes, he was right back in Solaris.

"If only we could say that our division was whole," Cooper replied sadly.

"It is," Alistair assured him. "Ash is just... well... across the Realm."

Craven grunted frustratedly. "It would be a miracle if every Ally could be awake and in one place for a change."

More people started to arrive. Ana and Morghan were first, both cradling cups of steaming coffee. Penelope's mouth watered at the sight of it. The Wolf caught her staring and begrudgingly handed it over. "Here," he said. "Knock yourself out."

Nodding, Penelope took her first sip. "Thank you, Morghan."

Not long after that, Lucinda walked in with Lady Evanora, a man that Penelope recognized as Sam Waters, and Malachai. She fought not to scowl at the sight of him and turned her attention to Aveo, who gave her a sympathetic smile.

"Your Highness," Evanora said, bowing. "It's lovely to finally meet you."

"It can't be any more lovely than it is to meet you, Lady Evanora. I've never admired someone so much," she replied, momentarily taking the elder's hand. "Pardon my appearance, of course. I had no idea I'd be meeting you so early."

"After the day you had yesterday, I wouldn't have complained if you showed up in a bathrobe," Evanora replied, chuckling as he gestured for Sam to step forward. "I'm not sure if you two have met, but this is my General, Sam Waters. He'll be spending a lot of time here in Dracus while we work on this alliance with Loren. I'm sure that you'll get along famously."

Had Evanora not remembered what Penelope had been forced to go through because of the Rebels, or was she dismissing that entirely? Her chest became tight, her blood beginning to heat. "Of course," she said, hoping her tone didn't give away her festering annoyance.

"Forgive us if we're hesitant when it comes to the Rebels," Marcus surprised her by saying. "There are plenty of people in this room who faced Hans of the Mist and Kurt Walsh head-on. It wasn't a pleasant experience."

Craven and Alistair nodded in agreement, while Aveo remained silent, portraying no emotion upon his face. However, Penelope could tell by his rigid demeanor that he was just as annoyed as she was.

"You all have much to learn about this organization, and why Lord Cedric created it," Evanora explained, her gaze drifting from face to face before ultimately landing back on Penelope. "I'll be here for a while, securing this alliance and helping King Loren restore order to his council and Kingdom. I hope that you'll all give me the chance to tell you his story in a way that he would want it to be told. Perhaps that would help put you all at ease. Of course, there's nothing that Sam or I can do to make up for what happened to

Princess Penelope. Walsh and his following have been dead for years. We can only move forward from here."

All eyes turned to Malachai, who'd slithered away from the group, lingering closer to the dais. "I'll have you know that I took a lot of joy in solving that problem for you all."

"Of course, you did," Morghan huffed.

"You're welcome," Malachai said, smirking devilishly.

Penelope had never wanted to rip out a man's throat more, and she'd come dangerously close to doing just that every time she'd trained with Aveo. "Why are you here?" she asked. "Don't you have some cell to rot in?"

"He's here because I asked him to be," Vincent said, walking in with Anderson and Benjamin on his heels. "I received a call from Beck this morning. He told me a few things that weren't included in the mass message we all received from him last night. I'd prefer to only have to say it all once, because just thinking about it makes me physically ill."

Vincent finished making his way over to the crowd, his complexion paler than Penelope had seen it in a very, very long time. Beads of sweat were visible along his brow, his chip clutched in his hand as if he were holding onto it for dear life. She sucked in a breath and held it for a while before exhaling slowly. Whatever he was about to tell them, it was bad. *Really* bad.

"You might want to sit down," Vincent suggested, pointing to the series of steps the dais consisted of. No one said a word and did as he asked, watching one another warily. Penelope made sure to stay as far away from Malachai as she could and chose to slide into a place at the very end of the dais step. Aveo took the place above her, while Alistair settled in on her side.

The overwhelming urge to bite her nails swept over Penelope as she watched her brother pace back and forth. "Thank you, Lady Evanora, for joining us. I figured you'd like to hear what I'm about to say," he started, his tone wavering with nerves.

"Thank you for thinking of me," she replied kindly.

"Of course," Vincent said before continuing with his pacing.

"Are you alright, Vincent?" Sam asked, breaking the lingering silence.

Vincent cleared his throat. "Far from it, actually."

"Did you want to tell us about it?" Lucinda asked, her voice as sweet as pie.

"I have specific instructions to do just that," Vincent informed her, scanning the faces of those now sitting on the steps. "Where's Lilly?"

"Lilly McBride?" Quinn asked, his brows pulling together.

"No," Morghan drawled sarcastically. "Lilly Calloway."

Penelope felt Aveo perk behind her. "Calloway?"

"Sorry, I was looking right at you," the Wolf explained.

"I *do* have an aunt Lilian, you know," Aveo informed him.

"Lilly's at the Infirmary with Maeve," Malachai said. "She was there when I went to check on her a half an hour ago."

"Do you want me to go get her?" Cooper offered.

"You're not allowed to teleport for at *least* two weeks," Malachai reminded him.

"I still have two legs, genius," the Archer growled.

Penelope might have laughed had she not noticed the tears beginning to form in Vincent's eyes. "Vincent," she said. "What is it?"

Sniffling, Vincent nodded and said, "Aries is dead."

Never before had Penelope heard a room fall so silent so quickly. The only thing that she could hear was the drum of her own heart beating. She stared at her brother, watching as his features crumbled no matter how badly he was clearly trying to hold himself together. No one said a word. Penelope wasn't entirely sure if anyone had thought to breathe.

"How?" Lucinda asked, abruptly breaking the deafening silence. "I don't understand. Beck sent us that message last night, and he said *nothing* about Aries having died. What, did he pass away during the night? Was he bleeding internally? Did the Elven Healers not notice? Of *course*, they didn't notice," she ranted. "It's always the fucking Elves."

Penelope felt Aveo grow stiff behind her. "Excuse me?"

"You heard me," Lucinda snapped.

"Guys!" Marcus chastised. "At least wait to hear an explanation before you shred each other into ribbons."

"Right," Vincent said, swallowing hard enough for everyone to hear. "You'll be wanting an explanation." He turned his attention to his chip, his hand trembling around the device. "Well, it says here that Aries' body was discovered in the same barn Ash was. There's evidence that she dragged him for quite some time. Thaddeus instructed Beck to wait until they had answers. By morning, a combination of Elven Healers and Sorcerers were able to discern what had happened to him. They believe that he was shot down by an invisible strike, likely meant for Ash. Given the state of his wings, he wrapped them around her to help cushion the fall. His back took most of the impact, though Ash's injuries line up with falling from great heights as well."

"An invisible strike?" Evanora inquired.

"Magic," Lucinda seethed. "It was the Witches, I'm sure of it."

"What sort of spell do you think was used?" Penelope asked, her chin trembling.

"A *moarte strike*," Lucinda replied through clenched teeth. "The Crimson Coven is famous for it. If it's done right, and the strike hits the target in the heart, they'll die instantly. What Vincent just described leads me to believe that whatever Witch is at fault for this missed."

"It's either that, or someone stopped them," Evanora contributed, drawing everyone's attention. "The Rebels are all on the move, migrating underground toward Central Idona where they're to wait for further instruction. They've seen that the Witches are on the move as well, migrating toward Solaris, but that there's more than one coven out and about. They've encountered members of the Unseen as well."

Lucinda and Morghan gasped in unison, drawing everyone's attention. "Irina," they both said, looking at one another.

"Looks like Veda finally crossed the final line," Malachai murmured.

"By Irina, you mean Irina Phantom, right?" Vincent asked. "I've read about her in dozens of history books."

"That makes sense," Lucinda told him. "She's been the High Priestess for centuries now. Every Idonian Coven is sworn to her. Her personal order, the Unseen, is only put into action when the covens step out of line. If I had to guess, I'd say that Veda is trying to swear herself to Xavier, and that Irina is the only thing stopping her. The odds are that the Unseen have been tracking the Crimson Coven members trying to escape to Solaris, and that some were caught in the act."

"You said that Ash was injured during all of this," Marcus said, steering the conversation back to the High Queen. "Is she alright? If she *was* injured, how did she manage to drag Aries from wherever they landed to that barn?"

Malachai snorted, earning quite a few glares. "I'm sorry, but have you met that woman? She's a Berserker. They find most of their strength through adrenaline. I bet she's exhausted today, and certainly paying for it, but she tried to fight me even after she was shredded by the beast. She could have won, too, I'm sure of it."

"Why didn't she?" Penelope scowled.

"You'll have to ask her that yourself next time you see her, because I have no idea what was running through her head," Malachai said. "Speaking of seeing her, when can we do that? Is she coming back to Dracus to heal here?"

"Not after Loren demanded I retract the Unity Bridge and disable all the portals," Benjamin chimed. "Besides, I'm no Healer, but I wouldn't recommend traveling in that condition."

"I can go to her and speed up the process," Malachai offered. "Besides, she shouldn't be alone there. You have to imagine what it was like for her to wake up to find Aries dead, and then doing all she did to get herself *and* his body to safety. She's surrounded by strangers right now."

Penelope's shoulders slumped, her stomach churning. She hated how much she agreed with the prince in that moment. "You're practically a stranger too. If anyone should go, it should be one of the McBrides."

"Send me," Quinn said, raising his hand.

"He's right. Someone familiar should be with her. The McBrides are the best choice. They know her better than anyone," Craven insisted.

Aveo opened his mouth to object. "I would advise sending someone else," he admitted, offering Quinn an apologetic look. "We have no idea if, or when Richard is going to strike again, and you and your brother can't miss a shot."

"Then I'll go," Alistair offered.

"No, we need you and your Dragon," Evanora replied.

"I can." Sam held his hand up.

"Yeah, let's send the *Rebel* General into the Kingdom of Elves. That's a fantastic idea," Malachai drawled sarcastically.

Sam's nose wrinkled with displeasure.

"I'll go," Penelope insisted, rising to her feet.

"I think not," Evanora chirped. "It's to my understanding that you've spent enough time here with Loren to know how he runs his Kingdom. Am I correct?"

"Well... yeah—"

"Good," Evanora interjected. "You'll be running it now, then."

Penelope blinked, lowering to sit back down.

"Alright, I'll go," Morghan insisted, stepping forward. "Ash and I hit it off pretty well when we first met on the Strip. I'd like to think that we bonded throughout the three tasks. Besides, Thad loves me. At least, he pretends to. Either way, I'm welcome in the Kingdom of the Elves."

"He's not wrong," Aveo added.

"You can take Lilly," Quinn offered. "It would get her out of Dracus. I hate to say it, but the Kingdom of Elves is safer right now. She'd put a smile on Ash's face, too."

Morghan started to shake his head. "Are you sure that's a good idea? She's young, and impressionable. What if the Elves try to use that to their advantage? The revival of the Arebus Archers is frightening, but that doesn't mean that everyone doesn't want a piece of the pie. She already has abilities now, at fourteen. Imagine how powerful she'll become as a full-fledged Archer. The Elves will no doubt think of that and try to befriend her."

"I wouldn't put it past them to try to adopt her," Penelope admitted, well aware of Aveo's eyes on her back. "They have a habit of acquiring children that might benefit them, is all I'm saying."

"Yeah, that won't happen," Quinn growled.

"Why, are you her legal guardian?" Benjamin inquired. "If not, then she's up for grabs, and she's too young to have a real say in the matter."

"I'm her eldest surviving family member." Quinn replied. "I'm pretty sure that makes her my ward."

Penelope exhaled slowly, shaking her head. Before she had a chance to break the news to him, Malachai beat her to it. "Unless you register in a Kingdom and file documentation stating that you're willing to take responsibility for her as her legal guardian, then she's not your ward in a way the Idonian Council will recognize."

"Then I'll do that, when we win back Solaris," Quinn snapped.

No one said another word about the matter and instead started planning Morghan and Lilly's journey to the Golden City. Using Lucinda's chrome sphere was out of the question, seeing as the Witches scattered across the Realm would be able to track them through Magic. Cooper wasn't able to teleport, and the portals were shut down. There was only one option left.

"Dragon it is, then," Craven said, clapping Morghan on the shoulder.

"You want me to do *what?*" the Wolf gaped.

37

Shortly after the meeting ended, Quinn and the others met in the fields behind the castle to see Lilly and Morghan off. There was no way of describing how badly it hurt to watch his little sister fly away after just getting her back, but he knew it was for the best. Someone needed to be there for Ash, and if it couldn't be him, Lilly and Morghan were the next best thing. He could only hope that Penelope was wrong, and that the Elves wouldn't try to take advantage of Lilly.

"Evanora was right," Malachai said, arriving at the Archer's side as Willa flew out of view. "Lilly is far too smart to be used by anyone. I haven't known her long, but within hours after I met her, I knew she was a prodigy. Actually, she reminds me a lot of myself when I was her age."

Quinn scowled. "That can't possibly be a good thing."

"Don't worry, she'll make better decisions," the prince assured him. "She didn't grow up with the father I did, therefore, she should be fine."

"She didn't grow up with a father at all, thanks to you," Cooper snapped, grabbing everyone's attention. Some winced, and others just looked away, unwilling to witness whatever happened next. "Funny, Morghan didn't grow up with his father, either. Neither did Penelope and Vincent. Alistair's sister didn't get to grow up at all."

The color drained from the Rider's face, his eyes flashing with pain.

Aveo stepped forward, setting his jaw. "That's enough, McBride. You can berate him all you want, but don't bring other people's trauma into it."

Quinn held his breath, a bad feeling pitting in his stomach. He looked toward Malachai, who appeared unfazed. He doubted that was really the case. Clearly, the prince had a heart. Most of it might be black, but it had changed for the better. Quinn could only imagine how difficult it was to move forward when everyone kept dragging you back into the past.

"No, it's not enough," Cooper argued. "I don't understand how you can all act like he hasn't done those things. You weren't there when Sam's father came up to the McBride Estate the morning after a Pandora attack to tell us that my father and his wife were slain by the Prince of Darkness himself. And you weren't there when Death Valley burned to the ground, and when Alistair's family died. Fuck, you all thought he was dead. His body wasn't found, but no one bothered to look for him. You thought he was just another victim. Well, we're all victims, aren't we? Because of *him*, and you let him stand here like he's done nothing wrong! Sure, let's let him help. He can be a Healer. He can tell us all of his father's dirty little secrets. That'll make up for it all."

Cooper's harsh words drove everyone into silence. Quinn's heart rate crept up as his gaze darted between the prince and his brother. He ignored his own pain resurfacing at the mention of his father's passing. He could still remember his funeral like it was yesterday. Getting lost in those memories wasn't an option right now.

"Penelope." The moment Cooper said the name, everyone in the field went rigid. "You, of all people, should agree with me. He took Cedric from you. You could be married right now, but instead you're here—"

"Stop. Right. Now," Quinn cut in, baring his teeth. But it was too late. Tears were already flooding the Princess's eyes. Cooper's words had already sunk in, and her current betrothed's face was becoming red with rage. "What do you think you're doing? Is your goal to make Malachai feel like shit? Well, instead you're upsetting everyone else."

"They're already upset, Quinn." Cooper insisted, throwing his hands up frustratedly. "We're all just playing along for Ash's sake, but that doesn't mean it's not unbearable for some of us. Can't you see that, or are you too blinded by your love for her?"

Quinn's fingers curled into fists, the blood racing through his veins coming to a quick boil. "I'll tell you one more time. Stop or—"

"Or what?" Cooper challenged, his fangs extracting. Ana and Craven caught sight of that and took steps toward him but remained at a comfortable distance. "What are you going to do? Nothing. Even if you tried, you can't do any worse than what Lincoln's already done because that *monster* took him from us and turned him into whatever sick thing he is now. He destroyed our family and obliterated everyone else's. He took our father from us right after we lost our mother, and we've lived every day in fear since."

"Your father wasn't innocent either," Malachai barked. "So before you start blaming every single struggle you've endured on me, maybe you should start asking yourself why the last Arebus Archer chose to lead everyone to believe your species was extinct while he hid away in the mountains. Maybe, just *maybe*, it was because he *wanted* everyone to believe that he was dead, so that he wouldn't have anyone breathing down his neck while he followed my father's orders. Did you honestly believe that he was just a simple, innocent farmer? Well, I have news for you. He is just as much at fault for the Pandora as I am, and when he couldn't handle what he'd done, he deserted the cause. I knew where he was the entire time, and I didn't say a word. I *wanted* to leave him alone, but my father discovered the truth, and he used his power to manipulate my every movement. He forced me to kill Pat and Celine as punishment."

Without any warning, Cooper disappeared, reappearing right in front of the prince. For a moment, Quinn thought that he'd gone against his Healer's orders and teleported but realized that he was wrong. Cooper hadn't teleported. He was just fast. *Too* fast.

Before anyone had a chance to react, or try to intervene, Cooper's fist was colliding with Malachai's jaw. The prince stumbled, momentarily losing his footing on the slippery terrain. Before he had a chance to correct himself, Cooper tackled him. Everyone watching began to shout in process, but not because they were worried for Malachai. They were far more concerned about what Malachai might do.

Lately, the prince had been acting docile and kind, but that didn't mean that he wasn't still a man that they should fear. He was still just as skilled in all forms of combat as he was a month ago. Quinn's breath hitched as ideas of what Malachai could do to his brother swam through his mind.

The others started to shout in protest as they watched Cooper drive his elbow into Malachai's ribs, knocking the wind out of him. Quinn gawked at the sight of his brother, fangs gleaming in the midday sun. He looked nothing like the man he knew. It was almost as if Cooper had been replaced by a rabid animal starving for a kill.

The pair continued to fight, Cooper landing punch after punch while Malachai fought to fend him off. Quinn wondered if he'd fight back at all. It was clear that he was trying his best *not* to, but a man could only take so much of beating before losing his composure.

Just as that thought fluttered through Quinn's mind, Malachai drove his knee into Cooper's gut and shoved him off, sending him sprawling into the snow. Quinn bit his tongue at the sight of Malachai struggling to his feet, spitting blood onto the ground. No one said a word. Instead, they watched, grimacing as the prince drove his boot into Cooper's side.

"That was for chipping a tooth," the prince explained, wiping his mouth with the back of his hand.

Cooper snarled, pushing himself to his feet, cradling his side with his arm. Without any warning, he lifted his free hand, blowing Malachai backward with a gust of air. Quinn's jaw dropped, as did Marcus's and Craven's. The prince landed a few feet away on his stomach, having fallen face-first into the snow. When he lifted his head up, he was wearing a glare unlike any other, his eyes flashing red.

"Cooper, stop," Lucinda warned.

Ignoring the Sorceress, Cooper stormed forward, fighting not to limp. The wind started to pick up, whipping through everyone's hair, sending snow flying back up into the air in angry gusts. A funnel started to form, reaching down from the clouds above.

Malachai stood up, visibly trembling with rage. Quinn moved to get between them, but Marcus pulled him back.

"I've been trying really, *really* hard not to snap your fucking neck," the prince admitted. "But because I somehow still manage to have some respect for you, and most importantly Ash, I'll refrain. This time."

A manic laugh escaped Cooper, the sound chilling Quinn to the bone. What exactly had his brother become? "There won't be a next time."

"You're right, there won't be," Valentina said from behind, pushing past the crowd of people to get to the pair. Everyone turned to watch as she approached, appearing as if she'd rushed there straight from the Infirmary. She was dressed in a pair of comfortable pants, fluffy boots, and a coat with a massive fur-lined hood. Her hair was a mess of tangles, her golden eyes wild and red. "If you don't stop this right now, I can assure you that you will not only affect the outcome of this war in a negative way, but you will ruin more than one life in the process. You will damn us all."

Quinn's stomach churned, his heart beating too fast for him to handle. "What do you mean?"

"The future is finicky, Quinn," Valentina said, arriving before him. "There are multiple timelines. What you're experiencing now is a defining moment. If this fight continues, and Cooper wins, the Pandora will continue to run rampant throughout the Realm, multiplying until we're completely overrun, resulting in the extinction of at least three species. If Malachai were to win, he'd be too ashamed to remain with us, and the Blood Oath he swore to Ash will kill him. If she were to choose to destroy the oath, he'd remove himself entirely from the war, leaving it for everyone else to finish. If that were to happen, we would fail. Everyone standing in this field would perish at one point or another."

Ana let loose a long whistle, slowly shaking her head. "That's heavy."

Valentina nodded agreeably before she started again. "The Realm is changing, Cooper. For the better. We've *all* been through the worst things imaginable leading up to this—Malachai included. I know that this is a difficult pill to swallow, but we need him just as much as we need the Allies. You might not have realized this yet, but there are very few strong warriors left in this Realm, and almost all of them are standing in this field as we speak. We're losing people left and right. We lost Aries, we almost lost you, and we're going to lose more. We need everyone that we can get."

Cooper clenched his jaw as the wind died down until it was no more than a gentle breeze. His attention drifted between Malachai and the Prophetess for a time before he took a few steps back. "Fine," he grunted, turning to head back into the castle. Quinn watched him go, at a loss for words.

"He's unstable," Lucinda said, her shoulders slumping.

"He's just endured an incredibly traumatic experience," Malachai reminded her. "We all fly off the handle when something terrible happens to us. I hate to say it, but I was in his position when I destroyed Death Valley."

"Why did *you* fly off the handle?" Craven asked with narrowing eyes.

"Well, the *first* time was when I showed my father the finished product for the Pandora injection and he turned around and drove it into my neck without my permission," Malachai replied bluntly, moving to follow Cooper into the castle. "It was all downhill from there," he shot over his shoulder.

38

After spending most of the day in the Healing Springs, Ash was brought to a suite that she was told belonged to Penelope and Vincent. Normally, she'd have looked around. After all, this was her siblings' home for so many years. Little pieces of them were scattered all over, but she couldn't bring herself to take her eyes off the window in front of her, and the unfamiliar Kingdom on the other side of it.

The last time Ash had woken up in a strange, new place, she'd thought she needed to fight her way out of it. And she would have. In fact, she had tried to, because she hadn't known then that her destiny had brought her there. Yet now, she felt the same way she did waking up in that Infirmary. Afraid.

Ash was surrounded by strangers once again. People who looked at her as if she were a charity case, in need of their pity. She was a wilding. A savage. Slowly, she closed her eyes, allowing her mind to bring her back to that moment Richard wrapped his hand around her throat. Instinctively, she reached to touch the places where the bruises had begun to bloom, her mouth growing dry.

Not only had Ash been betrayed. She'd also been dragged away from the people she cared about because of it, and, Aries had lost his life.

Up until that moment, Ash believed that she was incapable of shedding another tear. Her emotional wells had run dry. Yet, a few dripped down her cheeks, trailing down to her jaw. Shuddering, Ash pulled in a shaky breath, opening her eyes. She turned away from the window and approached the bed, breathing in the scent of her sister. She lowered herself onto it, pulling her knees up to her chest before wrapping her arms around her legs.

A knock on the door led Ash to jump out of her skin. She hadn't heard the front door open downstairs and wasn't fond of the idea that anyone could enter the suite at any time. Scowling, she bit her tongue, hoping that if she didn't respond whoever it was would think she was sleeping and leave her alone.

"Ash?" A shrill, female voice called.

Still, Ash remained silent.

"I know you're awake," the voice insisted. "I've only come to see how you're fairing."

Frowning, Ash figured it was best to comply. "You can come in."

The last person that Ash had expected to open the door was Princess Mika. The very sight of her caused every one of Ash's muscles to become as rigid as stone. "You can set everything over on the nightstand," Mika said just before a servant walked in carrying a tray of soup, fresh bread, and blood.

The servant walked across the room with slow, graceful steps. She kept her chin high, her back as straight as a rail, and her gaze fixed on her destination. Not once did she meet Ash's gaze. Whatever, she sighed, forcing herself not to give into the urge to roll her eyes.

"You may leave us now," Mika ordered once the tray was put on the nightstand. "Unless Her Majesty is in need of anything?"

Ash shook her head. "I'm fine, thank you."

After dipping into one of the deepest courtesy Ash had ever seen, the servant waltzed out, shutting the door behind her. "You are certainly not fine," Mika insisted now that they were alone. "Elves are an extremely intuitive species. We can sense when people lie." The Princess took it upon herself to sit at the end of the bed, crossing one leg over the other. "The Healers tell me that you barely uttered a word all day."

Turning her attention back to the window, Ash thought of how to respond. "Twenty-four hours ago, I was waking up next to the dead body of one of my friends," she said, her tone colder than ice. "I'm not in the talkative mood."

Mika offered her an understanding nod. "No one expects you to bounce right back after what happened. We're all mourning Aries. In fact, we should be mourning him together, which is why my parents would like you to attend dinner with us tonight."

Ash swallowed a groan before it had a chance to escape. There wasn't a single chance that she could stay in the Kingdom of Elves and avoid Thaddeus and Esmeralda for long. Of course, Ash had known that. She'd just hoped they'd give her another day.

It would be rude to refuse, therefore Ash didn't have much of a choice than to accept. "I'd like that." It wasn't necessarily a lie, but it was certainly far from the truth.

"I'll send my designer up to measure you for something to wear," Mika declared excitedly, rising to her feet. "In the meantime, have some of that soup to hold you over. You'd be surprised how uplifting a hot meal can be." She started toward the door, a certain pep in her step that hadn't been there when she'd arrived. "I'll come back to fetch you later. Unless you'd rather me send Beck?"

"Either one of you is fine," Ash informed her, though she'd much prefer the latter. The last thing she needed to do was send the Elves the wrong message, especially with their history of matchmaking. "But I do look forward to getting to know you while I'm here, Mika. It feels strange that we haven't had a chance to talk until now."

Mika brought a hand to her chest, her eyes wide and glowing. "It warms my heart to hear you say that."

The Princess left, and Ash immediately scooted across the bed to retrieve some of the fresh slices of bread from the tray. She took a bite and her shoulders relaxed, releasing all the knotted tension within them. As long as she could concentrate on her lunch, she could keep her thoughts off of dinner. By now, Ash was used to meals with royals, though Loren was a far cry from Thaddeus and far easier to talk to. She did, however, wish she didn't have to attend that dinner alone.

So, while Ash ate, she devised a plan. While she'd arrived in the Kingdom of Elves under unfortunate circumstances, it would benefit her to use her time there wisely. Befriending Mika was just the first step. Afterward, she'd find something to bond with Esmeralda over. Perhaps she'd entice the Elven Queen with thoughts of a future marriage. That would surely put her to work and keep her off of Ash's back. And there was Trinity, a six-year-old who Ash would undoubtedly get to love her. She already had Beck in the bag, so there was no need to worry about him.

Thaddeus would be Ash's biggest challenge.

ASH HAD SPENT THE LAST FEW HOURS BEING MEASURED AND FUSSED over, all while silently plotting. She thought of everything she'd say over dinner and how she'd portray herself. One thing that she knew she couldn't do was be herself. Instead, she'd have to act more like Penelope. A poised, proper woman. Something Ash was still learning how to be.

"Which color do you prefer, Your Highness?" the designer, a petite Elf with pastel blue hair, asked as she held up two gowns. One was emerald green, embellished with intricate Idonian knot patterns woven with shining golden thread. The second was silver, with a similar pattern woven with black thread instead.

Leaning forward in her chair, Ash's gazed shifted between the two, her brow furrowing with concentration. "Are you positive that I can't wear pants?"

The Elf snickered, setting both back on the rack she'd wheeled in just a few minutes prior. "Normally, that would be fine, but considering this is your first time joining us, and it's the Giving Day season, it's customary to spice things up a bit."

For the first time all day, Ash found herself smiling. "Very well then, Tila. I'll go with the green."

"Perfect!" Tila clapped once before beginning to prepare the dress. Ash continued to watch her curiously while another Elf started to curl her hair. The last thing Ash wanted to do was get transformed into some beautiful creature, but she knew this was what Penelope would do. So, she persevered. She started to build her facade, layer by layer, until she arrived in front of a tall mirror to see the final look.

Breathtaking, some might say, but that's not how Ash felt. She peered into the looking glass, tilting her head curiously, examining the stranger in front of her. She hadn't realized until then how easy it was to cover up every blemish or wrinkled worry. Truly, camouflage is all it was. A costume. A part for Ash to play until she could return to Dracus and shed the new skin she wore.

"Is something wrong, Your Highness?" Tila asked, appearing in the mirror behind Ash. "You look... distant."

"Not at all," Ash assured her, whirling around. "And please, call me Ash."

Tila's eyes bulged. "I couldn't possibly."

"I won't tell if you won't," Ash countered, chuckling beneath her breath.

Once again, a knock on the door startled Ash so terribly she thought that for a moment that her soul had left her body. Tila rushed to see who it was, leaving her on her own for a few moments, during which time Ash's gaze returned to her reflection. It reminded her of the one she'd seen in her strange dream. A perfect version of herself. The version she was meant to be before the Realm fell apart, and she was separated from her family.

Tila returned quickly enough, bowing at the waist upon her arrival. Ash purposely froze, just to keep herself from cringing. "Your Highne—" the Elf caught herself. "I mean Ash. Prince Beck has come to retrieve you for dinner."

Ash's brows flicked upward, her lips parting slightly. She'd assumed after her heartwarming comment earlier, Mika would have been the one to escort her. Clearly, that wasn't the case. "Great." She forced a smile, straightening her spine. "I'm starved."

After being led down to the suite's lavish foyer, Ash found Beck waiting, whistling a pleasant tune. Her breath caught in her throat at the sight of him. Of course, she'd always known that Beck wasn't only a General, but a prince as well. But she'd never seen him dress like one. He wore a fitted tunic in a shade similar to Ash's dress. Shining golden lace adorned the hem, cuffs, and tight, high collar. With his back turned to her, Ash could see the Tree of Life, the Chamberlain family symbol, embroidered on the back.

"Sorry to keep you waiting," Ash said, clutching the skirts of her dress.

Beck's eyes bulged ever so slightly as he turned around, a slight blush beginning to dust his cheeks. "No worries," he assured her, holding out his hand. Ash took it in her own, a shiver sweeping down her spine. "I'm just happy you're feeling well enough to join us tonight."

"Those Healing Springs of yours really work," Ash replied, allowing him to lead her out of the suite and into the elegant corridor beyond. She was easily lost in her surroundings, in awe of everything she set her eyes upon. Every painting was bright and so realistic that Ash wondered for a moment what would happen if she attempted to leap into one. The statues they passed were carved so intricately that they appeared real. The rug lining the corridor was woven with so much care that she felt guilty walking upon it.

"Feel free to use those Springs as much as you like while you're here," Beck told her, guiding her around a corner. "And after, of course. I'm sure my family wouldn't mind seeing you more often."

Nodding, Ash's stomach fluttered with both nerves and something like excitement at the thought. "Once things calm down, I look forward to spending time here."

"I'd like that," Beck admitted, his lips spreading into a crooked smile. "We might finally get a chance to duel."

Ash snorted. "I wouldn't want to hurt you."

"Oh please," he waved her off with his free hand. "That's what the Healing Springs are for."

When Mika had informed Ash about dinner that night, she'd failed to mention that it wasn't just the Chamberlain family she would be dining with, but the entire Elven Council as well.

The second Ash walked into the royal dining room, she wanted to turn on her heels and vacate the premises. Perhaps, if she were to make it past the golden gates without being stopped by guards, she could bribe a tradesman in the Lakelands to take her to Mayfire. From there, she could find a way to buy a horse and ride for six more days through Pandora territory until she made it to Witherow, a village she knew she could trust. They would help her get word to the Allies in Dracus and—

The sound of chairs sliding against marble pulled Ash from her thoughts. Every soul sitting around the long, extravagant table had risen to their feet, bowing their heads.

"Your Highness," they all muttered in unison.

Ash felt her cheeks flame with a furious blush. "You can all sit," she said, hoping her voice didn't waver. They all did as she requested, lowering back into their seats gracefully while Beck led her to one of the two remaining unclaimed chairs, which happened to be right next to one another. As luck would have it, Ash was given the chair beside a small, adorable Princess with pale curls and bright, curious golden eyes. Beck, on the other hand, wound up at the very end of the table, next to his father.

Across from Ash sat Princess Mika, who was grinning from ear to ear. "You look stunning. Tila did such a wonderful job. I knew she would. That's why I picked her."

"She was very kind," Ash replied as a waiter set a glass of champagne on the table in front of her. She wanted to reach for it and chug the contents, but knew she'd better wait.

"It seems that she forgot a crown," Esmeralda mentioned, swirling her glass of white wine. "That simply won't do."

Ash's heart sank at the sound of her words. "It's alright."

"Nonsense," one of the council members said, a tall, thin woman dressed in a gown that seemed to be made entirely with spring leaves. "You should wear a crown whenever you go out in public. And your designers across Idona should remember that."

That glass of champagne was starting to look even better. Ash watched all the bubbles rising, her mouth watering.

"You can have mine," the tiny Princess said beside her.

Shaking her head, Ash offered her the best smile she could summon. "Thank you for the offer, but that belongs to you. It looks so pretty that I couldn't possibly take it off your head."

Just when Ash had thought her big eyes couldn't brighten anymore, they did.

"Trinity, you can't just give all of your things away," Mika reminded her younger sister. "Even to the High Queen."

Trinity scowled, crossing her little arms. Ash fought not to laugh at the sight. "They're my things to give away."

Across the table from Beck, Esmeralda started to rub her temples. "We've been over this, Trinity. Last time we let you play with all the other children, you gave all the jewelry you were wearing, some of which being family heirlooms, to a four-year-old."

"We had to send Aveo to search for her," Thaddeus added.

"He quickly found out that the four-year-old was smart enough to hand everything over to her parents," Beck said, continuing with the story. "And they used everything to buy a nice plot of land for themselves, complete with a house and all. Aveo, being the softy he is, chose to leave them be and hunt down who they sold the jewels to. He wound up getting everything back, and the buyer didn't dare complain about it, especially since he threatened to drag the man in front of my parents and have him thrown in Namhain for willingly buying things he knew belonged to the royal family."

Intrigued, Ash leaned forward, yearning to hear more.

"I wound up paying these people a visit myself," Mika started, sipping her champagne, which gave Ash permission to do the same. "Words couldn't describe the look on their faces when they opened the door to find me standing there, on their porch. I asked Red to paint a picture of it, just so I could frame it, but he declined, and Aveo scowled at me for even suggesting it. But, that's not what matters," she paused to take another sip. "The only reason I went there was because Trinity missed her little friend. Clearly, her parents were too afraid to take her to that park after what they'd done. So, my mission was to clear the air. I invited them all to dinner, here at this very table. They told us their story, and we listened. And at the end, we all let bygones be bygones. We hired a few men to help them start a farm, and a few contractors to fix their house up. They're flourishing now, and Trinity is forbidden from wearing jewelry outside of the castle. Everyone won in the end."

The story had come to an end and Ash's heart had melted entirely. She wound up turning toward Trinity, who cowered slightly beneath her gaze. "You changed that little girl's life, and probably set her family up for generations. You're a hero."

The Princess perked, her smile returning quickly. "Like you?"

"I'm not a hero," Ash told her. "Not yet." How could she be, with Aries' and Archibald's blood on her hands? Soon, she'd have to kill Xavier too. As Evil as he may be, to her, it would still be another life stolen. Her throat thickened at the thought.

The first course was served, complete with seasoned, cooked shrimp positioned along the rim of a glass filled with cocktail sauce. Having never tasted shrimp before, Ash was a bit nervous to try it. She didn't want to offend the Elves, or their chefs. So, she took her first bite. To her surprise, flavor erupted upon her tongue. She loved it but paced herself. There was no way of knowing how many courses she would have to sit through.

The second course arrived less than thirty minutes later. A pot roast, with a side of mashed potatoes and asparagus sprinkled with salt and pepper, along with a goblet of wine. Ash ate slowly once again, gently cutting her meat and asparagus, plopping small bites into her mouth.

The third and final course came soon after. Desert. Apple pie. Ash beamed at the sight of the slice the waiter set in front of her, with a side of vanilla ice cream. "My favorite," she said with a grin, reaching for her fork.

"Cooper might have drunkenly mentioned that when he was here," Beck admitted, taking his first bite. "They paid a visit to my pub, after your coronation. I regularly serve desserts, so I gave them the pie I had on hand. He was ecstatic, and said something like you know, Ash loves apple pie. She'd have it for breakfast, lunch, and dinner."

Ash chuckled, dipping a piece into her ice cream. "What can I say? He knows me well."

"How well?" Mika inquired. "Are you two…"

Suddenly, Ash lost her appetite. "Absolutely not," she insisted, knowing all the eyes of the council were upon her. "He's my twin. Well, obviously not biologically. That's just what they called us because we were born so close together."

"They?" Thaddeus inquired, lifting a single brow.

Nodding, Ash said, "My adoptive mother and the McBrides."

"I see," the king responded, returning his attention to his drink.

"So, are you seeing anyone?" Mika pressed onward, resting her elbow on the table, setting her chin in her palm.

"I don't exactly have the time for that," Ash told her, pushing pie around her plate. She'd hoped to avoid such questions, but quickly remembered her plan to lure Esmeralda into a trap. "But this chaos won't last forever, and I have been starting to think about the future."

As expected, Esmeralda perked, her eyes shining mischievously. "I know every eligible bachelor in the Realm. Feel free to send me on the hunt. Unless you'd prefer for me to hunt for a bachelorette."

Ash reached for her goblet of wine, in desperate need of at least an ounce of liquid courage.

"Esmeralda," the woman in the green, leafy dress chastised. "You can't just question her sexuality at the dinner table."

The Queen shrugged in response. "Calm down, Camella. It's important that Ash knows she can be open and honest here."

"It isn't our business," another council member, a man by the name of Tristane, said. After that comment, the entire council started to council. Thaddeus remained silent, watching all the drama unfold from the head of the table. Beck beckoned a waiter over and asked for another drink. Mika inspected her fingernails. Ash wished she could slip into the shadows.

"I thought she was going to marry Beck," Trinity blurted, causing the entire room to fall silent at once.

Stunned, all Ash could do was stare at the young Princess.

"That's why she's here, right?" Trinity inquired.

"No, it's not," Mika spat. "She's here for other adult reasons. Perhaps it's your bedtime."

"It's hardly seven thirty," Trinity complained.

Before the sisters could argue any further, the castle started to shake around them. Ash gripped the table with one hand for support, holding on to her goblet with all her strength. Only two things could make such a ruckus—an earthquake, or a dragon. Ash was hoping for the latter.

The trembling faded away, and shortly after an Elven guard hurried into the dining hall. "Your Majesties," he started, bowing at the waist. "I apologize for the intrusion, but we have visitors."

"Tell Alistair he's a tad bit late for dinner," Esmeralda laughed. "But we'll make him a plate."

"It isn't Alistair Ward, my queen. It's Morghan Henning, and a young woman," the guard explained.

Ash's brow furrowed with confusion. "A young woman?"

Not a second later, Morghan walked into the dining room with none other than Lilly McBride at his heels. His gold locks were messy, blown back from the flight he'd clearly just endured. His caramel eyes were wide, dancing about the room. Lilly did the same, though she seemed far less unraveled. She smiled at everyone looking her way, offering them a wave.

The Wolf started toward Esmeralda and Thaddeus, snatching an untouched drink in front of their adviser, Griffon. He chugged the contents of the glass on his way to the end of the long table, all while Ash watched him with wide eyes.

"I was sent by Lady Evanora Ivanenko," Morghan started, completely out of breath. "To warn you about a potential Witch uprising, and to keep Ash company."

Gasp sounded around the table, flooding Ash's ears. But she hadn't gasped at all. She couldn't even bring herself to breathe. As if she could sense it, Lilly made her way around the table, completely ignoring the fact that she'd just walked straight into the lion's den. Ash shot to her feet to greet her, pulling her into the tightest hug she'd ever given, breathing her scent, losing herself within it.

"I can't believe Quinn let you come here," Ash whispered in her ear, finally releasing Lilly from her vice like grip. "With Morghan, nonetheless."

"Quinn?" Mika chirped.

"My brother," Lilly told her. "And, trust me, here is far better than there right now."

39

Once Morghan shared everything he needed to with the Elven King, Queen, and their Council, both he and Lilly were given plates of food. Chairs were brought forward so they had a place to sit. Ash watched them both dig in as if they hadn't eaten for days, though Lilly was far more graceful than the Wolf at her side. Mika, on the other hand, was having a difficult time hiding her disgust.

"The flight took five hours," Morghan explained once he'd finished. "We would have used the portal rooms, but we couldn't risk opening them again. I'm sure you understand why. Richard knows the codes to everything. Your portals, Loren's portals, Xavier's portals. He's a spider web of intel."

Lilly remained silent, smiling at young Trinity from across the table. The Princess grinned right back, which didn't surprise Ash at all. Lilly had always had a way with children.

"We could all use an update on what, exactly, is going on in Dracus," Beck informed the Wolf. "Craven has sent me a few messages, but not nearly enough. We're essentially blind over here."

Nodding, Morghan pulled in an audible breath. "Well, most of the council is still in the Infirmary. At least they were when Lilly and I left. I imagine they've all been released by now. Well, everyone but Loren."

Ash held her breath, warding off unwelcome memories of what had happened to the king.

"Loren tried to stop Richard from harming Ash, and lost his hand in the process," Morghan explained solemnly. "They weren't able to find it, and now suspect that the Air Clan Leader, Ariel Manchester, was able to take it and use it to get into his personal safe. We aren't sure what was taken yet. No one knows what was inside but Loren himself, and I'm assuming Richard."

Genuine sorrow flooded Esmeralda's features. "He lost his hand?"

"Yes," Morghan told her.

"Wouldn't he have kept the Emblems in his safe?" Griffon asked Esmeralda.

Ash watched both the queen and king pale. "I believe he did mention doing so," she replied in a horrified whisper, turning her attention back to Morghan. "You need to contact whoever is in charge of that investigation and have them check his safe for three identical Emblems. They look like large, golden coins."

Beck fished through his tunic, pulling out a strap of leather holding what Esmeralda had just described. "This is what they look like," he explained.

"What is it?" Ash asked, her stomach twisting with unease.

"What remains of the sixth Sectra," Thaddeus explained, his expression grim. "Three parts were given to each Kingdom. There are twelve altogether. When put together like a roll of coins, they mold into Amoria's Staff."

Ash's breath hitched. "I thought that was destroyed right along with the Realm."

"The rest of the Galaxy thinks the same. Only Aiden's council learned the truth. The Sectra couldn't be destroyed. It could only be broken down and molded into the Emblems," Esmeralda explained, fiddling with her napkin nervously. "They've been handed down to council members since. Gideon's set was stolen by Xavier during the Idonian Kingdom's fall. Now Loren's has likely been taken. If they manage to get their hands on Cleo's or mine…" she trailed, shaking her head as if to will away the thoughts.

Thaddeus nodded, his expression grim. "Who's handling this investigation? Richard was Loren's second. Who are we supposed to contact during his recovery?"

"Craven is handling the investigation, and Penelope is currently running Dracus in Loren's stead with Lady Evanora's help," Morghan explained, reaching for his goblet and taking a long sip. "In other words, everyone is in over their heads. If Lady Evanora hadn't shown up this morning and started ordering everyone around, we'd all be running around like chickens with our heads cut off. Technically, we're still running around like loose chickens, but our heads are attached."

"We had no idea that Evanora was in Idona," Esmeralda admitted, shifting in her seat. "We didn't find out until we saw the papers about Sam Waters. I take that it was true, then. The Rebels really do still exist, even after all that bloodshed."

Morghan and Ash nodded in unison. She pursed her lips, wishing someone would notice how low on wine her own goblet had become.

"Malachai destroyed a fraction of the Rebels that had gone rogue," Morghan said, pushing what remained of his food around his plate. "He had no idea that there was anyone left, let alone fifteen thousand people. He was just as shocked as everyone else was when Sam declared himself the Rebel General in the Infirmary."

Thaddeus tapped his fingers along the table's surface, his brow wrinkling with thought. "Will Loren be striking an alliance with them?" he asked in a calm, cool tone.

Ash sucked in a breath, her growing nerves causing her heart rate to spike. "He never shared his thoughts regarding the matter before the... incident. At our last council meeting, he said that he was waiting for Lady Evanora. I believe that he planned to speak with her before he made any decisions. Now, I'm not sure what's going to happen."

"We'll discuss it at the Idonian Council meeting at the end of the week," Esmeralda declared, waving a waiter forward to fill her glass. "Speaking of Malachai, Ash I have to say, as much as we despise that man, what you did was... well... genius, to say the least.

You've managed to trap one of Idona's biggest threats in a way that would have never crossed any of our minds. I have to ask. What do you plan to do with him now that he has no choice but to follow you for the rest of his days?"

The butler had taken notice of Ash's empty glass, and she waited for him to finish filling it so that she could take a sip before she answered that complicated question. "I plan to use him as a way to lure the Pandora away from Xavier. They'll follow him, and because of that, Xavier will lose more than half of his army."

Across the table, Mika spit out her drink, spraying it all over Morghan and Lilly. "Sorry," she said, reaching for a napkin to wipe off the Wolf's face. "It's just... you want the Pandora to fight *for* us? I thought the ultimate goal was to drive the species into extinction. I mean, they're savages."

"They *act* like savages," Beck said, taking Ash by surprise. "They're just people following orders. If Ash's right, and it's possible to use their originator and creator as a way to change who gives them those orders... war won."

"I'm not sure that it would be *that* simple," Thaddeus said, ruining the mood. "You'd have to worry about what to do with the Pandora after the fact. Not to mention, the Idonian people won't take too kindly to them roaming around free after terrorizing the Realm for as long as they have. The war might very well continue. The people could revolt. If you go through with this, you'd have to be prepared for something like that."

Most things that Ash had heard about Thaddeus were bad, but now that she'd met him, and was sharing a meal with him, there was no denying that he was a wise king. She'd expected for him to immediately object to her idea. She thought that most people would, which is why she was so hesitant when it came to even telling Alistair about it. Now, she was amazed by how the council appeared deep in thought, some of them smiling at the idea. Esmeralda seemed pleased. Thaddeus and Beck began to bounce a few ideas off one another, while Morghan winked at Ash from across the table.

Nice work, Princess, he mouthed.

The meal continued. Everyone worked to finish their dessert while they conversed about the Pandora, and what it would be like if Ash's idea actually worked. How quickly would all the attacks on the villages stop? Would the last Red Winter end early?

Before long, the conversation veered back to the Emblems, and Amoria altogether. Morghan had messaged Marcus, who had confirmed that Loren's set was missing. They still weren't sure if anything else was taken, and Malachai couldn't think of anything else Xavier would have wanted. What he *could* tell everyone was that the Emblem collection was supposed to take place *after* Idona's defeat, and that it was his sister Soroya that was in charge of that phase, therefore he knew little about what her plans were.

"Well, they won't be getting any more of them," Esmeralda said confidently after Morghan read Marcus's last message. "They must have plans to invade the other Realms then, seeking complete control. But why? What's the sense in causing so much pain and destruction throughout Si Realtra? Xavier won the High Throne. That should have been the end of it. Had he ordered his beasts to stand down and chosen to rule a normal Kingdom instead of focusing on all the other places in Idona that wanted nothing to do with him, we could have reached some sort of peace years ago. Instead, he wants to continue. What, will he never stop?"

Not until Amoria is restored, Ash thought, chewing on her inner cheek. She recalled everything that Jay had said to her, about who Xavier *really* was. It was hard to think of him as the grandson of the last Amorian King, knowing that meant that Malachai was a direct descendant of such Evil as well. Ash's blood chilled at the thought. She *wanted* to tell the Chamberlains and the rest of the Idonian Council the truth about what was really waiting for them on the other side of the Galactic Gates, but she couldn't bring herself to squash the tiny embers of hope in their eyes.

"He will when I kill him," Ash told the queen.

40

After his altercation with Cooper, Malachai had chosen to keep his distance from the Allies. He'd spent the rest of the day reading and revising his will before heading to the Infirmary the next morning to check on his patients. Once he arrived, he kept his head down and got to work, avoiding eye contact with every passing nurse and Healer. The last thing that Malachai wanted to do was converse with anyone that he didn't have to, which was fine by most people he encountered. No one wanted to talk to him anyway.

The last few days, Malachai had built a good reputation in the Infirmary. The patients were kind after hearing about all he had done to save so many others since arriving in Dracus. No one refused his service, which lifted his mood enough for him to smile halfway through his first shift.

"You should take a break," Ebony suggested while Malachai poured himself a cup of steaming, black coffee inside the Healers quarters. "You've been working since dawn."

"They're short-handed up in the maternity ward," Malachai replied as he took his first sip, burning his tongue in the process. "All the chaos sent a surplus of mothers into stress-induced early labor."

"You're *delivering babies?*" Ebony gawked.

Malachai snorted. "No. All I'm doing is helping with the newborns once they arrive. I don't mind. It's nice spending time with people who don't speak. I could deliver babies, though, if you needed me to. I've delivered plenty in the past. Once, I encountered a Witch who was traveling across the Regal Mountains in hopes to get home before her daughter decided to make an arrival. She was still days away from her destination when I found her laboring in a cave. Long story short, I helped her deliver the baby, and then remained with her throughout the rest of her journey. I stayed in her village for a while afterward, to make sure the baby was fairing alright."

"Hmm," Ebony huffed, eyeing him mischievously. "You are one of the most complex individuals I have ever come across."

"What can I say? I like to keep everyone on their toes," the prince drawled.

Not a moment later, Anastasia came barging into the room, tossing the doors aside so hard that they slammed into the walls, leaving dents. Malachai froze as he took in her appearance. Her white hair braid was askew, her cheeks red from the cold. Her breathing was ragged, as if she'd just run at Immortal speed for hours. Altogether, she looked like she'd just walked out of battle.

Malachai set his coffee aside, knowing full well that he wouldn't get a chance to finish it. "What is it?" he asked, looking her up and down once more.

"You need to get back to the castle," she said between deep breaths. "I heard screaming, so I went next door to Marcus's apartment. There's something wrong with his head."

Malachai's heart sank, fear beginning to stroke his spine. He didn't ask any more questions and ran out of the room, barreling through the Infirmary until he made it outside, where he transitioned into a hawk and flew as fast as he could toward the castle. The people crawling the streets stopped dead in their tracks, staring up at him with wide, fearful eyes. He tried his best to ignore them and focused on the wind rushing through his feathers instead.

As Malachai flew, a memory he'd buried long ago fluttered before his eyes. The day his mother told him that she was having another baby. He was fifteen at the time and had thought he'd never have the opportunity to call anyone brother or sister, but then Marcus came along. Pink, pudgy, and screaming at the top of his lungs. The moment he'd set his eyes upon him, Malachai had realized that he'd never loved someone so much in all his life. His heart still had yet to repair after leaving him behind, and he doubted it ever would, but the very idea that he was in enough pain to scream loud enough to wake his neighbors, Malachai couldn't stand it. His stomach was roiling with nausea as he landed on the castle's front steps and transitioned back into his Mortal form.

The guards didn't try to stop him as he made his way into the castle and rushed up to the third floor. There were guards everywhere, equally alarmed as the prince. They could all hear the screaming, yet no one knew what to do.

"We've already called for help," one of them said as Malachai passed.

"I am the help," he replied, arriving in front of Marcus's door.

"Prince Vincent and Sam Waters are already inside with Lucinda," the guard informed him as he opened the door. "Just... do whatever it is that you do."

Nodding, Malachai entered the suite and followed the screams until they became so loud that he could hardly stand the sound of them for another second. He found Marcus, surrounded by Vincent, Sam, and Lucinda in the kitchen. His brother had collapsed on the floor and was gripping his head, screaming louder than when he had the day he was born.

"Hey," Malachai said softly, sliding onto his knees beside the Mentor, placing his hands on his shoulders. "You're fine," he assured him, focusing on his abilities, listening to whatever it was that Marcus's body had to tell him. Silence fell as Malachai sorted through his thoughts. Once he realized what the problem was, he withdrew his hands, fighting to hide his surprise. "He's spelled," he said to Lucinda.

"By whom?" she asked, running her hands over Marcus's sweaty, chocolate locks.

Malachai had a feeling that he knew exactly who had placed a spell on Marcus, and what type, but he wouldn't share that information with Lucinda. Or anyone for that matter. Meera's secrets were Meera's secrets.

"I'm not sure, but it's a memory blocker," Malachai informed her. "It's still in place, but it's fragile."

Lucinda's eyes narrowed accusingly. "Oh."

"Someone put a spell on me?" Marcus managed to say.

Vincent hushed him, patting his knee. "Don't worry about that. The pain's gone, isn't it?"

Marcus nodded, however, his teeth were still chattering, and he was shivering from head to toe.

"Sam, go start a hot shower," Malachai directed. "Vincent, find him a change of clothes."

Both men nodded and hurried off to do what they were asked. Malachai turned his attention back to Marcus and placed a hand on his shoulder. "We'll get to the bottom of things," he assured him. "For now, all you need to worry about is getting comfortable. Let someone else do the cooking for once."

Lucinda snorted. "As if *that* would ever happen."

"He's under too much stress, and it's triggering the spell, attempting to break it. Just like the mothers I saw this morning, giving birth to early babies. Everyone's under too much pressure. We all need to breathe, before we snap, like Cooper yesterday," Malachai explained. "We don't need this spell breaking on its own, inflicting more harm than good. We need to figure out exactly what spell it is and undo it using Magic. Or we can leave it where it is and attempt to reduce his stress levels. Clearly, he's been doing just fine with it in place."

Marcus shook his head, opening his eyes for the first time since Malachai had arrived. "I want it gone."

"Are you sure?" Malachai asked. "You've been doing just fine—"

"I don't want anything altering my memories," Marcus snapped as he struggled to sit up. "I don't care if it was placed there with good intentions. My pain is *mine*, and I'll experience it, just like everything else."

Malachai's chest tightened. "Why would you think that it's blocking painful memories?"

"Consider it a hunch," Marcus retorted. "It must be if I can't remember my parents, or anything up until the age of ten."

A shower turned on in the distance. Soon after, Sam appeared in the kitchen, wiping his damp hands on his pants. "It took me a second to figure it out, but the shower is on."

"Come on, Marcus," Lucinda directed, helping him to his feet. "Let's get you cleaned up and in bed. When you wake up, you can supervise me cooking your lunch."

Malachai watched them walk away, pushing himself to his feet as well. He watched Sam walk over to the cupboard and grab two glasses. "Thirsty?" he asked, glancing over his shoulder.

"Sure," the prince replied, his stomach churning after all that had occurred.

"Don't worry so much," Sam directed, filling both glasses with water. "He's been through worse, just like the rest of us. A headache won't disable him for good. Besides, we have some badass blood rushing through our veins. It takes a lot more to bring down a Trevayne." He turned around, holding the glasses of water in his hands, his lips spreading into a knowing smirk.

Unsure of what to say, all Malachai could do was stare at the man.

"Oh, don't look at me like that. You don't think I didn't notice the family resemblance?" Sam inquired, setting one glass down on the island while saving one for himself. "Not *everyone* can be this handsome."

Malachai slipped his hands into his pockets and scowled. "Tell me that you weren't here to tell him."

Shaking his head, Sam said, "Nope. Vincent suggested that I come to ask him for advice. He's a Mentor, after all."

"What would you need a Mentor for?" the prince asked, lifting a brow.

"Well, I'm a Warlock, and Ash is going to awaken my gene... when she gets a chance," Sam explained. "That way, I can be the most powerful General in this Realm and lead the Rebels to success."

Malachai frowned, eyeing his cousin quizzically. "What makes you think that you're a Warlock?"

"Well, Constance is a Witch," Sam said. "And Warlocks are rare, but aren't as uncommon as people think. Some get lucky, and their gene activates on its own at some point during adolescence. But for those whose genes *don't* activate, all they need is a little help from a Sectra."

Malachai hummed, his lips pressed together. "Let me guess, you learned that from reading Pat's writings?"

Sam's lips stretched into a grin. "How did you guess?"

MALACHAI CHOSE TO REMAIN IN MARCUS'S APARTMENT, JUST TO ensure that he was alright. Hours passed, and eventually it was time to serve lunch. Lucinda handled everything while everyone else settled into chairs around the dining table. Sam and Marcus got to talking about his possible transition, but eventually, the conversation veered toward Constance.

Guilt gripped Malachai each time he heard her name. All he could think was about the last time he'd seen her, the moment he'd left Solaris. She'd been in the room as his father berated him over and over again before ultimately tossing him out, and she'd dared to speak up about it. She was a strong, intelligent woman, and she was trapped in a city where no one truly cared about her well-being.

Malachai had wanted to save her while he was in Solaris, but he knew that it wasn't possible at that time. If anything, Constance would need to save herself, and he'd be right there waiting for her when she figured out how.

"I'll get Constance back," Malachai blurted, his fingers curling into white-knuckled fists. "I hate that she's there just as much as you do."

Sam's features crumbled as if he'd been holding in every ounce of his sadness and devastation for years. Malachai knew that look. Sam was about to fall apart, no matter how hard he tried to fight it.

Unsure of what else to do, the prince stood from his chair and moved closer to him, placing a hand on his trembling shoulder.

"There is no hope for my sister," Malachai revealed. "But there *is* hope for Constance. Lincoln too. I promise you that I will fix this, and that your family will be together again. I will fix what I broke. You don't have to—"

"It's not just *your* responsibility," Sam interrupted, his voice wavering. "And it's not just *my* family. It's yours, too."

Vincent's breath audibly caught in his throat. "Wait, what?"

"Our mothers were sisters," Malachai revealed, dropping his gaze to the table. "Soroya and Celine Trevayne."

The color quickly drained from Lucinda's face. "I knew you were Soroya's son, but I didn't know—" she caught herself, pausing as if to rethink her next words. "I thought Celine had made it out of Idona before the Gates shut."

"No," Sam informed her. "She wound up in Crane, married my father, had my sister and I, and died when she was pregnant with our younger sister."

Malachai's hand fell off Sam's shoulder. He hadn't known that Celine was pregnant. He hadn't noticed. Constance hadn't mentioned, when she'd told him, that Celine was far enough along to know the gender. Now, the blood on his hands felt even thicker.

"I'm so sorry," Vincent said softly.

"It's my fault," Malachai admitted, his shoulders slumping. "I knew Celine and Pat were both in Crane, and I kept it from my father. I don't know how he discovered the truth, but he did. And my punishment was severe. He made me..." he trailed, tears beginning to well in his eyes. "What I said to Cooper was true. He used his power to... take over my body. I was still there consciously, but I had no control over what I did. He made me kill them both."

Lucinda shrunk further into her chair, holding a hand to her gaping mouth. Sam sat, shaking like a leaf. Vincent stared at the prince with bulging sage eyes.

"I didn't know that she was pregnant, though. Not until Constance told me," Malachai continued, finally bringing himself to meet Sam's gaze. "I'll never forgive myself."

A long silence ensued. The most insufferable kind, where everyone's hearts were breaking so badly that they couldn't bear to speak a word. Malachai returned to his seat, debating whether or not he should leave.

"Did you know that Ash was there?" Vincent asked abruptly.

Malachai froze at the sound of the question. "Yes."

Vincent's sage eyes narrowed accusingly. "For how long?"

"The entire time. I found out the day after she arrived."

"You left her alone," Sam concluded. "You could have taken her to your father at any point. Why didn't you?"

Shrugging, Malachai said, "I made a promise to Pat."

"I see," Lucinda whispered.

"Wait," Vincent blurted, shooting to his feet. "I know that you said yesterday that Pat played a large part in the creation of the Pandora, but how exactly did he wind up in Xavier's grasp?"

Leaning back in his chair, Malachai crossed his arms. "He was an Amorian descendant, just like me. We worked together for years, all day every day." He hoped that his voice didn't betray his evolving misery at the thought of the Archer. "He was my friend."

Vincent shook his head, as if trying to sort through his thoughts. "Pat was a teleporter. He lived in Crane." Backing away from the table, the prince began to pace back and forth. "You knew what your father's plans were, and you also knew where Pat had run off to."

Malachai's heart slowed to a stop. Vincent was putting all the pieces together right before his eyes, and he had no way of stopping it.

"Did you—" Vincent pursed his lips, meeting Malachai's gaze. "Did you warn Pat about the Dark Army invading the Idonian Kingdom?"

There was no sense in lying, so Malachai nodded, his expression grim.

"Holy shit," Lucinda breathed. "Pat was Meera's source."

"What do you mean?" Sam asked, tilting his head curiously.

All eyes turned toward Malachai in that moment, as if they were expecting *him* to explain. He sighed, straightening his spine. "It wasn't just Pat. I betrayed my father to help her prepare and defend her Kingdom, because I never wanted it to be taken away from the VanCamp's. I've never understood my father's goals, or the steps he's taken to reach them, but I've had no choice but to play along. Now, I'm playing my own game, and because of that, he'll never obtain what he really wants."

"What does he really want?" Lucinda whispered.

"Amoria."

Those sitting around the table fell silent, watching each other warily. Malachai waited for the backlash he knew was coming. *No one* spoke about Amoria. The Realm was dead, and that was that, but, Xavier and his ancestors had never believed that to be true. The descendants following him hoped and prayed that he was right. One way or another, whether through peace or war, they would go home.

"You're going to have to tell this to Marcus, and Penelope," Vincent divulged after a while. "If you're going to tell us any more, they should be here."

Nodding, Malachai sucked in a deep breath and said, "I'll tell you all anything that you want to know. Just promise that you won't try to kill me after."

Lucinda chuckled, her amber eyes alight with mischief. "If I wanted you dead, you would be."

41

Marcus sat at his dining room table, staring into nothing. The headache he'd just endured had drained every ounce of energy from his form, leaving him no more than a lifeless prop. He tried his best to appear present, but his mind was lost, drifting off to places that it shouldn't go.

Penelope arrived shortly after, though it was clear that she would rather be anywhere else. She sank into her seat, scowling at the drink they'd already set out before her. It was Malachai's idea. An attempt to make her feel welcome. *Comfortable.* As if that were possible after the way that he'd affected her life.

Once everyone had arrived, Malachai began to explain everything that Vincent had wanted him to. He described his lineage, and what it meant to the descendants supposedly scattered throughout the Realms.

On a normal day, Marcus's anxiety would have spiked, ruling over every breath and thought. After what he'd endured that morning, he could hardly manage to breathe, let alone react to every word the Pandora said.

"You say all this and maintain the idea that you care nothing about these Amorian descendants and what they want, yet you've dragged Ash into this mess," Penelope seethed. "Why involve her at all? Why suck her into whatever vortex you've created, *after* you attempted to end her life?"

"Out of all the people I've met, Ash's life was the *last* one I wanted to ruin. All I've done for the last eighteen years is try to protect her." Malachai's voice cracked around the last word. "I didn't know she'd become the Messenger, or an Immortal. I just knew she was somewhere safe, away from all these ridiculous politics. I thought we'd never meet. I should have just run the second my father tasked me to kill her. I was still stuck between my old life and the new one he forced me to create. I wasn't sure which way to turn, and I made the wrong choice. I tried to fix that by helping her fill the Scepter and setting her up for success. That's all I wanted to do. Keep a promise I made to an old friend. I didn't know that Cooper would wind up captured, and that she'd ask me to help. I didn't know Aveo would arrest me, and I'd become this *burden*."

Had Marcus known that it was possible for Malachai to react to his harsh words in such a way, he would have never said them. But a few things the prince had said struck a nerve. "You said you tried to protect her for *eighteen* years?" he asked, straightening his spine. "How?"

"That's what I came here to tell you all," Malachai told him.

The sound of the front door opening and closing startled Marcus. Naturally, he assumed that it was Lucinda and Sam returning with food. They'd been gone more than twenty minutes, after all. But it wasn't the pair. It was Penelope and Humphrey, of all people.

Malachai pulled in a shaky, audible breath at the sight of them. He hurried back to his seat, refusing to meet anyone's gaze. Marcus watched him wipe his eyes with his sleeve, his stomach twisting with regret.

"What's going on?" Penelope asked softly, staring at the prince.

Vincent crossed his arms, offering Marcus his best glare. "Care to explain that, Marcus?"

Swallowing hard, Marcus thought of what to say. "I upset him."

"Is that all?" Vincent snapped. "Marcus, you blamed him for events he had no control over. How the fuck is that fair?"

The sound of Lucinda and Sam entering in the process drew everyone's attention, and before long they were walking into the living room, unpacking the bags of food they'd retrieved, setting everything on the coffee table. "Sorry, guys, I didn't know you'd be here," the Sorceress said to Penelope and Humphrey.

"That's alright, Lucinda, we already ate," Penelope replied, her tone as sweet as pie. "Vincent summoned us both. Now we'd like to know why."

Vincent nodded, looking toward Malachai. "Care to tell us the story, now?"

All eyes turned to the prince, who cleared his throat in preparation to speak. "Five years after I forcefully became a Pandora, my father deemed the army ready to complete the next phase in his war. He and his council started to plan the attack on the Idonian Kingdom. I was given the privilege of attending the meetings, as the Dark Army's General. But, as I listened to what they planned to do, I started to panic.

"I knew that the most I could do was warn Queen Meera, so I sought out Pat McBride and asked for his help. At first, he didn't want to get involved. He'd deserted the Dark Army four years prior, and he'd started a family. Fuck, Quinn was the one to answer the door," Malachai explained, shaking his head in disbelief. "Pat was furious and sent him upstairs. We spoke in his foyer, and he agreed to teleport to Meera and tell her about my father's plans while I waited there at his estate."

Marcus stared at the prince; his eyes wider than they'd ever been before.

"He was gone for a long time. After a while, I was starting to think that something had happened to him. His family was starting to wake up, and Quinn came back downstairs. He asked me for breakfast. I started to panic, because I knew that at any second Pat's wife was going to come downstairs. But I heard a baby start to cry, Lincoln, I think. I knew she was occupied. So, I went into the kitchen and gave Quinn a glass of milk. That's when Pat finally teleported back."

Malachai started to shake, his face crumbling as he recited the memory. Lucinda was kind enough to pass him the rest of her wine, and he took it without question, taking a long sip.

"Pat told me something that I didn't know. He said that Meera was pregnant with twins, and due any day. He was adamant on finding a way to get the babies out of Solaris." Malachai met Vincent's pained gaze, the lump bobbing in his throat. "I'd heard of the teleportation hatches around the Realm. I knew that a newborn would be small enough to fit in one. The Magic involved might have been a risk, but it was worth it in our opinion. I wound up returning to the Regal Mountains, where I dug up all the information that I could find on them, but I couldn't find an exact list of the locations. So, I flew to the Safe Haven and stole them. Afterward, I gave them to Pat. I wound up spending another few hours waiting at his estate while he presented the idea to Meera. He came back at dawn, once again, while I was cooking eggs for his kid, and told me that she agreed."

The Realm started to spin as Marcus processed everything the Pandora had said. His throat became thick, preventing him from taking even, deep breaths. His heart was racing so terribly fast that he thought it might explode.

"Pat also told me that while he was there, she went into labor, and that she was likely giving birth in that very moment. I can't tell you how relieved I was. Meera would get two weeks with her babies before she'd have to send them away. Pat, of course, tried to convince her to do it sooner when he visited her a few days later, but she refused. I can't say I blame her, but it did make things difficult," Malachai informed them all. "We wanted to put people that we trusted at every hatch exit location. Meera insisted on her Black Knights."

Every word that came out of the prince's mouth was getting harder and harder for Marcus to hear. He closed his eyes, placing his head in his hands.

"Pat told her that wasn't a good idea, but she insisted. We all know what happened to those Knights that night. I tried to prevent it, but my father's scouts across the Realm beat my own men to every location," Malachai grunted frustratedly, finishing off the Sorceress's wine. "Anyway, Pat chose to leave the exit location in the center of the Realm off the list. He didn't want to give Crane's location away and swore that he'd check the location himself the night the Kingdom fell. Neither one of us expected one of the babies would wind up there."

"That's why I saw you near that cavern," Lucinda whispered with bulging amber eyes. "You were checking, to make sure we'd gotten them out."

Nodding, Malachai said, "I was. Unfortunately, I was followed."

Marcus's breath caught in his throat, memories flashing before his eyes of how painful that night had been. He could still feel all the claws dragging through his flesh, shredding him into ribbons. He could still smell the scent of his own blood emptying from his body, staining the snow around him. Shivering, Marcus fought to bury the memories once again, but failed. He shook, his fingers curling into fists, nails biting into the flesh of his palms.

"You knew where Ash was," Vincent presumed, the lump in his throat bobbing up and down. "The entire time."

"Yes, I did," Malachai confirmed. "But I made a promise to protect her from my father. So, I never told a soul."

Penelope scoffed, crossing her arms. "You could have mentioned where she was when you told me not to stop looking for her."

"Would you kill me if I said that I thought she was better off where she was?" Malachai asked. "I think that's what stopped me from telling you the truth. I wasn't sure whether she should be found at all, but I did want you to know that she was alive."

The Princess's features softened, her shoulders slumping. "I appreciate that."

"Anytime," he replied.

"So, you and Pat were Meera's source?" Marcus asked, staring at the Pandora disbelievingly.

Malachai gave him a curt nod. "Well, more or so Pat. I just provided him with some information."

"Wow," Humphrey said from where he stood, leaning against

the glass wall across the room from where Marcus sat on the couch. "What a plot twist."

"You can say that again," Sam finally chimed in. "Who knew Pat had so many skeletons in the closet?"

Lucinda snorted in response. "You have *much* to learn, my friend."

42

Two days had passed since Ash's stressful dinner with the Elves. During that time, they'd more or less left her to her own devices, which she was glad for. It gave her much needed time alone, to digress and ponder all that had occurred during the last week. Aries' demise. Her strange dream encounter with Pat McBride's younger brother.

Oddly enough, the Wolf had taken Lilly on as somewhat of an apprentice. At first, Ash had been surprised, but now that she'd witnessed them working together, she'd come to the conclusion that they were a perfect fit. Morghan had told Ash about all of his plans for her over coffee the morning after he'd arrived. Most importantly, he wanted Lilly to work on strengthening her telepathic ability.

During meals, Morghan would tell them both everything he knew about the Immortal communities in Idona, which was where Lilly's knowledge was lacking. As well as Ash's. She hadn't had much time to learn anything other than different ways to kill since she'd first arrived in Dracus, and listening to the Wolf talk turned out to be a welcome distraction from her tortuous thoughts.

At night, while Ash slept, she was tortured by nightmares. She'd wake repeatedly, covered in a cold sweat, shaking like a leaf. Every time she fell back to sleep, they'd begin again, like a vicious cycle. Various images would flash before her eyes, forcing her to return to moments in her life when she'd been most afraid. Once again, she was running from Pandora in Crane, fighting off a transition before vomiting blood on the East Cliff and passing out. Only in her nightmares, the Pandora caught up to her, pushing her off the cliff, sending her falling to her premature death.

If only that was the scariest of all the dreams.

Ash dreamed of Xavier, looming over her with a translucent complexion, entirely black eyes, and glowing orange veins. Black horns started to protrude from his skull, swirling like a ram's. He was turning into something monstrous. Something that should only exist in the Underworld.

A dagger made of dark matter began to materialize in his hand, shining like obsidian glass. Ash looked down to the weapons in her own grips. An enchanted dagger, and the Sovereign's Scepter. Her gaze shifted rapidly between the two, unsure of which one to use.

Xavier threw his dagger. It was headed straight for her. Ash needed to choose, but she couldn't form a single thought. She lifted the Scepter. Moonlight erupted around the room, but she was too late. The dagger was mere inches from her heart.

Closing her eyes, Ash prepared for impact, but it never came. Her eyes flung open, only to find a figure standing before her with massive black wings.

Aries.

"No!" Ash roared, pushing around him, thrusting her own dagger straight for Xavier's heart as the Fae dropped to his knees beside her. "Not again," she pleaded, staring down at the weapon protruding from his chest. "Not again!"

A pair of hands fell on Ash's shoulders, shaking her. She gasped, air filling her lungs to full capacity, thrusting her back into reality. Her eyes opened, only to find that sunlight had flooded her room. Dawn had come and gone.

Morghan was hovering over her, concern twisting his features.

"I had a nightmare," Ash admitted.

"No kidding," he replied warily. "I'm surprised guards aren't swarming this suite right now, considering how loudly you were screaming."

Gulping, Ash moved to sit up, a headache beginning to throb at her temples. "Sorry," she uttered, swinging her legs over the side of the bed. "It's just... ever since that day…"

"I've been there," Morghan admitted in a whisper, lowering to sit at her side. "After Death Valley, I saw it all happen over and over again, every night for years. I still get nightmares about it sometimes. But you know what helped me move forward?"

"What?" Ash asked, hoping she might be able to eventually as well.

"Confronting Malachai," Morghan said, taking her aback with surprise. "I encountered him in the city of Aren a few years back. The city is crawling with Pandora and Witches, but I was welcome there. I think *mostly* because Xavier hoped to recruit me."

Ash shivered at the sound of the king's name, knots beginning to form in her gut. "Why would he do that, when he had your entire species destroyed?"

"He knew the older Werewolves would never follow him. My grandfather moved them all from Amoria to Idona for a reason. Technically, Malachai wasn't supposed to leave me alive. But, since he had, and I was so young at the time, Xavier had hope that I'd join him. Fuck that," Morghan laughed, shaking his head. "Anyway, I was in Aren, mainly to stock up on supplies. I decided to stop at a tavern for a glass of ale, and perhaps to find a lady to spend the night with."

"Ew," Ash gagged.

Morghan shot her a dirty look. "Hey, when you roam around alone for decades like I do, occasional company isn't so bad. I'm a person. People have needs."

"Yeah, yeah." She waved him off. "Carry on."

"Alright," he said with a sigh. "I walked into this tavern—"

Ash snorted. "That sounds like the start of a joke. *A Wolf walks into a tavern.*"

"Can you let me tell the damn story?" Morghan grumbled. Ash nodded, pursing her lips, fighting against her growing smile. "Anyway, I walk into this tavern, and you'll never guess who's sitting at the bar. Malachai and Savron Phantom. At first, I turned around, figuring I'd find another place to get a drink. Aren's a massive city. There are plenty of taverns to choose from, but then a thought occurred to me."

Leaning forward, Ash yearned to hear more.

"I figure the only way to get closure or make peace with what he did to my species was to get a little payback," Morghan said, cringing. "In hindsight, it wasn't such a good idea. Attacking the Prince of Darkness on his own turf? Xavier might occupy Solaris, but Aren belonged to Malachai. Still does, probably. I must have had some sort of death wish, but I walked right up to that fucker, and I poked him in the shoulder."

Ash's eyebrows flattened. "You *poked* him? That was your retaliation?"

"The start of it," Morghan replied, leaning back on his hands, crossing his feet at the ankles. "After that, without getting into every grimy detail, we came to blows. In the end, he wound up paying for a *lot* of damage done to that tavern, but I won the fight, and Savron bought me an ale. We've steered clear of each other since. Until now."

Astounded, all Ash could do was stare at the Wolf. "So, beating up the man responsible for the near extinction of your species stopped your nightmares? I mean, it's a great story, and definitely amusing. I'll be sure to tease Malachai about it next time I see him, but I don't see how it'll help me."

"This situation is different. You'll need to find closure in your own way," Morghan informed her.

"But how can I find closure for something that hasn't even happened yet?" Ash asked, falling back onto her bed with a groan, staring up at the ceiling. "I'm not just having dreams about Aries. I'm having dreams about the beast, and running from Pandora in Crane, and fighting Xavier. I keep seeing him turning into this... monster. With horns and glowing orange veins."

Morghan stiffened beside her, so much so that she felt it and angled her head to look at him. His normal, tanned complexion had gone pale, his eyes wide with horror. "Did you say... glowing orange veins and... horns?"

"Yeah, why?"

"Ash, I'm not sure that you're having nightmares at all," Morghan whispered. "I think you're being warned."

Not thirty minutes later, Morghan, Lilly, and Ash were in the library. She wasn't entirely sure what the Wolf was looking for, but she helped in any way she could. But, for the most part, she was frozen with shock, her eyes darting in every direction.

The library in the Kingdom of Elves was more than three times the size of the one in Dracus. The rows of books on each of the four floors appeared endless. It would be far too easy to get lost there, so she tried to stick close to Morghan and Lilly.

"It might be easier to ask one of the attendants," Lilly mentioned, gulping as she looked the massive bookcases up and down. They were as tall as Giants, or so Ash imagined.

"I don't think that's such a good idea," Morghan admitted, keeping his voice low. "I don't want to tip the Elves off that we're dealing with an Amorian uprising without talking to the others about it first."

Ash lifted her brows in an effort to appear surprised. "You think this has something to do with the Amorians?"

"I'm certain," he replied, examining a shelf of books titled in a language Ash didn't know or understand. "What you described was almost identical to what legends used to say about Xanthius. If Xavier is somehow connected to him, that poses a massive problem."

A wave of nausea swept over Ash. She *wanted* to tell Morghan the truth but wasn't sure what to say. He'd want to know how she figured it out, and would he believe her if she told him that a Dreamwalker from the Underworld had paid her a visit?

"Maybe Aries learned something about Xavier in the afterlife, and he's trying to warn you about it from whatever Second Life Realm he's in," Morghan suggested.

"Second Life Realm?" Lilly inquired with a curious tilt of her head.

Morghan nodded, pulling out a book, flipping through the pages. "There are different layers to the afterlife, the same way there are levels to the Underworld. Legend states that if the Moons still need you, you're sent somewhere to wait. If they don't, you get to go to the *true* afterlife. No one knows what that's like. Some say you become a star. Others say you're taken to a new Galaxy, far away. Some people believe that your life begins again, in a new form. No one knows the truth."

The sudden urge to sit down came over Ash. She crouched, bracing her back against one of the bookcases. "You think Aries might still be needed?"

"Possibly," Morghan revealed. "I could see why the Moons would want to use him, but it's rare for someone from the afterlife to connect with a living person. The Moons have been known to occasionally provide people with special dreams. Like visions, but not as potent or vivid. Aries was smart enough to know that he could use the Amulet to make contact with you. Of course, he'd know that. Magical weapons were sort of his specialty. He did run the Safe Haven's vault, you know."

Ash's jaw dropped, her blood running cold. "My Amulet can connect with the dead?"

"Yes," Morghan said, giving her a look that made her feel daft. "You have a lot to learn about your Sectra. It's capable of far more than just entrapping Witches in rings of blue fire, and leveling city squares. When the Sorcerers and Elven Blacksmiths were constructing them, the Sovereign gifted them dust carved directly from the Moons, which means you're connected to them."

"Whoa," Lilly said with an awestruck expression.

Morghan nodded. "Whoa is correct."

"How do we know it's Aries and not someone else," Ash blurted, pushing to her feet. Maybe she could use this opportunity to tell the Wolf about her encounter with Jay. "What if it's a Dreamwalker?"

Morghan recoiled at the sound of the question before shaking his head. "That's impossible. There are no more Dreamwalkers. The Arebus Archers took care of that."

"What do you mean?" Lilly squeaked. "Why would they *take care* of Dreamwalkers?"

"I'm not entirely sure. I just know that when men and women were old enough to take the bow, their gifts would manifest as well. If that gift turned out to be Dreamwalking…" Morghan made a throat slitting motion with his hand.

A shiver swept down Ash's spine. If that was true, why was Jay still alive? She supposed that eventually she would get the chance to ask him, but right now, it was best that she focus all her time and energy on figuring out what sort of monster Xavier *really* was.

"What matters most is that you were warned, Ash. Now, we might finally know what Xavier has done such a good job of hiding, which means we can prepare you better, and come up with a proper plan. The best way to do that is to find books about Xanthius," he mouthed the name, as if fearing the attendants in the library might overhear with their Elven ears. "And, you know who knows this library better than anyone?"

Ash's shoulders relaxed, her lips tugging toward a smile. "Vincent."

A few minutes later, her twin brother was guiding them through the library, into one of the darkest, deepest corners via video-call. Thick layers of dust covered the books on every shelf. Cobwebs dripped from bookcase to bookcase. Spiders dangled from the ceiling.

"Well, I think it's safe to say no one comes to this corner. Not even the maids," Lilly chirped, delicately brushing cobwebs aside.

"People want to forget that corner exists, almost as badly as they want to forget that Amoria ever existed, Vincent explained. I hardly went back there, but Cedric told me about the books on those shelves, and what they were about. Stories of living nightmares."

The hairs on the back of her neck began to stand at an end. That was what she'd have to face. A living nightmare, just like the one that had just had her screaming in her sleep.

"I wouldn't be surprised if the Elves burned all of the books about... you know who," Vincent added. "Don't beat yourself up too much if you can't find anything."

"We *have* to find something," Ash informed him. "I *need* to know."

Why?

"Because I'm almost certain that Aries tried to warn me that Xavier is somehow connected to the last Amorian King," she informed him. Of course, she'd already known that, but was going to use this opportunity to break the news to the others. "I already have a good idea on how to defeat him. Nullify him with the Scepter's Moonlight, and then bury one of my enchanted daggers in his heart. But it would be nice to find out what he's actually capable of doing before I enter *that* particular arena."

"What makes you think you have to bury one of your daggers in his heart?" Morghan inquired, blowing dust off a book before picking it up and examining the cover. "If killing him is that simple, why did we just suffer through three tasks to get the Scepter?"

"It's just a hunch," she lied. "I chose the dagger in my dream. I didn't get to see him go down, but I'm pretty sure it worked."

"Interesting," Vincent mused. "Let me know if you find anything there. I'll look around here for you. But, while I have you on, there are a few things I'd like to tell you."

Vincent went on to tell Ash and the others about everything that had happened during the last few days. Cooper had attempted to kill Malachai shortly after Morghan and Lilly's departure to the Kingdom of Elves. Fortunately, Valentina had intervened, and Cooper was now mandated to receive counseling before he'd be allowed back in the field. Loren was still in the Infirmary, and actively refusing visitors. Axel was vetted and deemed a victim of Richard's and was allowed to resume his duties as the Draconian General. Penelope and Lady Evanora were doing their best to keep the residents of Dracus calm, while overseeing the reconstruction of the square. Craven was now insisting that if Ash wanted to follow through with her idea to recruit the Pandora, then she should have Malachai perform a Realm address by the end of the week to allow as much time as possible to integrate the beasts into one of the three armies. Ash wasn't sure how she felt about that, but she told her brother to tell Craven to start planning it anyway.

Malachai spent his mornings in the Infirmary and his afternoons and evenings working with Anderson and Grant to find a way to disable the portal. He'd also met with Axel and had provided the General with more intel about the Dark Army. Supposedly, the prince had been incredibly helpful the last few days and had even managed to shock everyone in ways that they hadn't thought possible.

"Well, the other night, Malachai might have told us a few interesting things. In short, he enlisted Pat McBride's help in warning Meera about the attack his father was planning on Solaris. Together, they came up with the idea to put us in that hatch. In short, they're the only reason we're alive."

Ash dropped the book she'd been examining at the sound of his words, her heart dropping into her stomach. "You're joking."

"Not one bit," Vincent informed her. "I'm surprised this is the first you're hearing about it. It was all over the paper this morning. The article was quite amusing."

"You guys keep looking for a book that might help us," Ash ordered, beginning to back away. "I'm going to find that paper."

43

Constance stared down at the paper Alrich had just given her, unable to believe what she was reading. Her mind swam, her heart racing at an incredibly unhealthy rate. "Xavier is going to implode," she concluded. As soon as the words sailed past her lips, the castle trembled with some sort of outburst upstairs, and the sound of animalistic roars reverberated throughout the halls, rattling the windows.

"Thankfully Richard is here now to take the brunt of Xavier's anger," Alrich mentioned, wincing as the words. "This *is* his fault, after all."

Nodding, Constance started to skim the article again. The entire thing explained how while Richard was a Rat in Dracus, Malachai had turned out to be a Rat in Solaris. The prince had detailed every incident where he tried to undermine his father, and there were too many to count.

To make matters worse, the article ended with *"Rats, you can't trust anyone these days."*

"Well, that was the final nail in Malachai's coffin." Constance cleared her throat nervously as she set the paper on her vanity. "What are we going to do now?"

"What do you mean?" Alrich inquired, pacing before her large, arched windows. "We do the same thing we've been doing—keep our heads down."

Constance scowled at the thought. "I'm getting really sick of pretending to be some loyal, long-lost niece. My mother is rolling in her grave as we speak. I'm sure of it. And Malachai is your *best* friend. Why aren't we following him? There has to be a way out of here. We can go to Dracus and—"

Alrich darted across the room in a flash and covered her mouth with his hand, preventing her from saying another word. She froze, staring up into his flashing red eyes, her throat thickening. "Not another word," he ordered, using that authoritative tone that she absolutely despised. "There are eyes and ears all over this castle. All over the *Realm*."

All Constance could do was nod, so she did. Not a second later, someone knocked on her door. Her heart leaped into overdrive, goosebumps pebbling the flesh beneath her black velvet dress. It wasn't lunch or dinner time. There were no events scheduled for Xavier to parade her around, and if there were, he'd probably have canceled them given today's paper. There was *no* excuse for Constance to be bothered. Unless someone had just heard what she'd said.

Alrich cursed beneath his breath, beads of sweat pebbling along his brow. Constance remained still, waiting for his direction. A second knock sounded, this one angrier. Alrich removed his hand from Constance's mouth, only to take her by the shoulders and kiss her. Deeply, and passionately.

The sound of Constance's door being thrown open flooded her ears, but she paid it no mind. Instead, she melted against the Pandora, wrapping her arms around his neck, pressing her body against his. He grunted approvingly, backing her against the vanity. She shuddered at the sensation of his hands running down her sides, forgetting all about whomever lingered at her threshold.

"Out of my respect for heated afternoon trysts, I'll tell my father you're indisposed," Soroya said before shutting the door, leaving them to their dirty work.

Alrich stilled, his lips abandoning hers. Constance panted,

having never been kissed in such a way. Her heart pounded furiously, her blood like molten lava, singing through her veins.

"My apologies," he said, equally breathless. "I... I had to make it convincing. I figured if they thought we were running away together..."

"It would be a lesser punishment," Constance finished for him.

Nodding, Alrich's gaze dropped from her face to her position on the vanity, remaining where he stood between her legs. The lump in his throat bobbed as he slowly backed away. Constance reached out, wrapping a hand around his black cloak, wrenching him back toward her.

"Let's make it convincing then," she said, flushing at the sound of her own words before she surged forward and reclaimed his lips, kissing him gently, waiting for him to deny her. He never did. Instead, he deepened their kiss, his hands returning to her waist. The next few moments were a blur of passion Constance had only read about in books. She wondered if they'd proceed further, and how she'd feel if they did. How much would it change between the two of them? Would it improve her life, or make it even worse?

Soon, those thoughts faded away, gone with the wind, and Constance lost herself in the man in front of her. Her hands moved up his chest, undoing his cloak. It fell to the ground at his feet, and for the first time, she got a good look at what was hiding beneath. A pristine, muscular form that led her mouth to water, her stomach fluttering. She ran her fingers down the soft, silky fabric of his black tunic until they made their way to his hips, grazing the waist of his pants.

Alrich paused, as if frozen in time. "We might have gotten carried away," he said, taking a step back.

Nodding, Constance hopped off the vanity, smoothing her skirts while he retrieved his cloak from the floor, throwing it around his shoulders, hiding that delicious form once again. She fought not to frown. "You're right," she agreed, despite her drooping shoulders. "We should keep this professional, if we expect to—" she caught herself, rolling her eyes. "Take the right steps."

"You're a lady," Alrich said. "You deserve better."

With that, he turned to leave. Constance watched him go, her heart in her throat, tears beginning to prick her eyes. She brought her fingers to her lips, still tingling from his kiss. Something had stirred, deep inside her, as if his touch had turned a light on. One that would quickly be snuffed out, if he believed that she deserved better than a man as loyal as he was.

Dinner that evening was a wreck. Constance wasn't hungry, and everyone noticed, despite her best efforts to hide that fact by forcing small bites into her mouth. She washed each bite down with gulps of sweet wine until her mind became fuzzy, blurring her memories of the hours leading up to that moment.

Xavier was in a similar mood. He didn't speak and hardly looked at anyone. Constance watched his facial expressions change rapidly, as if he were having some sort of internal conversation with himself. Richard and Ariel, their new guests, conversed amongst themselves at the other end of the table. Soroya snapped her fingers, beckoning a servant to bring forth another bottle of wine. Lincoln remained silent, having finished his plate not five minutes after it arrived in front of him.

Dessert was served. Chocolate pie topped with whipped cream and fresh strawberries. A dish meant for the Giving Day season. Constance's stomach churned at the thought of spending the precious holiday in Solaris, with all of these people who couldn't care less about her. Apparently.

The urge to look over her shoulder, to where Alrich lingered in the hall with the other guards was insufferable. Constance fought it, holding out her wine glass so that Soroya could refill it.

"Busy day?" Soroya asked with a devilish smirk.

Constance bit her tongue.

The hushed conversation at the end of the table ceased, and Constance could feel the Draconians eyes on her. "You know," Richard drawled. "I had the pleasure of meeting your elder brother.

What a nice young man. It's a shame that the Draconians got their claws in him." He clucked his tongue, reclining in his chair.

Refusing to give the Rat the time of day, Constance focused on her wine.

"I highly doubt he'll continue to be the General," Ariel added with a scoff. "Before we left, I put money on Calloway."

"Calloway?" Soroya scoffed. "An *Elf* as General of the Rebel army? You must be mad. And if you're right, then the Moons are too."

Ariel nodded, as if in agreement. "Everything is upside down these days, which is why I expected it. Whatever you *think* is going to happen, it'll wind up being the opposite."

To that, Constance raised her glass before taking yet another long sip. But, before the conversation could continue, Alrich stepped inside, bowing at the waist. "Your Majesty, I've just received word that Jax Phantom has arrived," he revealed, straightening. "Where should I send her?"

Xavier's eyes narrowed. "In here. Someone, make her a plate."

The servants rushed forward to do just that, all while Alrich went to fetch this *Jax Phantom*. Whoever that was. Constance could only assume that they were a relative of Savron, whom she despised. Just like everyone else in Solaris.

"You're going to feed her?" Soroya inquired, giving her father a long, disapproving look. "She failed you. She should be punished."

"Do not tell me how to reprimand my children," Xavier snarled so viciously that Soroya flinched. "I think I've learned from my mistakes. Would you rather me cast her out just like your brother, just so she can go join the Allies?"

Not a minute later, a woman around Constance's age waltzed into the room with the sort of grace a queen should have. Her long, silvery blond hair fell down to her waist, her pale gray eyes fixed directly on the king. She was dressed in leather, wearing the same cloak Alrich always wore. The only difference was that hers was lined with red silk.

"Father," Jax greeted, inclining her head to Xavier. "You told me to find you the second I arrived. I'm sorry to intrude on your dinner."

Xavier waved her off. "It's a *family* dinner. Does my blood not run through your veins?"

Jax offered him a bright smile. "That it does."

"If that's the case," Xavier started again. "Tell me why Ash VanCamp is still alive."

Never before had Constance witnessed a person become so still. Even her own heart was scared to beat as she waited for Jax to respond.

"Irina intervened, father." Jax's words wavered as she took a nervous step back. "There was nothing I could have done. The Unseen forced us to retreat."

Who the fuck is Irina and why do people listen to her more than Xavier? Constance thought, sipping her wine. *And where can I find her?*

"We were still able to take down Aries before she caught on to what we were doing. He was one of your biggest threats. That should count or something, right?" Jax asked, glancing about the room, clearly expecting someone to stand up for her. Constance didn't dare utter a single word. "You have to understand that Irina agreed to help you in Erim, but she didn't expect to lift a finger in Idona. We're blood bonded to her. She's our High Priestess. We have to do as she says."

"You know that the *entire* reason she stopped you is because she's too emotionally involved," Xavier snapped. "You should have known better than to listen to her at that moment. We could have dealt with her afterward."

"She won't condone you harming her blood," Jax said, her tone colder than ice. "You know that. Idona thinks the Messenger is the only being in this Realm that can end you, but we both know that's not true. Your orders harmed her family once. She won't let you do it again. Not through us."

Constance could have sworn that she watched Xavier's veins begin to glow like firelight, but the second she blinked, that sight had vanished. The king, however, was still furious, the entirety of his eyes having grown completely black. Everyone else pushed their chairs back, and the guards flooded into the room, Alrich included. He tapped Constance's shoulder, signaling her to leave.

She refused, opting to finish her glass of wine.

"You are Amorians, and you will follow. Your. Fucking. King," Xavier seethed, rising to his feet. "Your High Priestess is *nothing* compared to me. If she continues to defy me, remind her about what happened to the Werewolves. I'm itching for another culling."

"Father—"

Xavier held up a hand, stopping her from speaking another word. "Because you did succeed in slaying Lord Aries Blackwing, you won't be banished like your insubordinate brother. You will be punished, the same way he was, however. Only this time, I won't be sending you back to Aren. You'll remain here, to complete a simple task."

"What task?" Jax inquired, her expression grave.

"Training her," the king pointed toward Constance. "Starting tomorrow."

Constance choked on her wine, her eyes growing wide. She looked toward Jax, who was staring at her as if she were some sort of lowly peasant.

"You have one month," Xavier added, rising from his seat, pushing the chair aside. "You'll train every day, from dawn to dusk. By the end of it, Constance will be the lethal weapon we need her to be. At least *she* hasn't sworn a Blood Oath to another. She's *mine*."

44

The evening before Aries' funeral, five days after Ash arrived in the Kingdom of Elves, she found herself in a bit of a daze. Dracus was still on complete and utter lockdown. Loren refused to open the portals, extract the Unity Bridge, or even leave his chambers. Vincent had yet to find any information on Xanthius in Dracus, and after searching the shelves for days, Ash had finally given in and asked the library attendants. They openly admitted to burning all of the books pertaining to him a few centuries back, per the crown's direction.

Ash was at a dead end. And soon, she might very well be dead herself.

Malachai's Realm address was set to take place the day after the funeral. It was then that Ash would finally be able to join the other Allies because her presence was needed for the address to actually work. The Pandora would be better influenced with people like Ash, Beck, Axel, and Craven by the prince's side. They'd all agreed to participate, including members of the Idonian Council such as Lucinda and Valentina.

Aries would have likely participated too. A crack seared through Ash's heart at the thought of him standing on that dais, scowling eternally, his burgundy eyes fixed into a glare sharper than the Scepter's crescent blade.

Sadly enough, Ash was looking forward to the funeral. It meant that she'd see people she'd longed for in the past week. Not to mention, Giving Day was on Sunday.

If there was one thing that Ash refused to give up, it was spending the sacred holiday with the McBrides and the Waters. Of course, this year they wouldn't have Lincoln or Constance, but they'd be with them in spirit. And, they'd add new faces to the mix. Their treasured Allies. Ash couldn't be more excited. Even if they'd spend the evening stationed at various underground tunnel entrances, waiting for Pandora to answer Malachai's call.

Ash had just finished her new nightly routine, a hot bath with stress relieving scented oils and more bubbles than necessary, when Morghan barged into her room. She tightened her robe, summoning her worst glare.

"I might not act like it, but I *am* the High Queen," she hissed. "Knocking is necessary."

Morghan scoffed, rolling his eyes. "We're on the same division. I've seen everything and covered you during your bathroom festivities. I think that gives me the right to barge in when the Queen of the Fae is standing in our current foyer, asking for you."

Queen Cleo sat across from Ash, at her borrowed dining room table. Her magnificent, sparkling wings were hidden, allowing her to rest against the back of her velvet upholstered chair properly. The very sight of her filled Ash with awe and fear. The thin, white gossamer gown she wore was studded with enough shining diamonds that it could likely stand on its own. She sparkled like a lonely star amidst an impossibly black Galaxy.

Ash wished she could absorb into her shadow.

Servants had been kind enough to attend, filling much needed glasses of wine, providing treats Ash couldn't bear to eat. She was far too nervous, sick to the stomach. There was no need to guess why Cleo had chosen to pay her a visit.

"That little friend you brought here with you is very kind," the queen began, running her finger around the rim of her wine glass. "She gave me a hug."

"Did she?" Ash gulped, eyeing the threshold, well aware of where Lilly was lingering beyond. "I'm sorry if that offended you."

"Of course it didn't," Cleo insisted, straightening in her seat. "Listen Ash, I know you've spent a lot of time with the other royals, and that I haven't been very present, but you should know that I'm unlike them all. I believe in love and unity above all else. In turn, that means I appreciate simple acts depicting those two things, and I desire them more than I ever have before."

If only Ash had learned more about the rulers inside Idona before she'd joined them. She might have known what to say to Cleo, or all of the others. She was growing tired of playing every-thing by ear. *Winging it,* as Morghan often said.

"Forgive me," Ash said, biting her inner cheek. "I have much to learn about... well... everything."

"Understandably so," Cleo replied, taking a sip of her drink. "You spend most of your time out there, in the Realm, in places no ruler has dared to go during the last thirty years. We all commend you for that, even if the Elves do not show it."

Ash stared at her, unable to believe a word she'd said. How could every other ruler wear a shining crown, sitting as if some sort of stick had been sewed somewhere where the sun didn't shine, while Cleo was as normal as a pig farmer in Lorcan?

"How are you fairing?" Cleo asked once Ash had failed to respond.

"As good as anyone would in my position, I hope," she admitted, relaxing her shoulders, and her posture altogether. Something told her that she didn't need to pretend that she was anything other than what she truly was in Cleo's presence. And, after all she'd recently lived through, she appreciated that. "I'm terribly sorry about Aries. I take full responsibility. I know I can't make it up to you or provide you with an adviser as good as he was. He is irreplaceable. But I will help you in any way that I can. Call on me whenever you're in need, and I will come."

The air felt stale. Almost tainted with the very depression leaking from Ash's pores.

Cleo nodded, her eyes fixed on the glass of wine in her hand. "You remind me of your mother. Entirely oblivious, but braver than all the rest. Innocent, despite her upbringing. Beautiful, in spite of what was buried inside." Shadows were beginning to dance in the queen's eyes, a sudden sadness falling over the room like a wet blanket. Ash could have sworn that for a moment, the Realm had lost all color and drained of all its beauty.

An empty feeling evolved in the pit of Ash's stomach. "What was buried inside?"

The queen didn't respond. Instead, her gaze subtly moved toward the exits on either side of the room. With a wave of her hand, the doors shut, locking with a *click*. Ash's jumped, startled by the action. *I'll never get used to Magic. Never.*

"You do not say anything inside these marble walls that you don't want the Realm to know," Cleo advised. "They listen."

Ash's mouth dried up like a well in the heat of Summer Solstice. "Oh."

"Our Fae hearing is nearly as strong as theirs, but the difference between our species is that *we* respect the privacy of others," she explained, not bothering to whisper. "Anyway, my heart has crumbled to dust all over again. Losing your sweet, sweet mother tore me in two. Losing Aries... I'm not sure when, or if I'll ever recover. But queens do not get to mourn. We have kingdoms and the people who live within them to care for. What will happen to my precious, fellow Fae if I were to be held up in my quarters, lost in grief?"

"Like Loren?" Ash asked, cringing.

Cleo nodded solemnly. "Loren has the support of his council, and the Allies. I have neither of those things."

"You don't have a council?" Ash balked.

"My entire following is my council," she replied with a confident lift of her chin. "We make decisions as one, whole body. That way, everyone is happy. If someone desires a change, we discuss it. The only reason that Aries was named my adviser was because I needed someone to help me with the Idonian Council. Everyone else rules differently than I do. I don't understand the others, and I don't wish to. Aries did."

Another silence spread between them. Ash wasn't sure what to say, or how to act. There were no *right* words to say to someone experiencing such a loss.

"Truthfully, I don't believe that Aries ever belonged in the Safe Haven. He was too intrigued by everywhere *else*. It's why he ran the vault. He surrounded himself with historical artifacts and objects from other Realms. He practically *lived* in there. Most days, I felt so terribly sorry for him. Especially once the Dark War began, and we locked ourselves away. He roared at me for days after I turned the Enchanted Forest into what it is now. He didn't want to hide. He wanted to go out into the Realm and fight." Cleo closed her eyes, hanging her head. "But I couldn't let him."

Ash's eyes were becoming misty, which surprised her. She thought she'd have run out of tears by now. "Why?"

"Aries…" Cleo paused, pursing her lips. "He was… different compared to the other Fae. Born different, I mean. Some might say he was cursed, but I never thought that. Not for one second." She waved her hand a second time, opening the doors, which revealed Morghan and Lilly standing at the thresholds, listening in. Ash scowled at them both, opening her mouth to release the chastising words ready and waiting at the tip of her tongue. But, Cleo said, "It's alright. The lone Wolf and his apprentice may enter and properly listen to what I'm about to share."

Lilly skipped inside, claiming the chair at the head of the table. Morghan slipped into the chair beside Ash's, grinning at the servant who put a glass of whiskey in front of him. Lilly was given water, and she frowned. Ash snorted. "One day, Lillypad. One day."

"Is that what you call her? Lillypad?" Cleo inquired, holding out her glass to be refilled.

"Sometimes," Ash replied. "But most people just refer to her as Lilly."

Nodding, Cleo took a long sip of her wine. Afterward, she

looked toward Lilly, offering her a sweet smile. "Your soul is like a glowing white light. The sort of light people should follow." Nothing compared to the look of pure shock and joy upon Lilly's face. Ash hoped it wouldn't be the last time she ever saw her wear a look like that. "Anyway, Aries soul was like a flame. His was the first one I saw. If you didn't know, we were children together. Born only six months apart. I was older, and never let him forget it. I woke up with the Sight one day when I was seventeen, a year before our wings developed. I remember looking at him and just... seeing. There was a flame within him, so hot that I wondered how he wasn't burning from the inside out."

The Queen sucked in a breath before taking a moment to collect herself. Small snacks were served in the meantime. A few tiny cucumber sandwiches, cut into perfect triangles. Cheese and crackers. Cupcakes. No one reached for a thing. Ash wondered if Lilly and Morghan's stomachs were as sour as hers was.

"Turns out, it was the flame of a warrior," Cleo revealed. "But Fae... we're not warriors. We're gentle creatures. Our purpose is to use our Magic for the benefit of our Realm. But there are rare Fae, who are born to use their Magic for war." She looked toward Ash, who held her breath in response. "These Fae are called Blackwings. Only one lives at a time. So, when our wings developed and his turned out to be black, and feathered..." she trailed, shaking her head, as if willing away the memory. "The Safe Haven entered a state of panic."

Ash exhaled, all too aware of how quickly her heart was beating. "Why would they panic?"

"Because the last Blackwing to have lived turned out to be one of the worst enemies Idona had ever seen. His name was Orin. He was the first of his kind and was born two hundred years after the New Dawn began. It is said that Orin was born in a village that used to exist in Eastern Idona, long before the Draconians occupied that jurisdiction. This was when Fae lived everywhere, before kingdoms and territories were established. At first, High King Aiden wanted everyone to live together, you see. As one.

"However, when Orin came of age, and those magnificent black, feathered wings sprouted from his back, everything changed. Some people saw him as a god among men. Others saw him as the reincarnation of the Dark One. Those who believed in rebirth thought that Xanthius was reborn." Cleo shivered, the temperature in the room dropping as the wicked king's name sailed past her lips. "Orin loved all the attention. Both good and bad. And, once he realized that his Magic was different from all the other Fae, he thought he was meant for the High Throne. A sign from the Moons. He summoned all of his believers, and threatened to drain all the life from Idona, turning it into a wasteland, if the Cavanaugh's didn't evacuate *his* castle."

Images began to portray in front of Ash's eyes, as if Cleo had created a Magical screen—a window to the past, allowing Ash and the others to see all that she'd just explained. Ash saw Orin, and his following. Her blood chilled at the sight of him, with his long, black hair, pale skin, and bright, burgundy eyes. He was standing on a battlefield, armed to the teeth, wearing armor that looked more like obsidian glass. Everything about Orin was terrifyingly beautiful, in the most disturbing of ways.

Ash watched High King Aiden Cavanaugh approach the beautiful, blackwinged Fae on a battlefield. The king was alone. There was no sign of his historic council, or his white Dragon, Jakobi. He didn't appear to be armed, but she caught sight of the Amulet's enchanted chain peaking over the collar of his tunic.

One thing Ash noticed about the deceased First King was how much he looked like Alistair. In fact, the Rider was a spitting image of Cavanaugh. She wondered if anyone else had picked up on that.

"As you can see, Aiden tried to be amicable," Cleo started again. "But Orin wouldn't stand down."

Ash watched in horror as the Fae held out a hand with little effort, draining the life from the honorable king in front of him. Before the last bits of life left Aiden, Cleo willed all the images away.

"You wouldn't want to see what happens next," the queen insisted.

Lilly gulped. "You're right."

"Orin was, eventually, slain by Cavanaugh's dragon," Cleo informed them. Ash sighed with relief. "But not after he inflicted heaps of irreparable damage to Idona. No one could grow a thing. It was horrific. Mortals and Immortals alike were starving. It took my people centuries to return Idona to what it is today. But no Fae like him was born again, until Aries, five hundred years later. *That* was why everyone panicked. High King Lachlan VanCamp considered throwing Aries into Namhain. Beheading him was also an option. My mother agreed, but the rest of the Safe Haven didn't. They brought their concerns to her and voted she abdicate the throne. To Me. Because *I* would stand up for Aries. And I did. We came up with rules and presented them to Lachlan. After a long debate between the Idonian Council, Aries was allowed to live. Look at what he became."

Someone sniffled. Ash looked over to find that Lilly was wiping tears from her cheeks.

"What sort of rules?" Morghan asked.

"They weren't really rules as much as they were restrictions," Cleo told him. "Aries wasn't allowed to use his Magic, have any sexual relations, or marry. Even though it was proven that he wasn't at all related to Orin, and that another Blackwing wouldn't likely be produced from such acts. If he was caught even kissing someone, he would be thrown in Namhain."

Ash scoffed. "That hardly seems fair."

"Those were your great, great-grandfather's terms," the queen said. "I had no choice but to obey. Over time, Aries didn't mind so much. He got used to it. Life became more about studying or experiencing other things, but he was never *truly* happy. Not until the Five Realm War, anyway. That warrior's spirit of his had a chance to shine. Up until then, I hadn't seen him smile in over a hundred years. It's like he was *meant* for the battlefield. He was skilled enough with weapons that he had no desire to use any of his Magic. But that war eventually ended, and he slipped into depression again. He was so close to losing *that* battle. I could feel it. *See* it. In fact, I was waiting for him to come to me and inform me that he was making his ascension, but then he was summoned by Loren, to fight Ash and deem her worthy of the Sectra. I'd never seen him so overjoyed. I wondered if he'd return to me."

Ash quickly recalled that fight, her heart swelling at the memory. For a moment, she felt like she was there, staring down into those eyes of his that shined like red wine, pressing the tip of her sword against his throat. The way he gave her an approving smile before he left that battlefield, only to be replaced by Beck, who wouldn't fight her at all.

"When you requested his assistance with your third task, Aries was thrilled," Cleo claimed, staring at a spot above Ash's head. "Again, I thought he'd never return. I was right that time. He never did because you freed him. I can promise that he died happy, because of you."

One final crack appeared in Ash's heart. It had finally broken entirely. She sulked in her chair, hanging her head, allowing her hair to fall around her face, hiding her features. Hot tears began to prick at the corners of her eyes, threatening to fall in salty rivers down her cheeks.

"I'd have to agree with you," Morghan added softly. "Because lately, he's been trying to contact her through her dreams."

The entire room went still. The sound of erratic heartbeats flooded Ash's ears, scrambling her thoughts.

"What?" Cleo whispered. "Why?"

"He's trying to warn me," Ash revealed, lifting her chin, meeting the queen's wary gaze. "I think he discovered something, in whatever Second Life Realm he wound up in. He knows what Xavier is. He used my Amulet's connection to the Moons to show me. And now, unless I find some sort of written text about how Aiden Cavanaugh defeated Xanthius, I won't know what I'm walking into. All I'll know is how to kill Xavier if I even get the chance."

Cleo's bottom lip quivered. "I have some scrolls in possession. In the vault. I'll retrieve them for you and help prepare you in any way that I can." She rose from her chair, smoothing her immaculate skirts. "If Aries contacts you again… tell him that I'm glad his spirit is free."

In an instant, the queen vanished, leaving no trace of her behind. Ash stared at the spot she'd just been standing in shock and awe. "Well," she managed to get out. "That's one problem solved. Now we get to figure out how I avoid imminent death."

45

Quinn despised funerals.

He'd grown tired of attending them. The sight of caskets being lowered into holes in the earth made his skin crawl. But, most importantly, he was downright sick of saying goodbye to people. He hated the fact that he'd lived one day with someone at his side, only to have them gone the next.

The fact that he would never get to see their faces again drove him mad the most. Quinn could hardly stomach it. Watching Queen Cleo weep over Aries' casket made him want to sink into the shadows. He hated how badly she was hurt, even though he didn't know her at all. They'd never met, but he *had* known Aries, even if it was just for a short time. Because of that, he could understand why someone who'd stood by his side for two centuries would fall to pieces as he was being lowered into the earth.

King Thaddeus conducted the funeral, which took place on the sacred, invisible island of Cohmdhail in the center of Ardon lake. Aries was to be buried alongside past Idonian Council members, in a place so beautiful and untouched by all of the Darkness that had tainted Idona during the last thirty years.

The Elven King didn't seem like the type to do such a thing, in Quinn's opinion, but he did a good job, nonetheless. A few were starting to step forward to say a few words about the Fae, reciting their favorite memories of him. Lucinda was the first.

"I was in Ryiah when it came out that Aries had turned out to be a Blackwing Fae. I wanted to rush right home, worried that he'd be punished for it, but I had to wait a week, and finish the class I was teaching at the Elder's School for Sorcery. I tried to summon another Realm Sorcerer to take my place. Victor Frost came to my aid, and not a moment too soon. I wanted to get to Idona, to share my vote regarding Aries fate. I barely made it to the meeting in time. I'm sure Thaddeus and Esmeralda remember."

"We do," The Elven Queen and King answered in unison.

"Convincing Lachlan to agree to Cleo's terms was, and will always be, one of my biggest triumphs. It was a privilege to watch Aries grow into the Fae he became. I enjoyed seeing him every time I visited the vault, in search of ancient text. He was so helpful, intelligent, and genuinely good company. I knew he was meant for bigger, better things. And I believe that his journey is just beginning, despite his demise." Lucinda took a step back, fixing her gaze on her feet.

The next person to step forward was the Elven Adviser. Griffon, if Quinn remembered correctly. The man was in pieces. His eyes were swollen, red from all the tears he'd shed during the ceremony so far. His dark hair was disheveled, hiding his features. He kept a handkerchief clutched in his trembling grip as he approached Aries' grave.

"Thirty-five years ago, I sat around a table every month with Aries, Xavier, and Richard. I considered the three of them Allies. I might even call Aries my closest friend. And now, I stand alone, during such a trivial time in Idonian history. What will I do now that my fellow advisers are lost to me? Who shall I confide in when I feel the need?" Griffon sniffled. "I have no doubt that the Witches targeted Aries because of how powerful he truly was, even though he would never dare use his Magic. Xavier feared he might, and he is dead because of it. A martyr. One of many. I'm tired of losing good people."

Everyone nodded in agreement, but Quinn kept his head down, unwilling to watch any more.

While he didn't see them approach the grave, Quinn quickly learned that his own brother was the next to speak.

"I have Aries to thank for what little I know about teleportation. Our friendship was short, but I will never forget it. I'm sad to have lost him so soon. Not because he was a mentor of sorts, but because he was as genuine as they come. He fit right in with us in Crane. One might have thought he'd walked straight into his own house," Cooper said, chuckling beneath his breath. "I'd like to say a little something, on his behalf.

"*We are born in the shadows, and we return to the shadows. May the Moons carry you home, where we will one day meet again.*" Cooper finished, slinking back into the black-clad crowd while they subtly clapped. Quinn gave him an approving nod, his heart warming. Those were the words written at the very beginning of the book their father had written. *Arebus* words. The ones they would say to bid goodbye to those they loved.

A few more people stepped forward, most of which Quinn had never met before. He listened to their kind words, while also praying for the event to end. Not because he didn't care, but because he'd had his fill of throwing dirt into the graves of people he'd cared about.

It wasn't until Ash stepped forward that Quinn opened both his eyes and ears. His attention snapped to where she stood at the side of Aries' grave, tear drops dripping from her eyes. He wanted nothing more than to walk up to her and take her in his arms, if only to wipe them away, just as he did when Eliza's life came to an end. She focused on something in her hands, turning it over and over. Quinn's heart shuttered when he caught a glimpse of silver.

"I know that it is confirmed that the Witches are at fault for Aries' death," Ash began, her bottom lip quivering. "But I can't help but feel responsible. I was the one to draw him out of his Safe Haven. I just couldn't help it. The second we met, I knew that he was special, and that we would become Allies, before I even knew what that word would mean to me."

Every Ally standing before the grave inched forward, their eyes trained on the woman Quinn still saw as plain old Ash. A girl he'd grown to adore. They saw her as their leader. The High Queen. And what she was doing now proved that she had evolved.

"When Aries agreed to help me with my third task, I deemed him an Ally," Ash revealed. "And I shall uphold that promise."

The Allies took another step forward, along with the Idonian Council members. Quinn followed their movements, watching Ash like a hawk, unsure of what she'd do next. He wound up standing before the very end of Aries' grave, so close that one wrong movement would send him falling into it.

"I know that Valentina has expressed that we will receive an eleventh Ally, but I can't help but believe that we've already found another, and that we're saying goodbye to him today." Ash's tone wavered around her words, trembling like rippling water. Quinn wanted to reach out to her, to take her hand. He was so close that he could feel the warmth radiating from her form, but he didn't dare make a move. Not with all the spectators watching them.

Ash opened her palms, revealing what she'd been holding. An Ally badge. Two Dragons, curving in the form of a heart, yet separated by a sword. A symbol he'd grown to love. One that he was willing to die for.

"Cleo," Ash called, looking toward the Queen of the Fae.

The pair had clearly planned this ordeal, for Cleo stepped forward and opened Aries' casket without missing a beat or giving any warning. By the grace of the Moons, his body had been preserved. To Quinn, it appeared almost lifelike, as if the Fae was only sleeping.

Ash held out the badge before dropping it at the perfect place. It landed right where it belonged—above Aries' heart.

"I hereby claim Lord Aries of the Blackwing Fae as the twelfth Idonian Ally," Ash declared, her tone reverberating in the way that a Queen's should. "May he rest in peace, and may we meet again, when the Moons will it."

46

The last thing that Ash wanted to do after attending a funeral was head straight to a meeting. Unfortunately, that's exactly what happened. The second she finished using her earth ability to fill Aries' grave, Thaddeus requested that the members of the Idonian Council follow him to the mansion at the center of the island.

For a moment, Ash debated pulling rank and demanding that he postpone it for a few hours, so that she could spend some time with her Allies. She hadn't seen them in over a week, and all she wanted to do was hug them all, one by one. But, by the look on Thaddeus's face, Ash could tell that whatever he wanted to talk about was serious. So, she bit her tongue.

"I would like for the Generals and Aveo to join us," Esmeralda said. "In the meantime, the rest of you can explore if you'd like. It isn't every day that outsiders get to visit the island of Comhdhail. There are some rather majestic creatures that have taken refuge here. I'm sure that Lilly would love to set her sights on a Pegasus, or the historic White Stag."

"Once the meeting is through, you are welcome to join us in the Kingdom of Elves for a feast in Aries' honor," Thaddeus added before turning his back on them all, headed toward the mansion that loomed off in the distance. The council moved to follow him—

Ash included. She glanced over her shoulder, meeting Quinn's gaze. He gave her a nod and a wink before turning his attention to his younger sister, who was currently hurrying toward the hills with young Trinity and Penelope.

Ash pouted, wishing that she could follow them. She wanted to see a Pegasus too.

"Let me guess, you're jealous," Aveo commented from where he walked beside her, his own gaze glued on a particular Princess. "Is it sad that I am too?"

Beck laughed at him, earning quite a few glares from nearby council members. "Since when is the great Aveo Calloway more interested in Pegasi than battle preparations?"

The Commander's nostrils flared. "The White Stag is my family's sigil," he ground out. "And what makes you think that's what this meeting is all about?"

"Why else would they invite us?" Axel asked from Beck's other side. "I can count on one hand every time I was invited to an Idonian Council meeting. Every time, it was because they needed my opinion on something war related."

"Every Idonian Council meeting *is* war related these days," Lucinda said, startling Ash. She hadn't realized the Sorceress had moved to her other side. Her senses were clearly lacking these days. She'd need to work on that before the siege. Couldn't have just anyone sneaking up on her.

THE SECOND ASH WALKED INTO THE MANSION, SHE KNEW SOMETHING was wrong. The hairs on the back of her neck and along her arms began to stand on an end. Her skin crawled. Unease began to clench in her gut, the same way it always would when she first caught sight of red eyes while on watch back in Crane.

The door slammed shut behind her, causing her to jump. She whirled around to find that no one was there, but heard it lock, nonetheless. Her heart started to race, panic setting in.

"*That* was creepy," Beck said, visibly shivering. "Let's just get to the Round Table Room before my parents yell at us for dragging our feet."

Nodding, Ash figured that was for the best. She followed him over to the grand staircase at the far side of the foyer but noticed that Lucinda was still standing by the door, staring at the knob. Her wand fell from her sleeve, landing perfectly in her grip. Ash's breath caught in the throat at the sight of her attempting to spell it, only to be shocked in response. The wand fell, clattering to the floor.

Aveo froze, having witnessed the entire ordeal as well. "That can't mean anything good," he said, grinding his teeth.

Lucinda was trembling, holding the wrist of her right hand with the other, staring down at it with wide, amber eyes. "We're not alone on this island," she whispered.

"We have to warn the others," Axel insisted, hurrying up the stairs. Beck followed him. Once she saw Lucinda begin to make her way across the foyer to join them, Ash and Aveo followed too. The Commander kept reaching for a sword that wasn't there. Who brought weapons to a funeral? *Perhaps people should start.*

Thankfully, there was a weapon hanging around Ash's neck, and thanks to her complicated DNA, she *was* a weapon. But the last time she used the Amulet, she'd injured every member of the Draconian Council, and more. She wouldn't do the same thing to the Idonian Council.

After a few moments, she remembered the Scepter, waiting for her in her mindspace. A second later, it was in her grip. Aveo gasped, startled by the weapon's sudden arrival.

"How did you do that?" he whispered, staring at the Scepter in awe.

"Looks like you've learned how to use your mindspace. Good work," Lucinda said, patting Ash on the shoulder.

"Well, I really wish I were wearing pants too. Can I summon *those* from my mindspace?" Ash inquired, resuming her walking. She hadn't seen which way the Generals had turned at the end of the long hall, but Lucinda knew that place like the back of her hand. Directions wouldn't be an issue.

Aveo chuckled beneath his breath at the sound of her question.

"I imagine not. Perhaps you should start wearing them beneath your dress, like your sister does."

"How do you know what my sister wears beneath her dress?" Ash asked, staring in his direction with narrowing eyes. *I really need to talk to Penelope and figure out what the fuck is going on. One second, she's marrying Loren, the next, she and Aveo are attached at the hip. Why is she so confusing?* Ash began to twirl the Scepter in her hands. It moved as easily and gracefully as one of her limbs, almost as if they were designed for each other.

"She happened to tell me that she was wearing them earlier," Aveo explained. "She said something about how she wanted to be able to walk around the island without worrying about skirts."

Lucinda's breath caught in her throat. "I sure hope she's not hiking right now."

They turned the corner, and Ash caught sight of an open door at the center of the hall. Lucinda glared at the sight of it. No one was speaking within, and that wasn't exactly a good sign. Ash's heart started to race, beads of sweat pebbling along her brow. Her grip around the Scepter tightened, the orb hovering in the center of the crescent-shaped blade beginning to glow brighter.

"Stay behind me," Aveo mouthed.

"But you're unarmed," Ash mouthed right back.

Aveo looked down at his hands and flexed his fingers. "No, I'm not."

Rolling her eyes, Ash watched him approach the room, peeping inside. He went as rigid as a cat in water but walked inside. Ash waited another few moments before sharing a wary glance with Lucinda, who pressed her lips together and gave her a nod. They would enter together, wand and Scepter drawn, ready to strike.

Ash entered the room, taking in the massive round table. Nothing seemed amiss. Everyone sitting around it was supposed to be there. Or so she'd thought at first. When her eyes fell on a man sitting in between two empty seats, she staggered backward. The door shut, just like the one downstairs had. She was trapped.

"I don't know why you're just standing there," Xavier said,

looking at her as if she'd lost her mind. "Take a seat. And for Moon's sake, Ash, put down the Scepter. Your blinding Esmeralda."

The Elven Queen was, in fact, squinting.

Ash didn't put the Scepter down, but she did loosen her grip, softening the light radiating from it.

There were only two seats left, both on either side of him, meant for Lucinda and herself. Ash gulped. She wanted to remain where she was, but if the others had all followed his directions, she had a feeling she didn't have a choice. She chose the seat on the right, where Cleo sat on the other side, bearing no expression upon her face.

Xavier leaned forward, bracing an elbow on the table, resting his chin in his hand. He looked around the room, meeting everyone's gaze. "It's been a few decades," he eventually said. "Sorry that I've been so *absent*. You know how ruling can get. It's tiresome. Where's Loren?" he asked, pointing to where the King should have been sitting, which was where Axel was currently vibrating with rage.

"You know damn well where Loren is," the General spat.

"Oh, that's right," Xavier replied, sighing exasperatedly. "Mutinies are such a bitch. Let me know if he needs a hand with anything."

Ash's jaw dropped, and Axel shot to his feet, fists slamming down onto the table so fiercely that the room shook. The extravagant, diamond chandelier above them began to sway back and forth. "I don't care *who* you are. You will not offend my king again," he snarled, baring his sharp fangs.

Xavier wasn't phased in the slightest. "But only a few weeks ago, you were handing intel about him over to *my* men."

"You know just as well as I do that I was tricked into that arrangement," the General fumed.

"You poor thing," the Dark King teased. "I'm not here to banter back and forth with you. Sit down."

With the flick of a wrist, Axel was back in his chair, his hands resting on the arms as if tied to them by invisible chains. He struggled, veins beginning to bulge along his temples and neck. Valentina reached out to him, placing a hand on his forearm, forcing him to hold her gaze.

"Why *are* you here?" Thaddeus inquired, leaning back in his chair, as if *now* was a time to relax.

"Is this not an Idonian Council meeting, made up of the kings and queens of the Realm? Am I not one of them?" Xavier lifted a single brow, reaching the chalice in front of him. "I have every right to be here, Thad."

No one dared to argue. Technically, Xavier was right. He did occupy the Idonian Jurisdiction. There were more than one hundred thousand people kneeling before him, calling him king. If Ash remembered correctly, that qualified him. "Why did you wait until now to participate?" she asked, forcing her tone to remain even. She might not be able to hide how fast her heart was beating, or how shaky her hands were, but she'd be damned if she didn't at least *try* to appear stronger than she truly was. Even if all she wanted to do was flee the farthest corners of the Realm and hide for the rest of her days.

"He couldn't," Cleo revealed. "I personally made sure of it. I severed the connection from Solaris to Comhdhail."

Xavier nodded, sighing dramatically. "It's alright, Cleo. I forgive you."

Ash's gaze darted between the pair, and for a moment she wondered if the Fae was going to teleport to Xavier and rip his throat out before she remembered how the queen had said that the Fae were gentle creatures. The odds of *that* happening were slim to none, no matter how badly Ash wanted to witness it.

"That's all in the past now," Xavier insisted, fiddling with a ring on his left hand. A wedding band. Was he married? Malachai hadn't mentioned a stepmother. Who would be daft enough to marry the Dark King? Was that what he'd done with Constance? Ash's stomach became sour, the color draining from her cheeks. "You look ill, Ash. Is something wrong?"

Scoffing, Ash turned in her chair to face him. "Where is Constance?" she asked, eyeing his ring.

Xavier followed her gaze, snorting. "You can't possibly think that

I'd marry my own niece. We might not share blood, but there are lines that even *I* wouldn't dare cross." He shivered, as if disgusted by the very idea. "Constance is safe. Far better off than she was in that sink hole of a village you both hail from. I wear this ring to honor my belated wife."

Lucinda scowled, snorting with disbelief. "How sentimental."

"What is the purpose of your visit, Xavier?" Thaddeus demanded.

Finally, Xavier seemed to get serious. He straightened in his seat, dark eyes narrowing. "You have something that belongs to me, and I want it back."

"If you think we're going to willingly hand over the other Emblems, then you'd better be prepared to take our hands, or even our heads. We will never give them to you. I'd sooner toss them off the Galactic Bridge," Esmeralda declared, one of her tapered ears twitching, as if signaling someone. Xavier didn't seem to notice, but Ash certainly did. Her gaze subtly shifted over to Beck, just in time to watch him drop something into his shirt. His necklace.

Ash had forgotten that Beck was wearing one around his neck.

Fuck.

When Ash had learned about the Emblems at dinner a few days ago, she'd known they'd become a problem. She just hadn't expected to encounter that problem head-on at a funeral.

"I'm not talking about the Emblems, I'm talking about my son," Xavier said, his voice so low that it was frightening.

"Which one?" Ash inquired sweetly, despite her raging nerves.

The king's attention snapped in her direction. "The one that matters."

If Marcus was aware that Xavier was his father, and if he'd heard him say that, it would have broken him. Whether he loved him or not. To have your own flesh and blood throw you away like trash... Ash's blood began to boil, heating her face.

"He isn't here," Valentina said, speaking for the first time since that dreaded meeting had begun. "And, we had no part in him abandoning you. He made his own choice."

"He doesn't want to be one of your tools anymore," Lucinda

added daringly. "He's finished with being forced to complete the gruesome tasks you throw at him. Just be thankful that you didn't ruin him completely, and that there is still Light left in his soul."

The Elves didn't say anything about it. Neither did Cleo. But Ash could see in Aveo's eyes that he agreed. The way he avoided eye contact with the Chamberlains, and the way he clenched his jaw told Ash that he was biting his tongue, holding back whatever he wanted to say.

"That isn't his choice to make," Xavier said calmly, adjusting one of his cufflinks, feigning boredom. "If you give him back to me, I'll abdicate. I'll leave Solaris. I'll leave Idona altogether and become some other Realm's problem."

"The reason we shut the Galactic Gates was so that you *couldn't* become some other Realm's problem," Valentina argued. "The only people who know the code are Esmeralda and I, and neither one of us would willingly subject the rest of Si Realtra to whatever horrors you have planned. Do you think we're that selfish?"

Nodding, Xavier said, "Actually I do."

Ash looked toward Esmeralda, who bore no expression. She couldn't tell whether or not Valentina was right. Maybe Esmeralda *was* selfish enough.

Something told Ash that she was.

"Why do you want him so badly?" Cleo asked. "He betrayed you."

"That's none of your concern. He is my son."

Ash scoffed. *Son.* He had a perfectly good one right outside, yet he pretended that he didn't exist. "No," she said. "I've acquitted Malachai of all the crimes you *forced* him to commit, and now he's moved on. He is no longer your concern."

"Acquitted?" Thaddeus snapped. "Of *all* crimes? He murdered my nephew. Cedric was in line to become the next High King!"

"*Cedric* created an entire army right underneath your nose," Xavier told him. "I knew what he was doing the entire time. A noble lord, visiting even the dingiest of villages, searching for people to join his cause. He was forming some sort of resistance. I'm not an idiot. But I let him be, because, at the time, I didn't think he'd turn around and form an army of over twenty-thousand Idonians with the intent of rebelling against *my* throne. Not yours, or Loren's, or Cleo's. Mine. The only reason it even started to affect you at all was because he thought it was a great idea to recruit Walsh. That man was a psychopath. The only reason Gideon kept him around was because he was a champion in the war room. Walsh was a fungus, and it ruined that army. They were targeting everyone. Even people I wouldn't dare harm. So, we took care of it. Cut off the head of the snake. Fucking take me to court if you want. I did you a favor."

Ash held her breath, her gaze dancing between the two kings. The tension inside the room was so thick that she waited for it to smother her.

Xavier's gaze fell on the Scepter. Ash wondered what he'd try to do. Take it, so that she couldn't use it on him when the time came? *Good luck*, she thought, struggling against a smirk. Even if he *did* manage to get his grimy hands on it, he'd never get her daggers. If only she had one right then. How easy would it be to drive it into his heart while he was distracted and avoid the siege altogether?

Then again, when it came to Xavier, she really didn't know what she was up against.

"That's his blood on it," the king revealed.

"What?" Ash said, shooting to her feet, reaching to examine the weapon.

Xavier shrugged, as if everything he'd just said was obvious. "Cedric Chamberlain's blood is on that Scepter."

"How?" Esmeralda said through clenched teeth.

"He made it through the cavern," Cleo said, her words barely a breath of air.

"But the beast," Lucinda argued. "He couldn't have made it past that."

Ash quickly recalled all that Archibald had said to her, her eyes growing wide. "The beast told me that someone had come before me and spelled him so that he couldn't move," she revealed, her mouth growing dry.

"Cedric was a novice Sorcerer," Aveo mentioned. "He knew a thing or two."

Esmeralda nodded. "Which was why his quarters were covered in Ryiahn Ice after his fight with Malachai."

"And how he stopped the Amorian Fire at the Grimm Estate," Thaddeus added.

Xavier rolled his eyes. "Does any of it matter? We're straying too far from the subject. If my son isn't delivered to me by sundown, you're all dead."

47

Marcus was beginning to feel guilty for smiling so much, but he just couldn't help himself. Not when the sound of laughter flooded his ears, or when he was standing in the most sacred place in Idona surrounded by people he loved. Majestic beasts that Idonian eyes had not seen in decades stood everywhere that he looked. An entire herd of Pegasi stood in a meadow, munching on soft grass. Most of them were white, but a single black one stood taller than the rest, his massive, feathered wings reminding Marcus of someone he'd recently lost.

"That Pegasus is the closest thing we'll ever get to seeing Aries' wings again," Alistair declared sadly. "If we ever get to see it again."

The White Stag lingered in the tree line, observing the island's new guests, watching Lilly and Cooper play tag with the princesses. It wasn't a very fair game, when one of the players could teleport. Every time Trinity came close to him, Cooper vanished, reappearing somewhere else nearby. She squealed with excitement every time. The Stag didn't seem to mind.

"Do you think it'll come out?" Craven asked, coming up from behind.

"Who knows," Alistair replied with a shrug. "Can't say I'd blame him if he doesn't. We're a chaotic bunch."

Chuckling, Marcus couldn't help but agree. Just earlier, he'd watched Penelope tackle her brother to the ground out of nowhere. Poor Vincent had been talking to Morghan about something that appeared to be important when the assault occurred.

"How long do you think they're going to be in there?" Quinn asked, approaching with Mika on his heels. She was the only Princess who'd opted not to participate in the game of tag. Unlike Penelope, she hadn't thought to bring a change of clothes. Lilly and Trinity just didn't seem to care about their dresses. Why should they? Joyful moments were rare. They should make the most of them.

There was also the fact that Mika had *clearly* taken a liking to the eldest McBride brother. Such an attraction would not end well if her parents noticed.

"There's no way of knowing," Craven told him. "Idonian Council members have been known to last hours. Perhaps days, in some cases."

"What do you think they're talking about?" Alistair asked. "The siege? The new army? The Pandora? Malachai's Realm address?"

Marcus shrugged. "All of it, I'd guess. There's no way Thaddeus is going to just *accept* the fact that we'll be extending an invitation to the Pandora tomorrow."

"Actually, my father is rather fond of the idea," Mika revealed. "He's more concerned with how the Idonian people will react, and whether or not this will cause another war. Not to mention, the Pandora are aggressive. They've spent the last thirty years shredding flesh. People don't change overnight. We have to think about how their presence will interfere with our ultimate goal—peace."

Craven snorted, crossing his arms defensively. "If I remember correctly, the Elves thought the same about the Draconians."

"That's because when your species came into existence, they couldn't control their lust for blood. They'd raid villages. *Elven* villages. And, once they got a taste of Immortal blood—" Mika stopped herself, her tapered ears beginning to glow red with anger. It was evident that she was fighting against the urge to rant, and Craven looked as if he was about ready to rip her throat out with his fangs. Marcus prepared to intervene, while Quinn took a nervous step back. "Let's not pretend that Draconians didn't have a difficult past. It's common knowledge. The Scarlet Era was a trivial time in Idonian history, but your people proved to be civilized over time. They gained control. We highly doubt that the Pandora will be able to do the same."

Oddly enough, it was Alistair who spoke next. "You haven't spoken to one. You can't make a valid opinion until you have."

Mika blinked, surprised. She opened her mouth to argue, but something changed with Alistair. He went from being calm and relaxed to completely on edge. His muscles were so rigid, that if Marcus kicked him, he'd probably shatter his foot.

"What is it?" Quinn asked urgently.

Before Alistair could reply, Morghan ran up to them, his nostrils flaring. "Someone's here." His caramel eyes were fixed on the mansion off in the distance. "Smells like Malachai, but it's not him. Someone he's related to."

"He has siblings," Quinn said. "A sister, at least."

"He also has a father," Mika squeaked.

Craven sucked in a breath, closing his eyes, focusing on the scent. He was the only one among them who'd ever gotten *close* to Xavier. If the Dark King was there, Craven would be the one to confirm it.

When Craven's eyes flew open, horror twisting his features, Marcus's knees became weak. "We have to get in there," he insisted, gaze darting around frantically. Marcus knew that look. He was plotting. Taking charge. The Allies came forward, watching him, waiting for their orders.

"I can't teleport inside," Cooper revealed. "Just in case you were adding that to your plans."

"Shit," Craven snarled.

"But you can teleport to Dracus," Penelope mentioned. "Sneak into the portal rooms and get into the mansion through the portal there."

Marcus held his breath, trying to keep his mind off of the people that were inside that mansion. Valentina. Ash. Axel. Every ruler inside the Realm. He wasn't ready to attend any more funerals.

"Ebony only cleared me to teleport myself," Cooper reminded him. "I can't carry on any extra weight yet. I'm still unstable. *Apparently* in more than one way."

Shaking his head, Craven said. "You won't need to. You can gather whoever's willing and go through the portal."

Marcus watched Cooper's facial expressions rapidly change. He wished that he could change places with the Archer. Not only had he just *barely* survived being tortured in Solaris, but he'd been forced to become something he never would have become otherwise. He'd been through more in the last week than most people dealt with in their lifetime. Giving him such a stressful task wasn't the greatest idea, but the only other teleporter was stuck inside the mansion. Cooper was their only option.

The Archer didn't have a choice.

"Okay," Cooper said, though Marcus could see in his icy eyes that it was, in fact, *not* okay. "Who do I bring?"

"Malachai," every other Ally said in unison.

Cooper frowned, and Mika growled disapprovingly. "What if this is all part of some scheme? Maybe the prince was planning this the entire time. First, he gains Ash's trust. Then, he saves Cooper from Solaris, which gets everyone else to trust him too. After that, Xavier's Rat blows his cover, and every member of the Draconian Council was injured in the process. Dracus is extremely fragile now. Weak." Marcus flinched. The Princess was right, and he hated it. "After that, he comes up with some story about how he and Pat McBride were Queen Meera's source. Now, the entire Realm thinks he's some sort of hero. And, lastly, his father shows up to an Idonian Council meeting. Something he hasn't done throughout his entire reign. I can only imagine what he's demanding up there. But if I could guess, I'd say it's Malachai. And, once someone gives in and goes off to fetch him, they'll wind up leading the most notorious killer in Idonian history straight into a Round Table Room with every Idonian Council member within it. Not to mention *both* of our

Generals, and one of our Commanders—a man in line to become the next High King. It'll be a fucking bloodbath."

It was a sound argument.

Marcus cursed beneath his breath, his heart now beating far too fast for comfort. He worried that it might explode at any second. He silently weighed the two possibilities. What Mika didn't know was that *he* was the one Malachai had told that story to. Vincent and Sam were both there as well, yet neither one of them spoke up. Maybe she'd gotten through to them. Contorted their thoughts. But Marcus *knew* that the Pandora was telling the truth. He could see it in his eyes and heard it in his voice.

"You're wrong," Marcus told her.

Mika scoffed. "Am I?"

"Yes."

"We don't have time for this," Craven spat. "Is Cooper retrieving Malachai or not?"

All eyes turned to Cooper, and he shrunk beneath everyone's heavy gazes. "I will," he declared, both words wavering as he forced them out.

"Good," Morghan said. "Grab one of Ash's daggers too. I have an idea."

"What sort of idea?" Quinn asked warily.

"One that requires extremely good aim."

48

If only I had a dagger, Ash thought, clenching her jaw. *I could end this right now. There would be no need for a siege. No need to risk any more lives. The Dark King would be dead, and the Prince of Darkness would take over control of the Pandora. Problem solved. War won.*

Well, not entirely. Amorians lived in every Realm. Ash would undoubtedly have to deal with more uprisings, but that was in the future, and, right now, Ash could die any second.

"What will you do with him?" Cleo asked, her sparkling wings lying limp against her back. She was afraid, and she had every right to be. Ash knew that the Fae Queen could see far more than anyone else could. She had the Sight. Whatever power lingered beneath Xavier's surface, she knew about it. "Entrap him?"

Thaddeus shot Cleo a disapproving look, but she wasn't one of his subjects. She returned the favor, as if to remind him of that.

"That is none of your concern," Xavier told her calmly.

"How about a trade?" Beck asked. "Malachai for Lincoln McBride and Constance Waters."

Ash's brows flicked upward, her lips parting. She hadn't thought of that, and she certainly hadn't expected Beck to. However, she wasn't truly fond of the idea. She felt guilty for even considering it. For Malachai to finally escape his father's grasp, only to be betrayed and handed right back to him... her stomach churned at the thought. But if she had to choose between him and Lincoln...

The fact that Thaddeus was furious with his son was written all over his face, but he didn't say a word. Beck was acting like the General he raised him to be. Perhaps he'd forgotten that.

Xavier slowly shook his head. "I'm afraid I can't do that."

"Why not?" Valentina growled, clearly losing what remained of her self-control. "If Malachai is *so* important to you, why not release those that you've stolen? What is so special about Constance and Lincoln that you *need* to have them in your custody? Let the man return to his family. Let Constance return to her life."

The Dark King frowned at her. "Contrary to what you believe, I am not holding either one of them against their will. Therefore, I will not force them to return to lives they have no desire to return to."

"That's bullshit," Ash accused. "If you want to show up to *my* council meeting and threaten *my* council, then the least you can do is show me some respect and not lie straight to my face. I know that Lincoln was injected with something Malachai invented to erase his memories. He might *think* that he's there of his own free will, but he's certainly not." The room fell silent. Ash didn't hear so much as a beating heart.

"I already told you what I would do for you in return," Xavier said through clenched teeth. "Vacate Solaris. Move on. Is that not enough for you? My army will *stand down*."

"You mean Malachai's army," Ash corrected.

Xavier straightened in his seat, his dark eyes narrowing into deadly, sharp slits. "Malachai is the *former* General of my army. That does not mean that the army belongs to him. I'm the king. They answer to me."

"Except the fact that they don't," Lucinda spat. "Let me guess, you didn't take into account that these *beasts* you wanted so badly would actually function as *beasts*. They answer to an Alpha. Just like wolves, and lions, and so forth. You're not one of them. And, by the time you realized this might become a problem, it was too late to become one, because that would make matters even worse. You'd wind up at the bottom of the food chain, while your own son is at the top."

For the first time since that meeting began, Ash found herself smiling, and she wasn't the only one. Thaddeus had begun to smile too. They'd just discovered Xavier's weakness. He had no control over the people who followed him. Not when they looked at his son as their Alpha.

Malachai could very well steal his father's crown. Prophesied Dark King or not, the prince was a threat to Xavier's reign.

Ash, however, was an even bigger threat. Especially now that she knew for a fact that once Malachai made the Realm address the next day, Xavier wouldn't have a leg left to stand on. He'd lose his entire army. *That* was why he wanted him back so badly.

Don't forget that Xavier is powerful enough without an army, and that you'll still need to face him, Ash reminded herself before she got too carried away. *Not to mention, the lives of every soul in the room are in danger. And, unless I get my hands on one of my daggers, we'll be meeting our ancestors by sundown.*

"This isn't up for debate," Xavier reminded them, rising to his feet, turning toward the window behind him. "You might be right, Lucinda, but it doesn't change anything. Malachai will be returned to me. If one of you doesn't leave to get him right now, people will start to die. Did you think that I came here alone? Right now, there is an Arebus Arrow aimed directly at Princess Trinity's heart. Do I give Lincoln the signal, or not?"

Ash's heart took a flying leap off a cliff, her blood chilling to ice.

Beck was already on his feet, as if he could do anything at all to save his baby sister. Aveo had enough sense to drag him back down. Ash's gaze darted over to Thaddeus and Esmeralda. The King was the epitome of stone. If he was panicking at all, he showed no sign of it. Esmeralda, on the other hand, was shaking, horror etched in her features.

"You would harm a five-year-old girl?" Griffon asked so softly that Ash had hardly heard him.

"She'd be the first," Xavier explained, causing a cold sweat to develop beneath Ash's dress. Her tongue felt dry and too thick for her mouth, her throat too tight for her to breathe. "The Allies would scramble and try to save her. Cooper might teleport her to Dracus, but she'd already be dead. And, while they're all acting like frantic rabbits running from a wolf, Lincoln will pick them off. One by one. That's the beauty of being an Arebus Archer, you see. That's what makes them special; More powerful than any other Immortal species known to mankind. All he has to do is *think* about who he wants to strike. And, as long as he's within a three-mile radius, he won't miss a shot. No matter how fast Penelope runs, that arrow will follow her until it reaches its destination."

The Dark King's eyes fell on Aveo. "What a shame that would be," he drawled. "I wonder what he'll aim for. Her heart or her womb. She might survive if he chooses the latter. Again, Cooper might teleport her to Dracus fast enough for the Healers to stop the poison those arrows spread throughout the body. But there goes your chances of producing any heirs. Unless there's already one on the way...." he trailed, whirling around to face him. "What a shame *and* a scandal that would be."

Never before had Ash witnessed a man become so calm to so furious so quickly. While everyone else was simply terrified, morti-fied, and everything of the sort, Aveo was *livid*, but he remained in his seat, gripping the round table so hard to keep himself restrained that the wood began to splinter beneath his fingertips.

"After that, Lincoln will pick off the royals one by one. Then, he'll move onto the Allies and all of their little friends. His siblings might not go down so easily, as they're immune to the poison coating those arrows, but they'll go down, eventually. He might leave Morghan alive, so he can relive the travesty that befell upon Death Valley. He'll be too traumatized to be of any use to any of you. Might as well put the dog down."

Bile started to creep up Ash's throat, choking her.

"So yes, if you refuse to give me my son, you will disable my army. But it won't matter because there will be no one left to command any of yours. No Generals. No Allies. No kings and queens, and no heirs to take their places," Xavier declared, daring to chuckle. "And, of course, there's Loren too, but he has no fight left in him. He could have taken his own life while you were all here. Not that any of you will find out."

"Fine," Ash snarled, shooting to her feet. "Lucinda, give me your teleportation sphere. I'll get Malachai."

Xavier held up a single finger, as if to stop her. "I don't think so," he started, gesturing for her to return to her seat. "For all I know, you're realizing that you're in over your head and aiming to escape, leaving everyone else for dead."

"I would *never* do that," Ash fumed, silver flashing in her eyes.

"Oh, I upset the Berserker," Xavier said, shivering, feigning fear. "You'll remain here. Send someone else for him."

Valentina raised her hand, offering herself for the job.

"No, not you either," Xavier insisted, returning to his seat.

The Prophetess frowned, crossing her arms.

"I'll go," Beck offered.

"Nope," Xavier replied. "If Malachai fails to arrive, all royals die remember? Sorry, kid."

"Then send me," Axel said.

For a second, Ash thought the Dark King might agree. But, of course, he didn't. "You betrayed me. I don't trust you. You'll stay here."

"I'll go," Lucinda said with a heavy sigh, rising to her feet.

Finally, Xavier agreed. Lucinda opened a portal and disappeared through it. Ash could only hope that she thought of some sort of plan, and that she'd return.

"I call a recess while we wait." Xavier called, reclining in his chair. "Feel free to go to the parlor across the hall, pour yourselves some refreshments. I trust that you won't try anything ridiculous. There are eyes upon you."

The council stood in unison; Ash included. She moved to leave, but Xavier stopped her, wrapping his fingers around her wrist. "Not you, dearest."

Ash hung her head, having had a feeling something like this would happen.

"I'll stay too," Aveo offered, returning to his seat.

Valentina snorted from the threshold, drawing attention to herself. "Just as I thought."

The Commander lifted a single brow, giving her a long look that said, *what is it that you thought?*

"You're her Guardian," Valentina declared before slipping out of the room completely. Aveo and Ash shared a look of surprise. Something stirred inside Ash, like a buried door swinging open. A peaceful sensation swept over her, similar to what she felt when Malachai healed her with his abilities. She relaxed in her chair, smiling from ear to ear, just like the Commander across the table.

Xavier ignored them. A small gift.

"Was this what it was like for Penelope and Abernathy?" Ash dared to ask.

"I don't know," Aveo told her. "But, if it was, I feel even more terrible about what happened with that Sorcerer."

49

*L*incoln sat on a boat, a few miles off the coast of an island he could not see. His bow was loaded and drawn, images of a little Princess flashing through his mind. Something in his gut twisted. A subtle reminder of what he was about to do, and that he could never walk away from it. These actions would be set in stone. Unforgivable. But did he care?

Not a chance.

It looks like the council is complying, Richard's voice rang in Lincoln's mind. Right now, the Draconian was currently staring into a spelled fire, watching Xavier's every move. *You can lower your weapon. For now.*

MALACHAI WAS BEGINNING TO FEEL AT HOME IN DRACUS. THAT article in the paper had helped him immensely. The Draconians had started to see him less as a threat, and more as a hero. Benjamin had provided him with a chip, so that he could be contacted if anything were to go awry. People were beginning to *trust* him, and that was a feeling that Malachai had thought he'd never feel again.

The prince had settled nicely into one of Humphrey's spare bedrooms. Anderson had the room across the hall. They'd fallen into a routine of sorts. Wake up shortly after dawn, eat a small breakfast in silence, and then Malachai would head to the Infirmary while Anderson would head to the Communications Center. She would get straight to work with Grant, and by the time Malachai joined them later on in the day, they'd already have a slew of questions ready for him.

They were getting close and closer to finding a way to disable the portal. Malachai could feel it in his bones. While they worked on that, he would work on Lincoln's cure, or his plans to build Willa a saddle. He hadn't told Alistair about the project yet and doubted that the Rider would care much once he did. At least he'd be safer when riding the Dragon into battle. Alistair would thank him eventually.

"That's a *lot* of steel," Anderson mentioned, peeping over Malachai's shoulder to view the material list.

Nodding, Malachai continued drawing out his design. "Big beasts require very big saddles, and those require a lot of materials."

"Expensive materials," Anderson added. "Had I known you had *that* much coin, I'd have had you pay for that round of drinks last night."

"*I* paid for the drinks last night," Grant growled from where he sat, typing at his desk.

Before their conversation could continue, Benjamin walked into the lab, looking worse for wear.

"How's King Loren?" Malachai asked, temporarily abandoning his project.

The Head of Communications shrugged before falling into a chair, raking a hand through his sandy curls.

"As far as the injury goes, he's healing nicely. No signs of infection," Benjamin told him. "But he refuses to leave his quarters. He won't even go out into the rest of his suite. He remains in bed all day, staring at a mural on his ceiling. If he speaks, it's about Richard or Penelope. One second he'll recall some wonderful time with that Rat from his childhood, and the next he's saying something about how he's happy for Penelope and Aveo."

Malachai's brow furrowed. "Why shouldn't he be happy for Penelope and Aveo?"

"Oh," Grant said, sucking in a breath. "That's a long story."

"They were going to get married," Benjamin revealed to him. "But Penelope changed her mind. She was too afraid to piss off the Elves. Since then, her and Aveo have been getting along pretty well. There are whispers of them planning a small wedding to take place before the siege."

Wincing, Malachai could only imagine how Loren felt about that. "No wonder he won't get out of bed. The man's sick with heartache. Unfortunately, my abilities can't help with that."

"You know what they say, the best way to get over someone is to get under someone," Anderson mentioned as she returned to her station. "Maybe all he needs is a hot date."

"He lost a hand," Benjamin reminded her, scoffing with disbelief. "Trust me, it's going to be awhile before he has the urge to woo someone. If he ever does. I've known him all his life, and I can assure you that he's not the type to participate in a one-night stand. Anyway, whatcha working on, Malachai?"

Malachai glanced down at the papers in front of him, covered in calculations and the names of ingredients he might very well have to sneak back into Solaris to get. "A saddle and a cure for Lincoln McBride," he revealed with slumping shoulders. "Which will be extremely difficult to create now that I no longer have access to my lab. Which means, I don't have the proper ingredients, or a blood sample to test it."

"Sounds like quite the conundrum," Anderson said, pouting. "Maybe we could sneak in there?"

"Yeah, let's not do that again," Grant said, his lips dipping into a frown.

"You didn't even participate," Anderson reminded him.

"That might be true, but I was in Crane, listening in on every word. It was one of the most stressful things I've ever endured," Grant informed her, crossing his arms defensively. "Not to mention, we're down a teleporter, whose funeral we should probably have attended. I feel bad. We should be there with everyone else."

Benjamin nodded in agreement, but said, "Some of us needed

to stay behind. For Loren. Lady Evanora is doing her best, but she needs people to depend on."

"And, I wasn't invited," Malachai added. He'd known, the second that he found out about Aries' unexpected passing, that he wouldn't get to say goodbye to the Fae. Some might think that such a thing wouldn't bother him, but that wasn't true. Malachai had the utmost respect for Aries and had trusted him. That said a lot, considering the prince's past.

Everyone returned to their tasks. Benjamin read messages, Anderson and Grant continued their work with the portal, or black hole. At least, that's how Malachai saw it. They wound up needing his opinion on a few things, but most of the time he worked on Lincoln's cure. The undying urge to fix his mistakes pushed him to consider alternative ingredients. An entirely new formula, that might work the same way. Ultimately, he decided to get Ebony's opinion, and began to pack up his things. Just as he was turning to leave, Cooper appeared in front of him, one of Ash's Enchanted Daggers in his hands.

Malachai staggered backward, nearly tripping over his feet. He'd known that he and Cooper were still far from friends but thought that the Archer would follow Valentina's very clear directions. Don't kill each other. "*What* are you doing with that?"

Cooper sucked in a series of breaths. Clearly, he'd been running. "I need you to use it to kill your father."

50

Malachai had never imagined that his father would act so boldly. But, as he and Cooper raced to the castle, with Benjamin's key to the portal room, he realized that he'd underestimated him. A mistake that he would never make again.

"We don't know what he's saying in there," Cooper explained as they ran. "The only reason that we realized that he was there, was because Alistair sensed something weird and then Morghan picked up on his scent."

Nodding, Malachai tried to imagine what his father's goals might be. That was when a thought occurred to him. An extremely, terrifying thought.

What if Lincoln was there, too?

"We should hurry," Malachai insisted.

"We're running as fast as we can," Cooper argued.

Wrong, Malachai thought, transitioning into the fastest animal he could think of. A horse. All he had to do was give Cooper a look, and the Archer reached out, taking hold of him before swinging himself onto his back. *Odd,* Malachai grunted. *But, it works.*

Immortal speed in a Mortal form was fast, but Immortal speed in the form of a horse… they made it back to the castle in less than two minutes. Cooper dismounted, swaying back and forth. Malachai transitioned, reaching out to steady him.

"That was *fast*," Cooper blurted.

"Yes, it was. Now, let's get moving," the Pandora ordered, pushing through the castle doors. The guards paid him no mind. *Privilege of being Meera's source.* He headed for the stairs and was nearly there when a portal opened beside him, and Lucinda Cross stepped out.

The Sorceress took one look at him, enchanted dagger in hand, and said, "You can't walk in there dressed like that."

Malachai looked down at his attire and groaned. That morning, he'd dressed for leisure, not battle. He was wearing a plain white t-shirt and a pair of black denim pants. "Well, I don't have a uniform," he told her.

"Just use the one you wore on the last mission," Cooper suggested.

"I have no idea where it is," Malachai informed him. "I'm not even sure *who* it belonged to."

Lucinda looked him up and down with a steady, scrutinizing gaze. "Vincent," she said. "And I know how to get into his suite so let's *move*."

IT WAS IMPOSSIBLE TO DRESS WITH LUCINDA EXPLAINING EVERYTHING that had occurred. The amount of pressure upon Malachai as he pulled off his clothes, replacing them with a prince's uniform, was surreal. The Sorceress paced back and forth while the prince fumbled with zippers, buttons, and belts.

"I feel like I'm robbing someone, and I don't like it," Malachai admitted, tying his dark hair back with a leather strip.

Lucinda rolled her eyes in response. "You can terrorize villages, yet you feel strange about robbing a prince." She shook her head, scoffing with disbelief. "Vincent's reaction to your theft is the *last* thing you should be worrying about. Your father is holding the entirety of the Idonian Council hostage. Lincoln McBride is currently prepared to shoot down a five-year-old Princess. Right now, you're the only one who can stop that. If I don't return within a certain timeframe, everyone on that island will die one by one."

Nodding, Malachai sucked in a breath, stealing myself. "What do you think I should do? Barge into the room he's in, whip a dagger at him and *hope* it buries itself in his heart?"

"Yes," she told him. "That's exactly what you need to do, but I wouldn't barge in. I'd walk in, head held high. Pretend you're there to have a conversation. And then, hit him with the dagger when he least expects it."

Cooper appeared not a second later, dressed in his uniform, his massive black bow peaking over his shoulder. "Are we ready?" the Archer inquired, glancing between the pair.

"As ready as we'll ever be," Lucinda replied. "I'll open a portal to the mansion. There's no need to access the portal room. We'll leave from right here, the second you both give me the go ahead."

Malachai shared a look with the Archer, one filled with understanding. They would never be ready for something like this, not when so many lives hung in the balance. And, while they hardly knew one another, and had had their quarrels, one thing was clear. Together, they'd prevent any casualties. So, when the prince nodded, Lucinda threw her sphere to the ground and a portal leading to their fate appeared.

"Where are they?" Esmeralda demanded, eyeing the hallway from where she stood inside the parlor, her drink trembling in her grip.

During the last twenty minutes, Valentina had watched the Elves unravel like a ball of yarn. Thaddeus's stony facade had finally cracked the second he hurried to the window, staring out in hopes of catching sight of his daughters.

The Prophetess had done the same more than once, but she hadn't seen a soul. Wherever the Allies had gone, she hoped that it was somewhere safe, and that they weren't lying dead in the forest.

"I'm scared," Princess Trinity admitted from where she sat on a log in between Quinn and Vincent. Lilly stood behind her, watching the forest warily.

The Pegasi had followed them into the forest, clearly having picked up on Darkness's presence as well. The White Stag lingered nearby, the only thing standing between them and the mansion. Quinn couldn't help but think that he was trying to protect them. The only problem was that they were unarmed. And, that nothing would protect them from Xavier. Nothing.

Unsure of what else to do, Quinn wrapped an arm around the tiny Princess and pulled her closer. The other Allies were scattered about, ready for whatever might come. Morghan was in his Wolf form, standing nearby the Stag. Craven was perched in a tree, his violet eyes darting in every direction. Anastasia and Alistair were standing in front of Mika and Penelope. The Draconian's abilities were the only thing that could protect them.

The familiar sound of a sailing arrow rang in Quinn's ears. *Lincoln,* he thought, heart skipping into overdrive. The only chance he had to save whoever it was headed to was his senses, so he tracked it, eyes bulging once he realized it was coming in *his* direction.

In an instant, Quinn reached out, snatching the arrow out of the air, snapping it in two.

"Was that arrow meant for you?" Alistair asked in a demanding tone.

Shaking his head, Quinn said, "No. It wasn't."

All eyes turned toward Trinity, who hadn't dared to open her eyes. She was too busy curling into the Archer's side, her tears soaking his black button-down shirt. She hadn't noticed, but it didn't make a difference. Lincoln would realize that he missed his target, and he'd try again.

The Allies moved quickly, forming a circle around the log Quinn and Trinity were resting on. Penelope, Lilly, and Mika found their way inside, and together, they made a second barrier around the

Princess. Quinn helped, wrapping his arms around them all, determined to ensure that Trinity left that island without a mark on her. Even if that meant taking the arrows himself.

One look at Mika and Penelope told Quinn that they felt the same way.

51

*M*alachai passed through a portal, walking straight into a parlor filled with Idonian Council members. He froze, taking in the expressions upon their faces. So much hate lingered in all of their eyes. The prince's only saving grace was Valentina, who stepped forward, taking one of his hands in hers.

The Prophetess looked him up and down, examining his stolen uniforms. To Malachai's surprise, she laughed. "You're wearing the wrong color," she admitted, causing his brow to furrow with confusion. "Anyway, they're across the hall. He probably knows you're here. Ash and Aveo are inside. We haven't heard anything. I don't think anyone's been harmed."

Nodding, Malachai sucked in a breath. "We have a plan."

Cooper and Lucinda moved to stand in front of the council. The Archer drew his bow, pointing it toward the door. Lucinda's wand was gripped tightly in her hand, ready for anything that might come.

"What sort of plan?" Thaddeus asked.

Malachai withdrew the enchanted dagger stashed in his belt. "This," he told the Elven King, hoping that he'd understand. The odds were that Xavier could hear everything they were saying. "Lucinda will explain everything," he mouthed, gesturing toward the Sorceress before turning toward the hallway, his gaze falling on the door across the hall.

There was no sense in waiting another second longer. No matter what Malachai did, he would never be prepared. So, he rolled his shoulders, twirled the dagger in his grip, and made his way out into the hall.

ASH KNEW HE WAS THERE. SHE COULD FEEL IT IN HER BONES. THE urge to sigh with relief came over her, but she didn't dare. Instead, she stared across the table, meeting Aveo's gaze. No matter what happened next, they'd make it out.

The sound of glass shattering in the room across the hall had everyone shooting to their feet, Xavier included. "He wasn't supposed to start yet. Why did he start?" the king mumbled to himself, returning to the window, scanning the island.

Ash watched him warily. If Lincoln had started shooting without orders, how many of her Allies were dead? What had happened to Princess Trinity? She gulped, turning her gaze toward her Scepter. Without a second thought, she reached for it.

"What do you think you're doing?" Xavier snarled, whirling around to face her.

"What I was destined to do," she replied simply, aiming the weapon toward him.

"Don't," Xavier said. "If you do, you won't just harm me. You'll harm your mother too."

So, now you're using me as a pawn? MEERA SEETHED FROM WITHIN. *Against my own daughter? Just to save your own head, which was destined to be severed from your shoulders?*

Xavier ignored her, no longer in the mood to entertain. How could he be, when the ancient weapon created specifically to disable his powers was aimed directly at his heart? Now was *not* the time for Meera's complaints. Yet they continued anyway.

It's over Xavier. You failed. Amoria's resurrection wasn't meant to be. Accept it. Die honorably, so that we can both be free.

"I refuse," he said out loud, no longer caring about the witnesses in the room. "I will *never* accept death."

The Moonlight inside the orb at the end of Ash's Scepter began to glow brighter and brighter. Her unarmed Guardian moved to the other side of the table, taking his place at her side.

"That won't kill me," Xavier told her, cringing as the monster within him threatened to break free. He could feel himself beginning to change, no matter how badly he tried to fight it. His veins began to glow. The entirety of his eyes was swallowed by the Darkness. In a matter of seconds, the blood flowing through him began to heat, burning like embers in a fire. His head throbbed, horns beginning to threaten to break through.

The Dark One was angry.

"Do it," Aveo told Ash.

Moonlight began to emit from the orb, sailing toward him. Before it had a chance to grace Xavier's changing flesh, the door flew open, and the *real* threat emerged. Malachai. But, before he had a chance to say a word, he noticed a silver, enchanted dagger racing toward him. It buried into his chest, just barely missing his heart.

Good, the Dark One purred as Xavier ripped the dagger from his flesh, tossing it to the ground. *Let us take our leave. We are done here.*

No, Meera argued, fighting against the coming teleportation with all her might. *You won't escape. I won't allow it.*

Meera's words meant nothing. They escaped anyway, and the next thing Xavier knew, he was standing in his office back in Solaris. He collapsed, holding a hand to the wound in his chest. The Moonshade wouldn't kill him. It wouldn't travel throughout him, the same way it did to others, racing toward their hearts. He was safe. In pain, but alive. And he would remain that way. For now.

52

"It took you long enough," Ash growled, banishing her Scepter back into her mindspace. "I was almost certain that he was about to sprout horns."

Malachai didn't respond. Instead, he continued to stare at the place his father had just been standing, vibrating with rage. The Idonian Council members started to enter the room one by one, scanning it for any threats, eyeing the Pandora in their midst warily.

"Where did he go?" Cooper whispered, loaded bow still in hand.

"Not the Underworld, unfortunately," Aveo revealed, walking around the table to retrieve Ash's bloody dagger. The one that Malachai had missed his shot with. "But, he's gone, and that's what matters. Today, he had the element of surprise. He won't get that again."

Nodding, Ash looked toward Malachai, her heart sinking.

"I could have ended this," the Pandora said so softly that she'd hardly heard him. Cleo put a sympathetic hand on his shoulder, and the Elves averted their attention to the windows. "If I hadn't missed..." he shook his head, finally meeting Ash's gaze. "I'm sorry."

"Don't apologize," Ash demanded, walking toward him. "It was never supposed to be your burden to bear anyway. We all commend you for even trying. I'm not sure that anyone else in this room would be willing to kill their own father."

No one disagreed with her. And, as she surveyed their faces, she caught sight of the slightest hint of sympathy upon Thaddeus's face. It was gone in an instant. "We should get outside and check on the others. Lincoln could still act. Xavier will want revenge for what just happened." The king left the room, his wife and son following soon after. The rest of the council, and their new guests, followed in suit.

Malachai walked slowly, like some sort of undead creature, lost in his own mind. Ash eyed him, wondering what he was thinking. Was he still mulling over the fact that he'd missed, therefore *not* saving the Immortal Armies from a siege that would take many lives? Or was reality sinking in?

There was no going back now.

"Nice uniform," Axel said, pulling the prince from his thoughts.

Shrugging, Malachai said, "Couldn't walk in here in a t-shirt and jeans, now could I?"

"It looks good on you," Lucinda told him, flashing a too-white smile. It was evident that she was trying to lift his spirits. The odds were that that wasn't possible. She knew that feeling. *Failure.* It's how she'd felt, lying in the snow, bleeding out. Looking back, she was *glad* she'd failed. If she had tried to fight back, if she had killed Malachai, then who would have shown up today? Who would have had the guts to storm into a room and whip a dagger at the Dark King? Who would have healed her after her fight with the beast, and helped her fill the Scepter? Who would have saved Cooper?

Ash's throat became thick. She knew how the council would react to what she was about to do, but she reached out and took his hand anyway.

Malachai slowed his pace as they passed through the front doors, out onto the extravagant porch. He stared down at their hands, his brow wrinkling with confusion. Slowly, his gaze lifted to her face. He opened his mouth to speak, likely to warn her about why she shouldn't be touching him, but she cut him off.

"I'm proud of you," she declared, squeezing his hand once

before releasing it. "Now if you'll excuse me, I have six missing Allies and a few royals to locate."

THE ARROWS HAD STOPPED.

Four of them were currently embedded in Quinn's back, all of them intended for the Princess he held in his grip. He felt more anger than pain, though he was sure that would change later.

"I think he gave up," Penelope whispered, so close to Quinn that her breath tickled his neck. "We can probably separate now."

"I'd rather not," Mika squeaked, somewhere between Lilly and Penelope.

"Whether it's a good idea or not, there are four arrows sticking out of Quinn's back right now, some of which appear to be near extremely vital organs. It might be a good idea to get him some medical attention," Vincent said urgently, from right behind where Quinn fought to keep standing. "I hope Cooper was able to retrieve Malachai."

A small debate began to occur, one which Quinn didn't have the energy to participate in. His main focus was Trinity, who thankfully had stopped crying. She'd heard every arrow hit him. Everyone had. Anastasia had cursed so loudly, one might have thought she was hit.

But she wasn't.

No one else was. Only Quinn, as if Lincoln had known he was the one standing between him and his kill.

Lincoln's *kill* had been a five-year-old girl.

Quinn swallowed against the vomit sailing up his throat, unable to believe the last hour had occurred. Unable to believe that his own brother had attempted to do something like this.

There were some things that you couldn't come back from. Even *if* Malachai found a way to cure Lincoln, as he'd said that he would, he wouldn't be the same. Not once he learned about all he'd done. Quinn's heart broke for him, but less and less every day.

Footsteps sounded nearby. People were coming. A passing breeze carried Ash's scent, and Quinn sighed with relief. He released the princesses from his grasp, and the ring of people around them dispersed. Trinity remained where she was, clutching his shirt for dear life. Vincent remained behind him, examining his wounds without daring to touch them.

"Sit," Craven demanded. "Slowly."

Quinn did as he said, lowering himself back onto the log beside the tiny Princess, his back facing the other way. The last thing he wanted to do was scare her any more than she already was.

"Holy shit," someone said right before Quinn was swarmed.

Cooper stood at Quinn's side, staring down at him, complete and utter disdain twisting in his features. He glanced at Trinity and clenched his jaw.

"Malachai," Ash called, her voice trembling. "We have a problem."

The next second, someone was tearing Trinity from his lap. The Elven King. At first, she didn't want to let go, but once she realized her father was there, Quinn was chopped liver. He certainly *felt* like chopped liver.

"Get her out of here," Quinn ground out. "Get *everyone* out of here."

"Already on it," Lucinda replied, whipping her sphere at the ground. "I'll come back for you and Malachai."

"I'm not leaving him," Ash insisted.

"Yes, you are," Aveo argued. "If Lincoln is still in a three-mile radius and realizes that he has the perfect opportunity to get rid of one of Xavier's biggest problems, he'll do it. So, we're leaving. Now."

When the Commander gained the ability to command Ash, Quinn didn't know, but she listened. However, not without uttering some sort of crude comment beneath her breath. Quinn laughed, but that hurt him more. He stopped immediately.

The next few minutes were a blur of agony, and then the most calming sensation Quinn had ever experienced. "Damn," he muttered, his eyelids fluttering, threatening to close.

Once the prince had finished, Quinn sat up, amazed by how *good* he felt. "What happened in there?" he asked, figuring that was a good way to pass the time while they waited for Lucinda to return. "Looks like everyone got out fine. That's surprising, considering they were in the same room as Xavier."

"Let's just say that I had the chance to prevent Ash from ever needing to face him again, and I failed," Malachai told him, sulking against a tree, reaching to rub his temples. "I must have missed his heart by a few millimeters. I scared him away, but that's about it. Apparently, he forgot to call off his dogs. Now, Ash will still have to infiltrate Solaris, and Xavier will give her everything he's got. Because now, she isn't *just* the Messenger. She stole me away from him. Moons only know what he'll do to her. Scenarios are already swarming my mind. What if he keeps her alive? Tortures her? Wipes her memory and uses her during the rest of his escapades throughout the Realm? Maybe he'll make her a trophy wife, just to spite me."

Quinn stiffened. "Why would that spite you?" he inquired with narrowing eyes. *Don't tell me this idiot is after her too. First Beck, then Alistair, and now Malachai? Where the fuck do I fit in?*

"I refused to kill her, remember? I defied him because I saw something good in her. I'd been looking for an excuse to leave him for decades. Ash gave me one. Now, I can try to have a normal life. Be the Healer I was before he forced me into all this shit," Malachai explained. "He'd do anything to spite me for that. Including parading her around the Realms."

Quinn's mouth went dry. He tried to swallow and failed.

"And I just had a chance to kill him and take that burden off her shoulders and make up for the horrible things he made me do," Malachai added angrily, kicking at dirt. "I just want to apologize. To everyone. That was the *one* way I could do it and I *failed*."

The Archer watched his head falling into his hands. For a second, he thought he might be shedding a few frustrated tears. But Quinn was soon distracted by movement in the nearby brush. One of the Pegasi had returned. The only black one, with massive, feathered wings that mirrored a certain fallen friend's. Quinn watched in awe as it sauntered up to them, nudging the prince who hadn't seen it come.

Malachai lifted his head and was struck silent. Quinn could hear his heart, slowing. Calming. He watched them stare into each other's eyes. Understanding one another. Beast to beast. Whatever was happening between them, Quinn didn't know. He did, however, wish that it was happening to him. To have a majestic animal walk straight up to you, clearly with the intent of easing your pain... Malachai was a lucky man. Because Quinn had a feeling that he knew what was *really* happening in that moment.

Aries.

The prince reached up, running his hand along the creature's muzzle. After, the Pegasus bid him goodbye. It walked a few paces before taking off into the sky to join his herd.

"Feel better?" Quinn asked.

"I-I don't know what just happened," Malachai admitted, a bit flustered.

"You and I both know what just happened."

"I... think I might have been... tasked," he admitted, shooting to his feet, shaking his head as if to make sense of it all.

Quinn stood as well, watching the Pandora curiously. "What do you mean *tasked*?"

"I don't know," he said, his tone trembling. "It said things to me."

"Well, what sort of things?"

"He called me king."

"*What?*" Quinn blurted.

Malachai shrugged. "He called me by my true name... with king before it. But he told me that the only way to become that was to follow Ash. I'm supposed to remain by her side, and help her, no matter the cost. That the only way I will reach redemption is if we end this war. Together."

"Sounds complicated," Quinn replied, unsure of what else to say. "What's your true name?"

The prince's muscles went rigid at the sound of the question. "Why?"

"Is it not what you go by? Should we be calling you something else? Chai, perhaps?" Quinn asked, crossing his arms. "That's what my father called you. What I referred to you as, all those years ago."

"Oh," Malachai's posture softened, his face crumbling. "I didn't know you remembered all of that."

"Took me a second," Quinn admitted. "You make shitty eggs."

Malachai scoffed, tossing a twig at him. "I never said that I was any good at making them. But, when a toddler asks you for food, you can't exactly say no."

"So, did the beast call you Chai, then? Or did he call you something else?" Quinn wasn't going to let this go.

"Something else," Malachai admitted, staring at the Archer with the most serious look he'd ever seen him wear. "Can I trust you?"

"Have I given you a reason not to?" Quinn countered.

"Not exactly."

"Spit it out then. If you want me to help you with this task of yours, then I might as well know your real name," Quinn retorted.

"I didn't say you needed to help—"

"Spit. It. Out, *Chai.*"

Malachai pressed his lips into a hard line, his nostrils flaring ever so slightly. "Fine," he agreed. "But if you breathe a word to *anyone*, you won't just ruin my life, you'll ruin someone else's too. You'll take this to the grave."

"Okay," Quinn said, the word dragging on, his stomach beginning to twist with unease. The same way it always did when he felt like something bad was about to happen.

"Malachai Bonaventure," Malachai revealed, just as a portal opened behind them. Lucinda stepped out, staring at the prince with wide, surprised eyes. He didn't react to her presence. Perhaps he thought that he could trust her. Meanwhile, Quinn was at a loss for words, now recalling every second he thought that the prince had looked familiar. The truth came crashing down upon him, nearly knocking him off his feet. He stared at the prince, noticing all the features he shared with Marcus. The same sharp jawline, nose, and vivid green eyes.

It was only a matter of time before people started to notice.

No wonder Malachai had warned that his true name might ruin

someone else's life. If the Realm found out that Marcus Bonaventure, former Guardian to the High Queen, was Xavier's son all along... they'd think he played a part in the Idonian Kingdom's fall.

The portal closed behind the Sorceress, just before she said, "You're lucky I was the only one in the room I just opened that portal from." Quinn blinked, his brows flicking upward. She turned her attention to him, offering him a genuine smile. "Look at you, as good as new. Which is great. Dinner is in about an hour. It gives you both time to get cleaned up and change."

"Aren't you going to react?" Quinn asked.

"React to what?" Lucinda gave him the sort of look that made him feel ridiculously daft. "You don't think I already knew that? I know everything. I just never *say* that I know everything. That's why they call me the Sorceress of Secrets."

53

Malachai wished they'd taken him back to Dracus. There was no reason for him to be in the Kingdom of Elves. He was already wracked with nerves about what he'd have to do tomorrow. Address the entire Realm. Something he'd never done and had never thought he would.

To make matters worse, he'd had to sit through a dinner with the Chamberlains. Sure, he'd just saved their asses, but that didn't erase past discrepancies. He'd murdered their nephew, in that very castle. While they slept. On Giving Day, exactly three years ago.

Everything about Malachai's current circumstances were, in his opinion, fucked. He shouldn't be there. Nothing about being there felt right. He was sick to his stomach. It was after eleven at night, and despite how exhausted he was, he couldn't calm his mind enough to sleep. He tried to use his time wisely instead, working on random projects to take his mind off of everything. He sent over a few finishing details for Willa's saddle over to Benjamin for him to review. After that, he'd listed a few ingredients he thought might be able to substitute for the rare ones he would need for Lincoln's cure. That didn't last long.

Ultimately, he wound up pacing the length of his suite, glancing out at the familiar view. Something about it made his stomach stir, and he found himself heading out onto the balcony.

Malachai stared down at the Kingdom beyond, his mouth dryer than a Zerinian desert. Every soul living inside the great Golden City had decorated for the holiday. Despite the late hour, people were still walking the streets, buying hot chocolate and ice skating beneath twinkling lights. Couples walked hand in hand. Parents hurried to finish their last-minute shopping.

These people were *happy*, despite everything Malachai had done. They were doing all the things he *wished* he could do.

Leaning against the waist-high, snow-covered railing, Malachai resolved to watch them for a while. Perhaps live vicariously through the Elves and Mortals enjoying the late winter's night.

That was before he realized that he'd been in that part of the castle, staring out at the same view, if only for a few seconds. His blood ran cold, the color draining from his cheeks. Slowly, he looked up. There was another balcony above. One that he'd used to sneak into Cedric Chamberlain's suite.

Malachai started to shake from head to toe. Memories of that night began to flash before his eyes, but they didn't stop there. They went further back to when he'd first met the Elf, before his entire life had changed for the worst. They'd hit it off. Two bright minds, with their entire lives ahead of them. But Cedric had left to explore Si Realtra. Malachai had planned to do the same, before all his dreams were snatched away from him in the blink of an eye.

Now, the Elves were taunting him. Reminding him of what he'd done, and that they'd never forgive him. That he would *never* be accepted.

No matter how badly Ash tried to stand in between him and everything he deserved, it would never be enough.

Closing his eyes, Malachai fought to regain control of his emotions, but his anger for the Elves was bubbling over. How could he help Ash end the war, while constantly trying to outrun all he had done before he met her? The Pegasus *had* to be wrong. A man like him could never be a king.

Someone touched his shoulder, ripping him from his thoughts. Out of instinct, Malachai reached for their wrist, his eyes flying open. Once he saw that it was Valentina, he immediately released her, opening his mouth to apologize.

"I had a vision," she explained. "One that I wanted to prevent."

Malachai watched the Prophetess look toward the balcony and the ground below. His stomach twisted with unease, his nostrils burning with coming tears. "I-I wasn't——"

"Going to leap off this balcony?" Valentina supplied, giving him a disbelieving look. "You don't have to explain to me. It's not my business. But, before you go ahead and ruin our chances of using the Pandora against your father, therefore putting Ash in even *more* danger, you should probably know a few things. One, I know you were tasked today."

Unsure of how to reply, Malachai kept his mouth shut, hanging his head shamefully.

"That was before the Moons just woke me up out of a dead sleep, screaming at me to come get you," Valentina added afterward, crossing her arms in front of her silk robe. "If you die, so do our chances of winning this war. Every day, I see more and more about how horribly Si Realtra will be affected by it. This is bigger than any of us ever thought. You included. We need you. Don't be selfish."

Biting his inner cheek, Malachai offered her a nod.

"You know, after you ran off after dinner, the Allies decided to do a gift exchange. They all pulled names out of a hat. Yours was one of them," Valentina revealed. Malachai blinked, surprised. "But since you weren't *there*. You got the short end of the stick. You got *two* names."

Something twinged in Malachai's heart. Something *good*. "They... included me?"

"Yes," Valentina confirmed. "*Someone* is getting you a gift. And, you have some shopping to do right now, if you expect to participate. You *do* have a busy day tomorrow."

"I couldn't go out there," Malachai whispered.

"Yes, you can," Valentina insisted. "All the others are already out there. Well, everyone except Marcus. If you want, I can take you to him. I'm sure he'd be happy to take you along."

Though he tried not to, Malachai cringed. "I'm not sure *happy* is the right word."

"Oh, I can assure you he's in a pleasant mood," Valentina purred, turning to leave the balcony. "Grab your cloak and follow me."

"Where are we going?" Malachai inquired, hurrying to do as she asked.

"My suite."

Malachai stopped dead in his tracks. "What?"

"Don't look so surprised," Valentina said, winking at him over her shoulder.

"WHAT IN THE EIGHT LAYERS OF THE UNDERWORLD AM I SUPPOSED to get Aveo?" Anastasia grumbled, walking at Penelope's side. "And when are you going to explain to me why—"

Lucinda snapped her fingers, urging the Fire Clan Leader to shut her mouth. "Don't forget where we are."

Currently, Penelope was walking in between the two women down one of the busiest streets in the city. No one seemed to be paying attention, but that didn't mean they weren't listening in, hoping to hear a wisp of royal gossip.

"I think it's pretty obvious *why*," she whispered.

Ana gave her a nod, clenching his jaw. "But will you be happy?"

Nodding, the Princess said, "I do believe I can be."

"He's your sister's Guardian now," Lucinda mentioned. "Who saw that coming? Other than Valentina, of course."

"I certainly didn't," Penelope said with a snort. "I never saw Aveo becoming anything other than a Commander. Not to mention, he never really got along with the other species. Ash is all of them, and more. Lately, however, he seems to have changed quite a bit. He's warmer now. More accepting. For Sovereign's sake, he's shopping with the McBrides and Morghan right now."

Lucinda's smile grew wider, her eyes shining a bit bright beneath the twinkling lights wrapped around lamp posts and hanging from shop awnings. "He's come a long way from denying Quinn entry to the Kingdom," she chuckled. "Speaking of the Archer, I haven't the slightest clue what to get him. A hat, perhaps? Maybe some socks?"

Ana snorted. "Get him something cool, like a teleportation sphere."

"I can't *give* him one of those," Lucinda informed her. Penelope rolled her eyes, having a feeling that the Fire Clan Leader was going to get one lengthy lecture. "Those are given to Sorcerers who have graduated from their training and proven themselves worthy. Quinn is not a Magic wielder."

"Neither is Richard, but he clearly must have had one to escape Dracus," Penelope reminded her.

The Sorceress cringed. "I have a bad feeling about him. I think that he might actually be a Sorcerer. That he might even have been one before he became a Draconian."

An eerie silence fell over them, one filled with the hustle and bustle of the city that didn't appear to sleep during the holidays.

"We could rescue his betrothed from Solaris," Ana suggested abruptly. "Open a portal, drag her out. Boom. Happy Giving Day. Go make babies."

Penelope laughed, though it was hardly a thing to laugh about. She didn't know Sam well, and hadn't really made an effort to, but she knew that he missed his sister.

"I'm not entirely sure that betrothal is still on," Lucinda admitted. "I've seen the way he looks at Ash. She was all he talked about during our journey to the first task. He told Craven and I stories about her growing up. He rarely mentioned Constance."

Penelope hoped that one day, he'd tell *her* those stories. She might understand her sister better. Maybe even as much as Quinn did. A sinking feeling told her that she would *never* come close, but she was willing to try. Which was why she was out there shopping, when she hadn't plucked a name from the hat. She wanted her first Giving Day with Ash to be perfect. Even if her sister would be out in the field, waiting at a tunnel entrance for Pandora.

Suddenly, a thought occurred to her. "I have an idea."

"For Quinn or Aveo?" Ana groused.

"Ash," she admitted. "Cedric's collection of daggers. He'd want her to have them."

"Well, who pulled Ash's name?" Lucinda asked.

54

"What do you buy for a Sorceress?" Morghan asked Lilly, examining tables covered in silks and jewelry. "Lucinda doesn't seem like the materialistic type."

Lilly shrugged. "I don't know Lucinda that well, but I did watch her destroy a platter of cupcakes after dinner. She really seemed to like them. Maybe get her some of those."

Scoffing, Morghan could only imagine the look on Lucinda's face. "She might kill me."

"Lucinda is *way* easier to shop for than who *I* wound up picking," Cooper complained from a few aisles over. "I got Marcus. I hardly know the guy. He just feeds me."

Morghan gave Cooper a long look and said, "Marcus is easy to buy for. Actually, you don't need to buy him a thing. Give him something homemade. He appreciates shit like that."

"Not to mention, he's already getting another gift from Beck," Lilly added. "Only he already told us what his gift is. A night on the house at his pub, for everyone. One that I can't attend."

"I'm sure he'll think of something special for you," Morghan assured her.

"Oh, I don't care about getting anything special," Lilly told him. "All I want is for everyone to have a nice holiday. The biggest gift I could receive is seeing you all smile."

Cooper made some sort of choking nose, and Morghan looked over just in time to watch him melt, sparkles shining in his eyes. "How did something so *sweet* come from our father?"

"What do you mean? We're all sweet," Lilly argued.

"Uh, have you seen Lincoln lately?" Morghan countered.

Pouting, Lilly waved him off. "I don't want to talk about him. I just hope we can fix him soon, so he doesn't do anything else like he did today. If we can prove that outside of Xavier's control, he's a *good* man, we might be able to convince the Idonian Council to let him go home. Even if he's forbidden from ever leaving Crane's borders again. That's all we can hope for."

"I suppose," Cooper muttered, causing Lilly to bristle, which he noticed immediately. "Listen, you're not the one he shot four times."

"Quinn is just as hopeful as I am, even after the fact," Lilly insisted.

"Quinn isn't the only one Lincoln hurt," Cooper retorted harshly. "Don't blame me for being a little hesitant where he's concerned. He shot me down and then stood there and did nothing while Savron Phantom shredded me to pieces. My love was transferred from him to the people who saved me *from* him."

WHATEVER HAD HAPPENED INSIDE THAT SHOP MORGHAN AND Cooper had gone into with Lilly was horrid, and it ruined the Giving Day shopping spirit. But Aveo wouldn't let that stop him from trying to find a gift for Alistair, and Penelope as well. He couldn't complete either of those tasks if he didn't improve the mood.

After watching Cooper storm out of the shop, barreling down the street in a fit of emotions, Lilly and Morghan sulked out onto the street. "Okay," Aveo said, the word dragging on longer than necessary. "Does someone want to explain what happened so we can fix it and try to enjoy the rest of this night?"

Quinn was too busy staring in the direction his brother had gone. Aveo wondered if he was going to take off after him or give him space. Whatever happened next would help him understand the brothers more, which he desperately needed to do. Especially now that he was Guardian to someone who loved them wholeheartedly.

"He's more unstable than we thought," Morghan started to explain with a deep frown. "And, honestly, I can't blame him. Not after what Lincoln did to him. Because of his own brother's actions, everything changed for him. Even his DNA. Which he still refuses to accept. In case you haven't noticed, he isn't drinking any blood, which isn't good. Not to mention, he just said he transferred whatever love he had left for Lincoln over to the people who saved him."

"If he's not drinking blood, he could enter a state of bloodlust," Lilly whispered. "Remember what Mika said earlier about the Scarlet Era? How the Draconians couldn't control their lust for blood at first, and that once they got a taste for Elven blood…"

Cursing beneath his breath, Aveo could only imagine the catastrophe that would occur if Cooper lost his cool. "I'm going after him," he said, reaching into his pocket, handing Lilly an identification card. "Show this to shopkeepers, and they'll cover any costs. Find something for Alistair and pick out a ring for Penelope."

"Shouldn't you do that?" Morghan asked.

"Shouldn't *I* be the one going after Cooper?" Quinn added defensively.

Shaking his head, Aveo said, "Right now, it would be best that someone who isn't a blood relative try to calm him down. And yes, I'd prefer to pick out a ring, but the safety of my people takes precedence. If you happen to come across a Draconian, tell them to find me. I don't know shit about blood, other than how to shed it, and I sure don't know where to find it."

Morghan nodded. "I'll get in touch with Alistair."

"Good," Aveo said, turning his attention to Lilly. "Don't take what he says right now to heart. He's in a difficult place. Something that every warrior deals with at some point or another. I'm going to get him, get some blood in him, and then do what I do for every one of my soldiers that have a hard time."

"What's that?" Quinn inquired with narrowing eyes.

"Get him a case of ale."

"We *do* have a pretty big day tomorrow," Morghan warned.

"Healing Springs cure everything. Even hangovers."

"Why did *I* have to be the one to get Malachai," Alistair groaned, walking down a street beside Vincent, who was lucky enough to have gotten Craven. "*Me.* Of all people."

Shrugging, Vincent said, "I don't know, but you did. Maybe it's a good thing. By now, we all know Malachai left you alive on purpose."

"By now, we all know that might just be something he's saying to make himself look good. You know, like he did when he admitted he was Meera's source. Like he did saving the Idonian Council today." He paused, checking the time on his chip. "Or yesterday."

The prince at his side started to frown, slipping his hands into his pockets. "I know it's going to take time, Ward, but there's a lot left to be discovered about Malachai. He isn't who we thought he was. Maybe the Moons had you pick his name so that you'd start looking forward, instead of looking behind you. That *is* how you walk into walls, anyway."

"By looking forward?"

"No, by looking backward, idiot," Vincent shot back.

Before Alistair could reply, his chip started to vibrate in his hand. He glanced back down at it, only to find Morghan's name flashing across the screen. "Let me guess, you can't figure out what to get Lucinda," Alistair accused upon answering.

No, actually, we're pretty sure Cooper's experiencing some sort of bloodlust, and now he's loose in the Kingdom. Aveo went to chase him down. I need you to get some blood and then find them both, Morghan directed.

Alistair's heart shuttered. "What do you mean by *bloodlust?*"

He's still in denial, Morghan explained. *Unfortunately, with everything going on back in Dracus, he wasn't getting the attention he needed. We're not certain he's had even a* drop *of blood.*

"He's been a Draconian for over two weeks, *and* he's been in counseling," Alistair said, his throat becoming tight at the realization. "Ash passed out on the first *day* she didn't receive blood. Craven's still pissed at Marcus about it."

All the more reason to find him. Now, Morghan insisted. *And, if he refuses, hold him down and force it down his throat.*

"What's going on?" Vincent asked, the lump in his throat bobbing.

"I'm on it," Alistair replied. "Try to keep this quiet." After hanging up, he returned his attention to Vincent and said, "We need to find blood and get it to Cooper. Immediately."

55

Spending the evening Giving Day shopping with Marcus wasn't something Malachai thought he'd ever get to do again. The only difference was that now, he didn't know who he was, and that was for the best. Malachai had already made peace with the fact that Marcus would never know the truth. He would be forever oblivious to whom his relatives were.

But that didn't mean that Malachai wouldn't enjoy every second he had with him.

Their shopping had been easy, so far. Once Malachai had learned who he needed to shop for, he realized he already had something perfect in possession back in Dracus. Marcus had pulled Beck's name. The only logical gift for the General was a rare weapon, and Marcus had plenty. So, the first thing they did was find Lucinda, who happened to be with Penelope and Anastasia.

"Marcus and I will go back to Dracus and get the things," Lucinda declared. "You three find a present for Quinn."

"I've already asked Humphrey to retrieve what I need from my desk drawer," Malachai told her.

"Perfect," the Sorceress chimed before using her sphere to open a portal in a dark alley.

Marcus followed her, but not before meeting the prince's gaze. "You sure you're good?" he asked, nodding toward Penelope.

"Yes," the prince assured him.

Nodding, the Mentor disappeared through the portal. It closed shortly after, and Malachai turned around to face the Fire Clan Leader and the Idonian Princess. "Alright, who are we shopping for?" he inquired. "Other than Quinn." The best way to escape his depressive thoughts was to get busy and focus on something else.

"Aveo," Anastasia grumbled.

So far, the Elves hadn't paid Malachai any mind. Perhaps they were too lost in thought about the blissful holiday. Or maybe they didn't recognize him, given his recent haircut and change of appearance. Either way, it was incredibly refreshing.

Penelope, on the other hand, knew exactly who he was. And, considering this was the three-year anniversary of the day Malachai had killed her betrothed, one would think she'd refuse to be anywhere near him. Oddly enough, that wasn't the case.

Since Malachai had revealed that he was Meera's source, Penelope hadn't been unkind to him. They were still far from friends, and he doubted they ever would be, but they could withstand a short shopping trip together at the very least.

"I already got everything I wanted to get for everyone," Penelope declared happily. "But I do have an idea for Ash. I just haven't figured out who pulled her name."

"I did," Malachai revealed. "Well, she was one of the two names left that I got stuck with. Cooper was the other."

The Princess's smile slowly faded, her eyes widening with surprise. "Oh."

"Why?" Malachai asked with narrowing eyes.

"It's just... she likes daggers... and Cedric did too... and his entire collection is just sitting in crates right now," Penelope explained, gnawing at her bottom lip, avoiding his gaze. "But, if you're... okay... with that idea, I can still take you to them."

Malachai's stomach dropped, as if he'd just leaped off a cliff. Daggers *would* be the perfect gift for Ash, even if he'd just sent Lucinda to retrieve the gift he'd already decided on. But one of *Cedric's* daggers? The very concept felt completely *wrong*. Especially since he'd been haunted by that murder he'd committed since the second he arrived in that Kingdom.

However, Cedric was once Malachai's friend. And, if he knew the Elf as well as he thought he did, then Cedric would adore the idea of his beloved possessions going to people who would enjoy them as much as he did.

Anastasia let loose a long whistle. "Wow. Of all ideas. You two realize how wrong this is on so many different levels, right?"

"Yes," Penelope replied. "I mean, he killed Cedric, and he tried to kill Ash *with* a dagger. And, if he gives her one of Cedric's daggers for Giving Day…"

Malachai cringed. "Thanks for the elaborate explanation."

"Knowing Ash, she'd find that funny," Anastasia said. "It's worth a shot. But, if she slits Malachai's throat with it, that's on you, sugar."

Penelope gave her a long look. "He can say it's from both of us."

Malachai stared at her, unable to believe she'd just suggested that. Had she lost her mind? "Penelope, of all days—"

The Princess held up a hand, cutting him off. "I'm getting closure, so that I can move on with my life. I'm sure you can understand that. I don't know why, but I think doing this together might help with that."

"Alright," he agreed, lips curving into a smile.

"There wouldn't be anything for Aveo and Quinn in those crates, would there be?" Ana inquired on their way out of the alley.

THE SECOND MALACHAI SAW THE PAIR OF GOLDEN DAGGERS, HE knew they were perfect. He'd kill two birds with one stone and give one to both Ash and Cooper. He would still need to find a second gift for the Archer, to make it fair, so, they had a servant send the daggers up to Penelope's suite, where she'd wrap them later on, and headed back out into the city to finish their list.

"Why do I feel like we just robbed your deceased betrothed?"

Ana asked as they made their way into a shop made specifically for men.

Penelope cut her a harsh look. "We did not rob Cedric. We simply passed on something precious of his to people who will cherish them. He'd love that. That collection was his only legacy."

Inside the shop, Ana finally found something she thought Aveo might like. A simple ribbon. Malachai watched her hold it up, lips stretching into a sinister grin. "Here's an idea, tie this into a bow on your head and give him *you* for Giving Day," she suggested to Penelope, who bristled in response.

Malachai reached to pinch the bridge of his nose.

"Anastasia Volden," Penelope chastised, snatching the ribbon away.

Not ten minutes later, Ana found a *real* gift. A new scabbard fit for the duel broadswords Aveo was known for. And, for Quinn, Penelope eventually gave in and called him.

"What do you want for Giving Day?" she asked, lowering to sit on a park bench while Ana walked across the street to fetch them some hot chocolate with *Malachai's* coin. Not that he minded.

I didn't know you picked a name, the prince heard Quinn reply, though he didn't exactly sound joyful.

"I didn't," Penelope informed him. "But the person who did has *no* idea what to get you. So, what do you want?"

Well, I'm not picky. Usually all I get for Giving Day is a new hat, or a scarf, or something to help me on the farm, Quinn explained with a laugh that Malachai could tell wasn't real. Something was wrong. *You can tell whoever pulled my name not to worry about getting me anything. I already got the best gifts a man could receive. I got to know all of you.*

While that was a sweet thing to say, and Penelope was certainly melting, Malachai knew that he was deflecting.

"You're so impossibly sweet, if you were anywhere near me, I'd hug you as tight as I can," Penelope told him.

That would be a great gift, Quinn replied.

Malachai pursed his lips and crossed his arms. He wouldn't mind a hug either. Actually, he couldn't remember the last time he had one.

"You know, Quinn whatever-your-middle-name-is McBride," Penelope started, nothing but pure determination visible upon her features. "I'm going to make sure that this is the best Giving Day you've ever had."

The Princess hung up before she looked at Malachai and said. "Something is wrong with him."

"You noticed that too, eh?"

"I could hear it in his voice. He was trying not to cry," she informed him sadly. "His brother tried to kill him less than twelve hours ago. Maybe doing this gift exchange, night-out thing wasn't such a good idea."

Anastasia walked up, juggling three hot-chocolates in her arms. But, before she could make it across the street, someone ran past her, just barely nudging her arm. The hot chocolate fell out of her grip, splatting onto the cobblestone street.

"Sorry," Aveo said, turning back around, though it was evident that he didn't want to. "We have a tiny crisis. I'm trying to find Cooper."

"Why are you in such a hurry to?" Malachai asked, setting his jaw.

Aveo looked around, noting all the onlookers. "Let's just say he's having some *transition* problems."

Malachai's brow furrowed. "What do you mean *transition* problems?"

That was when it hit him. When he'd first met Cooper, during the Allies' first task, he wasn't an aggressive person, and he *certainly* wasn't the sort of man to start a fight. Since the moment he'd woken up, he'd been unstable. His temper was short, and his fangs were constantly out and ready.

Because he was hungry.

The realization hit Malachai like a bag of bricks. "I'm coming with you," he insisted.

"So are we," Anastasia said, flicking hot chocolate off her hands.

56

Ash had finished her Giving Day shopping relatively quickly. Morghan was easy to shop for. All she'd needed to do was go to Beck's pub and order a case of the Wolf's favorite whiskey, which the General wouldn't allow her to pay for. After arguing with him about this for far too long, she gave in and bought his most expensive bottle of wine when he wasn't paying attention.

"I can't believe you charged her for that," Beck growled at his barkeep, the same man he'd apparently bought the pub from to begin with.

The keep raised up his hands in defense. "She made me."

Beck turned his scowl in Ash's direction. "Why?"

"You have to pay him, don't you?" she asked, gesturing to the keep. "That's why."

The prince scoffed, crossing his arms. "I have enough coin to pay him for a century, thank you very much."

"Could I have that upfront?" the keep asked, flashing the General a wicked grin.

Beck shot him a dirty look.

"Listen, it's Giving Day. The entire purpose of the day is to *give*," Ash reminded him, snatching the bottle off the bar. "Now, if you'll excuse me, I'm going to go get Craven tipsy."

The Draconian, who'd watched all the drama unfold from a booth in the corner, shook his head. "We have a huge day tomorrow, and it's really late."

"Did I just hear *Craven Amsterdam* say he didn't want a drink in *my* pub?" Beck shouted, walking around the bar, a second bottle of the same wine in his hand. "I won't stand for this. I simply can't. Our lifelong friendship was built on drunken secrets. Do you not care about me at *all?*" the Elf clutched at his heart, all but falling to his knees in dismay and betrayal.

Craven groaned, falling back against the booth's cushions, rolling his eyes so extensively that Ash was certain that he caught a glimpse of his spine. "Why must you *always* be so dramatic?"

Ash slid into the seat across from him, just in time for the keep to deliver three wine glasses. She gave him a nod of thanks, her lips spreading into a knowing smile. He winked in response, returning to his place behind the bar.

Beck claimed the seat beside Ash, filling the three glasses. "Drink," he demanded. Ash did so immediately, taking a deep sip. Immediately, she could tell why that wine was so costly. Craven did the same, having lost the battle. "Great, now let's plan for tomorrow. Directly after the Realm address, we'll head to our assigned tunnel entrances, which will be in pairs. I've already spoken with Sam, who spoke with Lady Evanora, who said that the Rebels will spread out to each entrance to back us all up."

"Good," Craven said with a shiver. "What are the pairs and where are they going?" He pulled out a chip, and Ash did the same. If she didn't type whatever Beck said in her notes, she'd forget. Especially since the wine she'd chosen to drink was so incredibly potent.

"Glad you asked. I just got those results back from our friend Grant."

Snorting, Ash said, "Let me guess, he used that compatibility system again."

"Yes," the General confirmed. "And it works. I mean, look at how well our divisions performed during the tasks. Clearly, we can trust it. So, instead of pulling names out of a hat like you guys did with the gifts, I decided to reach out to Grant. Hope you don't mind."

Craven took another sip. "Not one bit. Tell us what he said."

From there, Beck explained in great detail who would be guarding what entrance, and with how many Rebels. Considering the fact that there were over forty tunnel entrances around the Realm, the list was lengthy. Beck gave them the pleasure of skipping past which soldiers Grant saw fit for what, and focused entirely on the Allies, and the people Ash and Craven were most concerned about.

Malachai and Quinn would stand by the entrance closest to Solaris. Marcus and Craven would head to an entrance just outside of Mayfire, one that the Draconian appeared to be familiar with. Lucinda and Alistair would head to Lorcan, close to the Regal Mountains. Vincent and Aveo would head toward the Forest of Fools. Ana and Morghan would go back to Olaigon. And Ash and Cooper would be somewhere between Redding and The Strip.

"I'm confused," Craven admitted. "If Aveo is Ash's Guardian, shouldn't *he* be her partner?"

"Technically, yes," Beck replied, filling a second glass. "But the system said otherwise for this mission. It considered every possible outcome for what's about to happen. If the Pandora chose to attack, it's best that Cooper's with Ash."

"Why?" Ash inquired.

"Because," Beck said nonchalantly. "Right now, Cooper's the weakest, and Ash is the strongest."

Ash choked on her wine, anger beginning to coil in her gut. "Excuse me?"

"Hey, that's not my opinion, it's the system's," Beck informed her. "But I will say that I can understand why. He's the youngest, and while he might be a teleporting Arebus Archer with a recently developed ability to manipulate the air, he has no idea what he's doing, for a lack of better words. Not to mention, he's been through a recent trauma, and that affects soldiers on the field. Trust me, I know. I've seen some men and women so shaken after fighting Pandora that I had to put them on leave. They never come back. And we know what happened to him was a lot worse." His voice got lower and lower with each word he spoke. "Truthfully, Ebony doesn't want him to participate in this. We had to hound her into agreeing, because we need to know how he'll react in the face of danger now. Axel agrees."

Ash's throat became unbearably tight. "Is this a test, then? For him?"

Beck nodded, his expression grim.

"What happens if he fails?" Craven said, swallowing hard enough for Ash to hear.

"He could temporarily lose his Ally badge."

"That's hardly fair!" Ash shouted before she could stop herself. "He didn't *choose* what happened to him."

"You're right," Beck said calmly. "He didn't. But, since he's woken up, all he's done is create problems for everyone else. He hardly shows up to any of the appointments Ebony made for him for counseling. He refused to receive a Draconian Mentor. I subtly mentioned the Healing Springs earlier, and he waved me off. Did the same to Mika when she brought them up."

Sighing heavily, Ash turned her attention to the window. Unfortunately, she wasn't there for him when he woke up, and hadn't seen him until Aries' funeral. They'd spoken a few times via Morghan's chip, but other than that, she learned everything he wasn't telling her from Quinn. He hadn't mentioned his air ability, or that he'd tried to use it to kill Malachai. What made matters worse, was that Ash was too busy dealing with her own trauma and struggles to make sure that Cooper was *really* okay, and not just pretending. He was her twin, no matter what biology said. She should have been there for him.

Just as Ash was preparing to reply to the General, she watched someone run past the window at Immortal speed. Not a second later, she watched a series of people follow. Penelope was the last of them, slower than the rest but determined, nonetheless.

"I wonder what that's about," Craven said, having noticed all the fuss as well. "Who would Penelope and Malachai chase?"

A distant shout rang in Ash's ears, sending her heart racing. "Whoever it is, they just caught him."

57

Despite Aveo's best efforts to catch Cooper, Alistair got there first. Just as the group he'd managed to form were closing in on the Archer, the Rider came out of nowhere, crashing into him. They fell to the snowy ground, causing the Commander to attempt to skid to a stop before he ran right into them. The slick cobblestone made that next to impossible. He managed to recover his footing at the last second, but Ana wasn't so lucky.

The Fire Clan Leader crashed into them, tripping over where they fought on the street. Thankfully, Malachai was smart enough to have transitioned into a hawk before he made any accidental contact, returning to his Mortal form in time to catch her before she wound up face-first on the ground.

Onlookers gasped, in awe of all the action.

"There's nothing to see here!" Aveo shouted over Cooper's snarling. The Archer was trying to break free, but he stood no chance against Alistair, Malachai, and Anastasia combined. "Go on with your business! That's an order!"

The Elves and Mortals surrounding them just stood there, motionless with wide eyes and hanging jaws.

"Did you not hear me?" Aveo bellowed. "Go one with your business! Commander's orders!"

Finally, they started to move, tearing their gazes away from the scene.

"And, if *anyone* dares to speak about this incident, I'll *personally* pay them a visit," Penelope added from behind. "This poor man put his life on the line today to save the Idonian Council. Show him some respect!"

They all nodded before hanging their heads in shame, making their way off the street. Aveo found that his heart was skipping erratically at the sound of Penelope's commanding tone. He whirled around to face her, suddenly overcome with the urge to pull her into his arms and do *far* more than hug her.

"Good work," he said, giving her an appreciative nod.

The slight blush that dusted Penelope's cheeks caused Aveo's desire for her to fester even more.

That was before Cooper tried to bite Anastasia, who yelped in response.

People started to flow out the pub across the street. Beck's pub. The second Aveo caught sight of Ash and his General, relief flooded through him.

"Here, bring him inside," Beck directed, though it was pretty evident that he didn't have the slightest clue about what was happening. But Aveo needed to get Cooper out of the open immediately, and the pub was their best option. So, he walked toward him and helped the others to drag him inside.

One thing that Aveo *hadn't* expected was for Cooper to be as strong and agile as he was. Even with five men almost twice his size in muscle, and in some cases stature, he almost slipped their grip more than once.

"He's absolutely feral," Craven warned on their way up the stairs, into the loft above the pub. "When was the last time he had any blood?"

"Morghan is pretty sure that the answer to that question is never," Alistair said.

Everyone stilled, despite the fact that they were still on the stairs.

"*What?*" Malachai gaped. "That's not physically possible. He's been a Draconian for weeks."

"Vincent went to get more information," Alistair informed him. "But I'm starting to think that it's true. I spend a lot of time with Cooper, and I've never seen him pick up a thermos, or a glass of blood. Quinn *lives* with him and has never seen him drink it, which he just confirmed in a message on my way over here."

Cooper roared, writhing, trying anything to break free.

They started moving again. Aveo could only hope that the loft was strong enough to keep the Archer inside.

"Did you at least bring the thermoses?" the Commander asked the Rider.

"Yes," Alistair told him. "I told Penelope where I left them."

As if summoned by the sound of her name, Penelope appeared at the bottom of the stairs. "Is it safe for me to come up?"

"If I were you, I'd hurry," Ash warned from the stop of the stairs. "Because the second this door closes, it's not opening until Cooper's back to normal. So, if you want to shut yourself in with a feral Draconian, that's your choice."

The sound of Penelope's footsteps on the stairs and her uneasy breathing flooded Aveo's ears. She'd made her decision.

Finally, they made it to the loft. Penelope shut the door behind her, locking it. Ash and Beck started to move furniture to fortify it. Craven moved to stand in front of the only window, purple shreds of electricity beginning to swarm his fingers.

"Should I shock him?" the Draconian asked. "Put him out so that we can force feed him?"

"That would traumatize him even more," Malachai said, shedding his cloak, pushing up his sleeves. "We need to get him to drink the blood willingly. And, I think I have a way of doing that."

In one, slick motion, the Pandora placed his hand against Cooper's chest. The Archer relaxed immediately. His snarls stopped, his eyelids fluttering as if he were dreaming.

"What are you doing?" Aveo asked.

"Using his healing ability." Ash was the one to reply. "It's an extremely relaxing sensation. It'll calm Cooper down enough for us to talk to him."

Malachai nodded. "Get the thermoses ready."

Penelope brought them forward, handing them off to Alistair.

The Rider dropped to his knees beside Cooper, thermos ready in hand. "Coop," he started. "Listen, I know you became one of us under some really bad circumstances, but it isn't so bad. It was a surprise to me too. You think I expected to wake up a Draconian?" The Rider laughed. "Not a chance. But I did."

Cooper's eyes fluttered open, fixing on Alistair's.

"I was mauled to death. Marcus was too. Ash didn't ask to have Draconian DNA either. All four of us became Draconians under painful and weird circumstances. But, once you make peace with it, it isn't so bad." Alistair brought the thermos a little closer. Malachai shuddered, still using his ability to keep the Archer calm.

As Aveo watched all of this unfold, something struck at the cords of his heart. He'd done this. *He* was the one to inject that venom into Cooper's veins. Should he have? Sure, the man was still breathing thanks to that act. But, to see the amount of internal agony he was in…

Penelope reached out, taking Aveo's hand. He flinched, having not expected the touch. She didn't say anything. Instead, she watched the scene playing out in front of her. She might have taken his hand because she needed comfort, but the truth was, so did Aveo.

"You're so lost in what happened, that you forgot about yourself," Alistair explained sadly. "Which sucks because you're so important. Our division wouldn't be the same without you in it, man. Now, we have even more in common than we did before. We can help you get used to all this if you let us. Just take some baby steps. Drink this blood before you hurt somebody, because the Cooper I know would never hurt a fly, unless it was a Pandora."

Ash snorted at the comment. Malachai sighed at the ceiling. Anastasia downright laughed. Beck just shook his head, kneeling at the Archer's side.

Malachai withdrew, eyeing Cooper cautiously.

"Thank you… again," Cooper said to the Pandora.

"We *have* to stop meeting like this," he replied, lips twitching toward a smirk.

58

After the Cooper crisis, everyone returned to their respective suits to wrap their gifts and head to sleep for the night. The next morning, chaos began again. Ash was awoken out of a dead sleep to Penelope shaking her shoulders, like a child on Giving Day morning.

Technically, it *was* Giving Day morning. It just didn't feel like it. There was no decorated tree out in the family room, with piles of presents beneath it. The McBrides were nowhere in sight. Nothing about the holiday felt like it should.

"Where's Quinn?" Ash asked Morghan, who walked out of the kitchen with two mugs of steaming hot coffee in his hands. She took one, sipping it greedily, burning her tongue in the process. "I figured he'd be here."

"The McBride brothers were summoned by Beck for a briefing," Aveo explained, clad in his normal uniform, decorated with shining badges and a silver cape. "They're Malachai's guard detail for the address. He wanted to make sure they were clear on what they were supposed to do if anyone were to strike."

Nodding, Ash pursed her lips.

"I know you've never spent a Giving Day morning without them," Penelope mentioned softly from where she sat, curled up in a nearby chair. "I'm sorry."

"It's fine," Ash assured her, just in time for Vincent to stumble down the stairs, yawning. "It's our first holiday together, anyway. We should spend it together, while we can."

Penelope's eyes shone a little brighter at the sound of her words. "We *are* your family too," she replied, looking toward Aveo. "The four of us will have a wonderful, granted quick, Giving Day breakfast together. As a family."

Ash could have sworn that the Commander blushed for a split second.

"I'm here too," Morghan reminded her.

"With Morghan," the Princess corrected.

AFTER BREAKFAST, ASH DRESSED IN HER ALLY UNIFORM AND THEN rushed to find Malachai before the Elves got their claws in him. She got there just in time, for the Chamberlains were already closing in on the poor prince.

Ash was told by a pair of guards that Thaddeus and Esmeralda had pulled him into the king's study, along with Sam. When she arrived, she found both Quinn and Cooper standing outside.

"There you two are," Ash grumbled as quietly as she was able. "I was hoping I'd see you this morning, before this day took a turn for the worse."

Quinn frowned, his shoulder's slumping. "Duty calls."

Wrinkling her nose, Ash slid her gaze over to the study door. "Which is precisely why I'm here." She didn't bother knocking before she entered the study, where Malachai was currently sitting in a chair in front of Thaddeus's desk, while Sam lingered in the back of the room, pretending the view out the window was more interesting. Ash could hear both of their pulses racing, and she could understand why. One of them had murdered Cedric, and the other had taken over his army.

It was no wonder why they were nervous.

"There you are," Malachai said in a calm and collected tone, though it was clear that he was overcome with relief at the sight of her. "I wanted your opinion on this speech before we went out there."

Lies. Ash lifted a brow. He knew better than to get her opinion on speeches. At least she hoped he did. "Of course," she said, reaching to take it from him. As she skimmed Malachai's immaculate handwriting, the Elves continued with whatever they were trying to drill into him before.

"Are you *positive* that you wouldn't rather use the one Griffon wrote for you?" Esmeralda asked with pleading, golden eyes.

Thaddeus remained silent, glaring at the prince from where he sat on the other side of his sprawling oak desk.

"If I were to do that, Your Highness, the Pandora would know that an Elf wrote it. I mean no offense by that," Malachai assured her, straightening in his seat. "But Pandora are intelligent creatures, and they know me well. They'll think you're pulling my strings, and that could very well stop them from listening to what I have to say."

"Which would defeat the entire purpose of this address," Ash added, handing Malachai back his speech, her heart warmed eternally by its ending. "Besides, I think what he wrote is perfectly fine. Inspirational even."

Esmeralda's nose wrinkled. Thaddeus's nostrils flared. "Very well," the king said. "What about that one? He hasn't been officially chosen as the General yet. And, while we value Lady Evanora Ivanenko's opinion when it comes to all things, from battle preparations to different types of tea, we have no idea who he is, or what he's capable of."

"I know who he is," Ash informed him. "We grew up together. He's saved my head on dozens of occasions. We were trained by the same people. Some might say he's even better with a sword than I am."

That grabbed Sam's attention. Finally, a smile blossomed on his lips. *He'll never forget I admitted that.* Ash swallowed a groan.

"And by the same people, you mean Pat McBride," Thaddeus assumed.

Ash stiffened, now feeling the urge to defend herself. "Partly, yes, but he died when I was six. I was hardly training with weapons at that age."

"What does Pat McBride have to do with anything?" Malachai asked kindly, clearly trying not to start an argument. "I thought you summoned us to go over the Realm address."

"That doesn't mean I can't ask things that I'm curious about," Thaddeus said calmly, though his eyes said otherwise. They flickered with a desire Ash knew all too well. A desire to reach out and rip out someone's tongue. "I'm beginning to notice a bit of a pattern. One that I'm not sure I can ignore."

Ash's heart stilled, her pulse thrumming in her ears. Now *she* was the nervous one. "What sort of pattern?"

"Pat's the one who found you and played a part in your survival all those years ago. Well, thanks to that article, we know that Malachai and Pat worked together. And, that the prince knew where he lived, and visited him on more than one occasion. Who's to say that he didn't visit him regularly?" Thaddeus inquired, leaning forward. "How do we know that you two haven't been working together far longer than you're letting on? And that this isn't part of some scheme?"

Esmeralda's jaw dropped. Clearly, her husband hadn't discussed any of what he'd just said with her. The poor woman had been blindsided.

Sam went rigid, taking a step forward, but he didn't say a word. *Good choice.*

"Malachai and I didn't meet until my first task," Ash replied.

"She's not lying," Malachai added for good measure. "I knew Ash was in Crane, but I never went to see her, or spoke to her. I left her alone because I promised Pat that I would."

"Wait what?" Ash gasped, her attention snapping in his direction.

The prince nodded. "We made a pact. I wasn't to say a word about where you'd wound up, and he'd make sure you were safe and warm. I was never supposed to go back to Crane. I didn't, until my father made me, when he discovered I was lying about Pat's whereabouts."

"I'm having a really difficult time believing that," Thaddeus told them both.

"You don't have to," Malachai replied with a shrug. "But whether you *believe* it or not, Ash and I working together is what's going to win this war. The fact that you're questioning your High Queen, and accusing her of such conspiracy, could get you dethroned. In case you've forgotten, she has the power to do that. She can appoint someone else to rule over the Elves if she really wanted to."

Ash held her breath, her gaze darting between the two men. Alphas. The kings of their prides, ready to rip each other to shreds. But who would win? She didn't want to find out.

"We only summoned Malachai here to make sure he was ready for the address," Esmeralda said in a tone as chill as ice. "Thaddeus, you're out of line. *Must* you always invoke anger? On a holiday, no less?"

The king paid his wife no mind. Instead, he rose from his seat, placing both palms on the surface of his desk. "Good work," he drawled with a smirk meant for both Malachai and Ash. "You made everyone believe you were a puppet, when you're clearly a puppet master, pulling Ash's strings."

A low growl reverberated in Ash's throat. She wanted to roar at him from the top of her lungs for making such assumptions, but she decided to take a different route. "Do you love my siblings?" she inquired, standing as well.

Thaddeus scoffed at her. "Of course, I do. I raised them."

"Yet you shun *me*," Ash retorted, losing control of her inner Berserker. She felt her eyes change, burning silver in the early morning light. Everyone in the room froze, now eyeing the exits. After what she'd done to Dracus's city square, they were likely imagining how a much smaller study might fare against her. "When all Penelope and Vincent wanted was to find me, you called off their search. Why? Because you were afraid you might draw too much attention to yourself, or because you'd deemed me a lost cause?"

The king recoiled, lifting his hands off the desk, curling his fingers into powerful fists. "Xavier had noticed—"

"Cedric *found* that village," Ash interjected. "He might not have sensed the invisible barrier protecting it, but he was there. He was close, and you made him stop. You banished Matt Abernathy and look where he is now because of it. Now, you dare to accuse me of scheming? Stop pretending you're innocent when everyone knows how familiar *you* are with schemes. You left me for dead, and now you're belittling the few people who tried to protect me."

That comment didn't just refer to Malachai, who'd gone to great lengths to save Ash's life eighteen years ago. It referred to the McBrides, and Sam, and Drake, and most importantly Eliza Snow —the only mother Ash had known.

Given the surprise written all over Thaddeus's face, at least Ash knew that *some* of her words had resonated with him and gotten through that thick skull of his. He was struck silent, jaw hanging open, eyes wide.

"I will say this once," Ash continued, her voice little more than a whisper. "Stop trying to turn me into something I am not. If I were some savage, wilding queen, do you think the Moons would give me a Guardian? One of your own Commanders, no less? You may not like what I stand for. Quite frankly, I don't care. I'm trying to save us all. What are you doing?"

There was no answer. And, if there was, Thaddeus wasn't willing to give it to Ash. So, she looked toward Malachai and Sam, nodding toward the door. "We'll see you at the address. Try to control your temper. Whether you like it or not, we need this army to flourish. If you stand in the way of that, you stand in *my* way."

Ash didn't bother looking toward Esmeralda before she started toward the door, Malachai and Sam following suit. She ripped it open, allowing it to slam against the marble walls, leaving quite the splintering crack. She hadn't expected to find that Quinn had been joined by so many others, including Beck and Mika Chamberlain.

"What?" she snapped, unnerved by the way they were all looking at her.

It was Morghan who began a slow clap.

Mika didn't move a muscle.

59

Malachai had never been so impressed by a person.

The way Ash had ripped into Thaddeus...it would live in his memory for the rest of his Immortal life, and he was glad for it. He hoped the image of how his face appeared would never fade. Why he chose to abandon his father for her was beginning to make more sense. So much so that whatever nerves Malachai had about this address had vanished. He knew that he was doing the right thing.

So, the prince approached the dais, stepping in front of the cameras that would stream everything he was about to say to every screen in the Realm, his eyes flashing red. He called upon those buried parts of himself—the ones that made people look at him and shiver. The ones that made him the enemy they feared, and not the victim he'd succumbed to be.

Ash stood to his right, though a bit behind. Both the McBride brothers stood on either side of the dais, black bows peeking over their shoulders, visible for all the Realm to see. Beck and Axel stood farther back, symbols of the other armies the Pandora willing to answer Malachai's call would fight beside. Esmeralda and Thaddeus sat on their thrones, with Mika standing at the queen's side, one hand resting on the throne's arch.

The Allies were scattered about, each of them focused on every direction, searching for anyone that might intervene. Willa hovered in the sky above the clouds, yet close enough for Malachai to hear the wind rushing beneath her wings.

Grant and Anderson had arrived from Dracus to assist with the address, and all Malachai needed to do was watch the former's fingers.

A crowd had developed in the Throne Room behind the Communications officers and the guard. Most of them were Elves, some Mortals, and very little Draconians. The most notable absentee was King Loren. Malachai could only hope that he was watching.

Grant began with five fingers, bringing down one at a time. The second he got to two, Malachai's heart began to race despite all of his preparations. He fought to maintain his lethal demeanor, the one that always got the Pandora's attention. *I can do this,* he reminded himself, biting his inner cheek.

The red lights blinking on all the camera's turned green, and Malachai knew that there was no turning back. The time had come to make his change permanent.

"My fellow Idonians," Malachai started, sounding far sterner than he'd anticipated. Far too much like the version of himself he'd left in Solaris. "I'd like to start by wishing each and every one of you a happy Giving Day, and I'm sorry to interfere with your festivities, but this is a matter of great importance.

"By now, you've seen the papers and have heard the whispers. You know precisely why I'm standing where I am. I made a choice, and I'm providing my fellow Pandora with an opportunity to do the same." A shiver swept down Malachai's spine. He wondered if anyone noticed. "The only reason that your species exists is because my father, your king, betrayed me. He ripped me away from my life and all of my accomplishments as a Healer and a Scholar. He ruined my future as a Black Knight. He shoved me in a lab with a few other unfortunate souls and demanded we use our knowledge to make him something vicious. Once we were done, he turned around and shoved that syringe into my neck."

Steeling himself, Malachai fought against the surge of emotions rushing through him. He could feel Thaddeus and Esmeralda's eyes burning into his back, searing through his black suit-jacket.

"Eighteen years ago, there were thirty-thousand Pandora, each of them injected with my venom. For those of you who were turned willingly, were you aware that I was locked in a cell? Your creator, your originator, and your Alpha was locked away, forced to sit through six extractions in a twenty-four-hour period. For. Three. Years. Straight." Malachai's words came out harsher and harsher, fire beginning to roil deep in his gut. "Now, you can get enough for six injections per one extraction. That's thirteen thousand, one hundred and forty injections a year. Altogether, that's upward toward forty thousand injections. I know for a fact that there were only ten thousand *volunteers*."

Gasps sounded throughout the Throne Room, looks of pure horror etched in the features of every soul in the crowd.

"Eventually, my father ran out of those injections. What do you think he did next?" Malachai inquired, shifting his weight from one leg to the other. "Why do you think the Red Winters began? Not for the sole purpose of terrorizing those still willing to defy Xavier, that's for sure. No. he needed to increase his numbers, and the only way to do that was through *me*. He wouldn't settle until there were more Pandora than any other species in this Realm. So, if I didn't provide him with three thousand new soldiers by the end of every Winter Solstice, I'm sure you can all imagine what he would have done to me as punishment. Another three years. Another forty thousand injections."

Malachai dared to look in Ash's direction. Her complexion had gone green, her eyes growing misty.

"That wasn't his only way of increasing his numbers," Malachai revealed, yearning for a glass of water to wet his impossibly dry mouth. Perhaps something stronger. "There was breeding, of course. Pairing the strongest, most promising Pandora with one another, and then taking their children, raising them to be emotionless assassins. I was clearly his first choice for this. Perhaps if *I* had a child, they'd produce venom too. I refused. No child of mine would be put in a cell and drained of venom six times a day. I'm sure you can imagine how he punished me for that. He tripled the amount of desired soldiers and quadrupled the amount of breedings. There are *children* as young as ten amongst your ranks, genetically modified to transition into their final forms by the age of seven."

Someone hurried out of the room, holding a hand over their month.

"How many Pandora have become a beast by force, only to have their children stolen straight from the delivery room?" Malachai asked, clutching the podium with all his might. "How many of you were stolen from your beds in the middle of night, forced to join a cause you don't believe in, all because you happened to be good at something? Like Bernardine Anderson, for example. Snatched from her bed in Redding a year ago, because of her vast knowledge of astrophysics. At least *she* came to her senses."

If Anderson were still in Solaris, Xavier would have demanded that she interfere with this broadcast. Malachai wanted to laugh at the thought but didn't dare. Xavier couldn't stop this.

"You do not have to endure this anymore," Malachai explained, softening his features. "This will be the last Red Winter, but it doesn't have to mean your deaths. There is no reason to fight for a king who has abused you in such ways, forcing you to head out into the Realm and put your lives on the line while he sits in his stolen castle, on his stolen throne. A throne that *we* gave him."

Malachai's heart was soaring at the sight of the crowd, nodding agreeably. If he'd gotten through to the *Elves*, then he had to have gotten through to the Pandora.

"I was banished by my father for refusing to kill the *one* person who could stop the horrors he inflicts upon us. Ash VanCamp could have killed me, and I would have deserved it, but she gave me a chance instead. One where I could take a new path, right my wrongs, and undo the damage I've inflicted upon our Realm. She, and every other person on this dais, is giving members of the Dark Army a chance to do the same. Fight for us. *With* us. Join an army designed specifically to bring peace. In exchange, you'll receive a full pardon," Malachai revealed, knowing that sentence would be the hook, line, and sinker. "Leave Solaris. Right now. Find your freedom. We'll be waiting for you."

60

The second the flashing lights on the camera flicked from green to red, the entire Throne Room erupted with applause. Ash sighed with relief, fighting the urge to double over. She wasn't sure she'd taken a breath at all during the address. In fact, spots were beginning to swarm her vision, but they'd done it. They pulled it off. And now all they needed to do was hope that it worked.

After the applause died down, the smiles started to fade from everyone's faces. They were remembering all the prince had revealed. The horrors he'd brought to light. Cages, breeding, kidnapping. Ash's stomach became sour all over again as she recalled every word.

Silence swallowed the Throne Room, smothering all sound. Ash's ears rang with the sudden difference. She cleared her throat, turned toward Malachai, and opened her mouth to speak. But, before she could, Beck beat her to it.

"I hate to rush everyone, especially after that, but if that worked, Pandora are fleeing Solaris as we speak," the General explained. "Malachai needs to suit up, and we all have a few prayers to say while we wait."

"Xavier won't let those Pandora go easily," Axel added, clenching his jaw. "It's going to be a bloodbath. We need to be ready to heal the injured. And, we only have one Malachai, so I'll go ahead and summon some Healers."

Esmeralda nodded. "We'll provide some too."

As expected, Thaddeus didn't say a word.

"Alright, scatter," Beck ordered. "We'll reconvene in the square in thirty minutes. Anyone that needs some liquid courage, follow me."

Aveo stepped onto the dais. "Come with me," he said to Malachai. "Benjamin sent over a Draconian uniform to wear. He thought the black and red might resonate with your fellow Pandora. I'll take you to it."

Malachai nodded, moving to follow him. Ash managed to catch his gaze before he left the room, offering him a wink as she hopped off the dais, joining her fellow Allies.

"Is it just me or did that entire thing just make Malachai look *ridiculously* hot," Anastasia mentioned, biting her bottom lip, staring at the door he'd just slipped through.

"Seriously, Ana?" Alistair groused. "Keep it in your pants."

"I could say the same to you," Quinn muttered, earning a harsh elbow to the ribs. Ash's heart stilled at the sight, her heart dropping into her churning stomach. Their eyes met, and she could see immediately that he'd regretted what he just said, but Ash didn't wait around for an apology. She walked out of the Throne Room without uttering a single word, headed to find Beck and that liquid courage. She didn't think she needed it before, but now she was certain that she did.

ONCE EVERYONE GATHERED IN THE SQUARE, ASH MADE A POINT NOT to look at either Alistair *or* Quinn. She was furious with them both, and as far as she was concerned, she had every right to be. The Rider had told their secret without consulting her first, to the *last* person she would have wanted him to tell.

All of this was reminding Ash why she avoided entertaining the idea of love.

There were a few occasions, while they were waiting for everyone to join them in the square, where Quinn tried to get her attention or speak to her. Every time he tried, she made a point to enter a conversation with someone else. She'd ask Craven and Marcus about their feelings regarding that day's mission. Or she'd talk to Ana, who was still drooling over Malachai, which was bothering Craven immensely, though he didn't admit it.

"I don't know how you haven't jumped his bones," Ana whispered. "I mean, the man left everything he knew for you. He just informed the entire Realm that *you're* the reason he gained enough courage to leave his abusive father."

Ash scoffed, wrapping her arms around herself. "There's no way that'll ever happen. The Elves have *barely* been able to stomach him staying inside their castle. Imagine how they'd react if they thought the entire reason we were working together is because we were *sleeping* together?" She kept her voice low, hoping no one was listening in. "Thaddeus already accused us of conspiring since my birth."

"*What?*" Vincent blurted.

Okay, someone *was* listening in.

Frowning, Ash turned to face her brother. "Yes. This morning, before the address. Don't worry, I put him in his place, and Esmeralda agreed with me."

Craven snorted. "How did *that* go over?"

"Fucking phenomenally," Sam insisted with a wicked grin.

Ash was sure that Sam would have continued with an incredibly detailed explanation of the encounter, including every word she'd said, had Malachai not decided to make his arrival. Clad in a Draconian uniform that clung to every muscle. He'd left his eyes red, likely so he could relate to his fellow Pandora during their difficult transition. The crimson stripe running diagonally across his uniform brought them out in the best of ways. Up until then, Ash had never thought them anything but haunting.

The prince had tied back half of his hair with Elven braids running along his temples in typical warrior fashion. Clearly, Aveo was at fault for that. The smirk her Guardian was wearing told Ash so.

"Okay, you look like some sort of Elven, Draconian, Pandora, badass Hybrid and it's working for you," Anastasia complimented. "If *that* doesn't scream unity, I don't know what does."

Aveo's smirk grew even wider. "That was the entire point."

"I'm *genuinely* a Hybrid," Ash reminded them all. "I'm walking unity. Just because Malachai braided his hair and put on a different uniform doesn't make him one."

That was when the Pandora flashed a set of fangs identical to a Draconians.

"That's just playing dirty," Marcus insisted. "Now, if you two don't mind, we have tunnel entrances to get to. Does everyone have their gifts for the exchange?"

Most people nodded in unison. Ash didn't because her gift for Morghan would need to be delivered. Which was in order, as far as she was concerned. If not, she'd have a lot of explaining to do.

61

By the time Malachai and Quinn made it to their tunnel entrance, Pandora were already flooding it, most of them leaking blood all over the snow. Axel had been right. The streets of Solaris were running red, and the prince could only blame himself for that.

Lost in his thoughts about how many Xavier and his loyal subjects had slain, Malachai forced a smile for the sake of those who'd made it out alive. He'd known, deep in his gut, that something like this might happen. The Pandora might be fast, but when it came to an Arebus Archer and Witches, they weren't fast enough.

Suddenly, Malachai wasn't in a very giving spirit.

"You did the right thing," Quinn reminded, watching the beasts run into the tunnel, where they were met by Rebels with blankets and med-kits. The sound of moans and painful screams flooded Malachai's ears a second later, causing him to grow stiff with both rage and regret. "These people will heal. They're free now. Free to choose what they want to do."

Nodding, Malachai chose to focus on those words. *Free. Heal.*

"You're right," he replied, pulling in a deep, rickety breath.

They stood in silence for a time, waving Pandora down, guiding them inside to safety. The Realm rumbled around them as stampedes of beasts dove through the tunnels beneath their feet, all while

Malachai kept his gaze fixed in the northern direction. He could sense something coming. Something familiar and dangerous.

Quinn could sense it too. Malachai could tell by the way he loaded his bow in a flash, his eyes transitioning from his usual cerulean to an eerie glowing blue. They'd both known the risks that would come along with guarding the tunnel entrance closest to Solaris. There was *bound* to be intervention.

"Who do you think it is?" the Archer asked through bared, clenched teeth. The Pandora passing between them were beginning to tremble. Those in their Mortal forms kept looking over their shoulders, lips quivering with fear.

"Savron," a passerby revealed, a man, drenched in blood from head to toe. "He followed us out. We didn't even know that he was *there*. Xavier had sent him back to the Regal Mountains. Banished him too, for what he did to that Archer."

Quinn flinched but offered the Pandora an appreciative nod. "Head inside. We'll handle him."

"Wait," Malachai called, just before the man was getting ready to drop into the tunnel. "Is Savron coming as a Warlock, or as a Pandora?"

The man shrugged. "I don't know, Your Majesty."

Your Majesty. The title echoed in Malachai's mind, chilling him to the bone. "Go on," he urged the man. "There are Healers waiting for you with food, water, and warm blankets. Just head toward the center of the Realm. There will be Rebels to guide you along the way."

"Rebels?" the man asked, his eyes bulging. "I thought you killed them all."

Malachai was getting pretty tired of hearing people say that. "Just the risky ones," he explained. "Now go, before Savron gets here."

The man was gone in a flash, transitioning into something fast. The other Pandora picked up the pace, hurrying to get away from the monster who followed.

Savron's scent grew stronger and stronger, but Malachai couldn't see him. He wasn't close enough. For whatever reason, he was surely taking his time. The prince waited impatiently, his mind swimming with ideas about how to defeat him. Arebus arrows wouldn't work. Not the way they were supposed to. And, even *if* Malachai found a way to kill him, Veda would bring him back all over again.

There was also the fact that Malachai wasn't sure he could kill one of his siblings, even if they weren't blood related.

When Savron finally appeared, Malachai realized that he hadn't come to start a fight, or to intervene. The very sight of the Warlock made the prince want to wretch into the snow. His silver-blond hair was caked with blood seeping from a wound at his temple. His left arm dangled, dislocated from his shoulder, his wrist barley hanging on by threads of gnarled flesh. His crimson coven cloak was torn to shreds, as was his flesh beneath.

Quinn lowered his bow, alarmed by the Warlock's appearance. "Holy shit," he breathed, eyes bulging as Savron arrived right in front of them.

"What happened?" Malachai asked, helping Savron to sit down.

"I'd gone back to father to plead my case and apologize for what I'd done to the Archer. And, perhaps to have a proper Giving Day with Jax since she was summoned to take my place. She's been training that Witch he made Lincoln bring in. That relative of yours." Savron wet his chapped lips. "I was in his study when your Realm address started. He lost it."

Malachai could barely think over the sound of his blood roaring in his ears. "He took it out on you." It wasn't a question.

More Pandora were beginning to pass by, eyeing the Warlock warily as he said, "He went full-on monster, Chai. I didn't even recognize him. He looked just like what the books said about Xanthius. How Aiden Cavanaugh described him. I couldn't get out of there in time. Either he didn't remember who I was, or he didn't care." Tears began to well in Savron's silvery gaze. "I barely made it out of there with my life."

"Well, as horrible as that all sounds, we can't exactly let him enter the tunnels," Quinn reminded the prince, his lips dipping into a deep frown. "Not after what he did to Cooper."

The Archer wasn't wrong. The Allies would kill Savron the second they set their sights upon him.

"I know," Malachai said solemnly. "But I can still heal him."

It took every ounce of the prince's energy to heal Savron, and in the end, his arm was still dislocated. That was something Malachai could do without his abilities. The cry that escaped the Warlock when he adjusted his arm, putting it back into his shoulder socket where it belonged, was oddly satisfying. Savron's current circumstances didn't change everything he'd done.

"There," Malachai said, a bit breathless. "That should make fleeing a little easier for you."

Savron nodded, pursing his lips. "Where should I go?"

"Anywhere but where Veda and the Crimson Coven are," Malachai explained, his tone laced with sincerity and warning. "They *will* hand you back over to him. Your best chance is to find a shadow and stay inside it."

"What about Trixa?" Savron asked, silver eyes flashing with worry.

"She can handle herself," Malachai told him.

"And the baby?" Savron pressed.

"Will be safe with Irina," the prince insisted. "You need to worry about *yourself*. You're surrounded by enemies in every direction. The Crimson Coven, the Unseen, Father, and the Allies all want you dead. So, go. While you still can."

Savron gave him a nod before taking off toward the west. The silence that followed his departure was unnerving. Malachai's skin crawled, guilt beginning to eat him alive. "That was another one of my mistakes," he told Quinn. "Savron was eight when his abilities surfaced. I made the mistake of telling my father, who thought that turning him into a Pandora would create one of the best weapons the Realms had ever seen. That was before he started sleeping with Savron's mother, in hopes to create more Warlocks, which is how our twin sisters were born."

"And you're just going to let him go?" Quinn asked, snorting with disbelief. "He's your brother."

"Via adoption," Malachai clarified. "He's also the reason your brother almost died. Now, let's focus on the fact that our tunnel has saved thousands of Pandora in such a short span of time. By now, most of them should be underground. Which means that we won today's battle, and now we can focus on more pleasant things. Like the gift exchange."

"You're deflecting," Quinn accused with narrowing eyes.

"So? I'd rather distract myself anyway. Besides, if the other tunnels are slowing down the way ours is, Lucinda could show up any second to start the process. Or, whoever has her sphere. So, if I were you, I'd get your presents ready."

Nodding, Quinn strapped his bow to his back and started to sift through his pack, retrieving three different things. One was a bundle of Arebus Arrows. The next was clearly a book, wrapped in black paper, and the third looked to be a ring box wrapped in silver paper, with a matching ribbon.

"You went all out," Malachai told him. "I'm beginning to think I didn't get enough."

Shaking his head, Quinn said, "These aren't all for one person. One's for Ash. I was hoping whoever showed up would be able to tell me who pulled her name, so I could give it to them."

"Well, you're in luck," Malachai informed him happily. "I did. But that doesn't look like something anyone but you should give her."

"It's not what you think," Quinn claimed. "It was her mothers. I tried to give it to her on her birthday, but we were rudely interrupted, which I can only blame Morghan for." He paused, rolling his eyes. "Anyway, I wanted to give it to her *before* she left Crane. I didn't get the chance. I've been looking for the right time to do it since."

Malachai cringed, unable to help himself. "And you think *I* should do it?"

"It doesn't matter how she gets it, just that she has it," Quinn declared.

62

Beck had been right. This *was* a test for Cooper. And, so far, he was passing it. Ash couldn't help but notice how calm he appeared when Pandora first began to barrel toward their entrance. Thankfully, most were uninjured, but there were a few things both Allies had witnessed that would forever haunt them.

Pandora carrying their young in their mortal forms, weeping with joy to be provided with safety. Everything Malachai had said about breeding replayed in Ash's mind, bile creeping up her throat. She did her best to remain strong, no matter how badly she wanted to cry at the sight of all the relief upon the faces of those that passed her by.

"We weren't exactly counting on children," Cooper mentioned, his brow wrinkling with worry as a woman passed by, both her hands wrapped around a set of twin toddlers. Pandora lingered behind them, helping to lower the young ones down into the tunnel. The sight warmed Ash's heart.

Until the sound of a newborn's cry pierced through the night.

Ash's heart skidded to a stop. She scanned her surroundings, searching for the source. The second she saw the woman, kneeling on the ground, covered in blood, holding a bundle in her arms, tears sprang from Ash's eyes without warning. She hurried toward her, sliding onto the ground.

"Hey," Ash whispered, slowly reaching to put a hand on her shoulder. The woman flinched, but not from fear. Pain. "Here, let me take the baby," she suggested. Whatever had happened to this woman, it was nothing like what had happened to the other Pandora. It was something worse.

The woman didn't have the energy to object. She handed the baby over, and Ash immediately brought it against her chest, horrified by how *cold* it was. "Can you walk?" she asked the woman.

"Yes," she croaked. "I think. I'm not sure. I ran so far, and so fast. All the way from Dairth."

Cooper let loose a long whistle, approaching from behind. "That's quite the hike. Why didn't you use one of the tunnel entrances closer to the Regal Mountains?"

"I couldn't." The woman gulped, shivering. "My husband was tracking me. He still is, most likely. He wouldn't let us go willingly. He called me a traitor and... well... you can see what he's done."

Ash clenched her jaw so badly that it hurt. The woman was suffering from multiple lacerations, her blood seeping onto the snow beneath her. Both her eyes were nearly swollen shut, already bruising. A glance at her hands told Ash that most of her fingers were broken, and she doubted that was the end of it.

"You're safe now," Ash said, her tone wavering. The baby shivered against her, whimpering. "Cooper, can you teleport this baby?"

"Where? Into the intersection? The Healers are overrun," he reminded her.

"To Jeremy," Ash told him. "He'll know what to do."

The woman didn't object. Instead, she remained silent, her eyes glued on the bundle in Ash's arms.

"What about her?" Cooper whispered. "Crane won't have what she needs to heal."

"I'll call Malachai."

The woman visibly stiffened, which only invoked a painful cry.

"Last I heard, Malachai had his hands full," Cooper argued. "Solaris wasn't exactly easy for the Pandora to escape."

"That was hours ago," Ash spat. "He'll come. I know he will. Besides, everyone's switching places by now. You know, because of the gift exchange. He could be anywhere else. He'll come," she repeated, silently praying that he would. "Just take the baby to Jeremy and stay with it until I say otherwise."

"If I leave you alone again, Quinn will kill me," Cooper insisted.

Ash's blood began to boil. "Quinn is not in charge of you *or* me. Now go," she demanded, handing the baby over to him. "*Now.*"

Cooper vanished without another word.

"You aren't alone," the woman said. "I'm here. I may be of no use to you in a fight, but I'm good for conversation. In fact, if I stop talking, I'll only think. And *thinking* is the last thing I want to do."

MALACHAI GOT THE CALL BEFORE ANYONE SHOWED UP TO REPLACE him. His chip started to vibrate, which couldn't mean anything good. Once he saw that it was Ash calling, dread settled in his gut. He answered anyway and listened to her explain what she'd just encountered. That a woman had been beaten so terribly by her Pandora husband that she'd needed to flee with her newborn, and that she'd had ran all the way from Dairth to Redding in the middle of Winter Solstice, the coldest part of the year.

"I'll be there soon," Malachai promised, his throat tightening unbearably.

"What is it?" Penelope asked from where she stood a few feet away, staring in the northern direction. She and Lucinda had replaced Quinn less than thirty minutes ago. The prince had found the present they gave him to be quite amusing, but all that humor had vanished.

"Ash," Malachai explained, heart thrashing against his chest. "She's safe, but I need to find a way to her. She's with an injured woman who desperately needs my help."

Lucinda cursed beneath her breath. "I sent the sphere with Quinn. Vincent probably has it by now. Or maybe Craven."

"I can fly," Malachai told her.

Penelope immediately shook her head, objecting. "No way. That could take more than an hour, maybe even two. Not to mention, your father will stop at nothing to punish you for what you did today. You're like a bright, blinking target."

"I don't exactly have another choice," Malachai reminded her. "Tracking down the sphere will take too long. Unless Lucinda can spell me a portal, then flying is my only option."

"If I *personally* made a portal, it would be just as Penelope described. A massive, blinking target," Lucinda explained, pulling out her chip. Not her wand.

"What are you doing?" Penelope growled.

Lucinda didn't respond to the Princess. Instead, she spoke with whoever she'd called. "Where's your Dragon?"

Malachai watched her, his eyes narrowing accusingly.

With Quinn and Aveo probably, why?

"We need a ride," Lucinda told him. "Immediately. Unless you happen to know where my sphere is."

Before Alistair had a chance to reply, a random portal opened behind Malachai. He whirled around, expecting someone to come out of it. Instead, he found himself staring into a window, where he could see Ash sitting on the ground with a woman.

"At any sign of trouble, I want you to run into the tunnels as fast as you can," Malachai shot over his shoulder, the words directed at Penelope. He wasn't sure who'd made the portal, but he had an idea who it might have been. However, he didn't have time to entertain that thought. He slung his pack over his shoulder and passed through.

The prince wasted no time getting straight to work. He healed the woman as much as he was able. By the end of it, while no physical wounds remained, he knew that the woman required a lot more healing. More than he could give her.

"Thank you," she said breathlessly. "I owe you everything. Consider myself in your debt."

Ash shot Malachai a disapproving look.

"You owe me nothing," Malachai replied, watching Ash's features soften. "The only thing I require of you is your *former* husband's name, so I can gut him."

The woman stared at him, her eyes still glassy from the effects of his abilities. "Ryole…"

Malachai choked on the air he was breathing at the time, his eyes bulging. "As in the *Commander*?"

"Yes," she confirmed. "We married three years ago. I fell pregnant in the Spring. He told me the second I delivered, I was to go to Solaris, so our baby could be raised the way a Pandora should. That *his* children would be the best. I gave birth three days ago. He never came. Then, I saw your Realm address. It gave me an opportunity to give my child a normal life. So, like every other Pandora, we started to flee. Ryole intercepted me on the outskirts of Dairth. I gave my daughter to a man—some Sorcerer. He ran with her, and after Ryole beat me to a point where he believed me dead, I waited for him to leave and then chased after the man. He was waiting for me a few miles away. After that, he disappeared, and I ran here. I was afraid if I used a closer entrance, it would be some sort of trap."

A Sorcerer. Malachai's eyes narrowed, his brow wrinkling with thought. First, a Sorcerer helps this woman, and then, a strange portal appears to take Malachai *exactly* where he needed to go.

"Storm," the prince declared, grinding his teeth. "If he keeps this up, he'll kill himself. That Blood Oath will tear him to shreds, especially if Jax finds out," he muttered to himself.

"What?" Ask asked.

"Nothing," Malachai assured her. "Where has the baby gone?"

"Cooper took her to Crane," she informed him. "We knew it would be too chaotic in the tunnels. We didn't exactly summon children. Not that we mind. We want to save everyone, but the intersection is no place for a three-day-old. So, I figured the village baker would be our best bet. He has everything she'd need."

The woman cleared her throat. "Besides me."

Malachai offered her a smile, reaching to squeeze her shoulder reassuringly. "We'll just have to find a way there."

A portal opened a second later, one that Alistair passed through, his brows raising with surprise. "I was expecting to arrive at the Solaris tunnel."

"Well, you didn't," Ash said, stating the obvious. Malachai couldn't help but notice how her demeanor had changed. She was as stiff as stone, a glare like no other upon her face.

Malachai chose not to comment on it, but he couldn't help but wonder what had gone wrong between the pair.

"Clearly," Alistair replied, shifting his weight uncomfortably from one leg to the other. "I was supposed to swap with Malachai, so he could go to whoever he needed to."

"I'm already here," Malachai admitted to him. "Don't you have a gift for me?" he teased.

The Rider's eyebrows flattened, his lips pursing. "I was told not to give it to you until the end, and to only take your place. That's all."

"Hmm," Ash hummed. "Then, if you're not busy, would you mind staying here so we can use the sphere and take this woman to her newborn in Crane?"

The Pandora had stopped coming, which was a sign that they were nearing the end. Alistair shouldn't have any trouble, and the odds were that they'd be summoned to the intersection within the hour.

"Yeah, no problem," Alistair told her with a half-smile.

Ash didn't return the expression. Instead, she took the sphere and tossed it to the ground, opening a portal to Crane. Malachai helped the woman to her feet, her knees wobbling so badly that he wrapped an arm around her, supporting her weight. They passed through the portal, arriving on Crane's main street.

One thing Malachai *hadn't* expected was for all of the villagers to be standing outside their homes and shops, staring at them. They brought their fists to their hearts, an action that made his sinuses burn with coming tears.

The sight clearly took Ash by surprise too. She slowed her walking, fingers wrapping around the chrome sphere. These were the people she knew. The ones she'd grown up alongside. Malachai could only imagine how strange it must be to have them look at her as anyone other than Ashlyn Snow.

"This way," Ash choked, pointing toward a building at the end of the long street, one with smoke billowing out of a chimney. The scent of fresh bread and pastries waffled through the air, causing Malachai's mouth to water. He hadn't realized how hungry he was. Had he eaten at all that day? He doubted it.

"This village is... adorable," the woman claimed, admiring all the cottages perched on cliffs and hills.

"And in the process of being reconstructed, thanks to *some* people," Ash threw over her shoulder, giving Malachai a deadly scowl that softened almost instantaneously. "But I forgive him."

"You do?" the prince blurted.

"I think they all do, Your Majesty," the woman mentioned, scanning all of the people watching them with kind eyes and smiles.

"You can call me Malachai," he told her. "No more silly titles. I think it's pretty clear by now that I was disowned."

63

Ash found Cooper in the bakery, where Jeremy was currently bossing him around while rocking the baby back and forth in front of his ovens. "Get goats milk. It'll be easier on her stomach. And go to Mrs. Meckellery's house. She'll have bottles. The woman has a child every year. Grab some clothes too, and blankets, and nappies, and—"

The baker paused the second he caught sight of Ash, the baby's mother, and the Prince of Darkness standing at his threshold.

"Don't stop," Ash instructed. "She'll need all of those things."

Cooper gave Ash a nod and then vanished once again.

"I've never been so happy to see a person in all my life," Jeremy said, eyes damp with tears. "I saw the address. Thought you'd all get yourselves killed. Then Cooper shows up with this little bean in the dead of winter, just like a little someone I happen to know." He winked, offering Ash a proud smile. "I'm glad to see that you're safe. *All* of you."

"I'm sorry I haven't been in touch since the Cooper ordeal," Ash told him, walking over to where he rocked the baby. The oven rang. Something was done within. Jeremy stood up to handle it, but Ash held up a hand, urging him to sit back down. "I'll get it. Just back away."

Malachai came forward, dragging the rocking chair Jeremy was sitting in backward. Ash slipped on a pair of oven mitts and retrieved the fresh pies from the racks inside, setting them on the nearby windowsill to cool.

"Apple," Ash mused. "My favorite. It's like you *knew* I'd show up."

"I make them every year, just for you," Jeremy replied, a certain twinkle in his eye that Ash hadn't seen in years. "But I imagine you'll need a place for this little one's mother to rest. I have a spare room upstairs. There are blankets in the closet. You know what I'm talking about."

Nodding, Ash pulled off the mitts. "Thank you, Jeremy," she said, leaning forward to plant a kiss on his cheek.

The baker blushed, waving her off with his free hand, the other still firmly securing the newborn. He looked toward the mother and said, "You rest as long as you need. The rest of us will make sure your baby is fed and safe. This isn't the first time we've done this."

The mother nodded, shadows dancing in her eyes. Ash knew, however, that after a few days in Crane with the people she knew and loved, she'd see light in those red eyes.

"Might we have your name, before you sleep for an unknown amount of time?" Malachai inquired.

"Fay," she replied. "And the baby is Jane."

"I betcha if we told that to Grandmother Opal, she'd have a custom blanket crocheted by dawn," Ash insisted with a chuckle. "Anyway, let's get you upstairs," she urged, gesturing for the woman to follow her.

Warmth radiated throughout Malachai's body at the sight of Ash, leading Fay upstairs. The way she'd acted beforehand, with the baker she'd known all her life, stirred something deep in his gut. He was in awe of her, no matter how hard he tried not to be. One second, she was the leader she needed to be, and the next, she was so loving. *Happy*. To see her smile, even after the day they'd just had was one of the best Giving Day presents Malachai had ever received.

Not that he'd ever really received one. His mother used to get him books, which he loved. But once she died, his father stopped caring about everything and anyone. Gifts were the least of his concerns.

The events of that day had been emotional, frightening, and chaotic, but Malachai could feel the weight lifting off his shoulders. To stand there in that bakery, or to walk down that street outside and have no one look at him like some sort of walking nightmare... he'd never thought that would happen again.

Ash had given him more than she'd ever realize this Giving Day. He wasn't sure that he'd ever be able to repay her.

When Ash returned, Cooper was just walking through the door, arms full of supplies. An old woman followed him in, carrying baskets that Malachai was happy to take from her. She took one look at the baby and melted.

"Grandmother Opal, I presume?" Malachai asked, looking toward Ash.

"You were paying attention," she mused, nudging him with her elbow.

"Of course, I was," he replied with a cocky smile, one that made her roll her eyes. "I bet she makes the most beautiful, crocheted baby blankets in Idona," he added for good measure.

Grandmother Opal's eyes twinkled, a prideful grin stretching across her wrinkled face. "Oh stop," she suggested, though it was clear she didn't mean it. She might as well have said *keep the compliments coming, I dare you.* "You're the one deserving of compliments this evening. What you did today was incredibly brave. And, if I do dare say so myself, that uniform suits you well."

Out of the corner of Malachai's eye, he watched Ash's mouth open and shut quickly, her eyes widening. His brows raised at the sight. *Jealous, are we?* "Thank you, Opal, but I'm sure it would look even better on you," he drawled.

Ash turned, gawking at him. Cooper choked on something

across the room. Jeremy shook his head, turning his attention back to the baby.

Opal's cheeks burned red, but that didn't stop her from saying. "You know, back in my day, men like you didn't exist, and I'm not just referring to your Pandora parts."

"*Opal,*" Ash gasped, bristling like a cat thrown in water.

"What?" the old woman asked, reaching into one of her baskets, retrieving a ball of pale purple yarn. "Just because I'm fifty years your senior doesn't mean I'm not in my prime."

Stunned silent, all Ash did was stare at Opal, her jaw hanging open. Malachai chuckled beneath his breath before saying, "We should be going. Wouldn't want to keep your Allies waiting. I'm sure that Opal and Jeremy have things handled here, but I'll make sure to reinstate my Wards around the village, just in case. Ryole is as bad as they come, and I know for a fact that he'll stop at nothing to get her back," he explained, gesturing to the baby. "I'll come back in the morning to check on her."

"I'll come too," Ash replied, giving Opal the side eye. The old woman snorted, her caramel eyes flashing with amusement.

"We should get back to Alistair," Cooper suggested, placing a fresh nappy and a bottle on the table beside Jeremy. "But, let me know if you need me to fetch anything else." He drove a hand to his pocket, pulling out a chip. "You can use this to contact me. There's a list of names. Pick any one of them. Whoever answers will get a message to me."

Just when Malachai hadn't thought it possible, Opal's grin grew even wider. "Is *his* name in there?"

Ash reached to rub her temples.

"You do remember *who* he is, right?" Cooper asked.

"Does that really matter anymore?" she countered.

"You call me whenever you'd like," Malachai told her, fighting the urge to laugh at the sound of Ash's following scoff. "But for now, we really have to go. Cooper's right. Alistair's alone. There's a reason we were put in teams of two."

"Ah, the Dragon Rider," Opal said with a sigh, lowering into a chair. "He's not bad to look at either."

"How much of Greg's Giving Day punch did you have, Opal?" Jeremy asked, his eyes narrowing accusingly.

"Not enough to keep me from helping with that baby," Opal insisted proudly. "Now, you three go ahead and get on your way. I'm sure that you'll be needed below ground at some point tonight. Not to mention, the night is still young, and you have lots to celebrate."

"We'll celebrate once my people are safe and healing," Malachai told her, turning toward the door. "Please tell Fay that if she requires any more of my assistance to not be afraid to call."

After that, they left the baker, all while Ash shook her head, mumbling beneath her breath.

"You know, if I didn't know any better, I'd say you were jealous," Cooper teased, poking her in the shoulder. "Is there something that you need to tell Malachai? Shall I leave, so you can speak in private?"

Nothing compared to the scowl Ash gave the Archer. Malachai shivered at the sight of it. "Well, he hasn't pissed me off today," she revealed. "I can stand being in his presence, unlike you right now."

"Okay, before you both start arguing, you should probably know that I have gifts," Malachai interjected before they had a chance to continue. "So, be nice, or neither of you are getting a thing."

"I didn't start this, you did," Ash argued.

"It's not my fault that women are attracted to me, Ash," he reminded her. "At least Opal was upfront and honest about it."

"What exactly are you insinuating?" she grumbled.

Shrugging, Malachai retrieved the teleportation sphere from his pocket. "Nothing," he assured her, imagining the place where they'd left Alistair. "I'm just saying, I like when women are straightforward."

"And I like men I can trust," she admitted. "I learned today that they're incredibly hard to find."

"Oh?" Cooper's brows flicked upward.

"Long story," Ash told him. "Just toss the sphere."

64

An hour later, the Allies, Malachai, Aveo, and Beck were all in the intersection, surrounded by chaos. Rebels and Pandora scrambled around, helping Healers with the injured, handing out blankets and bottles of water. Sam was clearly in over his head, but so far, it appeared that he'd handled the night well enough.

The next few hours were a blur. Ash did whatever she could, using her earth ability to create a garden, in hopes to add to the stocks of food the Rebels already had. There was only so much that she could do on her own and had no choice but to contact Shadow. Thankfully, the Earth Clan leader was gracious enough to send her thirty of his best soldiers. They would be there by the morning. In the meantime, Marcus started to create a stew in a massive cauldron, using a recipe Cooper had given him as a Giving Day gift, from Pat McBride's personal collection.

Ash was able to grow most of the ingredients, and the Rebels had already had enough beef stored. She promised to replace it as quickly as she was able and asked Beck if he could put in an order to the Kingdom of Elves immediately afterward. He got right on it, and soon enough, stew was being served in every container. Bowls, mugs, chrome thermoses—which Ash had used her water ability to clean out—and jars that had once held milk.

The children were fed first. Penelope and Morghan helped feed the ones too young to feed themselves, so their parents could finish being bandaged or rest. Aveo and Quinn started figuring out a place to put them all. Somewhere safe, where they could be protected. Staying underground wasn't an option.

"What if we took a base?" Ana inquired, wiping a hand across her sweaty brow. "We've done it before. We could do it again."

"Well, I sank the one in the Lakelands," Ash reminded her. "And Craven blew up the one near the Forest of Fools. The only base still standing is the one you took down, but so many Pandora just fled from there. They won't want to go back. We need to think of something else."

Aveo nodded in agreement. "We could construct one."

"That could take up to a year, maybe more," Quinn insisted. "We'd need to build hundreds of homes to fit all of these families."

"Well, without *Magic* it would take a year," Ana argued. "Veda was able to move a base. You can't tell me that it wouldn't be possible to *create* one, too."

Ash pursed her lips. "I think it's pretty obvious that Veda would be the *last* person to assist these people."

"Yes, but Lucinda is her nemesis," Quinn countered. "Which means our lovely Realm Sorceress rivals Veda in regard to power. She could very well be capable of doing such a thing. Not to mention, she has an entire league of Sorcerers to help her."

"Good point," Aveo commended. "Where is she?"

Ash scanned the massive intersection, her stomach sinking with dread. She knew, deep down, that Malachai had *saved* all these people, but all the carnage before her made her think otherwise. Now, they were homeless and in pain. On a holiday, no less.

"Over there," Ash revealed. "With Vincent, taking names."

"I'll go ask her," Ana said. "Ash, you look like you could use a drink. Blood, or whiskey. Either or. Get one."

Frowning, Ash watched her storm away, weaving through hordes of distressed people. She caught sight of Malachai, sewing together someone's wound. He'd run out of energy to use his ability more than an hour ago, but he wasn't useless. Not as long as there was anesthetic and suture kits. Or so he'd said.

What would have happened if she'd killed him, back on the East Cliff? Or, before that, in the forest where they'd first met? She'd known taking a chance on him would be a risk, and that she would lose the respect of every other Idonian or Amorian, she supposed.

A hand fell on her shoulder, startling Ash out of her thoughts.

"Here," Aveo said, handing her a glass filled three-quarters full of amber liquid. "Quinn went to hunt down some blood for you. I figured this would be easier to find. What possessed you to get Morghan an entire case of whiskey?" he asked, chuckling as she took the glass. "I mean, it came in handy. It's certainly calming a lot of Pandora nerves right now, but that's beside the point."

Shrugging, Ash said, "Morghan loves his whiskey."

"Most men do," Aveo replied.

"Perhaps I should order another," Ash said, brow winkling with thought. "If it's helping—"

"You need to worry about yourself for five minutes," her Guardian cut in. "So does Malachai. The two of you haven't stopped."

"Well, Malachai's the only one who can do *his* job. He needs to be here, with all these people that he summoned, and I need to be here to show that *we* support the Pandora too," Ash explained, taking her first sip, grimacing as the heat of it burned down her throat and into her stomach. "When they look around, they see Draconians, Elves, Rebels, Arebus Archers, a Werewolf," she paused to suck in a deep breath, exhaling slowly. "They know they're not alone, as long as we're here."

ASH DIDN'T AGREE TO LEAVE THE INTERSECTION UNTIL IT WAS nearing three in the morning. Malachai had outright refused until his own people growled at him to go and get some rest. Penelope and Morghan had left long before then, mostly because Ash's sister had fallen asleep while reading to a pack of toddlers a bedtime story. Aveo had taken one look at her, curled up amidst half a dozen children, and asked the Wolf to scoop her up and take her home.

Home today was the McBride Estate, and Quinn had left an hour earlier to start getting beds in order for everyone. Ash made her way up the path, Malachai trudging beside her, the Allies dragging their feet behind them.

Cooper barely made it up the front steps before collapsing on the porch. Ana dragged him inside before falling onto the foyer floor. She didn't get up. Morghan was already asleep in the family room, in his Wolf form in front of a fire. *Typical,* Ash chuckled.

"Penelope's asleep in Lilly's room," Quinn revealed on the way down the stairs, dressed in a pair of soft plaid pajama pants, no shirt, his hair still damp from a shower. "My bathroom is free for whoever wants to use it."

"Me," Lucinda blurted, shedding her cloak, hands already moving to the zipper on her uniform jacket. She traveled up the stairs so quickly that she might as well have been a blur.

"There's another shower downstairs, down the hall in the washroom," Quinn explained. "And another, in between Cooper and Lincoln's rooms. One across from Lilly's, and of course, there's Ash's, or the hose out in the barn. You can all fight over the last option," he said sarcastically before turning in the kitchen's direction. Marcus followed him, muttering something about putting on a pot of coffee.

Aveo chose the downstairs bathroom, while Ash, Alistair, and Malachai made their way upstairs, her legs barking at her with every step. She walked to her room in a daze, absentmindedly peeling off her uniform and her underclothes beneath. After making it to her washroom, she turned on the shower and unraveled her braid.

It was an effort to keep her eyes open as Ash stood beneath the steaming hot stream. Water ran in rivers down her entire form, drenching her hair, washing blood, dust, and grime from her aching flesh. She ran a bar of lavender scented soap all over before dropping and refusing to pick it up. Bending over would take too much energy, and she needed what remained of her reserves to get dressed and get in bed.

Shutting the shower off, Ash stepped out and wrapped her robe around herself, wiping her feet on the bathmat before walking over to retrieve her comb from where it lay on her counter. She put little effort into running it through her hair before wrapping a towel around it, drawing out as much water as she could.

Dressing was a gruesome task. Ash nearly fell four times while trying to shove her legs into soft black leggings. She pushed her arms through the sleeves of a red plaid flannel she'd stolen from Cooper a few years back, one that had once belonged to Lincoln, and then Quinn before him. It smelled of pine and campfires, no matter how many times it had been washed. Ash lifted the fabric to her nose, breathing it in deeply.

As Ash was fumbling with the last button, a knock appeared on her door. "Who knocks in this house?" she asked, her words slurred from exhaustion and whiskey.

"Me," Malachai replied, opening the door a crack. "Are you decent? Or do people not ask that question in this house either?"

"Actually, they don't," she admitted. "Modesty flew out the window a few years back when we were all swarmed by bees out in the fields and had to run to the pond, rip off our clothes, and jump in."

Malachai nudged the door with his foot, allowing it to open completely. Ash caught sight of a few presents by his feet, and two cups of coffee in his hands. "Mind if I come in?" he inquired politely.

"Did you ask my Guardian?" Ash said, lips playing at a teasing smile.

The Pandora rolled his eyes, entering the room, holding out one of the mugs to her. "I would have, but he's currently asleep out here on a bench in the hall. Some Guardian you have."

"Why's he sleeping on a bench, when Quinn set up beds all over the house?" Ash took the mug, taking a long, deep sip before she realized it wasn't *just* coffee. "Is that... Greg's Giving Day brew?" she asked, her eyes bulging.

"I kept hearing so much about it," he admitted, returning to the threshold to retrieve the presents. "And, once I learned Sam got his hands on some, I made him put some in a thermos to take home for this particular moment."

Ash gave him a long, scrutinizing look. "And what sort of *moment* is this?" she asked, hoping her voice didn't betray her evolving nerves.

"The moment where I finally get to give you your Giving Day gifts," he informed her, setting the small pile on the bed. "I snuck Cooper's into his room, even though Lucinda had apparently claimed that as *her* territory indefinitely. She also mentioned that she might sleep for a few days."

"I wish I could too, but there's still work to be done. I'm going to have to petition the Idonian Council, well... myself, for land to build a place for all the Pandora to live, and a proper base for the Rebels —one that isn't underground. A place where the two armies can train as one. You know, learn to work together—"

Malachai held up a hand, stopping her. "Enough working for the evening."

"Says the man who needed to be told by his own patients to leave," Ash countered, taking another sip before heading back over to her dresser, in need of a pair of wool socks. "You were really in your element down there," she added, setting the mug aside so she could pull the socks on. "I mean, we were surrounded by carnage, but I've never seen you smile like that."

"I haven't in a while," he admitted, lowering to sit beside the gifts on the bed before patting a spot beside him. A silent gesture, one that Ash couldn't refuse. "We make a good team, you know," he continued once she was settled, legs crossed like a pretzel, hot mug in her hands. "Well, when we're not at each other's throats. Not that I ever think we will be again. Or so I hope."

Shaking her head, Ash confidently said, "We won't. I don't think we could go through everything we have today and these last few weeks and even remotely revert back to how we were when we met."

Someone passed in the hall. Marcus, on his way to use the shower across from Lilly's room, his arms filled with clothes and a toothbrush. He stopped for a second, offering them both a smile, eyeing the gifts on the bed.

"Do you like my ribbon work?" the Mentor inquired. "Lucinda had her judgments."

"It's perfectly fine," Malachai told him. "She's just going to tear it off, anyway."

"You're not a chef," Marcus countered. "You don't understand how important presentation is." With that, he went on his way. The sound of the washroom door opening and shutting followed a moment later.

Malachai moved on to hand her the first present, a black velvet box wrapped in a red ribbon. Ash tugged at it, flicking it at him afterward. She opened the box, only to feel her heart drop into her fluttering stomach. It was a bracelet, but one of the most breathtaking she'd ever seen. There were no jewels, or anything of that nature, but the silver alone was beautiful enough to stare at for hours. It was woven into a pattern of Idonian knots and roses. Simple, yet extravagant all the same.

"It was my mother's," Malachai admitted before Ash had a chance to tell him that it was too much, and that she couldn't accept something so beautiful. "I found it in her things after she passed and carried it around with me ever since. Mostly, it just sat in a drawer. When I pulled your name, I knew I finally had a person to give it to you. Besides, I think my mother would have liked you."

Ash's mouth went dry, her pulse hammering in her veins. "This looks like something you should give your future wife."

Malachai waved her off. "I don't think that's in the cards for me. So, might as well give it to you."

"Are you sure? Opal seems pretty interested," Ash joked.

"I'm too busy. I couldn't give her the attention she deserves," he insisted, faking sincerity while he picked the bracelet out of the box and slid it gently onto Ash's wrist. It fit securely, refusing to budge. She could hardly feel that she was wearing it at all. "My mother was a Witch, remember? She cherished what little she had. It wouldn't surprise me if she spelled it to make sure it wouldn't fall off."

"Ah," Ash said, curiosity flashing in her eyes.

"And the next gift is from Penelope and I to both you *and* Cooper. But you can take a peak now, if you want," Malachai offered, holding out the larger velvet box for her. "She hunted down whoever pulled your name and *insisted* that they take something from Cedric's collection of daggers. Obviously, once she realized it was me, she was a bit hesitant, but she insisted anyway. Besides, I knew Cedric, and I know that he'd want his possessions to go to people that would appreciate them as much as he did."

Ash's throat became unbearably tight as she tugged at the ribbon, peaking inside the box to find two matching golden daggers. "You got me a dagger? One of *Cedric's* daggers?"

"I know," Malachai said, sighing at the ceiling. "The Irony."

"The Irony indeed," she replied, chuckling beneath her breath. "But thank you. It's beautiful. Cooper will think so too. He'll find it funny. The twins with twin daggers."

"He is aware that Vincent's your biological twin, right?"

"We're triplets," Ash argued.

Malachai snorted disbelievingly. "I see."

"Where *is* Vincent?" Ash asked. "I didn't see him leave with us."

"He decided to stay and help Sam. He'll come here in the morning," Malachai explained. "Anyway, that's all I have for you. Unless you wanted something else…" he trailed, eyes flashing flirtatiously.

Ash's eyebrows flattened, her lips drawing into a hard line. "You're something else, you know that?"

"Oh, I'm aware."

Ash's features softened, a heavy sigh escaping her. "You know what else I want?" she asked. "To sit here, finish these drinks, maybe make some more, and then pass out until noon tomorrow. Also, I'd like to give you a gift as well."

"Those weren't the rules," he said with a frown. "Besides, you've given me enough. I could get you a gift every single day for the rest of our Immortal lives and never come close to thanking you."

"What do you mean?" Ash asked, angling her body to face him completely. "After what you did for me on the East Cliff, and for

Cooper, on Comhdhail, and not to mention today... I think we're even."

Malachai shook his head, the lump in his throat bobbing. "We will never be even. Not when the gift you gave me was my freedom."

Ash's breath hitched, her lips parting. She stared at him, unsure of what to say. He stared right back, his gaze dropping to her lips for a fraction of a second before returning to her eyes. Her heart ceased to beat, her palms growing sweaty with unexpected nerves.

"Well, I should hunt down my bed," Malachai told her, rising to his feet. Ash did the same, but not to bid him goodbye. Instead, she reached for his hand and pulled him toward her until her body crashed against his, her arms wrapping around him, hugging him as tightly as she could. She buried her face in his chest, clamping her eyes shut, waiting for him to return the embrace.

At first, Malachai was as rigid as a marble statue. But, after a few moments, he softened, hugging her just as tightly. "Well, *this* is a nice Giving Day gift," he admitted.

"It's just a hug," Ash said, her words muffled by his shirt.

"Well, when you haven't had a hug in over a decade, it is," he admitted to her.

"Well, you can have a hug every day, then," she insisted.

"I'd like that."

65

Malachai awoke the next morning to the sounds of birds chirping outside Ash's window. He opened his eyes, took in his surroundings, and immediately started to panic. His eyes darted over to the closed bedroom door, a subtle sigh of relief escaping him as he rolled out of bed, carefully and quietly, not wanting to wake her. She was still fast asleep by the time he made it to the door, his fingers curling around the doorknob, twisting it gently.

The door creaked open. The Pandora held his breath, glancing over his shoulder. Ash remained where she was, curled up into a ball, surrounded by blankets and pillows. The chrome thermos that was once filled with Greg's Giving Day brew sat empty on her nightstand, their mugs sitting side by side. He wasn't exactly sure when they'd fallen asleep. Maybe pure exhaustion had gotten the best of them. Yesterday was long, and difficult, but that didn't mean it was a good excuse. The Allies might very well string him up for this.

Stomach rolling with nausea and regret, Malachai exhaled slowly, only to find Quinn in the hallway.

"There you are," the Archer said, as chipper as ever. "I've been looking everywhere for you."

"Uh...you have?" Malachai asked, his pulse pounding in his ears.

Quinn nodded, peaking through the open door behind the Pandora. He snorted, shaking his head. "She has that massive bed yet takes up a corner of it. Why do you think everyone opts to sleep in there with her? They get ten times more space than sleeping in the family room, or with anyone else. I'm not surprised you figured that out."

"It was an accident," Malachai assured him, shutting the door. Aveo was still passed out, only now he was on the hallway floor, not on the bench. "I only went in there to give her, her gifts, but—"

"That was last night, and we need to deal with right now," Quinn interjected. "I need your help with something."

Nodding, Malachai asked, "With what?"

"Do you have good handwriting?"

Ash was startled awake by someone banging on her door. She shot up in bed, gripping her sheets, covered in a cold sweat. Jay had visited her again. Mostly to congratulate her, but to offer her some more warnings. All of which involving Malachai. How the Dreamwalker had known who she was sleeping next to was beyond the lengths of her imaginations, but he was incredibly clear.

Whatever sort of *feelings* that might be beginning to bloom... Ash needed to bury them. It was one thing to bring unity between species, which would result in a peaceful Realm. It was another thing to become romantically involved with her former enemy. The Elves would have an absolute fit, along with the rest of Idona. If Ash felt the need to be with someone, it was best that she go with the Dragon Rider or practically *anyone else.*

Ash had, of course, insisted that she didn't think of Malachai in that way, and that a relationship was the least of her concerns right now. She had an entire population of people living underground who needed a home, an army that needed a base, amongst many other things, like training, armor, and the necessities. She had her hands full.

But still, Jay's words replayed within her mind relentlessly.

VanCamps and Bonaventures don't mix romantically.

"Ash," Alistair called from the other side of her door. "Breakfast is ready. Get your lazy ass outta bed, it's after ten."

Frowning, Ash shook away the thoughts of Jay and threw her blankets off her, turning only to catch sight of something resting on her pillows. Her heart skidded to a stop at the sight of the silver wrapped box, one she recognized from her birthday, before a Werewolf hunt derailed the entire event. A note sat beneath it, written with delicate, perfect script.

Ash reached for the note, her mouth going dry.

Ash,

I meant to give this to you before you left Crane. I never got the chance. I've tried on multiple occasions to give it to you after that, but nothing has worked out. Yesterday, I finally gave in and gave it to Malachai. But, once we all got back to Crane, we both decided that because of the nature of this gift, it was best that you open it on your own.

A few years back, before Eliza died, Lincoln asked for her engagement ring. I'm sure you can imagine why he'd do that at that point in time. But, a year later, he gave it to me. I decided back then, that before you left for wherever you chose to go, I'd hand it over, so that whenever you met the right person, you could use it. That way, wherever you wound up, you'd have that peace of your mother.

And a little piece of us too. A reminder of where you came from, and the people who love you endlessly.

Quinn and Malachai (because he wrote the letter. My handwriting is horrid).

Ash chuckled, tears dripping onto the parchment. Quinn's handwriting *was* horrid. She steeled herself, setting the letter aside and picking the box up, turning it over in her hands. She chose not to open it. There was no need. She knew what was inside, and what it looked like.

Eliza's engagement ring. The same one Ash had stared at for hours on end, mesmerized by the way it appeared when the sun shined off the diamonds. *Like a prism,* Eliza had told her. *So many faces, yet all it takes is one ray of light to make them all shine.*

Ash sucked in a breath before stashing the box in her nightstand, attempting to steel herself. The scent of bacon and eggs filtered through the air. Marcus had made himself right at home once again. She grinned at the thought of him bustling around the kitchen, fussing over every little thing. Making sure everything was perfect. *Presentation is everything.*

Once she was sure that there was no sign that she'd been crying, Ash made her way downstairs and into the dining room, where everyone was already piling their plates with everything from eggs to bacon, to sausage, and a stack of pancakes nearly as tall as Ash was.

"Did you sleep at all last night?" Ash asked Marcus, lowering into the free chair at his side.

"Not a wink," he admitted. "We have another big day ahead of us. Eat, so you don't run out of energy halfway through."

Ash didn't argue with that. She made her own plate, scooping things off of every dish passed around, and proceeded to eat it all greedily.

"Alright, here are the assignments," Vincent said, rubbing his tired eyes. "At least the ones that Sam and Beck came up with before they both crashed in an alcove. Ash and Lucinda need to call an Idonian Council meeting to start discussing where to put all these people. They needed to come up with a decision quickly. There are children who need fresh air, baths, and warm beds. As of this morning, Crane's Justice Keeper has returned and is in the process of converting the schoolhouse into a temporary relief center. It'll be better than living underground, but it won't last for long. The villagers are scrambling to make homemade meals, using the kitchens in the community center. That's Marcus's assignment."

Marcus nodded. "Understood."

"Cooper, I need you to fetch Lilly from the Kingdom of Elves so she can assist Marcus, in the event he collapses from exhaustion," Vincent added, pausing to take a sip of his coffee. "Craven and Alistair are supposed to go down into the intersection and start taking names. We need to know who's a warrior, and who isn't."

The pair looked at one another and smirked. It wasn't every day that they got to work together on an assignment.

"Morghan and Penelope, you're going to be leading the relocation of women and children to the school," Vincent informed them. "Aveo, you'll accompany Ash and Lucinda. Thaddeus and Esmeralda will be more amicable with all of this if you're there. Anastasia, you're going to be Malachai's assistant for the day."

"Wait, what?" the Fire Clan Leader blurted, mouth still full of eggs. "I know absolutely nothing other than basic first aid."

Malachai patted her reassuringly on the shoulder. "Don't worry. All you'll have to do is change a few dressings. On the bright side, you get to follow me around all day."

Anastasia's features softened. "Can't say I have anything to complain about *that*."

"And for Quinn," Vincent said, nearly out of breath by now. "You get the fun job."

The Archer's eyes narrowed. "What's the *fun* job?"

"We've received word from villages across the Realm. They're sending donations. Dry foods, blankets, clothes, medical supplies. Your job is to write down everything that arrives, from where, and then distribute. Don't worry, Dracus is sending some Communication Officers along with the Earth Clan members to help you with that."

Quinn fell back in his chair, his lips curving into a frown. "And what will *you* do?"

"Oh, I'm going to take a nap."

66

After eight hours' worth of going back and forth with the Elves, what remained of the Idonian Council finally came to an agreement. A village would be built, fifty miles south of Lorcan. The Pandora would reside there, in that unoccupied part of the Realm, where they wouldn't be bothered or harassed by what remained of the Dark Army. Lucinda's Sorcerers would set up barriers, and Malachai and Anderson would set up Wards.

A base for the new army to train and reside would be built between Olaigon and Lorcan, in a location preferred by the Rebels, yet close to home for the Pandora.

The only problem was that both locations were in the Draconian Jurisdiction, and Loren hadn't bothered to show up.

"I'll go back to Dracus and speak with him," Valentina said sadly, the only Draconian present. "I should be able to get an answer for you all in a matter of hours."

"Tell him that we'll start building tomorrow, whether he likes it or not," Ash said. She wasn't trying to be insensitive, but she'd had enough of Loren's absence. He'd locked himself in his chambers weeks ago, and had yet to appoint another adviser or second-in-command to handle his business. There was only Valentina, and what remained of the Draconian Council. "I understand he's lost a lot lately, but not only did he miss a fellow Idonian Council member's funeral and the catastrophe that happened afterward, he missed a historical occasion. Did he even watch Malachai's Realm address? Does he know that any of this is happening?"

Valentina bit her lip. That was answer enough.

"Yet you threaten to take *my* crown," Thaddeus uttered beneath his breath.

Normally, Ash would have shot him one of her worst glares, but Thaddeus wasn't wrong. He might have offended her in the worst of ways, but at least he was being proactive and *present*, trying to do what was best for his Kingdom and the Idonian people beyond it. Pandora included now.

"About the Ally celebration," Esmeralda mentioned, looking toward Valentina. "Would you like to postpone that further?" At some point during the last few days, the Prophetess had agreed to hand over the celebration planning to the Elves. Penelope had already done most of the work, and all they'd need to do is set everything up.

Shaking her head, Ash said, "No. Not any longer. The Allies deserve the night. And, we still have five days, correct? We should be able to get everyone relocated by then."

"My Sorcerers and I are confident that we can create the village in twenty-four hours. We'll use another twenty-four to do some final touches. We hope eventually, we can build it into a city. A true Safe Haven for them. But, for now, all we need are enough homes for everyone," Lucinda explained. "Last I heard from Quinn, who's in charge of charting all the donations, they should have enough food to last the rest of winter, not to mention other supplies. In the Spring, we'll help them get a head start on crops. In short, by the end of the week, all should be well."

"And the orphaned children?" Cleo squeaked. "What of them?"

Ash's stomach twisted into knots at the sound of her question.

"Less than seventy, thankfully," Aveo answered. "Most are over the age of three, but there are around twenty unlucky infants."

"If what Malachai said was true, the Dark Army will want those babies back," Griffon warned.

A shiver ricocheted down Ash's spine. "We won't let that happen."

"No, we won't," Cleo agreed. "I am willing to take them under my wing until the threat is eliminated. And, my Fae will assist your Sorcerers, Lucinda. Together, we should be able to make a miracle."

Before Ash left the Kingdom of Elves, Valentina handed her gifts. She said that they were for Alistair. Thinking nothing of it, Ash stashed them in her pack and walked over to where Cleo beckoned her.

"Yes?" Ash asked, offering her, her sweetest smile. The Elves had already left the room, along with Aveo, who wished to speak with them before they left. Lucinda had followed Valentina out, leaving Ash alone with the Fae Queen.

Cleo glanced around warily, as if the very wall had ears. But Ash knew for a fact that the Round Table Room was soundproof, to prevent Elves from listening in with their sharp hearing. Then again, she couldn't blame Cleo for being a bit apprehensive.

"I've wanted to talk with you, since what happened on Comhdhail," Cleo admitted. "But I haven't had a chance."

"I apologize. I've been a bit busy," Ash said, chuckling lightly. "Is something wrong?"

Nodding, Cleo looked down, examining her trembling hands. "I told you about the Sight, right?"

"You mean how you can look into someone and see their soul? Yes, you told me about that," Ash replied. "You said Lilly had a light inside of her. The kind that people follow."

"Yes, I did," Cleo confirmed. "But I saw something in Xavier too."

Ash's mouth went dry at the sound of his name, her heart skipping a beat in the worst of ways. "Let me guess, his soul is a black hole," she joked.

"It is strange. Ancient. Older than Si Realtra itself. Nothing like what I remembered about him," Cleo admitted, her lips beginning to quiver fearfully. "But the strangest part was that it wasn't alone. Something familiar was intertwined. Something that doesn't belong to him but belongs to someone else."

It was no secret that Ash had a lot to learn about her fellow Immortals, and things like Magic and everything else of the sort. Therefore, it shouldn't have surprised the Fae Queen that Ash looked at her as if she'd just spoken in another language.

"Belongs to who?" Ash inquired, her voice dangerously low.

"Meera VanCamp."

Ash felt as if she'd just been smacked in the face with a bag of bricks. She recoiled, eyes wider than they'd ever been. Xavier had warned her that if she killed him, she would kill her own mother as well, but she hadn't believed him. "How is that possible?"

"Do you remember what I said about Meera? Entirely oblivious, but braver than all the rest. Innocent, despite her upbringing. Beautiful, in spite of *what was buried inside?*" Cleo reached out, taking Ash by the hand, holding it tightly. "Your mother wasn't Mortal. She had the golden, shining soul of a Grand White Witch."

Staggering backward, Ash reached for the nearest chair and sank down into it. She stared up at the queen, who gave her a sympathetic smile, deep blue eyes twinkling like a midnight sky.

"It is my understanding that Meera fled from her family when she was around your age. I imagine she was put under a lot of pressure, considering what she was. The power she must have possessed could have rivaled Veda's, but Meera had no desire to rival anyone. I never asked her or brought up what I saw in her soul. I figured she'd made the choice to ignore it. But now, I wonder if she chose to call upon that power during her fight with Xavier. I fear that it went terribly wrong," Cleo confessed, each word wavering. "If I had to guess, and that's really my only option right now, I would say that she attempted a transference spell, but whatever power lays within Xavier was too strong. She wasn't successful, and as a result, only her consciousness was transferred. I believe that she might live within his mind."

Ash's chest tightened unbearably, a sense of dread unlike any other she'd felt before falling over her like a wet blanket.

"And Xavier," Ash asked, forcing the words out. "What of his soul? Could the power he possesses have once belonged to his grandfather?"

Cleo's perfect brows pulled together. "Who was his grandfather?"

"Xanthius, the last king of Amoria," Ash whispered, trembling from head to toe.

The queen's legs visibly wobbled beneath the fabric of her white organza dress. She reached for the marble wall behind her, bracing herself against it. "I didn't know…" her words were little more than a brush of air, barely audible. "I should have known…"

"No one did," Ash assured her. "Xavier went to great lengths to conceal his identity, and his true plans from the Idonian people. He made everyone believe he was just a self-righteous adviser who craved the power becoming High King could give him. The only reason I know any of this is because a Dreamwalker has been visiting me from the Underworld." She paused to examine Cleo's reaction. She seemed unfazed, and the relief that Ash felt to have finally told someone about Jay overwhelmed her. "All of this means, this war will not end when I defeat Xavier. There are descendants scattered throughout the Realms. Someone will try to take his place. I'm not entirely sure if Malachai knows any of this, either."

"It is said that Xanthius's power came from the Dark One," Cleo said, shivering. "If Xavier possesses the same power, then he had to have found a place to obtain it. It wouldn't be transferred through blood. If we can discover how he's done such a thing, then we can prevent someone from following in his footsteps."

"The Elves burned any and all information pertaining to Xanthius," Ash admitted to her. "There is none in Dracus, either."

Finally, something like a smile began to bloom on Cleo's pale lips. "Thankfully, I have a vault filled with Amorian artifacts and scrolls. I shall get to the bottom of things. All *you* need to figure out is how to defeat Xavier."

"I already have a good idea," Ash admitted. "The Dreamwalker gave me a few tips. I use the Sovereign's Scepter to nullify Xavier's power with Moonlight. Then, I bury one of my enchanted daggers into his heart."

"I see," Cleo said, pursing her lips. "That would explain the tethers."

Ash lifted a single brow. "What tethers?"

"Someone has connected to you," the queen explained, peering curiously in the direction of where Ash assumed her soul was. "I haven't seen anything like this, not recently, anyway. Whoever it is, they're extremely careful. They're hiding behind your lover's bond."

Ash's heart went still, her jaw dropping. "Er...you know about that?"

"I can see it clear as day," Cleo murmured, still examining her. "It's weak. You should probably strengthen it if you want it to do you any good. Unless you'd rather get rid of it entirely, in which case, I can assist." She held up a single hand, her fingertips beginning to glitter with frighteningly beautiful golden Magic.

"No," Ash said abruptly. "I... uh..."

"Would rather consult Lord Ward?" Cleo supplied.

Eyebrows flattening, Ash was beginning to wonder what she disliked more. The fact that Valentina knew every detail about her future, or the fact that Cleo could see everything about her present. "Yes," Ash admitted, crossing her arms, as if to conceal the queen from peering into her any further.

"If I may offer my opinion, I would strengthen it. Such a bond could assist you wonderfully, if you learn how to control it," Cleo informed her. "I can provide you with a book detailing ways to perfect it when I visit you in Crane to retrieve those babies tomorrow."

And how am I supposed to hide something like that in a house filled with Allies who snoop? Ash fought against the urge to frown. "Thank you," she replied. "I should really be going now. Please, let me know if you find anything helpful regarding this... uprising. Oh, and don't tell the Elves. Their relationship with Malachai and the Pandora is still extremely fragile. We don't want to risk any setbacks."

67

After finishing up with his last patient of the day, baby Jane and her mother Fay, Malachai and Anastasia started their trek back to the estate. The latter yawned on more than one occasion throughout their small journey, still reeking of Jane's spit-up. Malachai's nose wrinkled once a strong breeze carried the scent over to his sensitive nose.

"Don't make that face," Ana grumbled at him, kicking at a chunk of ice. "I *told* you I wasn't good with babies."

"You holding Jane is not what caused her to suddenly develop reflux," Malachai insisted.

Ana waved him off, returning her attention to the stain on her cloak. She attempted to wipe it away with her scarf, which only made matters worse. If she weren't so stubborn, Malachai might have told her to wait until they returned to the estate, where she could rub some dish soap and baking soda on it and leave it in the sink for an hour before ringing it out and hanging it in front of a fire to dry. Knowing her, she'd just use her fire ability to do that.

"She *was* cute, though," Ana admitted softly after a while, just as they were turning off the mountain path and onto the walkway leading up to the sprawling, cabin-like mansion. "She makes me want to go... shopping. For tiny outfits and ribbons."

Malachai laughed at that.

"What's so funny?" Ana scowled, shooting him a dirty look. "Just because I'm not great with babies doesn't mean I wouldn't spoil any nieces and nephews."

"Do you have any?" Malachai inquired out of pure curiosity.

"No," she answered quickly. "My only brother died during the Five Realm War."

Malachai clamped his mouth shut, his stomach twisting at the thought. It wasn't exactly a secret that the only reason the Three Realm War turned into a Five Realm War was because Anastasia's parents were murdered by Erminians on Minorian soil. The act was what sparked Idona and Minora's involvement in the war. Ana's parents were war heroes, known for their courageous acts during the Age of Monsters three hundred years ago, when strange, massive beasts hatched beneath the earth before making their way to the surface and tormenting every Kingdom, city, and village. It was the only period in Idonian history where every community was unified through a common enemy.

But the Pandora hadn't known Anastasia's brother had died during that war too. A crack seared through his heart at the thought.

"I'm sorry," he told her softly.

Ana demanded, "Don't be. That was a long time ago. Besides, I wasn't alone after the fact. I had Craven and the Amsterdams."

"Weren't they murdered?" Malachai whispered, afraid Craven might have already arrived at the estate, and might be listening from inside.

Stopping right in front of the porch steps, Ana turned to face Malachai completely. "They were," she revealed to him. "Thirty years ago. Craven and I were in Minora when it happened. No one ever found out who did it."

"Some things are better left undiscovered," Malachai said.

"Agreed," Ana replied, climbing the steps. "Do *you* have any nieces or nephews?"

"Not anymore," Malachai admitted, opening the door for her.

"Before I was disowned, I had a niece. She'd be around a month and a half old by now. I don't even know what my sister chose to name her. I doubt I'll ever be allowed anywhere near her."

Ana's features crumbled. "That's not fair."

"Ana, I betrayed my entire family," he reminded. "It *is* fair."

"So?" the Fire Clan Leader shot at him, kicking her boots off, shedding her spit-up stained cloak. "That baby would be far better off *away* from your family."

Malachai couldn't disagree with her, so he didn't respond. All he could do was hope that Trixa had everything handled. That she would protect their niece from harm. Even if that meant protecting her from her mother.

Savron had been right to worry about the baby. Perhaps Malachai should have told him to run and retrieve her and Trixa before going into hiding.

"You two are just in time for dinner," Lilly informed them, standing at the dining room's threshold. "I'd hurry before a certain *Commander* we know eats it all the second it lands on the table."

"Elves," Ana uttered beneath her breath, rolling her charcoal eyes.

Malachai found himself seated across from Ash, who was staring at him like she had something to say. But every time she opened her mouth, she closed it and turned her attention to someone else. He chose to focus on his meal, leftovers from the meal Marcus and Lilly had cooked in the village community center. Roasted pig, vegetables, and mashed potatoes.

There was no desert, only wine, which was perfectly fine. Malachai found himself so full from the meal that his eyelids were threatening to flutter shut.

"At least we finally found use for this dining room table," Quinn told Ash, who snorted in response, hiding her smile with her wine. Malachai couldn't help but wonder what she'd thought about her gift. Maybe that was why she kept looking at him. Perhaps she wanted to thank him for the well-written letter.

"Nice outfit, by the way," Quinn added. "I didn't realize you could wear my old flannels to an Idonian Council meeting."

"There is no written rule about it," Lucinda contributed from where she sat on Ash's other side. "And, the Elves might have thought it was distasteful at first, but I'd bet you they were jealous she was so comfortable four hours in."

Ash beamed at the comment, her smile growing wider.

Malachai averted his gaze, unwilling to get lost in the sight of it. Whatever he was starting to feel for her, he needed to ignore it. It would bring nothing but pain upon him. The last time he'd dared to love...it had ended terribly. In death. Bloodshed. His blood chilled at the very inclination of summoning those memories. He ignored those too, for his own well-being.

The way Quinn was staring at her, though, getting lost in that same sight...

"So, what did everyone get for Giving Day? We didn't really get a chance to talk about it," Vincent asked, eyes glassy from his drink. "Quinn gave me Arebus Arrows and one of Pat McBride's books."

From there, everyone described what they'd received, while Malachai sipped his wine, fighting the desire to chug the entire glass. Morghan had received a case of whiskey from Ash, which explained all the bottles being passed around in the intersection. Lucinda had received a bunch of cupcakes from the Wolf, which she'd passed out to passing Pandora. The Sorceress and Penelope teamed up to give Quinn an incredible gift; the keys to his own house, and the promise that from now until the siege, they'd all be able to live in it peacefully and unbothered.

Vincent had given Craven a picture of him from Penelope's eighteenth-year ceremony, one where he stood with all of the people who'd attended the mission to rescue the Princess beforehand. Craven rushed to retrieve it to show everyone, especially the people present that had attended the mission with him. It was passed around the table, and when it landed in Malachai's hands, sadness and regret started to stir in his stomach.

Beck Chamberlain, Aveo Calloway, Axel Graves, Craven Amsterdam, Marcus Bonaventure, Alistair Ward, Matt Abernathy, and Cedric Chamberlain. They were all standing in a row, wearing the biggest smiles, dressed to the nines, glasses of champagne in their hands.

"Man, I remember that night like it was yesterday," Alistair admitted with a dreamy sigh.

"So do I," Penelope said, eyes shining with joy.

"I don't remember much of it, if we're being honest," Aveo admitted. "I drank too much, but I do remember the mission. I don't think I could ever forget it."

Malachai handed the picture off to Anastasia, unable to stare at Cedric's face for a second longer and listened to everyone talk about what else they'd received.

Aveo had given Alistair a book about Dragons, one that had once been owned by Aiden Cavanaugh himself. Malachai wondered if the Rider had any idea how closely he was related to the original High King, and that he bore more a right to the throne than the VanCamp's sitting around the table with him.

Anastasia had given Aveo the scabbard Malachai had watched her buy, and he openly admitted how much he loved it. Marcus had given Beck Alexi Grimm's bow, even though the Elven General wasn't currently there to confirm it. He and Sam were both back to work in the intersection. Beck still, however, owed them all a night with free drinks at his pub.

"Malachai gave me a compass that belonged to my father," Cooper told everyone, causing the Pandora to stiffen at the sound of his own name. "Apparently, it'll lead you anywhere you want to go. It's perfect for a teleporter if they're teleporting into unknown territory. I'm sure it'll come in handy."

"That sounds amazing," Ash said, practically drooling. "But don't forget Cedric's golden daggers. He gave us those too."

The Archer nodded, smiling broadly. "Twins with twin daggers."

"Triplets," Vincent groused. "Only the triplet didn't get a dagger," he added in a harsh whisper.

Penelope snorted beside him. "Why don't you just go pick one out?"

"I didn't know I had the option," he told her. "But, if Cooper got two things from Malachai, what else did he give you, Ash?"

Ash brought her glass to her lips, taking a long sip. "He gave me a bracelet."

"The one you're wearing right now?" Lucinda asked, snatching Ash's wrist, ripping her sleeve back. Malachai's breath caught in his throat at the sight of it, his heart beginning to beat erratically. To see that bracelet... that she was still wearing it…

Swallowing hard, Malachai fought to hide his surprise and complete and utter adoration. He focused on his drink again, pretending that it didn't matter, as if the bracelet meant nothing to him—that it didn't mean everything to him to see her wear it willingly.

"That's gorgeous," Ana gushed at the Pandora's side. He sank further into his chair, taking a greedy sip of his wine. "Craven, next year you should consider something more like that."

"I thought you liked your new chains," Craven grumbled with a frown.

"I do," Ana assured him. "They'll gleam brilliantly with my fire."

Malachai didn't miss the curious glances being thrown his way, or the outright glares from Alistair and Morghan.

"Well, who got Malachai?" Marcus asked, meeting the Pandora's gaze. "What did you get?"

"My people's freedom," Malachai said, deflecting.

"Other than that," Penelope urged. "Who pulled your name?"

Refusing to look at the Dragon Rider, Malachai shifted in his seat, pondering how to respond.

"I did," Alistair revealed sadly. "I wasn't sure what to get him. Valentina said she'd help, but she never gave me anything…"

Ash shot out of her seat the second the words left his mouth. "Wait," she insisted, holding out a finger. "No one move a muscle."

Malachai watched her rush out of the room, his head tilting curiously. She returned a few moments later, her pack in hand. She dumped out the contents onto the table. Empty thermoses, a change of clothes, a spare uniform, a few daggers, and two packages wrapped in black paper with shining silver bows.

"Valentina gave me these earlier. She said they were for you," Ash said to Alistair.

"I take it that means they're for him," the Rider replied, gesturing to Malachai, sighing with relief. "Thank the Moons."

Ash pushed the packages across the table, practically trembling with excitement. "Well, open them," she urged.

The *last* thing that Malachai wanted was any more attention, but in that moment, he had no choice. All eyes were already on him. So, he reached for the smaller package of the two. A box, of sorts. He tore at the paper, holding his breath. What he found beneath was a wooden box, the Idonian symbol engraved upon it.

"You got a box," Morghan teased. "Congratulations."

"It opens," Quinn said, shooting the Wolf a damning glare.

Nodding, Malachai slid the top open, the Realm growing completely still at the sight of what sat within, resting on a black velvet pillow.

Ana caught sight of it first, practically falling out of her seat as if it were poisonous, surprise flooding her features.

"What is it?" Lilly asked from Malachai's other side, peering over. She too, seemed surprised, the color draining from her cheeks.

Shaking head, Malachai set it on the table for all to see, unable to believe it. He watched them all lean forward, gasps sounding throughout the room. He didn't dare look anyone in the eye. In fact, he wished he could run. He couldn't believe it. He chose *not* to believe it.

"Malachai," Ash said his name, slow and steady. "Open the second package."

Nodding, the Pandora did as she said, tearing into the paper, his hands shaking with nerves. Everyone around the table was holding their breath. No one said a word. He doubted that anyone was even daring to think a single thought.

Malachai's stomach churned with nerves, his thoughts swimming. It was impossible. It *had* to be.

A thin layer of black tissue paper lay beneath the wrapping, but there was no mistaking what lay beneath. The color stood out, clear as day.

An Emerald division Ally uniform, to go with the Ally badge he'd opened before.

68

For far too long, the dining room remained silent. Ash's eyes were glued to the badge and uniform. Her breathing became uneven, her heart beating erratically within her chest. She swallowed. Twice.

"The funeral," Marcus said, his voice little more than a whisper.

"The Guardian," Vincent added, looking toward Aveo.

"The eleventh Ally," Morghan finished.

Another silence evolved, one where Malachai stared down at his gifts, his expression unreadable. Alistair did the same, holding his hands up, as if to say that he'd had no idea. Ash knew that he hadn't known. She could feel his shock and surprise, which added to her own, making it all the more effective.

To think that Cleo wanted them to *strengthen* the bond... Ash shivered at the thought. She'd have to learn how to forgive him first, and that would take effort that she didn't know if she had.

"An *emerald* division Ally," Quinn mentioned, his lips twitching toward a crooked smile. "I think we can officially say that we have the sapphire division beat."

Ash's head jerked backward, as if that comment had thrust her back into reality. "*Excuse me?*" she asked. "We have a one enchanted sword holder, the last Werewolf, an Arebus Archer, a Berserker, and a *Dragon*. You think adding the Prince of Darkness to your team is going to make it so you contend with us? Think again."

"I have the Realm Sorceress," Quinn countered. "And the Electric Immortal, who also happens to be the lone survivor of the Idonian Kingdoms Ballroom Battle. Now, I have a shapeshifting, healing alchemist."

"I could kick your alchemist's ass. Actually, I have," Ash argued, crossing her arms defensively. "So has Morghan. He told me."

"Yeah, well, Craven can shock you to death without even needing to *think*."

Someone choked on their drink. Ash figured that was the Electric Immortal himself. She took a step forward, summoning her worst, most unnerving scowl. "And what will you do when I eventually wake up and use my *Sectra?*"

"Alright, let's just stop while we're ahead," Lucinda said, chuckling beneath her breath. "Besides, if you did that, you'd have to face my league of Sorcerers. So…"

"I don't think they'd stand much of a chance between an army of Dragons," Alistair chimed in, chin lifting with pride.

"Wow," Marcus said, sipping his whiskey. "Those of us on the onyx division will just go ahead and go fuck ourselves, then."

Everyone around the table started to laugh uncontrollably at the sound of the Mentor's statement, onyx division members included. Ash's shoulders slumped with relief, as did the Pandora's across from her. She wished she could use this moment to give him his daily hug but knew how odd that would look. So, instead she clapped and offered him a wink.

"Congratulations, Malachai," Ash said, unable to control her smile. "Looks like we're even after all."

Malachai shook his head, vivid green eyes glittering mischievously. "Never."

Ash sighed at the ceiling. *Anyone else.* Jay's words rang in her ears, his tone just as urgent as it had been when he'd said the words. *Anyone else.*

"A toast to our newest Ally," Vincent encouraged, holding up his glass. Ash did the same, hoping no one could see how horribly her hands were shaking. "To Malachai Trevayne."

Bonaventure, Ash inwardly corrected, taking a sip of her wine, her gaze shifting over to Marcus. He seemed overjoyed, just like everyone else. Even Alistair, which turned out to be the most surprising part of the evening for Ash. He'd opened his heart when it was sealed shut just a few weeks ago. He'd proven her wrong, and she was grateful for it. Forgiving him might be easier than she thought.

Maybe Cleo was right. Maybe they *should* strengthen their bond.

As if he could sense her thoughts, Alistair moved around Lucinda, his hand just barely grazing Ash's elbow. "I did *not* know that's what she picked out for my gifts," he admitted, chuckling beneath his breath. "Need a refill?"

Ash's immediate thoughts of the word *refill* reminded her of his blood. She trembled at the very thought, memories of that night in the cave flooding past her vision. Her cheeks heated with shame as a result. How could she be so distracted, during such a monumental moment? Why was she so affected by that memory?

Cleo and Jay's words both plagued Ash's thoughts. All she knew for sure was that she blamed them both for her current predicament.

"Ash?" Alistair asked, piercing through her thoughts. "Did you want more wine?"

Ash looked toward him, noting the sinister grin he wore. He knew. *Bastard.* "Sure," she replied, handing the glass over. "Fill it to the top."

"Understood," he replied with a curt nod.

Anyone else, Ash reminded herself, biting her inner cheek. *Anyone else.*

69

Five days had passed since Malachai had become an Ally. Four days since the village for his fellow Pandora had been built. Watching them all leave the intersection had shrunken his heart, and he wasn't sure why. Perhaps it was because for a single week, he'd been the leader he'd always wanted to be for them. And now, he had to watch them go and start their lives without him.

"You've done all you can for them," Ash reminded him from his side. "At least for now."

"All I did was nurse the wounds my address caused them," Malachai reminded her, wishing that for once she'd take his hand. It was a foolish wish. One he shouldn't entertain. "You should be getting ready for the celebration," he added, dreading seeing her in whatever dress the Elves had sent over. "That hair of yours likely takes hours to tame."

Ash snorted, which was considered incredibly unlady-like for a queen. He adored it. "They give up, usually. But you should be getting ready with everyone else. This intersection is empty now. We've done our part. Now, it's time to celebrate, with your *fellow Allies*," she trilled, elbowing him gently.

"Very well," he said with a heavy sigh, offering her his arm. She took it, albeit hesitantly. "So, have you decided who will escort you?"

There was quite the fuss about it the night before, when Penelope reminded her younger sister that that was necessary. Ash insisted that she didn't need an escort, but the Princess wouldn't relent, and neither would Lucinda.

"I didn't really have much of a choice in the matter at the end of the day," she revealed to him. "The Chamberlains picked for me. Beck will be there waiting the second we arrive."

ASH WAITED DOWNSTAIRS, DRESSED IN A SILVER GOWN STUDDED WITH jewels that shined like stars. She tried to ignore how exposed she felt with the low, scooping neckline, the dress's back dipping low enough to reveal most of her spine. At least the sleeves conformed to her arms, spanning the entire length of them. The fitted bodice hugged her curves, the ones she normally went out of her way to hide.

The satin sapphire sash draped diagonally across her was Ash's saving grace. It hid most of her more exposed parts, though she knew that's not what it was meant to do. It was meant to signify her division. There were three other people in the house that wore the same one, each of them embroidered with silver thread woven in Idonian knot patterns and adorned with their Ally badges.

The other divisions wore the same sashes in their own respective colors—Malachai included. Ash would never forget the look on Esmeralda's face when she told her they'd need another, and for whom.

"Everyone ready?" Lucinda asked, sphere in hand. She was dressed in a fitted, sparkling black dress. Her blood-red hair stood out so starkly next to it that it was impossible not to stare at.

"Yes," Penelope beamed, dressed in a breathtaking, silky red gown to match her escort's tie.

The Sorceress whipped the sphere at the floor, and everyone filed in line to pass through without a word. On the other side, Ash found herself in a hall in front of a set of massive double doors. Clearly, the party had already started within. She could hear the giggling, the music and dancing.

"Finally," the event coordinator, one of the council member's whose name Ash couldn't remember, gushed as she stormed forward. "I need everyone to line up in order of their divisions. Onyx will go first, after Princess Penelope and Sir Aveo are announced. Prince Vincent will lead you out, and we'll end with Marcus. Afterward, we'll start with Craven, go to Lucinda, and then Quinn. Finally, we'll start with Cooper, Morghan, Alistair, and then Ash and Malachai."

"But Malachai's a member of the Emerald division," Ash reminded her, pointing to the Pandora's very obvious green sash.

The Elf nodded, but said, "We understand this, but this is his reintroduction into society, and it would stand out more if you walked in together."

Great, Ash fought not to frown as they all got in order. She took Malachai's arm and waited for the announcements to start, pushing all of Jay's words from her mind before they had a chance to anchor within her mind once again.

As planned, Penelope and Aveo were introduced first. The attendees went wild at the sight of them, walking hand in hand instead of arm in arm, giving off the impression that they were in love. Vincent followed, dawning his sash with pride. A prince *evolved.* Anastasia sauntered down those steps, demanding respect in the way she always did, her long red dress trailing behind her so far that Marcus had to wait even longer, just so he wouldn't step on the train.

Then came Craven, Lucinda, and Quinn, to whom everyone raised their glass. Word must have gotten out about what he'd done for Princes Trinity. The Elves adored him, whispering praises as he walked down those stairs, his gaze fixed beyond them, to where the other Allies waited.

Cooper earned just as much applause, likely for what he'd endured in Solaris. Ash cursed beneath her breath, knowing all of it would only go to his head. Morghan came next, applauded as always for being the sole member of his species. Then Alistair, who invoked a strange silence.

Ash and Malachai, who waited right behind him, standing just outside of the view, stared at the Rider's back, their brows wrinkling with confusion.

That was when every soul in the ballroom dropped to their knees, holding a hand over their heart.

"Welcome back, Lord Ward," the announcer said proudly.

"They thought he died," Malachai whispered in Ash's ear, sending an unwelcome shiver down her spine, drawing goosebumps along her flesh. "There was a memorial for him, and the other Mayfire deaths. This is the first time he's come back."

"Oh," Ash said, gulping. Perhaps she hadn't realized *just* how important the Dragon Rider was. Not that that mattered. To her, he was still the same man who stood beside her during every difficult task she'd had to complete. From the elemental test to that very moment. "And now the man once suspected of his murder will be announced. Something doesn't feel right."

Before Malachai had a chance to respond, Alistair had made it down the red velvet lined steps, and it was their turn. "And now, last but not least, we have our High Queen, Sectra Holder, and the prophesied Messenger Ash VanCamp accompanied by her most recent Ally, Malachai Trevayne."

That's all? Ash wondered, moving toward the top step, staring down all that followed, her gaze fixed on the white marble floors. The room was silent, every soul within kneeling, performing that same symbol of respect. Malachai's back was ramrod straight, his heart thundering so viciously that it echoed in Ash's ears. They started their descent anyway, camera's flashing around them.

That's what this was. A publicity stunt. Ash's mouth dried up, her blood turning molten in her veins. *Sovereign help the Elves if they dare to speak ill of my name, or his,* Ash thought, gripping the Pandora's arm even harder.

The festivities were normal, for the most part. There was dancing, a delectable feast, drinks, and toasts to go along with them. Ash genuinely enjoyed herself. In fact, she couldn't remember the last time she'd smiled so widely than when she had Beck teach her the steps to a traditional Elven dance.

Some of the other Allies attempted to learn. Most of them already knew how to perform it perfectly and helped those who couldn't.

The entire premise was to stand in two lines, partners standing in front of one another. The dance would begin with a low bow, and the lines would join together. Right hand to right hand, the left held behind the back. Ash started the dance with Beck. They turned in a slow circle the second the music began, before he removed his left hand from his back and placed it on her own, causing her left hand to move to his chest. He led her through a set of simple steps afterward, the music in tune with the beats of his heart flooding her sensitive ears.

Once Ash found herself being lowered into dip so far that she feared her skull might rest on the marble floor, she was brought back up, handed off to the next partner to repeat the same exact steps. Cooper.

Ash knew right away that she'd have to lead, but the Archer

quickly proved her wrong. He spun her around and dipped her with ease, twirling her before she wound up in the arms of another, just in time for Lucinda to land in his own.

Craven repeated the dance, planting a kiss on Ash's cheek before handing her over to Alistair, just in time for Penelope to leave his arms and fall straight into Quinn's. The Rider was a professional and wasted no time reminding Ash of that fact. He pressed his warm hand against the small of her back, pulling her tight against him, twirling her around with ease. And, when he dropped her into that familiar dip and pulled her back up, he whispered something in her ear that left her at a loss for words.

Forgive me. Please. I can't stand this rift between us.

Ash's throat became thick as she was handed off to Quinn, her mind still whirling. She repeated the same steps, comforted by his familiar embrace. His presence always put her at ease.

"You look beautiful tonight," he told her, twirling her around once before pulling her back to him, in time with all the others.

"Thank you," Ash said as she dropped into the dip, her mind swarming from all the wine and excitement. "You're as handsome as ever," she admitted once he pulled her back up and kissed the top of her hand before handing her off to Morghan.

"Am *I* as handsome as ever?" the Wolf inquired as they repeated the dance once again.

Ash chuckled and said, "Of course you are."

Aveo was the next partner. While his steps were perfect, it was clear that his mind was elsewhere. When he brought her up from the extreme dip, he whispered, "I'm proposing when she returns to me. Pray that the Moons are favoring me tonight."

Nodding, Ash allowed him to twirl her into the next partner's arms. Vincent's. His cheeks were rosy with drink, eyes a tad glassy, a smile like no other playing at his lips. Ash hadn't thought of what it might mean to him to have all the Allies celebrating in the Kingdom of Elves, where he grew up. Her heart melted for him. And, when he handed her over to Marcus, she realized with a painful breath that there was only one person left in the line.

Malachai.

Ash's heart was beating so loudly that she was sure that everyone could hear it. If Marcus could, he didn't let on. Instead, he repeated the steps with perfect precision, likely eager to get back to Valentina, and handed her over to the Pandora without a thought.

Ash landed in Malachai's grip, heat coiling in her fluttering stomach. The sensation of his hand at the small of her back, the other positioned firmly on her left hip, led her breathing to quicken. She tried not to look into his eyes, afraid she'd get lost in the desire melting within them. But, once he dipped her, she had no choice. Everyone in the ballroom disappeared, and she was left with only him, staring down at her with the sort of look that brought a woman to her knees. His vivid eyes dropped to her lips, and she bit her own out of instinct, shuddering in his embrace.

The Pandora brought her back up so quickly that she stumbled, falling into him, her pulse thundering in her ears so hard that she couldn't possibly think. He corrected her, the lump in his throat bobbing. The music continued, blaring in her ears, drowning out her thoughts.

Anyone else, Jay's words repeated, reminding her of why she shouldn't just get it over with and kiss him, no matter how badly she felt the desire. Perhaps she should. She could always blame all the wine, and blood, and excitement.

Before she could make the choice, she was flung outward, landing back into Beck's arms. By then, the desire to have her lips grazed by another's had overwhelmed her. Ash reached up, framing the General's face in her hands, and surged upward to claim him with her kiss.

The music stopped, and the entire ballroom fell silent. Beck pulled away from her, cheeks flaming with embarrassment, eyes glittering with the need for more. They soon realized that the silence was not meant for them. The odds were that no one had noticed that kiss at all. Right down the line, Aveo had dropped to one knee, a ring box open in his hands, staring up at Penelope with hopeful bronze eyes.

"I know we're already betrothed," Aveo explained. "I know this isn't necessary, but I wanted you to choose. And now, I'm giving you the choice, because I love you. I have loved you since the second I set my eyes upon you, and I will love you for the rest of my Immortal days. I might not know how to show it well. I only know how to be a Commander. But I can learn how to be a husband, and a father. If you give me the chance. Will you marry me?"

Penelope was as still as a statue, staring down at the ring with wide eyes, her chin trembling. "Yes," she said abruptly. "I'll marry you, under two conditions."

Aveo stiffened, his brow wrinkling curiously. "What conditions?"

"That you marry me as soon as possible, before the siege," Penelope admitted. "And that you return to me afterward."

"When have I not returned from battle?" Aveo asked, plucking the ring out of the box, and sliding it on her finger with a cocky smile.

The surrounding observers clapped, cheering widely as Ash's Guardian rose to his feet, took his soon-to-be wife, and kissed her the way every woman deserved to be kissed.

Traditionally, Elven weddings took place over a span of two entire weeks. The first two would take place in the Kingdom of Elves, and, despite how much it infuriated Thaddeus and Esmeralda, the final ceremony would take place in Crane, because that's what Aveo and Penelope wanted. The Hidden Village was where they wanted to recite their final vows to one another.

"There's just something about that village that brought us closer," Penelope had explained to her adoptive parents. "Something we weren't able to do here, or in Dracus. We were able to be ourselves during that week we spent there. It's where we became... *us*."

There was no arguing with that, and Drake was more than happy to oblige. In fact, he was honored. The Elves sent him the supplies, and the villagers pulled together to make the square look like a dream.

After four days in the Kingdom of Elves—two days' worth of planning and preparing, and another two enduring Elven wedding traditions—Ash was able to return to Crane and see all Drake and the others had done. The entire village was transformed for the occasion. Paper lanterns hung from every clothesline. Rose petals of all colors were thrown over the cobblestone streets. Sheer fabric entwined with faerie lights draped over the square, forming a tent that fluttered majestically in the breeze. Every lamppost and tree was wrapped in lights, leading all of Crane to glow like a star against a black velvet sky.

The ceremony itself was beautiful, bringing all the guests to tears. Ash wasn't normally a crier, but even she was wiping a few runaway tears from her cheeks. In the end, her Guardian had become her brother-in-law, and her sister had become a Calloway.

In that moment, Ash was forced to acknowledge the fact that she would be the last VanCamp to hold the High Throne.

"I FOUND A FEW SCROLLS THAT MIGHT PIQUE YOUR INTEREST," CLEO said after the ceremony. "I left them under your bed."

Ash nearly choked on her champagne, swallowing it quickly so she wouldn't spew it all over the Fae Queen's velvet amethyst dress. "When were you in my room?" She could have sworn she locked the estate up when she and the other Allies hurried out, fearing they'd be late. "And, how did you know which bed was mine?"

"I was there about an hour ago," Cleo explained nonchalantly, sipping her own bubbling drink. "I followed your scent of course. It was a bit difficult. Exactly how many men have slept in that bed? I have to say, I must applaud you."

Eyebrows flattening, Ash brought her glass to her red-painted lips. "It's not what you think. There are spare bedrooms, but we haven't had the time to furnish them. So, the McBrides and I share. Wouldn't want Idona's Allies sleeping on floors, now, would we?"

"I doubt that you mind," Cleo insisted with a teasing wink. "Anyway, I'm sure that you can guess what the scrolls are about. Just let me know if you need help getting rid of any nightmares."

Ash's stomach churned at the thought, goosebumps pebbling along her flesh. "Thanks," she said sarcastically. "How are all the babies?"

"Wonderful." The queen's eyes shone a little brighter. "They fill a piece of my heart recently vacated. I enjoy spending my days with them, as do my fellow Fae. It's amusing really. I transformed the

Enchanted Forest to keep the Pandora out, yet I'm raising fifteen of them within."

"Does this mean you'll change it back now?" Morghan inquired, moving to Ash's side.

Cleo shook her head, a smirk playing at her lips. "Not a chance."

The next month went by in a blur. Ash spent her time keeping busy, afraid of what she might think if she dared to sit still. She studied the scrolls every morning, which often ruined her appetite for breakfast. Everything she'd suspected about Xavier had turned out to be true. That soul he possessed was not his own. It belonged to a being as old as the Sovereign herself. One that *she* had feared, so much so that she'd created a prison for him.

The Underworld.

What would happen to the Dark One once Ash slayed his current host was yet to be determined. How his spirit had escaped the Underworld was unknown. All that Ash knew for certain was that she'd have to track it and put it back where it belonged, all while dealing with an Amorian uprising in the other four Realms.

When Ash wasn't stressing over the scrolls, or the coming siege, or working with Alistair to strengthen their bond without drinking one another's blood, she was helping out with Lilly's training. Everyone else had stepped forward to assist her in some way, shape, or form. Morghan taught her about Immortal history, the only subject she was lacking in. Ash taught her how to throw knives. Aveo taught her the art of swinging a sword. Her brothers took turns helping her brush up on her bow skills. Craven taught her hand-to-hand combat. Marcus taught her how to track and make a mean chicken chowder. Vincent taught her everything he'd learned from Cedric Chamberlain about the other four Realms, along with their kings, queens, and courts. Alistair taught her about Dragon Riding, those lessons mostly consisting of him giving her rides on Willa, using the new saddle Malachai had made for him. Malachai taught her about alchemy, one of Lilly's favorite subjects, and a great deal about healing. Lucinda included her in the lessons she was already giving Sam when he had the time. And Anastasia taught her how to be a "*total badass.*"

Quinn put a stop to that the second he caught Lilly holding two flaming chains.

"Maybe *you* should attend my knife throwing lessons," Ash teased Malachai one day as they walked through the village, Aveo and Penelope trailing behind. "You know, that way next time you have to whip one to save my ass, you don't miss."

The Pandora sighed skyward. "If I'd known you were going to tease me, I wouldn't have let you tag along."

Ash snickered mischievously. "I'm only kidding. Besides, I want to see how Fay and Jane are doing."

"That doesn't really explain Aveo and Penelope's attendance," Malachai retorted.

"I'm sorry, am I bothering you?" Penelope inquired sweetly.

"Not one bit, Your Highness," Malachai replied. "It's just, I don't normally arrive with an entourage when I visit my patients."

Penelope quickened her pace until she was walking right beside Ash. "I'm only coming to pick out a cake," she claimed, but Ash knew the truth. She wanted to see baby Jane. Now that she was a married woman, that was all her thoughts consisted of; Either babies or making babies.

"Pick out a cake for what?" Malachai challenged.

"Oh, don't think I forgot your birthday," Penelope chimed, causing the Pandora to groan. "I caught a glimpse of your birth certificate when all of your records were transferred over to Dracus. The last day of Winter Solstice."

Ash's brows raised. "Funny. Mine's the first day of Winter Solstice."

"And that's still three weeks away," Malachai countered as they arrived in front of the bakery door. "And yes, I know when you were born Ash. Pat went to talk to your mother that night. Her water broke while he was still there."

Something in Ash's stomach fluttered, her heart swelling.

They entered the bakery, where Fay was working behind the counter, packing up an order. Her red eyes lifted from her work, a smile blooming across her lips at the sight of Malachai. "And here I was thinking you'd forgotten about us."

Unlike all the other Pandora, Fay had elected to stay in Crane. She'd taken up a job helping Jeremy in the bakery, and Ash had set her up in the same cottage she'd once shared with Eliza before they'd moved into the McBride Estate. It was the perfect place for a mother to raise her daughter, in Ash's opinion.

"As if I ever could," Malachai replied. "Where's little Jane? I wanted to make sure I fit her in before I head to Blackwing."

The new village the Pandora occupied, which they'd named after the fallen Idonian Council member. It was their way of showing respect to the council. Malachai liked to show his face there at least twice a week, though he mostly stayed in Crane with the other Allies.

"She's asleep in her cradle upstairs," Fay told him. "I can go wake her."

"No, finish what you're doing," Malachai suggested. "I'll wake her, and Princess Penelope would be more than happy to rock her back to sleep." He added the last part with a wink meant to tease Aveo over his shoulder. The Elf scowled at him in response, as if to say *don't feed the fire, shithead*—a name that Aveo had recently picked out for the Pandora.

They all wound up going upstairs, where Ash watched Malachai examine the month-old babe, her heart in her throat. It wasn't every day that she got to see a baby so small. The more she watched little Jane, the more jealous she became of Penelope, who was already preparing the rocking chair.

"There are ten fingers and toes," Aveo mentioned. "Isn't that all you need to know?"

"Are you joking?" Penelope choked.

Her husband gave her a wicked grin. "I'm only kidding."

"You'd better be."

Ash exhaled, slowly shaking her head. Newlyweds were insufferable.

"She's gained weight, and from what Fay told me last visit, she's stopped projectile vomiting all over Draconian Clan leaders," Malachai declared proudly. "I think it's safe to say that little Jane is growing wonderfully. I would feel better if there were an Infirmary here, though. One equipped to care for such small beings. I won't be here forever. Who knows when we're going to get summoned for the siege?"

"But Sam said the armor is still being made for the new army, and that we likely had another month," Penelope blurted, genuine fear flashing in her eyes.

Ash's stomach bottomed at the look on her sister's face. While Vincent, Aveo, and everyone else Penelope cared about headed off to fight in Solaris, she would be the only one left behind. It was decided that she'd go back to Dracus, to work with Grant and Anderson. But that didn't make it any easier.

"Here, focus on rocking Jane back to sleep while I review what Ebony sent me about her," Malachai suggested, handing the baby over to Penelope, whose features softened immediately. "And, once she's asleep, you can go and order me that cake. I prefer buttercream."

It was customary for newborn babies to be tested for certain abnormalities. Healers did this by taking samples of their blood, usually at birth. Ash had listened to Malachai go on and on about how horribly the Pandora were treated, left to give birth on their own, with no proper care. Since he didn't have access to his own lab, he drew blood samples and sent them to Ebony. Once she'd taken a look at them, testing them for abnormalities, blood-types, and all the other things they needed to know, she'd send all the information to the info-tab she'd gifted Malachai.

Ash waited, watching her sister rock the baby back and forth while the Pandora skimmed through all of Jane's results. Aveo watched her as well, something like adoration and desire glittering in his bronze gaze. Ash took that as a sign that she'd have a niece or nephew in the near future.

A strange sound escaped Malachai. One that had Ash whirling

around to see what was wrong. She found him staring down at the tablet, complexion blanched, brow furrowing with confusion.

"What is it?" Aveo demanded in a hushed tone, as if not to disturb the baby.

"Ash, you remember Fay telling us about what happened to her right? And, about who the baby's father was?" Malachai whispered, a muscle feathering in his jaw.

Cringing, Ash said, "Don't remind me. I can't wait to find out who gets to rip that prick to shreds."

"He's not Jane's father," Malachai informed her. "Her sample triggered a match for someone else's DNA."

"Whose?" Ash inquired. Given the state of the Pandora, it was clearly someone they both knew. "She's not yours, is she?"

Malachai shook his head. By the look on his face, something told Ash that even if she were, that would have been better news than what he was about to share. His gaze shifted to Penelope, then to Aveo, before ultimately landed back on Ash. "She said she gave the baby to a Sorcerer, who ran and then waited for her."

"Yes," Ash confirmed. "Smart thinking, if you ask me."

"Yeah, well, that Sorcerer was her biological father," Malachai revealed, handing Ash the tablet. She started to skim the document on display, completely unfamiliar with what she was reading. Her eyes landed on a specific name. One that stole the breath from her lungs.

"What's wrong?" Penelope asked softly.

Swallowing hard, Ash turned to her and said, "Don't panic."

"Why would she panic?" Aveo snarled.

"She's holding Matt Abernathy's baby."

72

Fay openly admitted to having an affair with the Sorcerer, and in the end, no one blamed her. Ryole, her husband, was an abusive piece of trash, and Abernathy—Storm—had shown her kindness. She was also able to provide Penelope with answers that she hadn't known she desired.

"He was tricked into a Blood Oath by a Witch named Jax Phantom," Fay had explained, holding Penelope's hand. "The terms of that oath were complicated. All I know was that he was forced to answer her every beck and call. He's her servant. He has to do whatever she says whenever she says it. For a while, he was free, allowed to roam as he pleased. That's when I met him. But afterward he was summoned to Solaris, where he was forced to create that portal. He came back recently. I'm not sure why she let him. He said she was in Solaris when he left. Her father, Xavier, demanded that she train someone named Constance."

Malachai cursed beneath his breath, his blood beginning to roar in his ears. He didn't dare look toward Ash. He couldn't bear to see the look on her face.

"He arrived in Dairth the day before Jane was born. Perfect timing," Fay explained, a blush creeping onto her cheeks. "But, once Malachai made that address, we knew we had to run. I gave Jane to him once I caught sight of Ryole. I found him after my husband beat me to an absolute pulp, and that was the last I saw of him. He gave Jane back to me and said he would get me help. I wasn't sure how, but I started running."

"The portal," Malachai blurted, jaw going slack. "A random portal opened in front of me, when Ash had called me to help you."

Silence spread throughout the bakery. The only sound was the oven going off. Aveo took the bread out, clearly unsure of what else to do with himself.

"Where is he now?" Penelope asked, her eyes fixed on the baby in her arms.

"I don't know," Fay admitted, shoulders slumping. "Jax probably summoned him."

"I want to know everything about this *Jax Phantom*," Ash said through clenched teeth, her words directed toward Malachai. "So I can turn her intestines into birthday streamers."

"You should," Fay admitted. "The only reason he was in the Regal Mountains was because he was looking for you."

"The next time you see me, I'll be with Ash VanCamp," Penelope whispered, her complexion paler than the snow falling outside. "Those were the last words he said to me."

Aveo remained silent. There was no readable expression upon his face. When he finally did speak, he said something that made Malachai's heart crumble entirely. "I didn't understand before. I hated that man. I didn't know why Penelope and he became so close. They were strangers before he was made her Guardian. I couldn't fathom how this random Sorcerer could just walk past those golden gates and become her absolute best friend. When I found him outside those cell gates in Solaris, I was furious. I didn't give him time to explain himself, because in my eyes, he'd betrayed Penelope, and everyone else as well. How could he, after that mission we attended to rescue her? How could he turn around and join the enemy?" The Elf took a moment to steel himself, turning away from everyone else, as if he feared how they might react to his stony facade cracking. "Then I became someone else's Guardian, and everything... made sense. I'd do anything for Ash. In an instant, she went from being my High Queen...to this person that *I* was chosen to protect. And, then she became my family," he added with a pained laugh. "I'll forever regret that fight."

"You didn't know," Penelope reminded him. "I'd have reacted the same way."

"Well, what do we do about it?" Ash asked, squaring her shoulders. "Can we find the contract? Destroy it?"

"Good luck," Malachai said, grinding his teeth. "No one knows where Jax hides anything."

"We could always kill her and break the oath that way," Ash countered.

The Pandora shut his eyes, sucking in a deep breath.

"I know she's your sister," Ash added softly. "But look what she's done."

"That isn't the only thing," Fay admitted, her voice cracking around the words. "He told me that she was the one who killed Aries. That she would have killed Ash too, had her grandmother not intervened."

Cursing beneath his breath, Malachai's head fell into his hands. *How* could Jax have become so Evil? He knew that he'd let Soroya slip too far away, but Jax? His stomach clenched, threatening to send his lunch up for a second appearance. He tried to breathe and failed miserably. To think that his own sister had been *seconds* away from killing Ash...

"Add her to the list," Malachai said to Aveo. "We'll take her out during the siege." He wondered if the Guardian knew how much those words had broken his heart.

Two months.

Constance had spent the last two months training with Jax, Soroya, and anyone else Xavier thought to throw her way. Each morning, she'd awake to Jax standing at her bedside with a hot coffee and a schedule. They'd practice for four hours, before Constance was handed off to Soroya, who'd teach her the more *dangerous* spells, like how to open portals with the flick of a wrist or change your appearance so convincingly that no one would be able to sense that you weren't who they thought you were.

In the evenings, Constance would train with Alrich. She'd practice her swordsmanship and other forms of close combat. To her benefit, she already knew how to handle her own without Magic. But that didn't mean putting the Pandora on his ass wasn't extremely satisfying, seeing as he'd barely said two words to her after their firework worthy kiss.

Twice a week, Constance would follow Lincoln around throughout Solaris. He'd explain how he was training the Mortals, whose abilities had grown stronger in recent months, and what remained of their ranks after Malachai's stunt.

There wasn't a day that went by that Constance didn't think of Malachai. She hadn't heard about him since that dreadful day, when Alrich had burst into her room and locked the door behind him. They'd sat on her bed, listening to the battle raging out in the city. Those screams of Pandora attempting to flee still rang in her ears, haunting her every thought.

Since then, Xavier had Veda place a barrier, one as black as night. It surrounded the entire city. Constance hadn't seen the sun since the moment it was put into place, trapping everyone inside. And those who wished to come inside could not. They had to fend for themselves. All while Constance wanted nothing more than to be on the other side, hunting down her cousin and joining him. She wanted to apologize for every harsh word she'd said to him. She wanted to make sure that he knew what he was to her. *Family*.

On the day that Constance was to be presented with her Crimson Coven cloak, she found herself staring outside her bedroom window, out into the darkness surrounding Solaris. There were no Moons. No stars. Just complete and utter emptiness.

A knock sounded at her door. Constance didn't so much as move a muscle, or think a thought before she said, "Come in."

"I'm here to escort you," Alrich said once he opened the door.

Without a word, Constance waved a hand, leading the door to slam shut. Her walls thickened a second later. No sound would pass through them. Slowly, she turned around to face the Pandora, offering him no expression as she'd been taught.

"They'll come any day now," she said, folding her arms in front of her chest. "What will we do once they arrive?"

"Find Malachai, or Ash VanCamp," Alrich explained slowly, keeping his gaze fixed firmly on her face. "We'll get out orders from them. Until then, we keep our heads down and play into Xavier's hand."

Nodding, Constance bit her bottom lip. "What about Lincoln?"

"He's beyond our help. Those injections Chai created haven't faded. Unless he brings a cure along with him, Lincoln will find a way to get himself killed. There's nothing we can do to stop that."

Every time Constance had found herself in Lincoln's presence, she'd wondered if some part of him knew who she was, or what they meant to one another. She'd wonder if he was aware that the only person who cared about him in that damned city was *her*.

Lincoln had made it abundantly clear that he didn't remember a thing. If his behavior didn't tell Constance everything she needed to know, his scent all over Soroya did.

For three months, Constance hadn't received her cycle. For two months, she'd blamed that on stress. First, Lincoln had vanished. Then Ash. And, then Cooper and Quinn had left. Everyone Constance knew or cared about had vanished in one way or another. Once Lincoln returned to retrieve her, taking her to a city no one dared to walk into, throwing her into a study with a king who thought he had some *right* to her, anxiety had ruled over Constance's every thought, breath, and heartbeat. It was no wonder why she hadn't bled.

It wasn't until Constance had started to find comfort in her current circumstances that she became worried. She knew she wasn't alone. Alrich kept her safe. Even Jax had sworn that no harm would come to her. Yet, she still hadn't received her cycle.

A month ago, Constance had come to the conclusion that something was amiss. She didn't dare ask for a Healer to confirm it. She knew she could survive through the siege. And, once she did, she'd find her father. She'd return to Crane. He'd likely rip her head off once he found out, but that was better than what would happen if Xavier did.

Four months. That's how far along Constance was. Her thoughts often drifted to the night the baby would have been conceived. The Harvest Festival. Lincoln had offered to walk her home, since Quinn had left with Lilly and Ash. One thing led to another, and the next thing Constance knew, they were meeting in secret. By the grace of some higher power, she wasn't showing. She could only hope that Ash's armies arrived before she was.

"You don't have to fight you know," Alrich reminded her, taking a step forward. "I can take you to the tunnels. You can escape. There's no reason to risk anything."

"No," she told him, lifting her chin, straightening her spine. "I want to. I want to be a part of the battle that ends it all."

Shaking his head, Alrich reached out for her, taking her hand in his own. "Don't let your pride get the best of you," he warned, staring into her eyes, allowing his own to transition from red to their natural blue. "You have more than one life to worry about."

"Don't try and tell me what you think is best for me when all you've done is avoid me," Constance snapped, snatching her hand from his grip. "You just told me that there was nothing we can do for the father of this child. I'm furious. I want to make them pay. *All* of them, for making me raise this baby alone. You can't stop me."

"I wouldn't dare try," he admitted, clenching his jaw. "You're right, I have been avoiding you. It's been decades since someone has made me feel the way you do. I've been foolish. *Scared*, even. But I would *never* leave you alone. I'd marry you in a blasted heartbeat if that child were mine. Fuck, I'd marry you anyway."

Constance's heart stilled, her breath escaping her. "What?"

"I said I'd marry you," Alrich repeated. "At the very least, I wouldn't leave you to do this alone. No woman should have to. Especially someone as beautiful, smart, cunning, and caring as you."

At a loss for words, all Constance could do was stare into his eyes. They were the shade of an autumn sky, the only hint of anything other than darkness that she'd seen in months. She wanted to get lost in them, to forget that she had somewhere else to be.

"Tell me that again once we're safe," she said, the words quivering in her throat. "Please."

Nodding, Alrich leaned forward, claiming her lips with his own. "I will."

Constance was led to the Throne Room, which was filled to the brim with Witches wearing the same cloak she was about to receive. Jet-black silk with the symbol of three intersecting swords embroidered with crimson thread, the same shade lining the underside.

An aisle sat before her, one leading straight up to where Xavier sat on his stolen throne, lined with candles taller than she was. Veda stood at his side, the epitome of deadly beauty. She wore her usual red cloak, her lips stained the same color, dark brown hair spilling over her shoulders in satin waves. Soroya stood on the other, wearing a dress of sheer black lace, her vivid green eyes narrowed into deadly slits.

Clearing her throat, Constance started her journey down the aisle. Minutes, or hours could have passed before she arrived in front of the throne, dropping to her knees with the sort of grace only a queen would have had. Her chin dipped toward her chest, her black hair falling in front of her face.

"You may rise," Xavier informed her, and she did as he said. Constance stood, squaring her shoulders, reminding herself that Magic thrummed in her pulse, raced through her veins, surged along with her blood. She was not harmless. "My precious niece, you have done more than please me. You are everything I have dreamed you would become and more. I am proud to call you family, just as Veda is proud to accept you as one of her own."

Jax stepped forward, a folded cloak in her arms.

"Constance Trevayne," Veda started, her voice reverberating throughout the Throne Room. "Do you pledge yourself to your coven, your sisters, and your High Priestess? Will you live alongside us, fight alongside us, and *breathe* alongside us until your time in this Galaxy comes to an end? Will you swear to serve your king, even if it costs you your life? Do you swear to fulfill the Prophecy, take your place as the reigning Trevayne of your bloodline, and commit to using your blood to release our fallen king?"

No one had mentioned such a thing before that moment. Constance had no idea that her initiation meant more than just becoming the average, Crimson Coven Witch. She gulped, daring to look in Soroya's direction. Her cousin nodded, urging her to do the same.

"I do," Constance said at last, inclining her head to the Witch.

"You do *what?*" Veda snarled.

"I pledge myself to the Crimson Coven, as my ancestors did before me. I will live alongside you, fight alongside you, and breathe alongside you until my time in this Galaxy comes to an end. I will serve my king, even if it costs me my life. I swear to fulfill the Prophecy and take my place as the reigning Trevayne. I will represent my bloodline and commit to using the blood racing through my own veins to release our fallen king."

Constance had no idea what any of what she'd said meant. All she knew was that she needed to do whatever Veda wanted until she received her chance at freedom.

Veda's lips spread into a satisfied smile. She reached into the folds of her cloak, retrieving a dagger with a blood-red blade. "Take this and slice your palm," the Witch directed, holding the weapon out to Constance, who took it without hesitation, drawing it across her hand, failing to do so much as grimace as the sharp blade bit at her flesh.

"Hold it above a candle," Veda ordered.

Sucking in a deep breath, Constance turned toward the nearest flame, holding her hand above it until a single drop of blood fell into the melting wax. The second it did, every candle in the room turned red, one by one, until the room was coated in an eerie red light, chilling Constance to her very core.

"Congratulations," Veda said, gesturing for Jax to fasten the cloak around Constance's trembling shoulders. "We welcome you as the newest member of the Crimson Coven. Now, your King would like to present you with a gift."

Xavier stood, his black robes fluttering with the movement. Lincoln brought forth a box, one long enough to contain a sword. Constance eyed it warily, holding her breath as the king took it from the Archer, prying it open before turning it around to give her a view.

Inside the box, Constance found a dual-ended sword, with a shining silver hilt in the center. Both serrated blades curved in different directions, taking on the appearance and color of a bright phoenix tail. The weapon looked like pure flame.

"This is the Phoenix Blade," Xavier explained. "A dual-ended sword, once owned by High King Seamus Grimm. If you spin it fast enough, you'll be able to hypnotize your opponents, bending them to your will. I thought you might appreciate it, and you've certainly earned it. Without you, I'm not sure how I would have survived the loss of my sons."

Nodding in thanks, Constance took the box, her heart crowding her throat. For the first time since she'd arrived in Solaris, guilt began to creep into her thoughts. This man, the husband of her mother's sister, thought that she loved him as a niece should love her uncle. He adored her enough to give her a weapon that had once belonged to a High King. She wasn't sure what to say, her mouth having gone so dry that her tongue stuck to the roof.

"You're free to go," Xavier told her, his tone as sweet as pie. "Celebrate tonight. You deserve it."

Constance took a step toward him, rising onto the tips of her toes so that she could kiss his cheek. "Thank you, uncle. For everything."

Afterward, Constance hurried back down that aisle, clutching the box containing the blade to her chest, her mind swarming a mile a minute. What she didn't know was that somewhere else in the

Realm, Savron Phantom was screaming out in agony, because her blood had severed his connection to the coven. The second her blood joined with that candle wax tainted by his very essence by Veda, Savron was as good as dead. He'd broken his vows, and Constance had taken his place. Now, the hunt was on.

73

For the last two months, Ash felt normal. She was surrounded by people that she loved, in the place she loved the most, preparing the plots for planting in the Spring. She'd studied, trained, laughed, and attempted to enjoy herself. She'd strengthened her bond with Alistair, learning how to control it in the process. Now, they could *choose* when they felt each other's emotions. Ash was no longer suffering from two different sets of feelings at once.

Unfortunately, every vacation must come to an end.

For the first time in nearly three months, Ash found herself standing in Benjamin's lab, inside the Communications Center. The scrolls Cleo had given her were unrolled on the long glass table for all to see. The first was written by Aiden Cavanaugh himself, detailing his fight against Xanthius. He'd drawn images of the weapons he used, and of how Xanthius had appeared.

The next two scrolls were about the Dark One. Ash had read them hundreds of times over the last few months, so the chilling details about how he arrived in Si Realtra after hunting the Great Sovereign for two millennia didn't faze her. As for everyone else, they were pale, their gazes distant.

"There's a gap," Ash explained, gesturing to the third scroll. "Here, we can see that the Dark One corrupted the beings our

Sovereign had created. The Arebus Archers and the Elves turned on one another. Mortals became aggressive, murdering one another left and right. The Dark One created crime. Sin. And it took our Sovereign over five centuries to find a way to contain him. She created the Underworld as his prison and threw all those that he corrupted in there with him. She tried to cleanse the Six Realms."

"And the gap is how this being's power came to be inside of Xanthius, and then Xavier," Benjamin concluded, rubbing his jaw. "I take it there's no scroll about who broke this monster out of prison?"

Ash shook her head, pressing her lips into a thin, grim line.

"What if it's genetic?" Lucinda asked in a hushed tone, all gazes turning to where Malachai leaned against Grant's desk. "That would certainly explain how Xavier wound up with that kind of power. Someone down his family line could have found a way to steal it from the Dark One, tainting their bloodline."

Malachai immediately shook his head, opening his mouth to object. "My father wasn't born the way he is. After my mother died, he mentioned going to some island. He never said where it was, or why he went there. He kept just as many secrets from me as I kept from him. But, when he came back from that island…" he trailed, shivering from head to toe.

"Perhaps Xanthius paid this mysterious island a visit as well," Aveo suggested.

Ash's stomach became sour at the thought. What if one of the descendants knew where that island was? What if they decided to go there themselves once they learned of Xavier's demise? She sucked in a breath, filling her lungs completely, holding that breath for a long minute.

"That'll be our first order of business then," Ash declared. "After the siege. I'll find the island, and I'll sink it."

"Is that even possible?" Quinn asked, eyeing her warily from across the table. "You'd need a lot of power to do that."

"You're talking to the girl who conjoined two lakes," Cooper reminded his brother. "And then fought an entire battle afterward. I think she could sink an island."

Ash inclined her head to him, offering him a silent thank you.

"We'll cross that bridge when we come to it," Benjamin informed them all. "For now, we focus on the siege. After this meeting, you'll leave with the Draconian Army. It'll take you four days to get there. That means four days to prepare for your assignments."

The Communications Head directed everyone to turn their attention to a nearby screen, the size of a wall. A list of names and objectives started to compile, some of which had Ash's heart skipping with nerves, hairs along her neck and arms beginning to stand on an end.

"Thanks to Anderson and Malachai's precious intel, we were able to identify our biggest concerns and assign our specialists accordingly. As you can see, Grant's compatibility system was able to pair you to opponents that would best suit your abilities and skills, increasing your success rates. Some of you will work in pairs, and some on your own. First, we have Marcus, who will take out one of Xavier's remaining Commanders, Ryole."

Plenty of people clapped at that. After what happened to Fay, the Allies would often fight over who'd get the chance to decapitate Ryole during the siege. Ash supposed they hadn't counted on Grant's system choosing on who got the honors.

"Next, Cooper will take out Xavier's second Commander, Glen. Supposedly, this particular opponent prefers to fight with poisoned needles, and has been known to dabble in Dark Sorcery. It's important that you don't get close to him, but as long as you're within three miles, one of your arrows will do the trick. Afterward, you'll join Vincent with his mission. Hunting down Alrich Undergrove and Constance Waters. Your task is to capture Alrich and rescue Constance."

Both men looked toward one another and nodded, lips spreading into wicked grins.

"As for Lucinda," Benjamin said the name and everyone froze, including the Sorceress. "You have three targets—Soroya Trevayne, Jax Phantom, and Veda."

Ash's breath hitched, her blood running cold.

"No worries," Lucinda said, reaching to tap her hand with her own. "I can handle them all."

"Since Jax is suspected of being the Witch responsible for Aries' death, the Elves would prefer that she is detained, so that she can be tried and convicted. But, since she's also suspected of tricking Matt Abernathy into a Blood Oath, which ultimately turned him into a weapon Xavier could use against us, the only way to stop that is to dispatch her." Benjamin offered Malachai a sympathetic look. All the Pandora did in return was nod solemnly. "As far as Abernathy himself goes, each of you will be provided with tranquilizer darts. Whoever sees him first gets the privilege of knocking him unconscious. Afterward, he's being transported back here to Dracus, where he will be detained until he can be cleared of all crimes and so forth."

Each of the Allies nodded in unison.

"Alistair and Anastasia have a different task, as you can see. The two of you will take Lilly McBride to the Dragon's Den, where you will gather however many Dragons you can. From there, you'll head straight to Solaris. Throughout the siege, you'll fight from the skies. Lilly will accompany Alistair on Willa, where she will be able to guide the fire using her telekinetic ability."

Quinn bristled, making no attempts to hide how furious he was that his fourteen-year-old sister was being considered a specialist. But he kept his mouth shut, and Ash was glad for it. If they expected to win, they needed all hands on deck.

"Morghan will be leading the Pandora portion of our new, united army. Under normal circumstances, we would have had Malachai take on this job. But he has a different task, one that Quinn will assist him with," Benjamin explained, pointing to their names on the screen. "They'll be hunting down Lincoln, shooting him up with the cure Malachai, Ebony, and Hartford spent the last two months perfecting. After they succeed, they'll jump in the fray. Malachai will heal the wounded, and Quinn will unleash his anger about me including Lilly in this on the enemy via Arebus Arrows."

Ash snorted, unable to stop herself. Amusement flashed in the Archer's eyes, his shoulders relaxing slightly.

"Humphrey will be the one worrying about Richard and Ariel," Benjamin added with a heavy sigh. "He's already left to give us intel on Solaris's current state. We don't need any surprises."

"I've had enough of them for a lifetime," Ash divulged.

"Haven't we all?" he countered. "Anyway, last but not least, we have Ash, Craven, and Aveo. Their mission is to infiltrate the Idonian castle and track down Xavier—"

"No," Ash objected. "I was supposed to go into that castle *alone*. Sending anyone else in isn't necessary." She fought to swallow her evolving anger, praying it wouldn't leak into her tone. "I'm the Messenger; they're not. I won't put them at risk."

"You don't have a choice," he insisted, clenching his jaw. "You said it yourself. You need to use the Scepter, *and* one of your enchanted daggers. You don't have enough hands. And you need Craven for the second part of your mission."

Malachai scoffed, disdain twisting his features. "You want her to slay the Dark King and then do something *else*? Is that not enough for you?"

"Trust me, I would rather her run for the hills the second that bastard is dead," Benjamin assured him, his voice dripping with venom. "But she can't. Anderson will explain why."

The Pandora took a step forward, clutching her info-tab to her chest, staring at the screen as it changed images. Ash sunk into a chair at the sight of the portal, nausea rolling over her.

"Grant and I spent three months trying to find a way to disable this thing," Anderson explained, her voice trembling as if she were afraid to continue. "We went over countless scenarios. At one point, we even considered petitioning the Idonian Council to allow Aries to use his Magic. It *was* Fae Magic that was used to create the damn thing. His was the direct opposite of that sort. His was *dark*. It could have obliterated that portal if he could fly close enough. Unfortunately, he is no longer with us, so this responsibility falls on the two of you."

Anderson took a breath, her gaze dancing between Craven and Ash.

"Between your Moonlight and Craven's electricity, that portal can be destroyed. All you need to do is stand at a safe distance away," Anderson explained, the image on the screen changing once again; this time to a picture of the Idonian Castle. "There are two bell towers on either side of the castle, connected by a bridge. The second you defeat Xavier, Aveo will head back out into Solaris to start getting people out. You and Craven will head to the towers. You'll wait a total of five minutes, then Craven will fire off a warning strike. After that, you'll wait another five minutes, and then you'll aim everything you have at that portal. There's just one problem."

Someone groaned. Ash looked over to find Alistair rubbing his temples.

"That much power will *level* the Idonian castle, quite possibly sink it into the ground. That's too much pressure. *Cosmic* pressure. You won't be able to run out in time," Anderson explained sadly. "And the Dragons won't be able to fly anywhere close enough to retrieve you. Which means that your only chance of getting out of there is either from Lucinda's sphere or teleportation."

"So, me," Cooper concluded. "Lucinda's sphere is the fastest way for people to get out of there before all of this happens. It'll have to be me."

Benjamin and Anderson nodded in unison.

"Unless Cleo is available," Morghan mentioned softly.

"She's the Fae Queen, and her people need her alive," Ash reminded him harshly.

"You're our High Queen and we need *you* alive," Quinn said with pleading eyes.

Exhaling slowly, Ash shook her head. "Not after today, I'm not. I filed my Will the second I got here."

"Oh?" Valentina squeaked. "Who did you choose?"

"You can open my Will after the siege and see for yourself," Ash informed her with a teasing smirk. "Now, let's suit up. We have a long journey ahead of us."

74

Ash despised goodbyes, but she gave one to Penelope and Valentina anyway. Her sister was shaking throughout the length of their embrace, sniffling terribly. "You have an important job too, you know," she reminded her, patting her back. "You're going to sit with Ebony, Grant, Hartford, and Anderson. You'll monitor our vitals, and at the first sign of danger, you can rescue us if we need it. That's extremely important."

"I know." The words were muffled against Ash's new uniform. "I just don't think I can take losing anyone else."

Nodding, Ash knew that feeling all too well. "Don't worry, we'll all come back to you. Afterward, you can go *home* and start that family you desire. Who knows, maybe that Guardian of yours will return to you."

"As much as I'd love that, I'm a bit more concerned about *your* Guardian returning to *me*," she admitted, giving Ash one last, good squeeze.

"Don't worry, I'll protect that new brother of mine, and when we get back, we'll have some of the most epic war stories to tell," Ash informed her with a proud smile, pulling away from her sister's grip. "People will write songs about our victory. And our children and their children and their children will dance to those songs."

"Will my name be included in those?" Craven inquired, stealing his own hug from the Princess.

Someone nearby released an exasperated sigh. "As if there aren't *already* a dozen songs about you," Axel spat.

"Alright, time to go," Shadow declared, clad in his new uniform as well. It was decided a few months back that all Realm armies would wear the same colors. Midnight blue and silver, with the Idonian symbol embroidered on the back. The Allies and the Draconians still adorned their usual diagonal stripe, only they were no longer color-coded. Instead, they all matched. There were no more divisions, at least for the siege. Along with all the other armies —the Idonian League of Sorcerers, the Elves, the Rebels, the Pandora, and the Fae... they were *one*.

"Let me guess, the Earth Clan is itching to feel the ground beneath their feet?" Shay teased.

"More like itching to bury some Witches alive," Shadow corrected.

THE MARCH BEGAN, WHETHER ASH AND THE ALLIES WERE READY OR not. They stood in a line, crossing the Unity Bridge for what could be the last time, an entire army at their backs. Ash kept her gaze fixed in front of her, on the Clan Leader's backs, all but Anastasia's. She'd left with Alistair almost directly after the meeting, since the Rider insisted it would take a few days to get the Dragons to cooperate.

See you at the siege, Ash said through their bond.

Good luck camping with a bunch of army brutes, was his response.

Good luck camping with Anastasia, she countered.

Ash could have *sworn* that she felt him flinch.

THEY MARCHED FOR TEN HOURS BEFORE THEY TOOK A BREAK, IN THE hills just a few miles south of Witherow. Tents were set up, fire pits constructed. The animals they'd managed to hunt along the way were skinned and cleaned for consumption, the blood drained for reserves in case the Draconians ran out along the way.

"So, drinking that deer's blood *wasn't* so crazy," Quinn mentioned, working to set up his own tent.

Ash scowled at him, sipping the tea she'd used her fire ability to heat.

"Do mine," Malachai requested, holding out a mug with a tea bag sitting in chilled water.

"*Please*," Ash said, lifting a single brow. "It's a word people use when they want something."

"Please," he obliged.

They drank their tea and ate in silence before crawling into their tents, where Ash failed to sleep. She was far too nervous to even dare, though some advice from Jay would surely be beneficial. So, she walked out into the camp, her gaze running over the fields covered in tents identical to her own. Smoke still billowed from faded fires, rising into the midnight sky, speckled with stars that shined like diamonds. The Three Moons were high, their light igniting the Realm around her.

Soon, it would be *safe* to camp out in the middle of nowhere. Soon, Ash wouldn't need an army around her. But the truth was that even with the seventy thousand surrounding her, Ash still felt death lurking behind, peaking over her shoulder. Watching her. *Waiting.*

An unending chill swept down Ash's spine, fear creeping into every thought. Images of those scrolls and what she would soon face flashed before her eyes. Her gifted dream from Aries replayed within her mind. Those horns... those veins, glowing like embers... that dagger made of Dark matter, sailing right for her.

Swallowing hard, Ash willed that fear away. There were four days left until she faced her fate. All of those people, sleeping in the tents surrounding her, might not walk out of Solaris. She might never see them again. She was the reason they were there. *Her* Prophecy was why they'd left their homes and their families. It was why they were risking their lives, well aware that they could very well never see their loved ones again.

Despite her best efforts, panic began to set in. Ash could no longer control her thoughts, her breaths, or her heartbeat. She began to shake, her bones trembling. The weight upon her chest started to crush her, threatening to bury her beneath the responsibility that had fallen upon her shoulders. All of these lives. All of these people.

A sob, or a scream, started to build in Ash's throat. She held it in, her eyes falling on the tent across from her own, and without giving herself the time to choose otherwise, she hurried toward it. She stomped through the fire pit, crushing embers beneath her boots, knocking over plates and cups that used to hold tea. She unzipped the flap and dove inside, startling the Archer trying to sleep within.

Quinn didn't say a word. He took one look at her and opened his sleeping bag. Ash kicked off her boots and crawled inside, surrounding herself in his warmth. She rested her head upon his chest, allowing the sound of his beating heart to sooth her.

Five months ago, Quinn was all she had. The only person she could confide in. The only person *fighting* for her. To keep her secret, to keep her safe. It wasn't just the two of them anymore. But, for the next four days, she'd pretend that it was.

75

When the Draconian Army made it to Solaris, the Elven Army and the Idonian League of Sorcerers were already there. Morghan headed off into the Idonian Forest, where the Pandora were waiting for his direction. It was there that they would wait for their signal. The Rebels were crowded in the same tunnel Malachai and Quinn had guarded a few months ago. When the signal came, they'd rush out with the element of surprise.

The only problem was the barrier surrounding Solaris.

Massive, and as black as the darkest night.

"Well, Humphrey didn't say anything about *that*," Ash grumbled, staring up at the massive, obsidian structure. "How are we supposed to get through there? And, Moons only know what Xavier has hiding behind it. We're practically blind."

Malachai pursed his lips, slipping his hands into the pockets. "The most my father has are whatever Pandora chose to stay, the Crimson Coven, and about five hundred Mortals with unknown abilities."

"Sounds like a real party," Beck said sarcastically.

"Well, I hope there are drinks, because I could *definitely* use one," Axel admitted, strapping his axe to his back.

The armies were getting in formation behind them. Everything was ready. The only thing standing in their way was the barrier.

Lucinda's Sorcerers were inspecting it. One even dared to poke it and said it felt like glass.

"Here's an idea," Craven started from where he stood at Ash's side. "Hit it with some Moonlight."

"That's our best bet," Lucinda said, storming over to where they'd all gathered in front of a lone, massive maple tree. "My Sorcerers won't try to use Magic to disable it. It's Black Magic. They refuse to be corrupted."

"Can't say I blame them," Beck chimed, crossing his arms in front of his heavily armored chest. "If Moonlight's our best option, we'd best fire that Scepter up, Ash. It's been waiting a millennium for action like this."

Nodding, Ash summoned the weapon from her mindspace. It arrived in her grip less than a second later, invoking gasps from the armies at her back. The other Allies step forward, staring warily in the barrier's direction.

"The second you shatter that, we'll be swarmed," Malachai warned, reaching for the sword strapped down his spine, his red eyes blazing. "Be prepared to run for the nearest sewer entrance. That'll be the only way you'll get into the castle."

"Everyone get in their pairs!" Ash ordered, hoping her authoritative tone hid her crippling fear. Aveo moved to her right, both broadswords drawn and ready. Craven drew Shadow Strike at her left, the obsidian blade sparkling with violet threads of electricity, snatching shadows beneath their feet. "Make sure your tech is working!"

Murmurs of *all clear* began to ring in Ash's ears.

Ash thought of something else to demand of them, just to drag on the time. It didn't matter that she'd spent months preparing for this moment, or that she'd fought against the Dark Army for the last eight years. She'd survived eighteen Red Winters, and this event would mark the last of them. None of that mattered. No amount of hard work would be enough to prepare her for what she was about to do.

A hand arrived on her shoulder, causing her to stiffen with surprise.

"On three," Quinn said calmly.

"One," Craven started.

"Two," Marcus continued.

"Three," Malachai finished, just as Moonlight shot out of the orb at the end of Ash's Scepter, barreling toward the barrier with impeccable speed. It slammed into it, the force of the impact driving Ash backward. Her boots dug into the icy earth, the sound of the barrier giving way crackling in her ears. All she needed to do was hold it long enough for it to shatter.

A pair of hands gripped her hips, stabilizing her. Just barely.

"It's working!" Beck said, his voice farther away than he truly was.

Ash shut her eyes, throwing all her energy into the act. She felt herself slipping, but more hands arrived around her, keeping her from faltering.

"It fucking better be!" Malachai ground through clenched teeth, pushing Ash forward even more. "I'm getting pretty tired of trying to keep this Scepter from blowing her off her bloody feet!"

The second the last word sailed past the Pandora's lips; the Realm shattered. The barrier imploded into billowing clouds of black mist and shards of glass, revealing what waited for the armies. A sea of red eyes, Mortals, and black-cloaked Witches ready to give Ash and the united army everything they had.

With a mighty roar, the Draconians took off, not giving the Dark Army a chance to make the first move. Waves of fire, light, and water hit Xavier's frontlines head-on. Pandora were incinerated, the Witches and Mortals screamed, the scent of burning flesh and smoke filtering through the air. Steam rose into the air from where the fire water became one, melting whoever stood in its bath to the bones.

"Alright, draw them out!" Axel ordered, gesturing for Shadow and the Earth Clan to step forward and take their shot. "Specialists move out!"

The armies were scattering, fearing they'd be buried alive.

Cooper gave Ash a wink and a crooked smile before he took Vincent by the hand and vanished right before her eyes. Lucinda whipped her sphere at the ground, stepping through a portal that led into the city. Marcus followed her through, Whitefire gleaming in his grip. Morghan's roar reverberated off in the distance, the Pandora army pushing forward, ready to meet their shape shifting kin head-on.

"Time to go," Malachai said to Quinn, twirling his sword in his grip.

"Us too," Craven told Ash. "There's a sewer entrance to the east. We can make it there before all the armies collide if we hurry."

Ash's grip tightened around her Scepter, the Amulet beginning to glow around her neck, like a beacon to those who had just left her, and those who should fear her. She started to walk away, to follow Aveo and Craven, when someone wrapped their grip around her wrist and pulled her back. A second later, Quinn pulled her into the tightest embrace she'd ever endured.

"Until we meet again," he whispered in her ear, planting a kiss on the top of her head.

"Ash!" Aveo growled. "We need to *go*. Now."

Sucking in a breath, Ash nodded slowly. "We will," she promised Quinn, her gaze shifting to where Malachai waited, scanning the battle forming before their eyes. "Go. Get Lincoln and bring him *home*."

THE SEWERS REEKED OF DEATH AND DECAY. ASH BROUGHT HER MASK up over her nose, her eyes burning as if she were walking through acid clouds. She pushed onward, following Aveo and Craven's lead, ignoring the way her stomach twisted and turned with nerves. The dagger stashed in her boot rubbed against her sock. The pair on her hips felt heavy. The Amulet burned at her chest, its power creeping beneath her flesh, pleading to be unleashed.

They'd traveled at Immortal speed on and off, careful to reserve their energy for the fight they'd have to endure. They kept silent, afraid to do so much as breathe.

There was no word on whether any others had completed their

assignments. The bug in Ash's ear was as silent as the dead of night. The only sounds she heard were from the ongoing battle above them. The clash of swords, the whizzing of arrows, claws tearing into flesh, and the screams. The scent of blood seeped through the sewer cracks, so thick Ash could choke on it.

"We're getting close," Craven warned, his voice little more than a whisper. "Be ready. There's no way that Xavier didn't assume we'd use the sewers. They'll be waiting for us."

"I'm counting on it," Aveo admitted, rubbing his broadswords against one another, sharpening the blades.

Ash rolled her shoulders, cracked her neck, and said, "It's judgment day."

76

Months ago, Constance had endured the worst battle she thought she ever would. Thousands of Pandora versus a few hundred unequipped Mortals in a village so deep in the Strip that the possibility of outside assistance was entirely null. Constance had thought she would die that day. But all of that was *nothing* compared to the Immortal Armies infiltrating Solaris.

"I'm beginning to wish that I *had* died that day," Constance uttered beneath her breath, staring out at the battle unfolding, perched on a rooftop in the center of the city.

"What?" Alrich hissed.

"Nothing."

The Draconians alone could have torn through the Dark Army's front lines with little to no effort, and they had. It took them less than half an hour to take out a quarter of the remaining Pandora, and most of the Mortals Lincoln had recruited. Constance tried not to think about them. They hadn't chosen to be here. They weren't fast enough to run when Malachai gave them the opportunity. They had no choice but to fight and die.

After the Draconians made it through the frontlines, the Elves, and the Idonian League of Sorcerers followed. Constance held her breath, watching in awe as various Sorcerers joined together to perform a mass inceptstasis spell, freezing Witches in place, giving the Elves time to cut them down. It was brutal. *Magically* brutal.

"Smart," Alrich said, grimacing. "Cruel, but smart."

"The Elves might be the strongest in regard to brute strength, but they're the most susceptible to Magical attacks. The Draconians have elemental abilities. And, even if they don't possess one, they're still faster. Without the Sorcerers, the Elves wouldn't stand a chance in a battle like this," Constance explained, scanning the city for any of their targets.

Alrich flashed her a wicked grin. "Someone's been studying."

"Sorta had to, with Jax and Soroya breathing down my neck," Constance reminded him. "You see any Allies?"

"Not yet," he replied. "I have a feeling trying to find Malachai in this mess is going to be next to impossible. Like trying to find a needle in a mountain of other needles. And the odds are that Ash is already in the sewers, headed straight for Xavier."

They would have to settle for anyone, then. Constance clenched her jaw. The other Allies, aside from the McBrides, wouldn't know her face. They'd see their Black Legion cloaks and strike without a second thought. They *needed* to find someone familiar.

"And I'm assuming you can't track him by scent."

Alrich scoffed. "You *do* see how many Pandora are out there, right? Not to mention everyone else. There are well over a hundred thousand warriors. I wouldn't even recognize my own blasted scent in this mess."

Groaning, Constance reached to rub the back of her neck. The Phoenix Blade felt heavy on her back, begging to be used. She *wanted* to get down there and fight. She *wanted* to shred through the Witches and beasts, and all of Xavier's assets, to punish him for tearing her from the life she knew and forcing her to become this... weapon.

That's all Constance ever was to him. Another tool. A pretty niece to flaunt around. All he wanted to do was use her the same way he used Malachai. It made her sick. Those words she'd said to the prince haunted her every thought. He hadn't deserved it. *Any* of it. There's nothing she wanted more than to apologize to him. But, as she stared out into the raging battle, she was beginning to doubt she'd get the chance.

"We can't stay up here," Alrich reminded her. "Soon enough, the Rider will arrive with an army of Dragons. I can sense them. They'll spot us. We need to find someone, and soon."

Nodding, Constance decided to turn her focus toward the east. That was when she saw it. A burning white flame, off in the distance. "Look!" she said, elbowing the Pandora in the shoulder. "Whitefire!"

"Marcus Bonaventure," Alrich said, exhaling slowly. "He's pretty far."

"Yeah, well, he's our best shot right now. Let's move."

THE FACT THAT MARCUS WAS COMBING THROUGH SOLARIS'S STREETS for the first time in eighteen years chilled him to the bone. He could hardly stand to see what had become of the city where he'd grown to be the man he was today. Where he was born, raised, and trained to be the Black Knight he'd always dreamed to be. Now, the streets were running red, blood splattered across the side of every building. Shop windows were shattered. Homes were on fire.

Solaris was burning. But cities could be rebuilt. *Empires* could be rebuilt just as easily as they were destroyed. Marcus would see the light returned to the city he loved. Even if that meant it needed to be reduced to rubble to make that happen.

"Any luck tracking Ryole?" Cooper's voice rang in the Mentor's ears, piercing through his thoughts.

"No," he replied, grinding his teeth. "How about you?"

"I haven't killed Glen, but I know where he is. The only problem is that he's with Lincoln. If I get close enough to take Glen out, I'll be close enough for Lincoln to take me out."

Marcus groaned, driving Whitefire's burning blade through the heart of a Witch. "Which means your brother and Malachai won't be able to get close enough either."

"Hence why we need to find a way to split them up," Vincent

contributed. "I'm almost certain that Ryole is with them. Smart. If they stay together, Lincoln can pick off anyone that tries to make a move on them."

"Whatever you're going to do about him, do it now. The fucker's taken out at least eighty of my Elves in the last half hour," Beck snarled. "Who's capable of firing arrows that fast, anyway? It should be impossible. I thought it *was* impossible."

"Well, if we can find a way to get his bow away from him…" Marcus trailed, carving through a hoard of Pandora, the scent of their burning flesh filtering into his nostrils, gagging him.

"Does anyone know if Alistair is in range, yet?" Malachai inquired. "I have an idea."

FLYING INTO BATTLE WITH THIRTY DRAGONS AT HIS BACK WAS THE most exhilarating thing Alistair had ever experienced. He could hardly handle the anticipation. The two-hour flight from the den felt more like eight. The entire time, all he could do was imagine what it would feel like to fly above that city, unleashing fire that Idona hadn't seen in over five decades.

"We should be in range soon," Ana called over from where she flew on Oberin, a massive, red-scaled wyvern four times Willa's size. Up until the moment she met the beast, Alistair had never seen her tremble with fear. But that only lasted a second before Oberin leaned forward, lowering for her to board him. Now, Alistair was sure that Ana was having the time of her life, and that her ego had grown tremendously during the process.

"Are you ready?" Alistair asked Lilly, who sat in front of him, strapped into the saddle Malachai had created.

She nodded, her lips pressed into a thin line. She'd hardly said a word since they left the den, her heart beating so ferociously that the sound of it crowded Alistair's thoughts.

"As ready as I'll ever be," Lilly squeaked, rubbing her hands together in preparation. "Let's roast these bitches."

Ana's laughter echoed in the night, the most joyful sound

anyone might hear on such a dreadful occasion. Solaris came into view, glowing like an ember surrounded by darkness. Black smoke billowed in thick clouds above it. The sounds of screams and the scent of burning flesh was carried by the breeze ruffling Alistair's locks and Lilly's long golden braids. His lips twitched toward a smirk as Willa's snarls reverberated throughout his form. The Dragons behind them roared, baring rows of razor-sharp teeth longer than the Rider's arm.

"I second that," Alistair said to Lilly. "Let's roast these bitches."

ust *one* dragon was enough to aid Aiden Cavanaugh in taking Xavier's Grandfather down. But thirty? His blood chilled the second he watched them fly in, all different species and sizes, their scales various colors. Under different circumstances, Xavier might have found himself enamored by their beauty.

The sight of a specific Black Dragon with an even more specific Rider led Xavier's face to twist into a scowl. *Cavanaugh,* something deep in his tainted soul seethed.

Oh look, another thing Malachai lied about, Meera drawled. *Aren't you glad he didn't kill him, like he was supposed to? If he had, this historical occasion would have never occurred.*

Malachai was somewhere out in Solaris, killing the men he used to command. Xavier had chosen not to think about him, or the shiny new badge upon his chest. The fact the Elves had even allowed him to make that Realm address in their own Throne Room was shocking. Now, the Draconians had made him an Ally, of all things.

"Enough about my son," Xavier snapped. "I can't afford the distraction. The Messenger is *here.* And she's brought friends. That wasn't a part of the Prophecy."

Yeah well, this entire stunt of yours wasn't part of the Beautiful Mind Prophecy, was it? Meera sneered. *Apparently, all that matters is that prophe-*

cies are fulfilled. What people are willing to do to get there... well... there are no rules, are there?

"Calloway and Amsterdam's presence changes nothing." Xavier turned away from the window, flexing his jaw. "Ash could have brought every Ally in here to face me, and it wouldn't have made a difference. I've had eighteen years to prepare for this occasion. I've reserved every ounce of my power. I'm ready. Ash, on the other hand, has no idea what she's just walked into."

ASH AND THE OTHERS HAD INFILTRATED THE CASTLE, ARRIVING IN the dungeons. Xavier was waiting just a floor above them. Ash could sense him, and it chilled her to her very core. Whatever dangerous power he possessed seeped through the castle walls, surrounding her, tickling the nape of her neck, swarming her senses.

The Scepter in Ash's grip reacted to it, glowing angrily, lighting up the darkness around them. The weapon remembered, which confirmed her suspicions. Ash was about to face off with a power so ancient that it had existed before Si Realtra. She would have to defeat something that even the Sovereign had feared enough to create the Underworld, just to contain it.

"Alright, is everyone okay with the plan?" Aveo inquired.

Craven nodded, taking a sip from his thermos before handing it over to Ash.

No one dared mention anything that they planned to do, since it was evident that Xavier's power was beyond limits. He could hear every word they said. Ash could *feel* him listening.

"This is it," she whispered, glancing between the two of them.

"Not quite," A voice echoed from nearby.

Ash knew that voice. She whirled toward it, her eyes burning sapphire blue and silver, flames beginning to swarm both of her hands. The sound of flickering electricity greeted her ears. Aveo found his way to her side, both swords drawn, bronze eyes narrowed into slits sharper than daggers.

"I heard about the wedding," Richard crooned, closer than he was before, yet remaining out of view. The scent of blood began to seep into the air. *Draconian* blood. Ash bared her teeth, releasing her most vicious snarl. "It came as quite the shock, seeing as the last I heard, pretty Penelope was betrothed to Loren, not you."

Aveo didn't so much as flinch.

"Doesn't that bother you?" Richard pressed. "How close she was to becoming a *Mason* instead of a Calloway? To betraying you *and* the Chamberlains?"

"Don't answer him," Craven growled.

To Ash's surprise, Aveo obeyed.

"Then again, neither you *nor* Loren would have been in such a position had the prince you all praise not slaughtered Cedric, would you?" Richard inquired. "If he were to come back from the dead right now, Penelope would forget your name. She'd fall into his bed before you'd even have a chance to blink."

"*Don't* react," Ash hissed.

Aveo remained as still as a statue, bearing no expression upon his face.

"Craven," Richard drawled, moving on to his next target, his voice growing closer and closer. "How are you faring, being back here in the castle? Are you receiving flashbacks of the Ballroom Battle, where you acted as the fail-safe? You know, that plan where the other warriors told you that if they were overrun to shock everyone in the ballroom, not just the Pandora? To murder them all in hopes that would deter the Pandora from pushing any further?"

Ash's breath hitched, but she didn't dare look toward Craven. She could feel his anger accelerating, the electricity swarming his sword and hands sparking even brighter, popping in her ears.

"Weren't Aveo's brother and six of his cousins in that ballroom?" Richard asked. "How many Draconian nobles were in there with you? How many of those people did you go to lessons with as children, and fight alongside in the Five Realm War as adults? What about the Fae that were there? Queen Cleo's daughter, do you remember her? Not even her superior Magic could keep you from having to act. But you'd made a pact, and the scent of their frying bodies still taints these halls to this. day."

Without warning, a thread of electricity shot straight between Ash and Aveo, sailing right for the masochistic monster standing at the end of the hall. He swerved at the last second, causing it to land inside a cell instead, bouncing from wall to wall until it imploded, sending shreds of purple crackling light in various directions, one sailing straight back toward them.

Ash held out her hand, trusting in the Amulet to deter it back where it belonged, straight inside Richard's black heart. It ricocheted off her power, changing directions once more, barreling toward the treasonous bastard. It hit him, sending him shivering, dropping whatever he'd held in his hands.

A head.

Humphrey's head.

A mortified scream escaped Ash as she held out the Scepter, unleashing every ounce of power on the adviser before he had a chance to recover from the shock. He was thrown into a cell, the door slamming, locking behind him. She stormed forward, refusing to look at the head of her friend on the ground, and brought one steaming hand to the lock, melting it beyond measure.

There was no chance that Richard would escape if he'd even managed to survive her strike.

Afterward, Ash sank to her knees, struggling to regain control of her breathing. She refused to look behind her, to see Humphrey's wide, fearful eyes, empty of all signs of life.

Aveo approached her from behind, placing both of his hands on her shoulders. Behind them, Craven started to inform the others what had happened.

"We have a specialist down," he explained, every word trembling. "After an encounter with Richard in the dungeons, we discovered that he previously killed Humphrey. Cause of death was decapitation. Richard has since been detained, locked in a cell by Ash. She melted the lock. If he's not dead yet, he will be when we crumble this castle."

LUCINDA STOPPED DEAD IN HER TRACKS AT THE SOUND OF THE NEWS, tears immediately pricking at her amber eyes. Humphrey was dead. Of course, she'd known that the odds of everyone she cared for surviving this treacherous battle were slim to none. But, like a fool, she had hoped they all would.

Later, once the battle was won, she would mourn her old friend. But for now, she had three targets she had yet to find. It was crucial that she did before they had a chance to harm anyone else that she loved.

There was no sign of Veda or Jax, but Lucinda had sensed a power that could only belong to someone like Soroya on more than one occasion throughout her hunt.

"Are you alright?" Malachai asked, his question clearly directed toward the party inside the castle. "Does anyone need any medical attention?"

"All we need is therapy," Ash retorted.

"Join the club," Cooper told her.

"Is everyone in position?" Marcus ground out. "Alistair, is Lilly ready?"

"Ready for what?" Lucinda asked. Had her bug been off? Did she miss something? Perhaps she'd heard it all but was too busy tracking Soroya to notice. She was currently nearing the city square, where the fighting was the thickest. Pandora ripped into one another, some good and some bad. The Elves and Draconians focused on the Witches since they weren't sure which beasts to attack. Morghan whizzed past the Sorceress, a blur of gray fur amidst a sea of black.

A black Arebus Arrow sailed past Lucinda's face, driving into the heart of an Elf. She stilled, summoning her scythe from her mindspace. She was in Lincoln's range. But, if he didn't see her, he wouldn't know that she was. And, if she could sneak up on him, she might be able to spell him to sleep, giving Malachai and Quinn time to inject him with the cure.

All Lucinda needed to do was figure out where, exactly, Lincoln was.

Quietly, Lucinda snuck around the block, following the sound of firing arrows. She gripped her scythe in one hand, and her wand in the other. "I'm approaching Lincoln," she whispered, hoping someone heard her.

"Fall back," Marcus ordered, close enough for Lucinda to hear him both through the bug in her ear *and* in person. She froze, her gaze darting in every direction. "Let Lilly do her job. Right now, every one of our targets is staying close to him. Soroya included. Once Lilly takes his bow, we can all strike at once."

Lucinda's eyes widened. How had she missed all of that? She chose not to ponder it and instead dropped into a crouch, peering around the side of a building, catching sight of Lincoln firing arrow after arrow. Both Ryole and Glen were nearby, cutting down anyone that dared to get close. Soroya stood, cloaked in black, observing the battle from a rooftop.

Smirking, Lucinda thought of the *perfect* spell to take her down. She readied herself, the words to complete it resting on the tip of her tongue.

"We're close. Get ready," Alistair ordered.

"Oh, I've never been *more* ready," Lucinda sneered, twirling her wand.

78

*L*incoln could sense them coming. He knew they were there, surrounding him. However, he chose not to shoot. He chose to appear oblivious, firing only at Elves, Draconians, and Pandora that dared to strike at him. Whatever they were planning, it wouldn't work. Between him, Ryole, Glen, and Soroya, the Allies didn't stand a chance.

At least, that was until a Dragon flew overhead.

Ryole and Glen scattered, Soroya vanishing in the blink of an eye, leaving Lincoln to his demise. His blood boiled like molten magma, racing through his veins. Rage coiled deep in his gut, flames licking up his throat. "Cowards!" he roared, turning around in a slow circle, searching for his next target. If he was to soon become a Dragon's dinner, he'd get one last kill first.

Lincoln's eyes fell on the Archer he'd once shot down inside the castle, perched on a rooftop *just* outside of his radius. Cursing beneath his breath, he loaded his bow, searching for a closer target. He caught sight of a certain enchanted sword. Whitefire. A beacon in the darkness.

Chuckling beneath his breath, Lincoln prepared to let loose his next arrow, but, before he could release it, his bow was torn from his grip. The Archer froze, watching it rise upward, landing in the grip of a young girl perched on the jet-black Dragon hovering above. His quiver was next, taken while he was still overcome with shock at the sight of her glowing blue eyes.

Snarling, Lincoln knew he wouldn't survive that battle without a replacement. Lucky enough for him, he knew where to find one. He started to run, as fast as his Immortal body would allow, stealing a short sword from a fallen warrior on his way. He kept to the shadows, pushing toward his destination with all his might. The Allies would catch him if he wasn't fast enough. He *needed* to be fast enough.

"Lincoln, *stop!*" someone bellowed. Whoever it was, Lincoln didn't care.

Lincoln had prepared for this night for months. He wouldn't let one little bitch with the ability to move things with her mind ruin his moment of glory. He would *get* that second bow, no matter how. And with it, he would kill every single Ally until there were none left. Until every threat to his king was vanquished.

The second Archer dropped from the rooftop in an attempt to intercept him. The Realm Sorceress rounded the corner behind him. Vincent VanCamp followed her. There were more Allies coming, likely intending to block him in. They would fail.

In one quick movement, Lincoln whipped the short sword at the second Archer's throat, reveling in the sight of it barreling through his flesh. He fell to his knees, his bow falling out of his grip, the arrows in his quiver scattering onto the cobblestone street.

"*No!*" the Sorceress shrieked, but before she had a chance to retaliate, Lincoln snatched the bow and quiver and turned in the opposite direction, pushing past anyone that tried to stop him.

Penelope hadn't taken a deep breath since the battle had begun. All she could do was stare at the screen displaying all of the specialist's photos and vitals, her hand constantly hovering above the button that would signal an alarm for aid. Ebony and Hartford did the same across the room, the former biting her nails.

One second Humphrey was fine, and the next he'd flatlined.

Penelope wasn't given a chance to press the button. He was alive, and then he wasn't. The transmission Craven had admitted less than fifteen minutes later had explained what had happened. Richard.

The Healers crowded around her wept instantly, but Penelope couldn't bring herself to. She needed to focus, because the next time someone went into a critical condition, she would hit that button. She would save them because it was all she could do.

When the alarms started blaring, and Cooper's picture started flashing red, Penelope brought her fist down onto that button so hard that she could have broken it entirely. Healers started reaching for their bags, zipping up their uniform jackets. The portal sphere one of Lucinda's Sorcerers had lent them sat ready on the table.

"Malachai's already on scene," Ebony announced, turning up the transmission so they could hear what was happening.

"He's bleeding out too quickly," the Pandora said, his words hurried and laced with panic. "I can't stop it. Nothing I'm trying is working."

"Describe the injury," Ebony demanded, her voice cool and calm.

"Lincoln threw a sword through his fucking throat," Lucinda revealed.

"I don't know how his head is still attached," Vincent said, his voice little more than a whisper. "What can I do?"

Penelope's heart cracked, her jaw dropping, tears beginning to slip from her eyes.

"Anything!" Quinn bellowed. "Do anything."

A sob began to creep up Penelope's throat.

"That's a fatal injury, even for a Draconian," Ebony explained, placing both of her palms on her desk, leaning forward, her eyes shut tight. "Malachai, you know that the most you can do is keep him comfortable until he passes."

"I refuse to believe that," Malachai shot back at her. "There has to be *something*. Some sort of spell."

"His vitals are dropping even further," Hartford warned.

"There's no spell that can keep someone from dying," Lucinda argued.

"Then what the fuck is the purpose of living in a Galaxy with Magic if you can't use it when you fucking need it," Malachai seethed.

"Bite him," Penelope suggested. "Draconian Venom kept him from death before. Pandora venom should be able to do the same. *Bite him.*"

Malachai didn't respond, and Penelope soon realized why. Cooper had flatlined as those words sailed past her lips. He'd died. Right there, when so many people were working to save him. He was gone. That picture of him on the screen was now boarded in red.

"Call it," Ebony directed, forcing the words through clenched teeth, tears spilling down her cheeks.

"We have an Ally down," Malachai said, each word shaking. "Cooper McBride. Cause of death... Lincoln McBride. Time of death, half-past seven p.m., seventy-first day of Winter Solstice, year one-thousand and forty-nine."

NOTHING WOULD STOP QUINN FROM HUNTING LINCOLN DOWN AND beating him to a pulp *before* Malachai had a chance to cure him. Quinn would prefer not to cure him at all. He wanted him dead and didn't care whether they shared blood, or that he was under the influence of some memory erasing serum. What he'd done was unforgivable. But, if he *had* to be cured, that at least he would eventually return to normal, only to suffer because of what he'd done to his own brother.

"You need to slow down," Malachai insisted. "Lincoln won't hesitate to kill you, either."

"He'd fucking better," Quinn shot over his shoulder. "Because, if he doesn't, he'll be forced to live with me holding this over his head for the rest of his pathetic life."

Malachai didn't respond. Instead, he picked up the pace, now walking beside the Archer, his red eyes gaze darting in every direction. Most of this part of Solaris had been reduced to ashes, yet the Dark Army still fought, desperately trying to win a battle where they couldn't possibly be the victor. By now, Ash, Aveo, and Craven were closing in on Xavier. Any second, they'd hear the fight begin. Two unfathomably powerful beings, at each other's throats. Both destined for what would occur between them on this night.

"There he is," the Pandora said, grabbing Quinn by the hood of his uniform, ripping him backward. "We need to be *extremely* careful about how we proceed. If he sees us, he'll kill us both."

Quinn didn't really care if Lincoln tried to kill him. So, he wrenched himself free of Malachai's grip and barreled toward the Archer, a mighty roar ripping from his lungs. His body flew into Lincoln's, tackling him down onto the cobblestone street, sending Cooper's bow flying out of his grip. Morghan appeared in front of them, snarling down at Lincoln, his sharp teeth just inches away from his throat, his claws digging into both of his shoulders.

"Now!" Quinn ordered, just in time for Malachai to slide onto his knees, the syringe ready in his hand. He watched, trembling with fury as the Pandora drove it into his brother's neck, knocking him out cold just a mere second before a hard force knocked into him, sending him and Morghan both sprawling in different directions. The Wolf flew through a wall, weakened by fire, the sound of his yelps echoing throughout the night.

Staggering to his feet, Quinn found himself standing on wobbling legs, face to face with one of Lucinda's targets. Soroya. Malachai stood over Lincoln's unconscious body, sword drawn and ready. For a split second, Quinn felt terrible for him, before he remembered how cruel siblings could be.

"You can't stop this, Soroya. It's already done," Malachai informed her. "It's over."

Soroya snickered, examining their surroundings, eyeing the battle still raging around them. "It doesn't *look* like it's over," she claimed. "Your precious High Queen has *no idea* what she's walking into."

"She does," Malachai assured her, lip curling above his teeth. "She knows *exactly* how to kill him. And she will."

"If only he were her only problem," Soroya drawled, the entirety of her eyes beginning to turn black. Quinn watched, jaw dropping with horror as her veins started to burn like embers, her complexion paling beyond comprehension, until it was translucent. Horns began to protrude from her skull, her long black hair unraveling from its braid, flowing with the breeze like a sheet of silk. "You see, brother mine, once you abandoned us, and Savron proved himself unworthy, the responsibility to carry on our family line fell upon *my* shoulders."

Pandora started to scatter, as did the Elves and Draconians nearby. Quinn couldn't bring himself to move.

Soroya's haunting, empty gaze shifted over to Quinn. "I'm sorry about your brother. Truly, I am. What a waste." Lightning crackled through the sky, striking in dozens of different places around them. Even the Witch seemed startled by it, her lips pressing into a thin, grim line. "It seems that either backup has arrived, or that I have another traitorous bastard in my midst."

A man cloaked in a black hood that shielded his face stepped out of a nearby alley, surveying the sight set before him before uttering a word. "Soroya," he said, inclining his head by way of greeting.

"Storm," she replied, baring her teeth. "What are you doing?"

No one missed the wand in the man's hand, and the way it glowed with a spell ready to be released.

"Just making sure you don't need my assistance, is all."

Soroya snorted with disbelief, threads of pitch-black mist beginning to swarm her fingers. "I don't."

"Are you sure?" Storm countered.

"Positive."

Quinn sucked in a breath, filling his lungs to capacity. Malachai looked between the two, as if trying to decipher the situation unfolding before them. Storm was a threat to both parties. He made that extremely clear with his entrance. But, why Soroya, who had clearly been blessed with the same power her father had, was so unnerved was yet to be determined.

"Does Jax know that you're here?" Soroya inquired, taking a nervous step back.

"She has enough problems on her plate," he informed her, fishing in his cloak for something. "She sent me to fight in her place. What a treat for you."

Quinn and Malachai shared a wary look, but neither dared to move a muscle. The Pandora remained where he was, standing over Lincoln. Quinn kept his back pressed against the building he'd been thrown into. Morghan had yet to resurface.

Something fell out of Storm's pocket. A clear, shining crystal. He pretended not to notice, even as Soroya scrambled away from it, her features the epitome of horror. Quinn watched her, his brow furrowing with confusion. Who would be afraid of a rock?

Soroya continued to stare at it, holding out her hand as if it were about to jump up and leap down her throat. Yet, while she was transfixed, worried about the crystal, someone else took the opportunity to take her down.

Thousands of crystal arrows came from every direction, striking Soroya down. One flew through her right eye, the next few into her heart, and before long, she was impaled by so many that Quinn was unable to see her form through them all.

Malachai had looked away, the lump in his throat bobbing.

Storm vanished.

Lucinda came forward, examining her kill.

"I'm sorry," Quinn said to the Pandora.

"Don't be," he ground out, walking toward the wall Morghan had crashed through. "Just get Lincoln to the tree. I'll get Morghan."

62

After their encounter with Richard down in the dungeons, Ash and the others made their way up to the first floor. Their comms died a second later, leaving nothing but static in their ears. They found Humphrey's headless corpse shoved into a corner, blood pooling beneath it. Ash's stomach lurched, her hand flying to cover her mouth. She squeezed her eyes shut, holding in a scream threatening to rip from her lungs.

Craven turned his back on the sight, his complexion ghastly. Aveo did the same, his lips disappearing into a thin line.

"Give me one good reason not to go back down there and tear Richard limb from limb. *Slowly,*" Aveo demanded, his fingers curling into trembling, white-knuckled fists.

The only answer Aveo received was the changing atmosphere. The air became thicker, the shadows stronger. Ash froze, the hairs on the back of her neck rising as goosebumps pebbled along her flesh.

Craven and Aveo drew closer to her, their sharp gazes shifting about the long corridor. A harsh breeze swept past them, blowing out every sconce along the hall, leaving them with only the Moonlight streaming through the windows to light their way.

Soft, eerie laughter echoed down the corridor. Ash peered down it, into the Darkness at the end.

"Craven, turn on the lights," Ash requested through clenched teeth.

They flickered a moment later, momentarily revealing a figure standing at the end of the corridor with a familiar, pale face. Ash's breath hitched, her connection to the Amulet around her neck growing stronger. But the next flash of light revealed that he'd vanished. To where, Ash didn't know. She wasn't sure that she wanted to find out.

"He's toying with us," Aveo snarled.

"Of course, he is," Craven seethed. "Why wouldn't he?"

Ash cleared her throat, tightening her grip around the Scepter's staff before taking a few steps forward. "We should have expected nothing less from him. But we can't stand here and wait for him to strike first. So, let's go. We can't drag this on all night. We still have a portal to destroy." With that, she pushed onward, the Moonlight emitting from her Scepter leading the way. Aveo and Craven followed without question. They had trained for this. They were ready.

Halfway down the corridor, they passed a row of windows, offering them a view of the battle raging outside. Solaris was burning. Flames roared, ashes mixing in with the falling snow. The cobblestone streets ran red with blood. Bodies of Elves, Draconians, and Sorcerers littered the ground. Pandora tore at each other's throats. Arebus Arrows flew in three different directions.

"Which way?" Craven asked. They'd arrived at the end of the corridor, where they were faced with a choice. They could either go right or left. The blueprints Ash had studied of the castle told her that if she were to head to the right, she'd eventually find her way to the Throne Room, where the final showdown would undoubtedly take place.

However, Ash's gut screamed to go left.

"We head left," she declared, turning in that direction.

"Why?" Aveo asked. "The Throne Room is the other way."

"That's where he *thinks* we'll go," Ash said, biting her inner cheek. "Being predictable is what'll get us killed in a fight like this. We need to keep him on his toes."

"I'm not sure that's possible," Craven whispered. "'Do you think Aiden Cavanaugh marched into Xanthius's Black Fortress with the intent to *keep him on his toes*?'"

Ash scowled over her shoulder at her former Mentor. "That was different." *Just like it was different for Jay. At least* he *was able to kill Xander in his sleep.* "Aiden had a Dragon."

Coincidentally, the castle started to rumble as if struck by an earthquake. Ash hurried forward, yearning to get to the nearest window. She sagged with relief the second that she did.

"And we have thirty," Aveo mentioned with a snort. "And look, they've all arrived."

Twenty minutes had passed without any sign of Xavier. The castle halls were empty. No sconces were lit. The lights flickered endlessly, giving off the impression the once beautiful castle was no more than a haunted shell.

Ash paused at the end of each hall, looking both ways. Every time she ascended into darkness, she struggled to contain the panic crawling at her insides. Her heart thundered behind her sternum so loudly that she was sure it had become a distraction for her comrades.

"We're approaching the east wing," Craven announced in a whisper. "This was where your ancestors resided. The royal dining hall is just down this hall."

Nodding, Ash swallowed against the lump crowding her throat. She desperately needed to get a hold of herself. If she was so afraid of dark, empty halls, there was no way she'd be able to withstand facing Xavier.

Someone put a hand on Ash's shoulder, and she all but leaped straight out of her skin. "Relax," Aveo said calmly. "There are three of us, and only one of him."

"Yeah, well neither one of us has the soul of a being so ancient and terrifying, that the Sovereign created the Underworld just to keep it contained," Craven argued.

"Says the only man able to get close enough to Xavier to steal something and live," Aveo countered.

The sight of a shadow darting into the dining hall caused Ash to skid to a stop. "What was that?"

"What was what?" Craven and Aveo replied in unison.

"That shadow," Ash informed them. "You didn't see it move?"

"There are shadows everywhere, Ash," Craven reminded her, moving his enchanted sword back and forth, calling them all to the shining obsidian blade.

The orb at the end of Ash's Scepter grew bright, as if the weapon had noticed it too. A shiver slithered down her spine, goosebumps pebbling along her flesh. "Something's here," she declared, sapphire eyes narrowing at the dining hall's entrance.

After a quick glance at her comrades, Ash started toward the dining hall, ignoring the fear now stroking against her spine. She paused just in front of the entrance, sucking in a deep breath, holding it for a time before releasing it all in one huff.

The Scepter's light grew even stronger, as if to tell her that they had company.

I can do this, Ash told herself, turning around to face the dining hall. At first, all she saw was a long, extravagant table surrounded by twenty empty chairs. Cobwebs dripped from the crystal chandeliers hanging from the ceiling.

The moment Ash stepped inside, her vision distorted, leaving her in the dark. Her heart leaped into overdrive, panic beginning to set in. "Craven!" she called, turning around to reach for where he'd been standing behind her. "Aveo?" Her voice cracked around the name. "I-I can't see."

Ash heard the muddled voice of someone responding, but they sounded as if they were all underwater. Her breath hitched in her throat and remained there, choking her. She fought to regain control of herself, but it was impossible. Whatever trap she'd walked into could very well be the end of her.

A cold, wet sensation surrounded Ash. She shivered from head to toe, fearful tears puddling in her eyes as she was thrust through the surface of some sort of indoor pool. She gasped, air filling her lungs as she swam toward the edge of it and pulled herself out. She sat on the stone floor for an extra moment and scanned her surroundings while she worked to collect herself. Windows lined the room, and through them Ash saw the remnants of what was once a large city. All that remained was smoldering rubble. Magma moved across the ground in smoking rivers. The sky looked as if it was on fire. The sight of it all led Ash's jaw to drop, every one of her muscles growing rigid.

Wherever Xavier had brought Ash, it wasn't in Idona.

Pushing to her feet, Ash approached the windows and gazed out into the wreckage. Charred bodies were floating in the lava, their bones disintegrating right before her eyes. Her eyes bulged, a horrified shout building in her throat as she staggered away, unwilling to watch anymore.

"Craven," Ash called again. "Aveo?"

There was no sign of her comrades. Ash was alone, which was the *last* thing she wanted to be. Sucking in a breath, she started toward one of the entrances and made her way further into what appeared to be some sort of fortress, rather than a castle. Cracks seared through the floor and walls, steam pouring through them. The ground trembled every few seconds, leaving her stomach churning with fear as she started toward what was once a grand staircase. She'd made it halfway up when she encountered a large gap, likely caused by one of the tremors.

Ash would have to jump if she wanted to make it to the next level. Frowning, she looked down, noting the lava visible through the cracks in the floor. Her main objective was to get as far away from it as possible, so she took a few steps back and sucked in a breath in preparation for her giant leap. She cleared it, just barely. Her foot slipped, and she caught herself on the railing, praying that it would hold. She hoisted herself up while whispering a prayer beneath her breath and climbed the rest of the staircase.

The next level was seemingly untouched, but the tremors became worse. Ash fought to keep her footing as she started down a long corridor. She made it halfway through when she heard something roar. Her heart took a flying leap off a cliff as it rattled in her ears. She forced herself to keep walking, no matter how badly she wanted to run in the other direction.

Ash made it to the end of the corridor, where she turned right, only to find out that half of the fortress had been blown to bits. She walked down what was left of a hall and out into the open, where she was provided with a horrifying view of what was beyond. A stark-white dragon was barreling through the air, its Rider holding a familiar, enchanted sword. Dragon's Breath.

"Aiden Cavanaugh," Ash whispered, bringing a fist to her heart.

"Enjoying the view?" an eerie voice asked.

Ash jumped, whirling around to find a male figure made of pure, black mist standing behind her.

"Hurry, or you'll miss the best part," the figure urged, pointing back to the Dragon. Ash returned her attention to it, just in time to watch it dip from the skies, sailing right toward a monstrous man below. Ash's skin crawled at the sight of him. Burning orange veins glowed in stark contrast against his jet-black flesh. Horns protruded from his skull, as sharp as the claws he had for hands.

Xanthius.

Ash held her breath as she watched Aiden pull a shining, silver dagger free from his boot. She could hardly believe what she was witnessing as he whipped it through the air, sending it sailing straight toward Xanthius's heart. She flinched when it struck him, exhaling slowly as he dropped to his knees, grasping at the dagger. His form began to transition back to its mortal state as he took in his final, labored breaths.

"All it took was a simple dagger, and a bit of luck," the figure drawled. "Yet this event sparked a fire that still burns a millennium later. The Bonaventures are cockroaches. They've survived all these years, scurrying in the shadows, inciting an infestation. Every once in a while, someone like you, Aiden, or Jay comes around to put them in their place. You might very well succeed today, but it won't be the end. Another will rise, and then another, and the fire will burn until there's nothing left to fight for. The Sovereign herself couldn't stop this, and you won't be able to either."

Ash opened her mouth to argue, but everything went dark, just like it had before. She found herself enduring the same, strange process, until she was thrust back into her own time. This time, she landed on a cold, hard marble floor.

"Oh, there you are," Xavier said, causing Ash to open her eyes and leap to her feet, only to find him sitting upon his stolen throne. "Tell me, did you enjoy your glimpse into the past? Do you understand what you're *really* up against now?"

Nodding, Ash felt her Amulet grow hot against her flesh as it began to cast its sapphire light around the room. The Scepter arrived in her grip a second later, the orb at its end burning so brightly that the Dark King squinted against it.

"It's over, Xavier," she insisted. "There will never be another Dark King, or another Messenger. This war ends with you and me. Right now."

MARCUS HADN'T STUCK AROUND TO WITNESS COOPER'S DEATH. Instead, he took off after Ryole, chasing the bastard across the city, Whitefire gleaming in his grip. He pushed all thoughts of the fallen Archer from his mind, focusing on his own task instead. This wasn't the first time the Mentor had lost a comrade in battle. He was certain that it wouldn't be the last. What mattered in the end was that those good men and women hadn't died in vain. That they succeeded, no matter the cost.

Ryole transitioned into a bird, flying onto a rooftop. Marcus snarled, leaping onto the side of the building, using loose bricks as stepping-stones, hoisting himself up and onto the roof where the Commander waited for him with a sinister smirk.

"It's a pity about that little friend of yours," Ryole drawled, racing for hilt of the sword strapped along his spine. "Then again, you can only escape death so many times. Cooper had it coming. And so do you."

Baring his teeth, Marcus took a step forward, twirling Whitefire. "You must have mistaken me with yourself."

Constance's legs were threatening to give in. She'd never run so fast in all her life, weaving through hordes of Pandora, Elves, Draconians, and Sorcerers. She ditched her cloak less than ten minutes after she started her run toward Marcus. Alrich had done the same, his eyes now blue instead of their usual red.

They were able to track Marcus all the way across the city, to an abandoned building. The sound of clashing swords and the heat of flames greeted Constance upon her arrival. Using a tracking spell, she was able to see which way Marcus had gone. He'd climbed straight up the side of the building, which was something she couldn't risk doing in her condition. So, she decided to enter the warehouse instead. There *had* to be a roof access somewhere.

"That's Ryole up there," Alrich warned, on her heels as usual. "Maybe we should leave him to handle this himself."

A cry of agony pierced through the atmosphere, the sound of bones snapping following not a second later. Constance cringed, pushing through empty crates and boxes on her way to the stairs.

"I'm seriously advising you *not* to intervene," Alrich hissed.

Something in Constance's gut, perhaps even her *soul*, told her that she needed to. So, she started the climb, hurrying up the steps, her gaze fixed on the exit out onto the roof. Halfway up, she snatched the Phoenix Blade from her back and started to twirl it. Ryole wouldn't stand a chance against *two* enchanted swords.

One swift kick sent the door leading out onto the roof off its hinges, flying into none other than Soroya. The Witch hit the shingles, groaning.

"Your entrance could have been kinder," Soroya snarled, pushing herself to her feet, blood seeping from a split in her lip. "What took you so long? I haven't seen you all night."

Constance's thoughts swarmed, searching for a spell that would apprehend Soroya before she had a chance to inflict anymore damage. She settled on something simple and started to spin the blade in her hands even faster, sending Soroya into a confused gaze.

She staggered toward the roof's ledge, gripping her head. Her knees wobbled, causing her to sway back and forth.

Faster, Constance pleaded, twirling the blade as hard as her muscles would allow. Across the roof, Marcus and Ryole continued to fight ruthlessly, the former's right wrist hanging on by skin alone. His eyes were glazed, swirling even. Blood leaked from a wound along his temple.

"Alrich, get in there!" Constance demanded.

Ryole was *fast*. Faster than any being Constance had ever seen. Every movement he made was as fluid as water, taking Marcus by surprise. Against an opponent like that, it didn't matter what sort of weapon you held. Constance ground her teeth, returning her focus to Soroya the second Alrich advanced, interrupting the scrimmage.

"S-stop!" Soroya screamed, stumbling further toward the roof's edge.

"No," Constance retorted, storming forward, allowing the blade to stop in time to drive it across Soroya's chest, sending her toppling over, falling onto the ground.

The sound of animalistic snarls flooded Constance's ears as she turned away from her former opponent, rushing toward where Marcus had fallen, bloodied, bruised, and broken. Alrich and Ryole were going head-to-head, two superior Pandora at each other's throats.

"Hey," Constance whispered, pulling Marcus further away from the altercation. "Are you still with me?"

A groan was her only answer. Marcus whipped his head to the side, revealing something shining in his ear—some sort of communication's device. Without words, she fished it out and put it in her own, hoping she could figure out how to make it work.

"Hello?" Constance asked. "Is anyone there?"

"I am," an unfamiliar male voice replied. "Who is this?"

"Constance Waters," she replied, swallowing hard against her nerves. "Marcus Bonaventure is gravely injured. He can't continue. We're on the rooftop of an empty building a few miles north of the square."

"Constance?" Sam's voice was like music to her ears. "Are you alright?"

"Yes," she replied. "But Marcus isn't, and Alrich is still fighting with Ryole. We are in desperate need of assistance."

"Who's closest?" the first voice inquired.

"I can get there in less than two," a new voice insisted. "We're within three miles. Tell Alrich to hit the ground."

"Hit the ground!" Constance roared.

Both Alrich and Ryole ceased their fighting, just in time for the latter to get a black Arebus Arrow through the throat. Constance's eyes bulged, her throat tightening at the sight of the Commander stumbling backward, gripping at the wound, blood spilling over his lips as he fell over the roof's edge to his death.

A few moments later, the massive Black Dragon that Constance had once seen save Crane hovered above her. "Thank the Moons," she breathed at the sight of Lilly McBride and her glowing blue eyes.

80

Aveo had watched a cloud of black smoke envelope Ash before she disappeared right before his eyes. He'd immediately tried to step into the dining hall, but Craven had pulled him back to prevent him from falling into the same trap. "The last thing Ash would want is for us to follow her into a trap. We need to be smart about this. The odds are that Xavier moved her somewhere else in the castle to separate us, and all we have to do is figure out where," Craven explained, his gaze darting between both ends of the hall. "I say we go this way, toward the suites."

"Why would we do that, when we know the fight will probably take place in the Throne Room?" Aveo asked, starting in the opposite direction. "We'll go there and wait."

"We *think* that the final fight will take place in the Throne Room," Craven replied, chasing after him. "What if we're wrong? What if it'll take place outside, somewhere in the city?"

Aveo might have laughed at the question under different circumstances. "If there's one thing that Xavier *isn't* going to do, it's subject himself to the armies. Trust me, he's still in this castle."

"Alright, but what if Ash isn't?" Craven countered, now walking at Aveo's side, picking up the pace to keep up. "What if he moved her elsewhere? She could be anywhere in the Realm."

Slowing his pace, Aveo considered that idea. "You really think that he'd just *remove* Ash from the equation?"

Craven released a frustrated grunt. "I don't know. Maybe he wasn't expecting an army this size, and he's doing whatever it takes to bide his time. Right now, I think that whatever he's doing is working. We can't proceed without Ash. We lost the bloody Messenger *right* before she was going to fulfill the Prophecy. We're screwed."

Aveo snarled, whirling around to grab Craven's shoulders and shake some sense into him. "We are *not* screwed. Ash gave us each one of those daggers. If we can't find her, then we're going to have to finish this ourselves."

"That isn't the Prophecy," Craven reminded him. "We're just... helpers. We *need* Ash, and if we don't find her—"

"We're going to find her," Aveo insisted, releasing the Draconian from his grip. "Get yourself together, Amsterdam. *You're* the only other person who's been in this position before. You're the closest thing to Ash that we can get. *I* need you. If I don't return home to Penelope—" he stopped himself, sucking in a deep breath. "She can't lose me too, Craven."

Craven nodded, swallowing hard. "Right," he replied. "Let's make her proud, but I swear you'd better name your first son after me or so help me—"

"Let's not get ahead of ourselves," Aveo interjected.

The pair started onward, combing through the castle, searching for any sign of Ash or Xavier. They found nothing. The place was empty, aside from shadows and terrifying memories. Every time they passed a window, they got a glimpse of the battle raging outside. The Dragons were wreaking havoc on what remained of the Dark Army. Witches and Sorcerers were still going head-to-head, while the Elves and Draconians secured the city walls. No one would escape. Xavier and his people would experience the same pain High Queen Meera and her people had the night the Idonian Kingdom fell eighteen years ago.

81

"What a shame that you've been separated from your entourage," Xavier crooned, rising from his throne. "All of your predecessors were strong enough to face the Dark One on their own. Then again, they were men, not a woman the size of a pixie."

Ash sucked on her teeth, wiggling her fingers around her Scepter. "Are we going to stand here and chat or are we going to finish this?" she asked, her sapphire eyes narrowing into sites. "I'd prefer to be on my way sooner rather than later, if it's all the same to you."

Xavier's lips curled into a mischievous smirk. "In a rush, are we?" In a flash, he was in front of her. Ash stood her ground, staring up into his empty eyes. She buried any ounce of fear threatening to overtake her. This was her fate, and it was time for her to face it.

"Aren't you scared, child?" Xavier inquired, his hot breath dusting over her cheeks.

"Aren't you?"

"Fear is not an emotion that I'm familiar with," he replied, reaching to run his finger down the Amulet. "But joy is. And I'm so pleased that you've brought this back to me."

Taking a step back, Ash allowed a sliver of power from the Amulet to seep out of her. Invisible, yet powerful. She felt it reach toward Xavier, snagging on his cloak just enough to get a glimpse at the shirt he wore beneath. Black, still concealing his heart, but she didn't need to *see* it to know where it was. She could feel it, beating evenly, as if this encounter were no more than a chance to catch up over cups of steeped tea.

Xavier shivered, his teasing smile transitioning into a frown. "Are you sure you want this, Ashlynn?" he purred. "You can surrender. Join us. Amorian blood runs through your veins as well. We can avenge our fallen Realm. *Together*. We can bring the true king *home*."

Ash's heart dropped at the sound of his words. "No part of my blood is Amorian."

"Don't play daft with me," he snapped. "You know very well how your mother's soul came to be intertwined with my own. You just haven't dared to learn the truth. I can give you all the answers you need, and more. Meera VanCamp was once called Meera *Phantom*. She's the daughter of Idona's High Priestess, Irina, and had a sister named Kiara, whom I married and produced two children with. She had a son before we were married, of course. Savron. What a waste, that one."

Ash shook her head, refusing to believe a word of it.

"Your mother was destined to become a Grand White Witch...one so powerful that she could have replaced her mother as High Priestess and ruled over this Realm. She could have grown to be more powerful than Queen Cleo, had she not run away to Solaris in hopes to start a new life. She tried to bury her past, but I discovered her secrets the moment we met. An Amorian *always* knows another Amorian."

"Stop dragging this on!" Ash roared as Xavier turned his back on her, hints of orange beginning to glow in his veins. "Either fight me or stand. The. Fuck. Down. I don't have time for history lessons. I'm far too busy trying to *make* history!"

As Xavier turned back around, a wall of Darkness began to rise up from the floor, stretching all the way up to the cathedral ceiling, swallowing the entire Throne Room whole. Within seconds, Xavier was no longer recognizable. He'd become something else. Something ancient, powerful, and unfathomably dangerous.

The robes Xavier had been wearing melted away, the fabric not at all meant for such a being. His heart was visible, glowing orange, a beacon for the dagger Ash snatched from her hip.

The beast Xavier had become snarled at the sight of the weapon in her hand. His gaze fixed upon it, his blackened, rotting fangs bared as he snarled. He stepped forward, knocking the throne aside, the crown resting upon the cushion crashing to the ground. He stormed forward, claws outstretched, pure Darkness seeping out of his every pore.

Ash moved, but it wasn't fast enough. He caught her by the sleeve of her uniform, claws tearing through the impenetrable fabric as if it were made of butter. He snatched her wrist, flinging it outward, sending her dagger skittering across the marble floors. "You underestimate me," he seethed, his reeking breath invading Ash's nostrils. "This entire time, you've underestimated me. You think that because I've hidden inside this castle for so long, that I am incapable of defending myself. That isn't true. Not in the slightest. I stay in here because you Idonians are not *worthy* of my attention!" he thundered, tossing her aside, throwing her onto the floor with the amount of effort it took to squash a bug beneath one's boot. "Why would I waste my time picking off such weaklings? Why bother when you're so fucking good at destroying yourselves? You might think you're united, but it's for this night alone. You will *never* be united. Either the Elves will find a way to wage war against the Draconians, or vice versa. The Pandora will be reduced to absolutely nothing, hunted by every Idonian, both Mortal and Immortal. No one will *accept* them after what they've done. That pretty little village you've built will be nothing more than smoke and ashes by the end of Spring Solstice, I can assure you. You're all wasting your time."

Ash glanced at where her Scepter lay a few feet away, her pulse pounding in her ears. Xavier followed her gaze and stormed forward. Cursing beneath her breath, Ash forced herself to her feet and managed to beat him to it in time to unleash the weapon's Moonlight upon him. A burning, white beam erupted from the Scepter's orb, sailing right toward his gut. The moment it collided with Xavier; the entire castle began to shake. The chandeliers hanging above them dropped, crashing onto the ground, sending particles of glass and metal flying in every direction.

Xavier roared as the Scepter's power pushed him backward, his orange veins burning brighter and brighter by the second as he fought to overpower it.

The dagger in Ash's boot was calling her name, but she couldn't reach for it without taking the Moonlight off of the king. She ground her teeth, desperately trying to think of what to do next. Before long, she realized that her only option was to let go of the Scepter and go for the dagger while hoping Xavier would be far too stunned to move so that she could throw it into his heart.

Just as Ash was about to drop the Scepter, she watched Aveo and Craven run into the Throne Room. Her heart leaped out of her chest, her shoulders slumping with relief as she met her Guardian's gaze. "Here," she called, tossing the Scepter over to him.

Aveo didn't show an ounce of fear. Instead, he caught the weapon and kept pouring the Moonlight into Xavier's terrifying form. A few moments later, Ash watched as Xavier started to transition back. He screamed at the top of his lungs, clearly trying to remain as he was, but the Moonlight was too strong.

Daring to smile, Ash looked toward Craven and pulled the dagger from her boot. He did the same, twirling it in his hands. She gave him a nod before taking off in the opposite direction of him. *This is going to work.* Ash knew it. She could tell by the way the Dark King slowed, the massive white beam driving him backward. He was far too busy focusing on how to push through it to notice two different daggers sailing straight to his heart.

The first one buried Xavier's shoulder, causing him to stumble. The second struck him in the side. A miss, but that didn't matter. Ash had one last dagger sheathed at her side, and she'd be damned if she missed the shot.

Without thinking, Ash took off, hanging her head, closing her eyes, and trusting in her aim. She let the last dagger loose, waiting to hear it pierce flesh. The second it did, she allowed her eyes to open, only to find that all of Xavier's power had abandoned him. Slowly, but surely. It evacuated, leaving him as a Mortal man with various fatal wounds.

Xavier fell onto his back, gripping the dagger driven into his chest. He sucked in a series of staggering breaths, choking on the blood crowding his throat. "Do you not realize that killing me means killing your own mother?" he managed to get out, his breaths becoming shallower and shallower by the second.

"My mother died two years ago," Ash retorted, unleashing the Amulet's blue fire upon him, burning him to a crisp. She waited until he was reduced to nothing but ash and one single, black heart to stop. Golden mist rose from the ashes, filtering through the air, sailing right for Ash, swarming around her in the form of a warm embrace before it sailed through the shattered window, off into the night beyond.

82

The time had come for Ash and Craven to head to the bell towers, but their comms had yet to come back to life, even after Xavier's suppressing power had vanished.

"We need to move," Craven insisted, a muscle feathering in his sharp jawline. "Every second we delay is another that puts the other four Realms in harm's way."

Nodding, Ash turned toward Aveo, holding her hand out for her Scepter. He didn't give it to her.

"No," Aveo said. "If I could use it on Xavier, I can use it to destroy the portal. You should go. You've done enough."

Ash shook her head, her stomach sinking with dread. "Aveo, this is why I was destined to retrieve the Scepter. Not just to nullify Xavier's power, but to destroy this portal. I can feel it in my bones. It's my destiny, not yours. You should go. Start getting people out of here. No more people should have to die tonight, Dark Army included."

"I'm your Guardian," he argued. "I can't willingly let you go and sacrifice yourself. You're right. Your destiny was to retrieve this Scepter, but that doesn't mean you have to be the one to wield it. Because *my* destiny was to protect *you*. Let me do that."

Shaking her head, Ash said, "I can't."

"Why not?" he growled. "And don't try to tell me it's because

Penelope needs me. Cooper will retrieve me. All I'm doing is putting you out of more harm's way and taking what remains of all this pressure off your shoulders."

"It's not that," Ash informed him, continuing to hold her hand out for the Scepter. "Please, give me my Scepter."

"No," he said, the word sharper than a knife. "You don't have to do this. Craven and I can handle it."

"You don't have a choice," Ash snarled, lowering her hand. "Give me my Scepter and get. Out. Of. Here."

"No," he repeated.

"Yes," Ash thundered.

"Why?" Aveo asked, his tone more demanding than ever. "Why you and not me?"

"Because," Ash started to explain, "you're the High King."

Aveo's jaw went slack, his bronze eyes growing wide. "*What?*"

"I chose you," Ash explained. "For a bunch of reasons, but most importantly, there isn't a person that I've met these last five months that is more dedicated to Idona than you are. I listed all the other reasons in my Will. You *have* to go. You're not my Guardian anymore, Aveo. You're Si Realtra's Guardian and my brother. So, please, let me do this so you can return to your wife, ascend to your throne, and restore peace to this Realm. *Please.*"

"Where's Aveo?" Vincent asked, storming toward Quinn. "Has anyone seen him?"

The first warning strike of electricity had sailed through the air less than five minutes ago. The Commander should have made it out by now. Quinn scanned the city for him but saw nothing.

"We don't know," Lucinda said, placing a calming hand on Vincent's shoulder. "But I'm sure he'll be here soon. Don't worry so much about Aveo. He knows how to handle himself. Instead, worry about Ash and Craven. They have no idea that their only chance of escape is—" she never finished her sentence. Instead, Quinn watched her gaze drift toward where Cooper's body was lying beside the lonely maple tree in the center of the field.

Willa landed nearby, and the Archer watched Alistair dismount before helping Lilly down, taking her by the hand and leading her toward where the Allies had gathered. He couldn't stomach how it felt to see Lincoln's bow strapped to her back.

Anastasia landed a second later, the massive red wyvern she'd flown upon all night immediately taking off into the skies, headed home just like all the other Dragons. She walked toward them, her expression grave. The second warning strike seared through the air, causing them all to flinch. Quinn could only hope that Constance was somewhere far away from there with Alrich and Sam, hurrying toward a safer place.

"It's starting," Malachai mentioned warily.

"It's ending," Lucinda whispered in response.

IT HAD ALL WOUND DOWN TO THAT MOMENT. EVERYTHING ASH AND Craven had worked for had led them to those two bell towers, throwing everything they had at the portal raging above them. The second her Moonlight met his electricity, Ash could feel the Realm shift. Those two substances were *not* supposed to be together, and it was clear as to why.

The power erupting above them was unlike any other Si Realtra had ever known. Ash found it difficult to keep her vision on her work, but all she could think of were Craven's last words, right after he'd hugged her and kissed her cheek. *It's alright Ash, I always knew that I wouldn't survive this Kingdom falling a second time.*

Before long, they realized that Cooper wasn't coming to retrieve them. There was only one explanation for his absence, and it shattered Ash's heart beyond repair. She'd looked toward Craven as soon as the realization hit her, only to find that he was watching her as well. He knew. These were the final moments of their lives.

Hot tears streamed from Ash's eyes as she prepared for their end.

I deserve this, Ash told herself, continuing to hold the Scepter up. *I did what Idona needed me to do, and now it's my turn to die.*

The bell tower Ash was standing on started to buckle beneath her. She could feel it giving way, sending her heart leaping into overdrive. Panic was setting in, but she didn't stop. Craven didn't either. They kept going, despite the castle trembling around them, threatening to send them falling to their deaths. Ash might be a Berserker but surrounded by such impeccable power that wouldn't make a difference. She'd be buried alive by rubble in a matter of minutes. That was her fate, and she accepted it.

The portal erupted around them, shattering entirely just as the bell towers snapped in unison. Ash refused to let go of her Scepter. She refused to stop shining her light until she hit the ground. She wanted the Allies watching out in the field, by that lonely tree, to know that she was with them until the bitter end. Her light would never go out. Even as she continued to fall, she stared up at the Three Moons, and she thanked them. Through them, her light would shine bright for the rest of time.

EPILOGUE

Ash's eyes fluttered open, her eyelids heavier than lead. Her entire body felt stiff, every single one of her bones aching. She didn't dare move. Instead, she stared above at the crystal ceiling and the bright twinkling lights shining down upon her.

People moved nearby, shuffling around, whispering.

Someone took Ash's hand, wrapping their warm grip gently around it. "You're awake," a familiar voice cooed.

Ash angled her head toward the voice, to view who stood at her bedside. Not just one person, but three. The first she knew, and the very sight of her sent tears springing to her eyes, steeling the breath straight out of her lungs. The second was familiar, in the sort of way that made Ash believe she'd seen her picture somewhere before. And the third was a man. A Fae. Aries.

"Mom?" Ash asked, choking on the word.

Eliza only smiled at her, pale blue eyes shining with tears.

"Am I dead?"

"No," the voice of a fourth person rang in Ash's ears. She turned her head in the direction it had come from, her eyes falling on a tall, beautiful male Elf with long black hair and shining silver eyes. "Not yet, anyway."

ACKNOWLEDGMENTS

Back in 2012, I had an idea. Low and behold, the Five Realm Chronicles was born, and it's been quite the wild ride. It's been almost a decade since this crazy journey has begun, and along the way I've met plenty of people who played a part in its fruition. Without the support of friends, family members, coworkers, readers, and strangers on the internet, I wouldn't have gathered the guts to publish this first Five Realm trilogy.

First, I would like to thank my mother, and my biggest critic. She was the first person to read the very first version of book one, and I was expecting her to hate it. She didn't, to my surprise, and I'll be forever grateful for the words of encouragement she gave me. Since then, she's remained by my side through thick and thin. She's the first person I go to when I get an idea. My readers can likely thank her for the fact that some of their favorite characters are still living.

A massive thank you goes to my best friend of sixteen years, Liz. I can remember sitting at a table in our favorite Greek restaurant for hours when I first told her about the Five Realms. I'm not sure what I would do without her. This past February, we sat in her living room for most of a day trying to come up with the perfect title for this book. She's the first to call me out for using too many adverbs or writing too much fluff, yet never fails to remind me of how much I've grown as an author.

I'd like to thank Gina, for ensuring me in those early days that I was talented enough. She read everything I finished, and let me rant and rave about new plot ideas and characters endlessly without complaint. Because of the support she gave me in the beginning, I gained the courage to keep writing.

Of course, I can't forget my husband, Joshua. He was there when I first started writing this series and he's still here today, celebrating each amazing milestone with me.

Another huge thank you to the best beta reader an author could ask for — Mags. We met by chance, and I'm so incredibly grateful for all the feedback she gave me on A Clash of Crowns. I can't wait to work together again in the near future.

Last, but certainly not least, I'd like to thank the wonderful team of people I work with to perfect these books. My editor, Maggie Kern at Miss K Edits, who ensures that each book I write is the best it can be. Moorbook Designs, who never fail to create captivating covers that always take my breath away. Zoe at Rainbow Danger designs, who not only helped me create a wonderful map, but turns each book into an artistic masterpiece with her wonderful formatting gifts.

Thank you all for making this first Five Realm trilogy possible. Here's to the next one!

ABOUT THE AUTHOR

M.L Darlow was whisked away at the sparky age of seventeen and embarked on a magical journey called The Five Realm Chronicles which came to light seven years later in 2019. Since then, she has continued her mission and pursued A Wicked Fairytale along the way.

M. L Darlow plans to take The Five Realm Chronicles as far as she can, with no end in sight.